PRAISE FOR

CLASH
— OF —
EMPIRES

'Fans of battle-heavy historical fiction will, justly, adore *Clash of Empires*. With its rounded historical characters and **fascinating** historical setting, it deserves a wider audience'
Antonia Senior, *The Times*

'**Grabs you from the start and never lets go**. Thrilling action combines with historical authenticity to summon up a whole world in a sweeping tale of politics and war. **A triumph!**'
Harry Sidebottom, author of the *The Last Hour*

'The word **epic** is overused to describe books, but with *Clash of Empires* it fits like a gladius in its scabbard. What Kane does, with such mastery, is place the big story – Rome vs Greece – in the background, while making this a story about ordinary men caught up in world-defining events. **I haven't enjoyed a book this much for ages. There aren't many writers today who could take on this story and do it well. There might be none who could do it better than Ben Kane**'
Giles Kristian, author of *Lancelot*

'**Exceptional**. Kane's excelled once again in capturing the terror and the glory . . . of the ancient battlefield, and this story is one that's been begging for an expert hand for a long time'
Anthony Riches, author of the Empire series

'**Carried off with panache** and Kane's expansive, engaging, action-packed style. A complex, **fraught, moving and passionate** slice of history **from one of our generation's most ambitious and engaging writers**'

Manda Scott, author of the Boudica series

'It's a broad canvas Kane is painting on, but he does it with vivid colours and, like the Romans themselves, he can show great admiration for a Greek enemy and still kick them in the balls'

Robert Low, author of the Oathsworn series

'Ben Kane manages to marry broad narrative invention with detailed historical research . . . in taut, authoritative prose . . . **his passion for the past, and for the craft of story-telling, shines from every page**'

Toby Clements, author of the Kingmaker series

'This **thrilling** series opener delivers every cough, spit, curse and gush of blood to set up the mighty clash of the title. Can't really fault this one'

Jon Wise, *Weekend Sport*

'A **powerful** and **vivid** historical novel that moves along at chariot-race speed'

Helena Gumley-Mason, *The Lady*

'Ben Kane's new series **explores the bloody final clash between ancient Greece and upstart Rome**, focusing on soldiers and leaders from both worlds and **telling the story of a bloody war with style**'

Charlotte Heathcote, *Sunday Express S Magazine*

'**A thumping good read.** You can feel the earth tremble from the great battle scenes and feel the desperation of those caught up in the conflict. Kane's brilliant research weaves its way lightly throughout'

David Gilman, author of the Master of War series

CLASH
OF
EMPIRES

Kenya born, Irish by blood and UK resident, Ben Kane's passion for history has seen him change career from veterinary medicine to writing, and taken him to more than sixty countries, and all seven continents. During his travels and subsequent research, including walking hundreds of miles in complete Roman military gear, he has learned much about the Romans and the way they lived.

Nine of his eleven novels have been *Sunday Times* top ten bestsellers, and his books are published in twelve languages; a million copies have sold worldwide. In 2016, his research was recognised by Bristol University with an honorary Doctor of Letters degree. Kane lives in Somerset with his wife and children, where he writes full time.

CLASH
OF
EMPIRES

BEN KANE

ORION

First published in Great Britain in 2018 by Orion Books.
This paperback edition published in 2019 by Orion Books
an imprint of The Orion Publishing Group Ltd
Carmelite House, 50 Victoria Embankment
London EC4Y 0DZ

An Hachette UK Company

3 5 7 9 10 8 6 4 2

A CIP catalogue record for this book is
available from the British Library.

ISBN (Mass Market Paperback) 978 1 4091 7339 7
ISBN (eBook) 978 1 4091 7340 3
ISBN (Audio) 978 1 4091 7341 0

Typeset by Input Data Services Ltd, Somerset

Printed and bound in Great Britain by Clays Ltd, Elcograf S.p.A.

MIX
Paper from
responsible sources
FSC
www.fsc.org   FSC® C104740

www.orionbooks.co.uk

For Sam Wood and Dylan Reynolds

– cyclists, gentlemen and since the Hannibal Trail in 2016,

good friends.

'It would be best if the Greeks never made war on each other, but could ever speak with one heart and voice, repel barbarian invaders together and unite in preserving themselves and their cities. If such a union is unattainable, I would counsel you to take due precautions for your safety, in view of the greatness of this war in the west. It is evident that whether the Romans or Carthaginians win this war, the victors will not be content with the sovereignty of Italy and Sicily. They are sure to come here and extend their ambitions beyond the bounds of justice. Therefore I implore you all to secure yourselves against this danger, and I address myself especially to King Philip.'

Agelaus of Aetolia, conference of Naupactus, 217 BC

A SHORT NOTE ABOUT GREEK
CITY STATES

Ancient Greece contained a confusing plethora of similar-sounding city states and regions. Most readers will have known of Athens, Sparta and Macedon, but not necessarily of Aetolia, Achaea, Athamania and Acarnania. Thermopylae and Marathon will be familiar, but it's less likely for modern readers to know the towns of the Hellespont and the mountain towns between Macedon and Illyria. It took me some time to familiarise myself with these political and geographical entities, and so to increase your enjoyment of the book, I urge you first to spend a little time looking over the maps.

Two of the following series of maps are slightly altered versions of the same map. One is from the Roman perspective, with place names in anglicised Latin, and the other is from the Greek perspective, with names in anglicised Greek.

Ben Kane

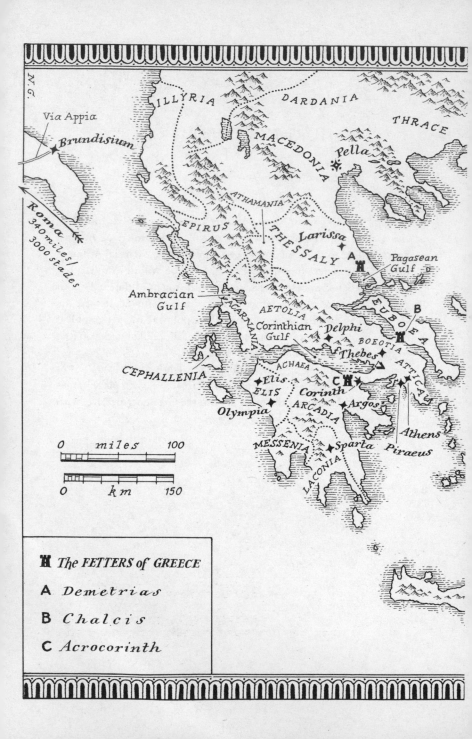

N.G.

Via Appia
Brundisium

Roma
340 miles/
3000 stades

ILLYRIA
DARDANIA
THRACE
MACEDONIA
Pella
ATHAMANIA
EPIRUS
THESSALY
Larissa
A
Pagasean
Gulf
Ambracian
Gulf
ACARNANIA
AETOLIA
EUBOEA
B
Corinthian
Gulf
Delphi
BOEOTIA
CEPHALLENIA
Thebes
ATTICA
ACHAEA
C
Elis
ELIS
Corinth
Argos
Olympia
ARCADIA
Athens
Piraeus
MESSENIA
Sparta
LACONIA

0   miles   100

0   k m   150

The FETTERS of GREECE

A   Demetrias

B   Chalcis

C   Acrocorinth

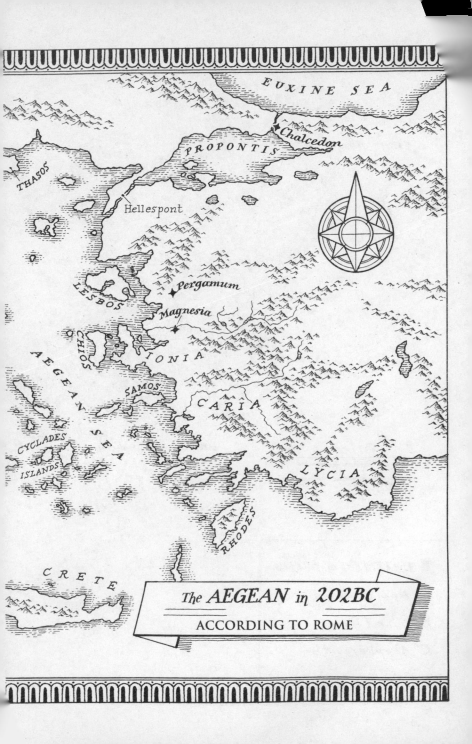

EUXINE SEA

PROPONTIS

Chalcedon

THASOS

Hellespont

LESBOS

Pergamum

Magnesia

CHIOS

IONIA

SAMOS

AEGEAN SEA

CARIA

CYCLADES
ISLANDS

LYCIA

RHODES

CRETE

The *AEGEAN* in *202BC*

ACCORDING TO ROME

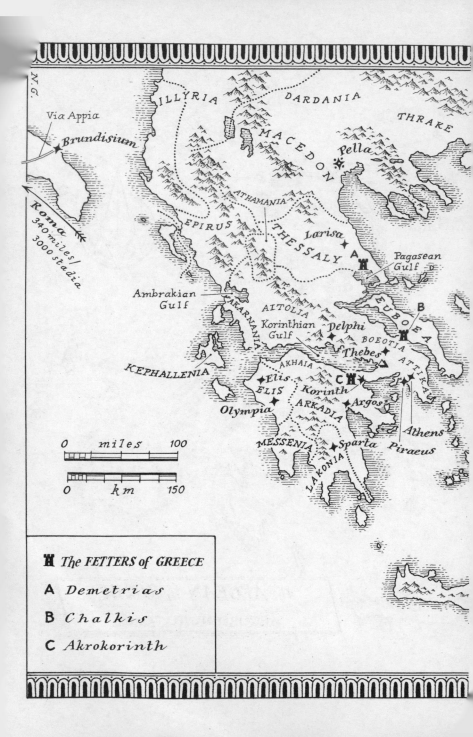

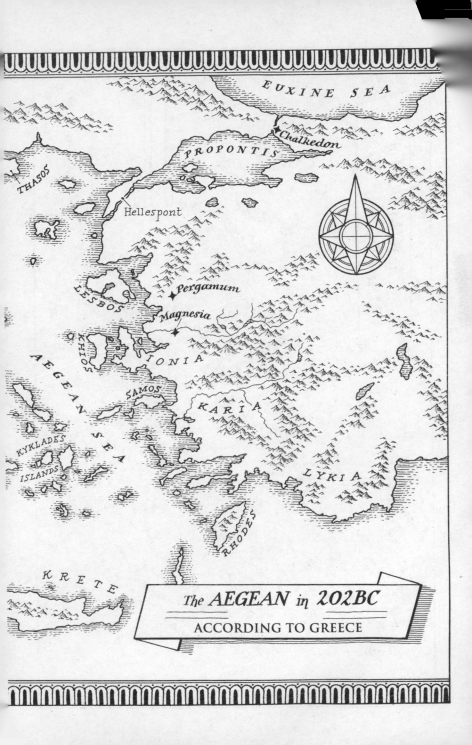

EUXINE SEA

PROPONTIS

Chalkedon

THASOS

Hellespont

LESBOS

Pergamum

Magnesia

CHIOS

IONIA

AEGEAN SEA

SAMOS

KARIA

KYKLADES
ISLANDS

LYKIA

RHODES

KRETE

The AEGEAN in 202BC

ACCORDING TO GREECE

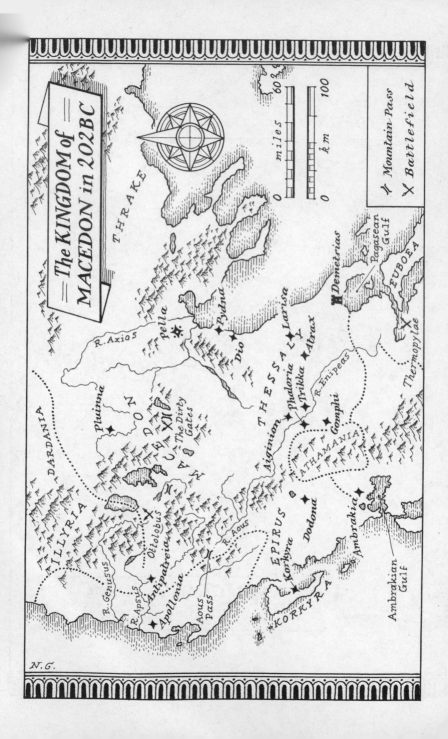

The KINGDOM of MACEDON in 202BC

0 miles 60
0 km 100

⚔ Mountain Pass
✗ Battlefield

THRAKE

R. Axios

Pella

Pydna

Dio

Pluinna

DARDANIA

ILLYRIA

R. Genusus

R. Apsus

Oklolobus ✗

Antipatreia

Apollonia

Aous Pass

R. Aous

EPIRUS

Korkyra

Dodona

KORKYRA

Ambrakia

Ambrakian Gulf

P A I O N I A

The Dirty Gates

Aiginion

Phaloria

Trikka

Gomphi

ATHAMANIA

R. Enipeas

THESSALY

Larisa

Atrax

Demetrias

Pagasean Gulf

EUBOEA

Thermopylae ✗

N.G.

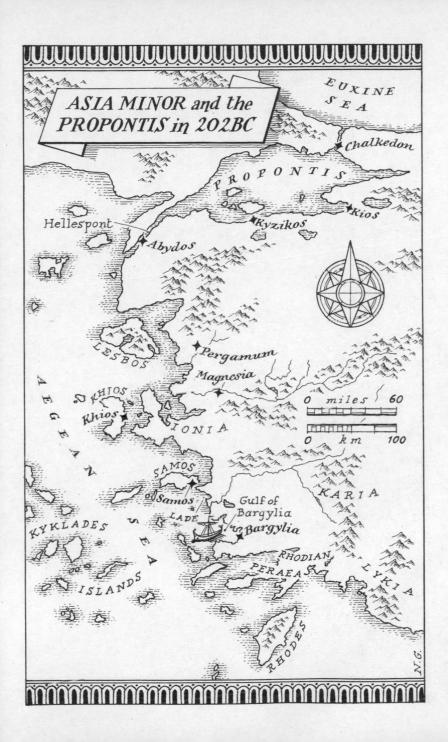

ASIA MINOR and the
PROPONTIS in 202BC

EUXINE
SEA

Chalkedon

PROPONTIS

Kios

Kyzikos

Hellespont

Abydos

LESBOS

Pergamum

Magnesia

0   miles   60

0   km   100

KHIOS

Khios

IONIA

AEGEAN

SAMOS

Samos

LADE

Gulf of
Bargylia

Bargylia

KARIA

KYKLADES

SEA

RHODIAN

PERAEA

LYKIA

ISLANDS

RHODES

N.G.

PROLOGUE

Off the southern coast of Italia,
early summer, 215 BC

I t was a beautiful evening, balmy and windless; the sea resembled a sheet of hammered bronze. A dozen small fishing boats were homeward bound, shadowed by screeching gulls. Light winked off soldiers' helmets on the coastal road. In the western sky, the mountains of Bruttium were dark shadows against the slow-sinking, golden orb of the sun. North-eastward, somewhere in the heat haze, lay the great city of Tarentum. Further out on the water, a squadron of Roman triremes beat a passage across the great, square-edged bay that cut deep into Italia's southern shores.

The ships were in two lines of five, and the front central vessel was commanded by the admiral Publius Valerius Flaccus. He was in no hurry – the three-day patrol, as far as the town of Locri and back again, had been uneventful – and they would reach their home port of Tarentum by sunset. Flaccus had decided that writing his report and other such duties could wait until the morrow. After a bath and a change of clothes, he was looking forward to an evening in the company of his mistress, the widow of a nobleman who had fallen at Cannae.

Flaccus was a short, determined individual. A fleshy jowl and receding hair took nothing away from his commanding presence, which was accentuated by a pair of bright blue eyes. It was these last, he was sure, together with his high rank and city graces, that had seen the widow succumb to his advances. Tarentum was no backwater, but those from Rome had a more cultured air; Flaccus knew how to milk that invisible superiority to the last drop. It had worked on his mistress-to-be the first time they'd met, at a recent feast to honour his arrival in the city. His lips twitched. He had bedded her the same night.

Just the right type of plump, she had soft, perfumed skin and remarkably pert breasts. Her bedroom tastes, wide-ranging and insatiable, were an endless source of surprise and pleasure. Flaccus reined in his imagination; like his officers, he sported a short tunic at sea rather than the cumbersome toga of his rank.

From his position close to the steersman, he had a view along the length of the ship. A central walkway connected the bow to the stern. To either side, three banks of oarsmen sat on benches, their bodies and outstretched arms moving back and forth in perpetual rhythm. At the front a flautist played, his melody setting the beat. The oar masters, standing every twenty-five paces along the walkway, rapped their metal-shod staffs on the planking in time to the tune. Currently the slow cruise, it commanded a steady speed that the rowers could keep up for hours.

It excited Flaccus to think that with a single word, he could have the entire squadron move to ramming speed. He had done so before, during training exercises, and by the gods, it stirred the blood. It would feel different when closing with an enemy fleet, of course; thrilling and terrifying at the same time. Quite how frightening, Flaccus had no idea, but imagining a ram's ridged bronze snout punching through *his* ship's hull was enough to make his belly tighten. Sinking to a watery grave was not how he wanted to end his life – nor was being sucked under by a passing vessel, or being speared in the sea by the foe. Sending a Carthaginian ship to the bottom, now that was an appealing thought. So too was running down the side of an enemy trireme, shearing away oars, and turning the vessel into a useless hulk to be boarded at one's leisure.

'Sail!'

The lookout's unexpected cry focused everyone's attention, not least Flaccus'. Fishing boats, plentiful and unthreatening, didn't warrant a shout. Trading vessels did, but with nightfall approaching, most round-bellied merchantmen would already be moored in a harbour, or anchored close to shore.

'Another sail!' cried the lookout. 'Three, four – I see five, dead ahead!'

Flaccus hurried to the prow, the captain on his heels. An oar master goggled at him, and Flaccus snapped, 'Maintain the rhythm until told otherwise, fool!'

He shoved past, the yells of the lookouts on his other ships increasing his unease.

It seemed doubtful the intruders were Carthaginian. Since Rome's huge naval victories during the last war, thought Flaccus, the *guggas* avoided encounters with Roman fleets wherever possible. Another alternative, Macedonian warships, seemed as unlikely. King Philip had attacked the island of Cephallenia two years before, it was true, and there were rumours of his designs on Illyria, but he wouldn't have the gall to send ships into Italian waters. Flaccus put the notion from his mind.

He reached the lookout, a skinny lad with wind-tousled hair. 'Where?'

The lookout gave him a nervous salute, and pointed a few degrees to starboard. 'There, sir. About two miles away.'

Flaccus raised a hand to his eyes. Far in the distance, outlined against the dark sea, were three white squares – sails. His heart thumped. He waited, spying after a moment two more. The ships were heading southeast towards the headland that formed Italia's heel, and any hope of a successful pursuit once they rounded that would be lost, he judged.

'Shall we give chase, sir?' The captain, a bow-legged old salt whom Flaccus had grown to like, was by his side.

'Aye. They're not Roman, that's certain. It would be best to find out what they are doing in these waters.'

'With the sun behind us, sir, they won't know we're coming until we are good and close.' The captain's leer revealed half a dozen peg like brown stumps. 'Gives us a decent chance, that does.'

Flaccus nodded. 'Good.'

The captain waved at the flautist. 'Fast cruise!'

A quicker melody started, and at once the oar masters took up the new rhythm. The rowers bent their backs and heaved, and within ten heartbeats, the trireme's speed had doubled. The ram scythed into the waves, as if it could sense their new prey.

The chase was on.

It was a close-run affair in the end. Flaccus' ships had come to within perhaps three-quarters of a mile before their quarry realised a thing. Quite what gave them away at that point was unclear – the sun was so low that anyone staring west would have been almost blinded – but suddenly, the five ships' speed increased to match that of the Roman triremes.

The headland was close, and the open sea beyond beckoned. Flaccus threw the dice, and gambled all.

'Ramming speed!' he bellowed.

It was a Herculean task to expect his oarsmen to sustain a chase with that distance remaining, but there was nothing to lose. At worst, the ships would escape, Flaccus decided, and his crews would face a long pull back to Tarentum under the stars. At best, their quarry would be brought to bay, and he'd discover why they had run like startled deer.

In the event, the breakneck-speed chase was short. Two of the vessels they were pursuing broke away, but the crews aboard the rest were no match for Flaccus' oarsmen. Seeing their fellows' plight, the front pair of ships came to a stop in the water. Cumbersome craft though they were, and outnumbered by his triremes, Flaccus took no chances. He sent four ships to surround the front two, and with the five remaining and his own vessel, crowded in around the slowest.

Shouted commands saw the three merchantmen's oars shipped. No one armed could be seen on their decks, and Flaccus' initial unease was replaced by a calm smugness. His plan had been well executed; resistance appeared unlikely. He had time to discover the ships' purpose, treat them accordingly, whether that be to fine their captains or impound their vessels, and still reach Tarentum before moonrise. His evening with his mistress was not under threat, an immense satisfaction.

Anticipation rising, Flaccus watched as the oarsmen eased his ship alongside the largest merchantman, a round-bellied craft with a square canvas sail. The port side oars rattled and dripped as they were drawn in. The ships slid past one another, scraping timbers; grappling hooks thumped onto the deck and were made fast. The sailors on the captured vessel shuffled about, faces tight with fear. Close to the mast, a small group of richly dressed men shared nervous mutters.

'Send over a boarding party,' Flaccus ordered. 'Find out who's in charge, and bring him to me.'

The gangplank dropped with a bang, and a score of marines clattered across, led by an *optio*.

Four soon returned, leading a stout figure. 'Says he's the commander, sir,' declared the optio. A none too friendly shove propelled the captive closer to Flaccus. Middle-aged, with a neat beard, he had intelligent

4

eyes. An embroidered himation, gold finger rings and his confident carriage marked him as a man of means. He bowed to Flaccus.

'Xenophanes of Athens, at your service, sir.' His Latin was accented, but good. 'Might I know your name?'

'Publius Valerius Flaccus, admiral.' He studied Xenophanes' face for signs of guile, but could see none. This meant nothing. In times of war, thought Flaccus, a man could trust no one save those who had proved themselves worthy of it. The Athenian hadn't made a good start. 'You fled from my ships. Why?'

Xenophanes' fingers fluttered. 'My apologies, admiral. We took you for pirates. Coming from the west, with the sun at your backs – it seemed sure that we were being attacked. There are a few weapons on each ship, but these are no warships. Flight was my only option.' A nervous smile. 'Not that we got far. Your oarsmen are to be commended.'

Flaccus ignored the compliment. 'What is your business in these waters?'

Xenophanes' expression grew confidential. He leaned closer, but the distrustful optio seized him by the shoulder. Xenophanes raised his hands. 'I mean the admiral no harm.'

'Keep your distance then, savage,' growled the optio.

Anger flitted across Xenophanes' face, but he gave Flaccus a practised smile. 'I wish to speak in confidence, without other ears listening.'

'Say what you have to say,' said Flaccus, already tired of whatever game Xenophanes was trying to play. In Tarentum, his mistress was waiting.

With a dark glance at the optio, Xenophanes muttered, 'I am an emissary of Philip of Macedon.' Seeing Flaccus' astonishment, he added quickly, 'As a neutral, the king deemed it easier for me to seek a meeting with your consuls and Senate; my purpose was to seal a pact of friendship with Rome and its people.'

This Flaccus had *not* expected. 'These are strange tidings. Philip has borne the Republic ill will of recent years.'

'A misunderstanding, nothing more.' Xenophanes' tone was bluff.

It was hard to see how invading Cephallenia was to be misunderstood, thought Flaccus. 'I am unaware of any Macedonian embassy journeying to Rome.'

'You have heard nothing of my task, admiral, because we failed to reach Rome. Landing at Juno's temple near Croton, we travelled overland towards Capua. Encountering Roman forces, we met with the *praetor* Laevinus. He was a generous host, and provided an escort to guide us on the safest routes, protection from Hannibal's army.'

Flaccus hid his surprise. Laevinus *was* a praetor operating in Campania. It seemed doubtful that Xenophanes could know of him unless he had met with the man, but that didn't explain why he, Flaccus, remained unaware of the Macedonian embassy and its unexpected mission. News of a possible alliance with Philip – welcome after the disaster at Cannae the previous year – would travel fast, thought Flaccus. And yet, Xenophanes' story wasn't beyond the realms of possibility.

'You were attacked by the Carthaginians, I assume. Is that why your journey to Rome failed?'

Xenophanes looked strained. 'Aye. Numidian cavalry are as deadly as they say. Several of our escort were killed, and their commander deemed it too unsafe to continue. On our return to Laevinus' camp, I pleaded for further aid to no avail. All his troops were needed to fight the enemy, he said. Without military protection, there was no chance of reaching Rome; I was forced to abandon our mission. You find us on our way back to Macedon.'

'Have you proof of Philip's intentions?'

'Of course. The documents are in a chest in my cabin. Say the word, and I will have them brought across.'

Flaccus rubbed his chin. Previous hostility between Rome and Macedonia wouldn't prevent Philip from seeking an alliance. Keenly aware that the fast-approaching onset of night would delay his return to Tarentum – and the willing arms of his mistress – by a considerable amount, Flaccus came to a decision. If Xenophanes' papers seemed genuine and a search of his craft brought nothing else to light, he would have little reason to detain the Athenian further.

'Let me have a look.'

Pleased, Xenophanes nodded. Cupping a hand to his mouth, he shouted an order at the nearest of his sailors.

Flaccus' good humour was returning. 'Wine?' he asked.

'I would be honoured, admiral.' Xenophanes' bow was a good deal deeper than before.

They had toasted each other and drunk by the time the documents came aboard. Flaccus cast a critical eye at the two parchments, one of which was in Carthaginian and the other in Greek. The wording of the former seemed to bear out Xenophanes' testimony; he assumed the latter to read the same. Stamped with a Macedonian seal, with a bold signature from Philip himself, both appeared authentic. His decision confirmed, Flaccus signalled for more wine. Smiling, Xenophanes accepted a refill.

'Let us hope that your next attempt to reach Rome succeeds,' said Flaccus, saluting Xenophanes with his cup. 'Here's to long-lasting friendship between the Republic and Macedonia.'

'May the gods grant it so,' replied Xenophanes, returning the gesture.

Cup drained, Flaccus glanced at the optio. 'Escort this gentleman back to his ship. Check the boarding party have found nothing important, and have them return.'

'My thanks for your hospitality,' said Xenophanes.

'Neptunus watch over your ships,' Flaccus replied.

'May Poseidon do the same to you.'

'Captain, make ready to shove off,' ordered Flaccus.

Xenophanes had just set foot on the gangplank when a commotion broke out on his ship. Raised voices came from below decks. Two marines clambered into sight.

'We've found something, sir!' they shouted at the optio. 'More like some*one*,' added the tallest.

Flaccus was by the rail in a heartbeat. 'What is it?'

'We discovered three men in the bottom of the hold, sir,' said the lead marine. 'Right behind a load of stacked amphorae, they was. If one hadn't sneezed, we never would have found them.'

Flaccus' eyes shot to Xenophanes. The Greek was halfway across the gangplank, and his pace had noticeably quickened.

'Halt, Xenophanes!' bellowed Flaccus. 'Get him back over here, optio.' To the marines, he said, 'Bring them up. Quickly!'

Soon a trio of swarthy men stood blinking on the deck opposite Flaccus. With a look of grim satisfaction, the optio pushed Xenophanes to stand alongside. The Athenian ignored the newcomers, and Flaccus' suspicions returned with a vengeance. With their dark complexions, oiled ringlets, and long tunics, they resembled the Carthaginians he'd encountered. 'Well, Xenophanes?'

They stared at one another in silence.

'They're paying passengers,' Xenophanes admitted. Spots of colour marked his cheekbones. 'I knew it wouldn't look good to have their type on board if we were stopped by Roman ships.'

'What type would that be?' asked Flaccus, sneering.

Silence.

'Well?'

'Carthaginians.'

As Xenophanes spoke, understanding blossomed in Flaccus' mind. 'Search the guggas.'

Inside twenty heartbeats, a separate set of documents was in his hands, discovered under the tunic of the most senior Carthaginian, a proud-faced man with a hawkish look. The emissary soon lost his composure under a rain of blows from the optio and his men; Xenophanes yelped like a whipped child as he too was beaten. Flaccus, whose nod had initiated the assaults, paid no attention. The tip of his tongue stuck from between his lips as he laboriously read the Greek. More shocked than he'd have thought possible, he reread the letter three times before trying to comprehend its full significance.

Flaccus caught the captain's eye. 'Change course. We sail for Rome.'

The old salt looked startled. 'Rome, sir?'

'You heard me. Send a message to the other ships. Three will accompany us. The others are to return to Tarentum with the merchantmen.'

'Aye, sir.' The captain shouted to the oar masters, who rapped out a set of orders. At once, the rowers on one side of the ship heaved their oars out of the water, while those on the other dug deep, turning the ship around to face the west.

Flaccus watched impatiently. He wanted to order ramming speed, but there was no point exhausting the oarsmen. Despite his urgency, the capital was at least two days' voyage away.

'We're bound for Rome, sir?' The optio had moved to his side.

'Aye.'

'Can I ask why, sir?'

The optio could speak to no one else of importance on the ship, Flaccus decided, and besides, the news would spread the length and breadth of Italia before the month was out. 'You are to keep this to yourself.'

'On my life, sir,' said the optio

'Philip seeks an alliance with Hannibal.'

The optio looked confused.

'Here's the proof!' Flaccus brandished the letter.

In the light of the setting sun, the writing on the parchment took on a blood-red hue.

A worse omen Flaccus could not imagine.

PART ONE

CHAPTER I

Thirteen years later . . .

*Near the town of Chalkedon, on the shores of
the Propontis, late summer 202 BC*

Demetrios didn't like hiding in the trees, but near the tents, it was easy to be spotted. Pilfering was a dangerous occupation. He'd been caught and badly beaten a couple of times; now he spied out the ground before risking his skin. Here on the fringes of King Philip's camp, among the evergreen bushes and cork oaks, he could pick the right moment. The only people about were soldiers seeking a quiet place to empty their bowels, and men with that on their minds paid little heed to a loitering youth in a ragged *chiton*. They'd take him for one of the hundreds of opportunistic tag-alongs following the Macedonian fleet along the Propontis.

Demetrios was no scavenger, but an oarsman on one of Philip's ships. Not on a glorious trireme, with its shining ram and patterned sail, or on one of the nimble *lembi*. His floating home was a pot-bellied, low-in-the-water transport vessel. It wasn't his choice of career, gods no. Since he was a boy, Demetrios had wanted to be a soldier who fought in the mighty phalanx. Now the chance of that seemed harder to reach than the summit of Olympos in mid-winter. It *might* have happened, thought Demetrios, if Ares hadn't turned his face away, if the other gods hadn't conspired against him.

His shepherd father had been poor, but he'd proudly served as a slinger in his younger days. He had taught Demetrios how to hunt, and sent him to learn pankration and wrestling with the wealthier farmers' sons. Lean, and wiry, strong from hard labour on the farm, he had learned fast, which was as well, for the richer boys had made fun of him at every opportunity. Stubborn, he had persevered, always thinking of his father's words: with the right introductions when he was older, becoming a *phalangist* could be arranged.

If only Father wasn't gone, thought Demetrios, his grief cutting him like knives. But he was, murdered by sheep rustlers on a filthy autumn night two years back. Orphaned – Demetrios' mother had died when he was five – and beggared by the theft of the entire flock, he had been reduced from shepherd's son to landless peasant at one stroke. With winter coming, even the kindest neighbours were able to feed him no more than for a few days. Soon he'd been forced to Pella, Macedon's capital and the nearest town of any size. Friendless, alone, his life on the streets had not been pleasant; he had survived by labouring in the market and on the docks.

In the spring just gone, when news spread that the king was to carry war to the Propontis, a sudden need had sprung up for crewmen on merchant vessels; Philip's soldiers would need vast quantities of food on their campaign, and ships to carry it. Sick of living hand to mouth, eager to be near the army, Demetrios had signed on with the first captain who would take him – which was how he found himself on the outskirts of the Macedonian camp, thousands of stadia from home.

His dream of becoming a phalangist hadn't quite vanished, but his day-to-day struggles ensured that he scarcely gave it a thought. The physical demands of rowing were immense, the oar masters overfond of using fists and feet. The rowers toiled from dawn to dusk under the burning hot sun. Water was passed around regularly, but rest periods were rare. After wolfing down his meal each night, Demetrios often had the energy only to lie down with his blanket. Sleep was hard to come by, thanks to those of his fellows who prowled the decks in search of flesh. After a near escape soon after joining the ship, he had formed an unofficial alliance with a couple of the younger rowers. They weren't friends as such – Demetrios knew this because they'd both stolen food from him – but come nightfall, the three stayed close, and took turns to stay awake. The arrangement meant he got a little more rest than before, but his sleep was fitful, and he always kept a dagger clutched in his fist.

Advancement from the benches seemed improbable; his hope of becoming a shepherd again was more realistic, but it would take a year at least to save the coin for a few sheep. Demetrios concentrated, therefore, on getting through each day, and trying to fill his belly as often as possible. Eighteen, still growing, he was always hungry. Aboard their ship at least, oarsmen's rations were poor quality and served in miserly portions. Stealing provisions was a daily, necessary task. Mornings were no good – Demetrios had had to grow used to his growling stomach at these times – but at the end of the day, as the sun set, when soldiers and sailors were tired, the pickings were better. He had learned to choose the tents where most men were absent, leaving the soldier whose turn it was to cook.

One such lay not fifty paces away, the closest to his position in the trees. An iron tripod stood over a small fire; dangling from its chain was a pot. Saliva filled Demetrios' mouth at the thought of the bubbling stew within. Despite its appeal, the risks were too great. Running with a vessel full of boiling liquid – a nigh-on impossible task – would end badly. Less tasty, but easy to steal, were the flat breads that had been set to cook on stones around the fire. Two or three would sate Demetrios' hunger. He might also trade one with a crewmate for a morsel of meat, or some olives.

His hopes that the soldier would be distracted by a neighbour had thus far come to naught, and so when the man gave his stew a good stir and then aimed for the trees with a determined gait, Demetrios grinned. Gods, let him need a shit rather than a piss, he prayed. He waited until the man, a tough-looking *peltast*, had drawn near before leaving the treeline, at the same time making a show of adjusting his chiton in the manner of someone who has just visited the latrine. Avoiding eye contact, Demetrios angled his walk away from the fire with its all-important bread. Close to the tents, a surreptitious glance told him the peltast had vanished into the woods.

Demetrios changed direction. Twenty steps, and he was standing by the tripod. The rich aroma of pork and herbs filled his mouth with saliva. Snatching up the cook's ladle, he scooped up a great mouthful. It was better tasting food than he'd had in days. His belly screamed for more, but time wasn't on his side. Demetrios grabbed three flat breads, and then, unable to stop himself, a hunk of cheese as well. Dropped into his loose-necked chiton, they were held in place by his belt. He looked to the trees, and was relieved to see no sign of the peltast. When his theft *was* noticed, thought Demetrios, he would be long gone.

Whistling his father's favourite tune, he sauntered off between the tents. Tonight, he would sleep on a full stomach.

*

15

There was no pursuit from his well-executed crime. Success made Demetrios cocky. Rather than eating in the relative safety of his ship, he made the mistake of stopping a *stadion* from the peltast's fire. One flat bread wolfed down and still ravenous, he opted next for a bite of cheese.

A voice drawled, 'What do we have here?'

Pulling food from his clothing did not look good; Demetrios decided to brazen it out. He shrugged at the group of young slingers who'd appeared from between the tents to his left and said, 'Robbing from your mates isn't a crime. They steal from us, we steal from them – you know how it is. Tomorrow the bastards will be prowling around, looking to repay the favour.'

The youth who'd spoken, a broad-chested individual with black hair held in place by a leather thong, let out an unpleasant laugh.

'Except you don't have any mates round here, sewer rat. We camp in the same spot every night; a man gets to recognise his neighbours. I've not seen you around before, which means you're a thief, plain and simple.' His friends rumbled in agreement.

Demetrios bridled. 'What's it to you?'

'Hear him! That's as good as a confession if I ever heard one,' said the slinger with a sneer.

Demetrios wasn't sure why the slinger cared what he'd stolen if it wasn't from his own fire, but one thing was certain: a beating was imminent. His accuser had four companions, not all large, but every one capable-looking. They fanned out and walked towards Demetrios with purposeful glares.

Slingers were fleet of foot, he thought, and these seemed no different. Even if he outpaced them to his ship, there was scant chance of help from his fellow oarsmen. In the pecking order of the rowing benches, Demetrios was near the bottom. He tried another option.

'D'you want some cheese? I have bread as well.'

Jeers and laughter followed.

'We'll take it after we've kicked the shit out of you,' said the leader.

Demetrios' thought had been not to resist, but the leader's arrogance was unbearable. 'Screw you, and your mother!' he cried, and lunged at the leftmost slinger. With four paces separating them, his target had time only to gape before Demetrios' right shoulder drove into his belly. Winded, he dropped like a stone down a well. Demetrios spun,

16

and smashed a left hook into the next man's jaw. Pain lanced from his hand, but the slinger's knees buckled. Demetrios fled, his ears ringing with outraged cries of 'Thief!'

He darted and weaved through the tents, leaping over guy ropes and at one point, a fire. Maintaining his lead, he began to entertain hopes of reaching the relative sanctuary of the anchored ships. The slingers wouldn't dare follow him out to those – although the fleet was part of Philip's host, there was a good deal of animosity between soldiers and crewmen.

Demetrios never saw the foot that tripped him. One moment, he was aiming for the gap between two tents, the next, the ground was hurtling towards his face. His outstretched hands took some of the impact, but the air still left his lungs with a whoosh. He rolled, desperate to get up, but the foot's owner gave him a mighty kick in the gut that sent him earthward again. Demetrios retched and a heartbeat later, spewed up the bread he'd swallowed. As he tried to push himself up on his elbows, a blow to the ribs knocked him back down. He sucked in a ragged breath, and wondered what in Tartaros he could do now.

Feet pounded. Voices drew near.

'Is this who you're chasing?' someone asked.

'Looks like it,' said the slinger who'd challenged Demetrios.

'He a thief?'

'Aye. Our thanks, comrade.'

The slinger's sandal-clad pair of feet halted in front of Demetrios' face. One kicked him, hard.

'Up, whoreson.'

Demetrios was at the slingers' mercy, but he wasn't ready to give in. Lunging forward, he sank his teeth into the slinger's ankle. A cry of pain and his victim stumbled backwards. Somehow he got to his knees. A shocked-looking peltast – it was he who must have tripped him, thought Demetrios – saved the slinger from falling. Behind the two, he could see angry faces – the other slingers. He punched the peltast in the balls, and as the man bent double, groaning, stood up.

The rest might kill him, but Demetrios didn't care. All his grief and fury at his father's death, at the harsh existence life had dealt him since, came boiling to the surface. If things had worked out as planned, he'd have been a phalangist by now, with no need to steal food. Instead, a lowly oarsman, he would die at the hands of the murderous slingers.

Demetrios set his back to the tent, his only defence, and clenched his fists. 'How many of you does it take to beat one man?'

The insult was too much. The slingers and peltast swarmed forward. Demetrios landed a couple of punches and a headbutt before a hail of blows sent him crashing to the ground. Stars burst across his vision; waves of pain battered every portion of his body. He did his best to curl into a ball. Protect his head, and there might be a chance of survival.

He lost consciousness soon after the stamping began.

Water splashed into Demetrios' face, and he came to, spluttering. He was lying on his side. There wasn't a part of him that didn't hurt. Clots of blood filled his mouth; rooting with his tongue, he found a loose tooth, and with difficulty, spat it out.

'He's alive.' The voice was amused. 'It's a wonder, considering how many of you jumped him.'

Feet shuffled. Demetrios didn't understand why no one answered. Cold fear uncoiled in his belly. An officer had come on the scene. When he heard the reasons for the attack, Demetrios' fate would be sealed anew. Resignation swamped him. The Fates were in a foul mood today.

'Can you move?' asked the voice.

Demetrios tried, and found he could. Wiping crimson-tinged drool from his bruised lips, he struggled into a sitting position. Sweet agony emanating from the right side of his chest signified cracked ribs; this was but the worst of his discomfort. He glanced up at the plain-cloaked man who'd spoken. Slim, bright-eyed, and with a beard, he reminded Demetrios of someone.

His eyes took in the slingers' and peltast's nervous expressions, and beyond them, an awed-looking crowd of soldiers. Realisation sank home. He'd heard the rumours of Philip wandering through the camp in plain attire, talking to his troops; it seemed the tales were true. Demetrios' stomach rolled. Whatever punishment he might have received would be worse now – the king would want to set an example.

He rose, wincing, to one knee. 'Sire.'

'These men say they caught you thieving bread.' Philip jerked a thumb at the slingers.

Demetrios hesitated. Denying the accusation would look as if he were lying to save his skin. He glanced at his pursuers, who were openly gloating, and fury took him. 'That's not how it happened, sire.'

The lead slinger let out a contemptuous laugh.

'So you didn't steal anything?' Philip's tone was hard. Dangerous.

'I did, sire.' Demetrios pulled out a misshapen lump of bread – in the fight, his ill-gotten haul had been macerated. 'But they didn't see me take it. No one did.'

Something that might have been amusement flitted across Philip's face. 'How then did they come to attack you?'

'I was starving, sire, so I stopped to eat some of it. The slingers saw, and not recognising me, presumed I had stolen the food.'

'The slingers' tents are a decent distance from here,' said Philip. 'After you ran, they gave chase?'

'Not before I'd knocked two down, sire.'

'How many were they?'

'Five, sire.'

Philip's eyebrows rose. 'Five. Against you.'

'Yes, sire.'

'Are you a soldier?'

'An oarsman, sire.'

'On one of my warships?'

'No, sire. A merchant vessel.'

The lead slinger flushed with shame. His companions looked embarrassed and furious. Philip, on the other hand, seemed intrigued. 'How did they catch you?' he demanded.

'That peltast–' Demetrios pointed '–heard their cries, sire, and tripped me.'

'Men don't like a thief,' said Philip. 'That's when they beat you senseless.'

'Aye, sire!' cried the lead slinger.

'I gave you something to remember me by,' retorted Demetrios. 'Your ankle will hurt for days. And I gave the peltast a good thump in the balls.' Someone began to chuckle; it took a moment for Demetrios to realise that it was the king. Sure that it presaged a dreadful death, he hung his head.

'My slingers are among the best in the world, or so they boast. Am I not right?' demanded Philip.

The lead slinger found his voice. 'Yes, sire.'

'Yet five of you were reduced to three by an oarsman. *An oarsman.* You only caught the mongrel because someone else intervened. Even then, he managed to injure two more of your number before you got the better of him.'

Silence.

'Speak, fool!' Philip's tone was murderous.

'You have the right of it, sire,' muttered the lead slinger.

'Get out of my sight,' snapped Philip.

Demetrios watched, disbelieving, as the slingers slunk away. If they'd been dogs, he thought, their tails would have been tucked right up between their hind legs. His delight was brief – the king would be punishing him too. Theft was theft; Demetrios had once seen a man executed for the crime. At the least, he could expect to have his right hand amputated. Panic swelled in his chest. Maimed, he couldn't row. When the fleet moved on, he'd be left behind, to die of starvation.

'You.' Philip was talking to the peltast.

'Sire.' The man's gaze was fixed on the ground.

'You did what you thought was right – I cannot fault you for that. Being taken off guard by the boy, however . . .' Philip paused, and the peltast looked up, naked terror in his face. The king laughed. 'Consider the pain in your groin punishment enough. You may go.'

Gabbling his thanks, the peltast disappeared into his tent.

Demetrios closed his eyes. Now it comes, he thought. Let my end be quick, great Zeus.

'On your feet.'

'Sire.'

Philip was going to execute him standing, thought Demetrios. Gritting his teeth against the pain, he got up.

'You're proud. You fight like a soldier.'

Confusion took Demetrios. 'I— sire.'

'You stole because you were hungry?'

'Aye, sire. They never give us enough.'

Philip's expression blackened. 'Merchant captains are paid sufficient funds to feed every man in their crew twice a day. What's your ship's name?'

'*Star of the Sea*, sire.'

Philip gave him a nod. 'On your way.'

Demetrios gaped. 'Sire?'

'You are free.'

'You're not going to kill me, sire?'

Philip's lips peeled back in amusement. 'I'm not.'

Demetrios gave Philip the deepest bow he could manage. Unable to believe his good fortune, he shuffled back the required ten paces before turning around and limping for the shoreline.

Halfway back to the ships, a quiet giggle escaped him. He still had the bread and cheese inside his chiton.

CHAPTER II

The forum Romanum, Rome

Titus Quinctius Flamininus was still a distance from the Comitium, the area for political assembly, when he signalled to his *lictores*; at once they moved to a quiet spot by a temple on the forum's eastern side. It was impossible to remain invisible thanks to his escort, but the great open space of the forum was busy enough that he wouldn't be spotted immediately. His fellow politicians were gathering outside the Curia, or Senate house, awaiting the arrival of emissaries from Aetolia in Greece. They had come, as everyone knew, to beg for Rome's aid against the warlike Philip of Macedonia – a king with whom the Republic had fought an inconclusive war some years before.

Flamininus had no intention of missing the important meeting, but before joining the throng, he wanted to see who was muttering in whose ear, and who was ignoring whom. He had spies in Rome, but much could also be gleaned by observation. Information was power, and for a man as ambitious as Flamininus, was worth its weight in gold. Roman politics was dominated by factions; the balance of power tended to move between perhaps half a dozen families. Too busy fighting Hannibal to visit Rome, Publius Cornelius Scipio remained the Republic's darling; his faction was the largest, outnumbering the second biggest by some margin. Neither of these two groupings matched in number the senatorial families whose allegiance swung to and fro, however. These were the senators whose support was crucial to anyone seeking office; they included Flamininus. Over the previous few years, his family had tended to support Scipio, but that was not Flamininus' purpose on this occasion. In his mind, alliances were like cloaks, to be worn and exchanged for another dependent on one's need.

Today he was accompanied by his elder brother Lucius, an athletic man whose face marked him as close kin. Rather than stay with the group, he had climbed the temple steps for a better view of the goings-on. Flamininus made to call his brother back, then thought twice. Lucius could cause no trouble there, and with time pressing, Flamininus was eager to spy out what he could.

Not thirty years old, he was a short man, his brown hair close-cut in the soldiers' fashion, and his beard trimmed. He was no Adonis, with eyes that verged on protuberant, a long, pointed nose and fleshy lips, but made up for his lack of looks with unbreakable confidence. When he'd tried to ride his father's horse at the age of four, it had been there, as when he had demanded to assume the toga a full two years before his fifteenth birthday. The beatings he'd had on both occasions had strengthened his self-assurance, which helped him to believe it was gods-given.

Scion of a faded patrician family, and bitter at his own lack of fortune in life, Flamininus' father had been a rigid taskmaster, easy to anger and hard to please. Locked in an unhappy marriage, his mother had been a shrew of a woman. From a young age, Flamininus had chafed to leave the family home; within a year of taking the toga, he had cajoled his father to introduce him into public life. He could yet feel the joy that had swept him as he rode away, towards Rome. He had taken his own path since. Legal assistant first to a town justice and then a prominent lawyer, he had cut his teeth on jobs that were integral to the running of the Republic. Well known despite his youth, adept at making allies, there had been an inevitability to Flamininus setting his foot on the political ladder more than five years prior.

His current role was that of *quaestor* at Tarentum, with a praetor's extra powers. He'd been appointed soon after the great southern city had been retaken from Hannibal; the post had been trying to say the least. Astute, not averse to taking bribes, Flamininus had discreetly amassed a fortune during his office. If things continued as they were, there was a good possibility that the position of consul might be his within two to three years. If matters went *exactly* as he hoped this afternoon, it might happen sooner.

He controlled his excitement. 'Only a fool puts the cart in front of the mule,' his old tutor had often repeated, and he'd been right. Spontaneous, Flamininus' move today was unlikely to succeed, but it was worth the gamble. Before the exalted office of consul could be considered probable, he needed widespread support among the senators, and that took time to secure. Old allegiances would have to be weakened, even broken, and new ones forged. Bribes would be paid, weaknesses found, and threats implied. On occasion, brute force might be called for. Flamininus wasn't as popular as Scipio, say, but he was determined, and his bag of tricks deep. In addition, generous use of his fortune saw his network of spies grow by the month.

'Good things come to the patient,' Flamininus murmured, his gaze roving over the toga-clad figures milling in front of the Curia, alighting on a man in late middle age. Even at a distance, the ex-consul Galba's gaunt figure was recognisable; if Flamininus listened, his melodic voice carried over the crowd. Thirty or more senators were hanging on his every word; as Flamininus watched, others drew close.

'Rome has no need to involve itself with Greek affairs,' he said, voicing Galba's oft-spoken opinion. 'Is Hannibal not enough for the Republic to deal with at one time? What need has it of a fresh war with Macedonia?'

Galba's stance wasn't surprising. The Republic had seen sixteen years of continuous, bloody conflict with Carthage. It had lost tens of thousands of its sons, and at various times, seen half its Italian allies swear allegiance to the undefeatable Hannibal. An end to the war was in sight for the first time, pleasing everyone, but Galba had his own reasons for avoiding conflict with Macedonia. According to Flamininus' spies, he was set on an important magistracy in Hispania. Even more than Flamininus' quaestorship in Tarentum, foreign positions carried with them the chance – through business deals, siphoning of taxes and so on – of becoming wealthy beyond one's dreams. Clearly Galba could not serve as a praetor in Hispania *and* prosecute a war with Philip, but if he prevented the latter, his many rivals would be denied the chance of fame, glory and riches in Macedonia.

Whether Galba knew it or not, Flamininus was one of those rivals. Before commanding Rome's legions in Macedonia, however he had to persuade the Senate to help Aetolia. After that, he would have to win election as consul. Both were huge obstacles.

Time, Flamininus thought. If only I'd had more time.

News of the Aetolian embassy had reached him six days before. He had wasted two days instructing his subordinates in Tarentum; the remainder had been taken up by a difficult voyage up the west coast. Docking that very morning, he had arrived in Rome not an hour since. His worry now was that while he'd been *planning* to lobby every senator in Rome, Galba and his supporters had been doing just that for at least half a month.

Flamininus took heart as Galba hailed a party of a dozen senators, only for the leader to stalk past without any acknowledgement. Twenty paces from the former consul, the dozen joined a larger group. All was not lost, Flamininus decided. It was time to speak with the anti-Galba faction. With luck, his words would find fertile ground. His head twisted, searching for Lucius. He had not moved from the top of the temple steps. Flamininus' gaze followed his brother's, and he frowned. Lucius was ogling several half-clad youths who were wrestling one another in the alley by the side of the temple.

'Come on, brother!' Flamininus called.

'All right, all right.' With a final, lust-filled glance, Lucius obeyed.

'Could you be more obvious?' asked Flamininus acidly.

'I wanted to be noticed,' replied Lucius with a nonchalant shrug. 'A shame none saw me. I'd have enjoyed a quick fumble while you press the flesh.'

Flamininus' temper began to rise. 'We are here on serious business.'

'We? It's always about *you*, little brother.' Lucius made a face.

'You like being *aedile*, do you not?' Flamininus shot back. It was he who had secured the post for Lucius.

Silence.

'Well?'

'I do.' Lucius' tone was grudging.

'If my trajectory rises, dear brother, so does yours. When I am consul, you shall be a *propraetor* or praetor, and there's nothing to say you couldn't be consul after me. Whatever benefits you enjoy now will be as nothing beside the opportunities that will fall into your consular lap. Understand?'

Lucius' pout vanished. 'Aye.'

Several hours passed, and the Aetolians arrived at the Graecostasis, where foreign embassies awaited their invitation to enter the Curia. Inside, the three hundred senators stood in their factions. Thanks to his rank, Flamininus had secured prime positions close to the consuls' chairs for himself, his brother and their supporters. The consuls for the year, Tiberius Claudius Nero and Marcus Servilius Pulex Geminus, were both present, attended by their lictores.

Perhaps eighty senators – in the main, Galba's and Scipio's political enemies – had promised to vote with Flamininus, but they would not be enough to carry the day. It was nonetheless a solid number. If this much support could be garnered in a few hours, the future was bright.

Nor had Flamininus given up all hope for the day. He was a skilled orator, and the senators were men, like any others. Raise their emotions enough, and they might be swayed into helping Aetolia. He'd seen similar things happen in the Senate before. The pleasing notion made him raise a mocking eyebrow at Galba, who affected not to notice. Annoyed, Flamininus scowled. Galba's lips twitched in reply, and Flamininus cursed inwardly, to have been so easily goaded.

Elmwood rods rapped on the floor. Heads turned, the murmur of conversation died away. It was indecorous to step onto the strip of tiled floor that ran from the bronze doors to the consuls' chairs, splitting the room in two. Instead Flamininus leaned outwards, not enough to appear eager – although he was – yet sufficient to afford a view of the entrance, where he saw two waiting figures.

'Euripidas and Neophron, emissaries from Aetolia in Greece, are come to speak with the Senate!' cried a senior lictor.

An expectant hush fell. Leather slapped off the floor. Flamininus could feel his heart pounding as the Aetolians approached.

Calm yourself, he thought. Victory will not be yours today. This is but the first skirmish in a war.

Euripidas and Neophron walked past, their gaze fixed on the two consuls. Dressed in fine woollen himations, both were middle-aged. Euripidas' grey beard afforded him the look of an elder statesman, while the wrinkles at the corners of Neophron's eyes proved he was no stranger to humour.

The serious and the comedic one, thought Flamininus. Interesting.

Reaching the consuls, both Aetolians bowed.

'I bid you welcome. The Republic and Aetolia have long been friends,' said Claudius, the more senior consul, 'although of recent years, that friendship has been sorely tried.'

More than one senator tittered, and Flamininus thought, this will test the emissaries' self-control.

At one stage during the long war with Carthage, the enemy had gained the upper hand against Rome. Aetolia had been left to its own fate. Unable to fight Philip alone, the weakened Aetolians had sued for peace three years before. Although it was they who had been the architects of the situation, most Romans would never admit that.

'It is our old friendship that made us journey from our home, sir. Aitolia would renew its ties to the Republic.' Neophron smiled, acting as if the barbed insult had passed him by.

Servilius would not let it go. 'The last I heard, Aetolia had made a treaty with Philip of Macedonia. With a king as a friend, what need have you of allies overseas?'

Euripidas let out an awkward cough, but Neophron pulled an even wider smile. 'That agreement is three years old, sir, and Philip is mercurial – you may have heard this. Of recent months he has abandoned the treaty by campaigning along the Propontis, where he has besieged and captured Aitolian towns, among others. It concerns him not an iota that the people whom his soldiers murder and enslave are freeborn Greeks.'

'The Greeks are ever at each other's throats. Were they not quarrelling on the very eve of Marathon, and the battle of Salamis?' observed Claudius, half-smiling as a ripple of amusement passed down the chamber.

'You speak true, sir,' said Euripidas with a rueful nod, 'yet it is rare indeed for us to make slaves of one another. Philip goes too far. Strongly worded letters have been to Pella; there has been no reply. Even if he has received them, it seems probable that our protests would fall on deaf ears: as I speak, he leads his soldiers against Kios, another Aitolian town on the Propontis.'

'Which is why the Assembly has sent us here to Rome,' continued Neophron. 'To ask, nay, beg Rome for assistance against this power-mad, murderous tyrant. It is too late for Kios, like as not, but other settlements are at risk.'

'Aetolia may be dismayed by the loss of a handful of inconsequential towns in Asia Minor,' declared Servilius, 'but the Republic is not.'

Cries of support came from Galba's faction.

Neophron acknowledged the sarcastic comments with a courteous half-bow. 'So a man might think. Yet if Philip's successes continue, he will soon control the Propontis, and with it, the grain trade from the shores of the Euxine Sea.'

'The citizens of Athens might lament that outcome,' said Claudius with a dismissive gesture, 'but again, it is no concern of the Republic.'

'Philip will not stop there. Since coming to power, he has done little but wage war,' said Euripidas. 'When his eye falls on Aitolia again, as inevitably it shall, our army might stem the tide for a short time, but he will emerge victorious. Aitolia *will* fall.'

Claudius' face was impassive; Servilius shrugged.

Flamininus watched Euripidas cast about, seeking a sympathetic reaction. Opposite, Galba was whispering in his neighbour's ear; his supporters acting as if the Aetolians weren't even there. Around Flamininus, however, a few senators were muttering. He listened.

'Philip should not be allowed to ride roughshod over anyone he pleased.'

'He could turn into the next Hannibal.'

'Vipers are best stamped on before they creep into your bed.'

The voices were muted, however. If anyone was to speak out, thought Flamininus, it would have to be him.

'Why should the Republic come to Aetolia's aid?' demanded Claudius. 'It was faithless Aetolia that abandoned the alliance between our peoples, not Rome.'

Silence fell in the chamber. Everyone knew that it was Rome's withdrawal from the conflict that had forced Aetolia to seek terms from Philip, but to lay the blame at the Republic's door would cause grave insult. Even so, it took Neophron's restraining hand to keep Euripidas from replying. A high colour marked the grey-bearded emissary's face, and he glared at Claudius.

Neophron pulled a placatory smile from somewhere. 'We Aitolians can only apologise. Our situation was desperate, but it was a mistake to make peace with Philip. A future alliance between our peoples would be sacrosanct – may the gods strike me down if I lie.' He glanced at Euripidas, who nodded in vigorous agreement.

'Once an oath-breaker, always an oath-breaker. Not one senator has spoken in your favour either,' said Servilius harshly. He shot a look at Claudius, who nodded in agreement, before flicking a finger at the door. 'I wish you a pleasant voyage back to your homeland.'

Again Neophron had to prevent an angry Euripidas from speaking. They bowed – more stiffly this time – and turned to go.

'The consuls lead Rome in times of war, but they do not make its every decision.' Flamininus pitched his voice to carry. 'Should the senators not vote on this important matter?'

The emissaries' gaze – along with everyone else's – shot to Flamininus. This venture may be doomed from the outset, he thought, but it is time to lay down a marker. To show the senators that I am a force to be reckoned with.

'*Quaestor* Flamininus, is it not?' Galba's emphasis on the first word made clear his contempt of the lowest-ranked magistrates.

'I hold the position with praetorian imperium, as well you know, Galba. I wish to vote on this matter, as I am sure do a number of my fellows.' Flamininus waited for the many loud cries of 'Aye' to die down before he continued. 'You seem to forget the previous war between the Republic and Philip. It may have been inconsequential, but that does not mean he is an enemy to disregard. He tried to ally himself with Hannibal some years ago, remember. In my mind, those who stand against him should be supported, not spurned.' He gave the Aetolians a friendly nod, and received the same in return.

'Never let it be said that I stand in the Republic's path.' Servilius' tone was smooth, but his eyes – fixed on Flamininus – were as murderous as Galba's. After a short exchange with Claudius, Servilius declared, 'Let us see what the Senate wishes. All those in favour of offering assistance to Aetolia, raise your right hand.'

Flamininus lifted his arm in the air, and his followers did the same. Some senators opposite also showed their support for the motion, but it wasn't many. Around Galba, not a single man had his hand up. Flamininus' gaze met that of his rival for the first time; it was Galba's turn to raise an eyebrow. 'Is that the best you can do?' he seemed to ask. Flamininus held the stare long enough to show Galba he wasn't scared, and then he watched the pacing lictores make their count. When a total of seventy-nine was called out, Flamininus decided that despite its failure, his provocative act had been worthwhile. The next time such an important vote came around, a network of spies would have made him better informed even than Galba. At least one of the consuls would already need to be on his side, and allies would be required throughout the Senate. Then success would be his.

'Seventy-nine,' said Servilius with evident satisfaction. 'And those of you who are against helping Aetolia?'

The second count took a little longer, but came back as two hundred and ten. 'Eleven senators are absent,' declared Servilius. 'Which means that even if they had all voted with *Quaestor* Flamininus, the result would have been no different.'

Flamininus dipped his chin in acknowledgement.

'Rome has spoken,' Claudius told the disappointed emissaries.

The pair bowed and made for the entrance. Catching Flamininus' eye, Neophron mouthed, 'Gratitude.'

I made an ally there, Flamininus decided. His skin tingled, and to his disquiet, he found Galba regarding him as a snake studies its prey.

From this point on, thought Flamininus, he would have to take care.

It had not been his intention, but he had made a real enemy in Galba.

CHAPTER III

Outside the town of Kios,
southern shore of the Propontis

The sun forged a path into the clear sky, burning off the last of the morning cloud. Demetrios' scalp prickled. His tunic was wringing with sweat, his face and arms were a deep shade of pink. Several hours had passed since dawn, and still the king had not appeared. All they could do was wait; one of Demetrios' fellows muttered, 'Wait and burn.'

'Don't like it?' another replied. 'Say something to the oar master.'

That silenced the grumbler.

Demetrios was as uncomfortable as the rest, but he kept his peace. The oar master, patrolling their ranks, needed little excuse to start wielding his staff. So Demetrios copied the old rowers, the men with lined, nut-brown faces, and hands with skin as hard as leather, and kept his head down. The crew were among hundreds who'd been ordered off the ships, their task to push siege towers towards Kios when the attack began. Each would receive two days' pay if the assault succeeded. That promise alone had made Demetrios happy. He wasn't a phalangist, but this worthy labour made him feel part of the army. It was better than breaking his back at the oars, that was sure.

Kios was not a large settlement, which explained its need for an alliance with a greater power. The townspeople had chosen Aitolia, Philip's enemy of old, which had made them an obvious target for the king. His eagerness to re-establish Macedon as a power in Asia Minor remained unabated; rumour had it that Kios would not be the last town to be attacked before the fleet's voyage home. And yet, despite the overwhelming forces surrounding Kios, and the scores of Macedonian vessels offshore, the inhabitants had decided to fight rather than accept a new ruler. Other towns along the Propontis had opened their gates and accepted Macedonian garrisons, but not Kios. No one knew why

– to Demetrios' mind, it seemed madness to resist – but the defenders' intransigence made him happy. Once the town fell, he could follow the soldiers over the walls in search of plunder. The risks of being killed were worth the gold or silver he might find. With such riches, buying a flock of sheep would become possible, rather than remaining an almost unattainable dream.

Demetrios glanced to his left. 'How long have we been here?'

'Three hours, maybe,' answered Onesas, one of the rowers he slept beside.

'How much longer will Philip be?'

Onesas glared. 'How would I know, fool?'

Demetrios didn't bother asking Theokritos, the last member of their little group, who was on his right. The smart answer would only be the same.

Cheering broke out among the infantry moments later.

'The king! The king is here!'

'Your friend,' said Onesas, nudging him. Theokritos snorted with amusement.

Demetrios ignored them, and craned his neck to see. The pair hadn't believed him when he related his encounter with Philip; they wouldn't change their minds now.

Magnificent in ornate armour, wearing his red-crested helmet with ram's horns, and astride a feisty Thessalian stallion, Philip rode forward of the siege towers. Everyone could see him. He spent some time surveying the town, which increased the tension – as was his intent, thought Demetrios. When the king turned, he was smiling.

'It's a long way to Pella from here,' said Philip. 'Are you ready to go home?'

After a brief, shocked silence, thousands of voices bellowed, 'NO!'

'I jest,' cried Philip. 'I sent messengers to Kios yesterday with terms for their surrender. The council rejected my offer out of hand. I am not their king, they say.'

An angry roar met his words.

'The town sits yonder for the taking, like a ripe apple on a tree. Are you ready to seize it for Macedon?'

Demetrios' voice mingled in the thunderous cheering that followed.

Philip gave a signal, and the trumpets sounded. The infantry formed up in blocks behind the towers. The king rode back to join his Companions.

'Time to push, you whoresons!' cried Demetrios' oar master. 'Move!'

Demetrios moved to the base of the tower with his companions. Like the rest, it had been hauled into place by mules. A sturdy, four-wheeled affair, three storeys tall, it had a covered platform at the top. The hides of fresh-slaughtered cattle had been stretched into place on the sides as protection. Buckets and buckets of seawater had been emptied over the tower from base to apex, in case of fire arrows.

'Into position!' ordered the oar master.

Demetrios and the rest had worked out the best method for moving the tower. He and eleven others placed themselves along the width of its back. A similar number moved to each of the wheels. Knees bent, hands gripping the wood, they looked to the oar master, who chopped down with his arm.

'Push!' he ordered. 'Push, as if your lives depended on it!'

Demetrios shoved with all his might. Nothing happened. He heaved. Beside him, Onesas' sandal skidded on some gravel, and he went down on one leg. Demetrios gave him an encouraging nod and together they pushed again.

'Put your backs into it!' cried the oar master, pacing up and down. 'D'you *want* the other crews to beat you to the wall?'

No one had the breath to reply, but his words hit home. The men pushing the first tower to reach the defences would receive an extra reward, a large amphora of wine. Groans of effort mixed with the noise of sandals scraping the ground. Men fell, bloodying their knees, and without a word rejoined their comrades. Demetrios strained again, pushing with all his strength; sweat dropped from his face to the dirt.

Creak. The wheels juddered. Creak. The tower shifted forward a pace, then another.

An animal groan left Demetrios' lips, and from deep inside he found more energy. On either side, Onesas and Theokritos heaved like men possessed; their companions did the same. Slow but steady, the tower rumbled towards the walls of Kios. Demetrios began to count his footsteps. Four hundred paces they had to travel. Twenty score until they had to scramble to safety as the infantry poured in and up the stairs to the top, there to throw themselves at the enemy. The first men onto the ramparts would die – and so might many of the oarsmen, as they fled from the defences and the deadly artillery. Demetrios tried not to think of that. Push, he told himself. Concentrate on beating the other rowers. Ten paces, and the going was a little easier. Twenty, and they had achieved more momentum. Fifty paces, and he had almost forgotten the danger they were in.

He couldn't see where the other towers were in relation to their own. 'Are we in the lead?'

'Aye,' came the reply from someone with a view. 'By a score of paces.'

They had covered perhaps a quarter of the distance by Demetrios' rough calculation, which meant the other oarsmen *could* be beaten. Urging each other on, he and his fellows heaved and strained, moving the tower over the bumpy ground at a steady speed.

A whooshing, unfamiliar sound carried from behind the defences. Something – a stone? – landed with an almighty crash somewhere to Demetrios' right.

'They're shooting at us!' cried the oar master. 'Push, you filth!'

Demetrios had seen catapults, but he'd never witnessed them being used. A quick glance behind, and his belly tightened. The boulder he'd heard was bigger than his head, and had gouged a long, deep line in the earth. Any man in its path would have been pulverised.

Crash! Another stone ploughed into the ground, closer this time.

More were landing by the other towers. A man who'd had both legs crushed lay and screamed at the sky. Oar masters shouted and used their staffs with liberal abandon. Fresh men replaced Demetrios and his comrades, who continued to walk behind the tower.

Another fifty paces, and several stones had hit their tower, tearing through the wet cattle hides. Demetrios and his comrades rejoined the men pushing without being asked. Their efforts weren't enough. Halfway to the walls, and the tower had gaping holes everywhere in its superstructure. The ladder between the first and second storey was gone, yet the oar master drove them on. 'The attack goes ahead!' he bellowed. 'Heave!'

A dozen heartbeats later, a stone smashed the left front wheel, killing an oarsman and maiming several more. Destabilised, the tower lurched to one side. It stopped, then listed further. Cries of alarm rose, and men scrambled to get out of the way.

'Push,' roared the oar master, who couldn't see what had happened.

'It's going nowhere,' said Onesas. 'The wheel's fucked.'

Scowling, the oar master stalked around to see. In the time he was gone, two more stones had landed, one destroying another section of ladder. A third hit the ground nearby, bounced up and beheaded an oarsman. Crimson and brain matter sprayed, and the corpse tottered and fell. A grey blur, the stone mowed down two more men and travelled a hundred paces to their rear, injuring several soldiers.

The officer in charge of the infantry to their rear took charge. 'To the other towers!' He was out in the open, pointing to their right. 'Quickly!'

Demetrios' mouth was dry, and his heart pounding, but the promise of two extra days' pay was huge. He took a step away from their sheltered position. A powerful grip pulled him back – Onesas. Demetrios looked, and understood why. The nearest tower had just gone down, two of its wheels shattered, and the next was faring no better. The fourth was close to the wall, but it had a dangerous tilt, and to reach it would mean exposing themselves to the deadly enemy artillery. The fifth and sixth towers were too far away to see.

'Move, curse you!' bellowed the officer.

No one stirred. The officer pointed with his sword at Demetrios, who was closest.

'Move, you sewer rat!'

There was murder in the officer's eyes. Demetrios took a step, then another.

'Faster!' The officer gesticulated at Onesas. 'And you!'

Thunk. The sound made Demetrios look up. A stone came arcing up from the ramparts, and his eyes traced its likely path. Before he could think, he sprinted forward, heaving the officer to one side.

'Have you taken leave of your senses?' Spittle flew from the officer's lips.

Crash. Thud. Thud. Thud. Puffs of dust rose as the stone smacked into the earth right where they had been standing. Mesmerised, both men watched it bounce away, leaving large divots in its wake.

Self-conscious, Demetrios released his grip. 'Apologies, sir. There wasn't time to warn you.'

'No.' The officer looked embarrassed. 'I— well— no.'

There were no more orders to run to the other towers. From the relative safety of their wrecked structure, the oarsmen watched the fourth tower rumble in towards the wall. Soldiers had somehow managed to clamber to the top, and were hurling spears at the ramparts. Brave men, thought Demetrios. Twenty paces out, a pair of long, forked poles were thrust out from the walls. After several attempts, the defenders shoved the tower sideways, in the direction it was already leaning. With an horrific cracking noise, leavened with men's screams, it crashed to the ground. Cheering broke out along the rampart, and the officer spat in disgust.

'Pull back,' he shouted at his soldiers. 'And watch out for stones from those bastard catapults.'

The oar master was quick to repeat the order. Demetrios and his comrades needed no telling. They ran from Kios, casting frequent looks over their shoulders.

Philip was furious with the failure of the first attack, but rather than sail away, he set the oarsmen to felling more trees. Several days passed. Fresh siege towers were built – a dozen – and when the next assault began, three attacked each of Kios' walls. The enemy artillery could not cope. Buoyed up by Philip's promise of even more pay, Demetrios and his crew reached the walls first. They watched, mesmerised, as the soldiers atop the tower leaped onto the rampart and hacked a path for their comrades to follow.

Before Demetrios could think of joining the attack – despite the danger, he was keen to join in the search for booty – he and the rest were ordered to help push another tower. The enemy artillery had caused heavy casualties among other crews. By the time they had again reached the walls, screams were audible from inside the town. Demetrios' desire to join in the sacking melted like frost under the morning sun. Taking a fine sword or purse from a warrior he'd fought would be one thing, he decided, but it was another to attack defenceless women. His companions were not put off, however. Scaling the tower, they seized discarded weapons atop the walkway and disappeared into the town. Not wanting to be called a coward later, Demetrios followed. Prudence prevailed, and he armed himself with an old but serviceable spear.

His desire to be a soldier was put to the test not long after, at the entrance to a large house. Four well-armed servants defended it; as Onesas drew near, one shot him through the throat with an arrow. Baying their fury, the oarsmen charged. Onesas hadn't been much of a friend to Demetrios, but he had been a comrade. He ran after the rest, spear at the ready. The fight was brutal. Inexperienced, lacking basic skills, the oarsmen were easy targets. Another three were slain almost at once, and the others quailed before the servants' determination. Demetrios' skilful overhand thrust, which skewered one through the eye, gave them heart. Two more oarsmen died, but the overwhelming odds soon told against the defenders. When a second was injured, the remaining pair could not defend the wide, chest-high gate alone. They turned, abandoning the entrance. As the oarsmen cheered, Theokritos scaled the portal and opened it. Demetrios watched his comrades charge in.

Feet pounded. A party of phalangists, minus their cumbersome spears, ran by, and Demetrios' long-buried hopes of joining their number surfaced, fresh as they had ever been. Reality sank in. He had no chance of joining their number. His best chance was finding some coin; with that, he could buy sheep. A man could start a flock with a dozen; one day, he might even have the money to buy a farm of his own.

'You're that mad bastard who saved an officer's life the other day.' The voice belonged to a grizzled phalangist with a short beard. Limping, he was trailing in his comrades' wake. A bloodied *kopis* dangled from his right hand; in his left he bore a brazen-painted *aspis* decorated with the Macedonian sixteen-pointed star

Stunned at being recognised, in awe of the fearsome-looking soldier, Demetrios flailed for an answer.

The phalangist stumped right up to him. 'It *is* you.'

'Aye,' muttered Demetrios, embarrassed now.

'Great Zeus had his hand over you that day, that's certain. What were you thinking?'

'I wasn't,' said Demetrios truthfully.

A hearty laugh. 'You couldn't have been. That officer's a good four-file leader, but few of us would have risked ourselves like that, even if we'd been near enough.' An appraising glance at him, then the bodies of his comrades. 'Oarsman?'

'Aye.' Demetrios hated the flush staining his cheeks.

'Ever used a spear before today?' The phalangist was staring at the crimson-tipped blade of Demetrios' weapon.

'In my village.' The memories came flooding back. Training with the old soldier whose task it was to make men out of boys. Boxing until his arms felt like lead weights. Wrestling with bigger opponents, and being pinned down with an arm twisted back so far it felt as if one shoulder would dislocate. Watching the men of the village dance to the god Ares every summer. Glorious visions to a boy, Demetrios had vivid memories of their shining bronze helmets and cuirasses, and how their spear points had glittered in the firelight. 'Father wanted me to be a phalangist. I learned pankration. Wrestling and boxing too.' Although he was telling the truth, he couldn't lift his gaze from the dirt.

'Your father was a soldier?'

'A slinger. After the army, he kept sheep,' said Demetrios. 'It was a small flock, but he said that didn't matter. A citizen is a citizen. If a youth is strong and skilful, he can be chosen for the phalanx.' That would never happen now, he thought bitterly.

'Your father spoke true,' said the phalangist. 'In the past, only wealthy men served, but things are different these days.' He glanced at his right leg and grimaced. 'I turned my fucking ankle climbing over the rampart.' With a nod, he walked away.

'Wait!' cried Demetrios.

The soldier turned. 'Aye?'

'Y-you're saying I could become a phalangist?'

A loud chuckle. 'I didn't say that, boy.'

'Oh.' Demetrios' hopes sank.

The phalangist looked him up and down again, as if for the first time. After a moment, he said, 'Find me in the camp. We can see if you really know any pankration.'

Demetrios' hopes shot skywards again. 'And if I do?'

'We'll see.' The phalangist walked away.

He had almost reached the nearest corner when a sudden realisation struck Demetrios.

'What do they call you?' he cried.

'Simonides.'

'Simonides,' Demetrios repeated, as pleased as Jason when he had claimed the Golden Fleece.

CHAPTER IV

Zama, south-west of Carthage, autumn, 202 BC

High in the autumn sky, vultures soared over a great grassy plain bounded by low, tree-covered hills. They rode the currents in tight circles, layer upon layer of them. Patient. Keen-eyed. Silent. The first had had the air to itself for a time; others had joined in ones and twos. Now there were fifty at least, and numbers were growing. From a distance, men might have suspected the presence of large amounts of carrion, but nothing had died below the circling birds yet.

Anticipation was everything.

More than one hundred miles from the great city of Carthage, the flat ground below was a perfect location for two armies to meet, and from it came the sounds of men and animals and trumpets. Dust rose in great clouds. Light flashed off helmets, weapons. Three hours had passed since the arrival of the first troops, but many thousands of soldiers, horses and elephants were on the move. Full readiness took time. Infantry units had to reach their appointed positions. The cavalry on both sides needed to assemble on the flanks. Elephants had to be chivvied into place by their handlers. Midday arrived; a layer of high cloud moved in, keeping the sun at bay and the temperature down.

The plain was where the Roman general Scipio was about to confront Hannibal Barca, most famous son of Carthage. This was a clash long awaited by both sides, and its outcome would determine the victor in the bitter sixteen-year conflict. Rather than a siege against the mighty, miles-long walls of Carthage, or a naval attack against its twin ports, this was to be a face-to-face battle between armies.

In the Roman army's second rank – made up of *principes* – stood Felix, a tall, sturdy legionary with a friendly face, and his older brother Antonius. Both were in their mid-twenties, black-haired and olive-skinned; Antonius was short where Felix was not, and stern where he was easy-going. Farmers from south of Rome, they had enlisted together seven years before; both were seasoned veterans of the fight against Carthage.

Felix felt relief to be here at last. Scipio's army had been in Africa for months, and in that time, the Carthaginians had been beaten twice. Stubborn to the last, their leaders had refused to accept terms, and in a final act of desperation, had summoned Hannibal back from Italia. Rumour had it that many of his troops were poor quality new recruits, but until they were defeated, the war could not be declared won.

Felix glanced upwards, and wished he hadn't. Even if Scipio emerged victorious, there would be dead Romans aplenty for the vultures by sunset. Keep your hand over me, Great Jupiter, Felix asked, as you have for the last seven years. Prayer finished, he buried his worries as best he could.

More time passed. Feet pounded the earth, and horses whinnied. Officers shouted. Elephants bugled to one another. Among the princ-ipes, nothing happened. They were in position. Ready for battle, but powerless to act until orders came. Men prayed, or talked in muted voices. Some cracked overloud jokes; others made surreptitious checks of their equipment. Fierce-eyed centurions paced to and fro, cajoling and threatening by turns.

Felix began to grow bored. Devilment took him at last, and he nudged his brother. 'Will we win?'

Antonius glowered. 'What kind of question is that, now?'

Once Felix would have been cowed by such scorn. Four years younger, poor at his studies, he had grown up in his smarter brother's shadow, but the war with Carthage had changed their relationship – Antonius might have excelled during their training, but it was Felix who had first been promoted from *hastatus* to *princeps*. 'There's no harm in a joke,' he retorted with a curl of his lip.

Antonius seemed about to reply, but took a sudden interest in the dusty ground between his feet. Their comrades did the same.

'You doubt we will be victorious?' barked a familiar voice.

Felix's heart sank. Despite his undertone, their centurion Matho had still heard his comment. It was uncanny how he managed it time and again.

Slam. Stars burst across Felix's vision as Matho's *vitis* clattered his helmet.

'Speak up, maggot!' Matho shoved the end of his vine stick into Felix's face. 'You don't think Scipio will triumph?'

'That's not what I said, sir.' Felix admired Matho, who was tough, capable and a good leader, but it didn't do to get on his wrong side. Mercurial, unpredictable, he'd been known to beat a man half to death for the smallest infraction.

'What *did* you say?' Matho's teeth were cracked and brown; his breath reeked of wine and onions.

'Just that there's no harm in a joke before a battle, sir.'

'We mustn't mock the gods.' Matho cast an eye skywards, then glared at Felix. 'And every man must play his part.'

'I'm proud to fight for Rome, sir,' said Felix, hiding his resentment. 'Always have been.'

'No more jokes.' Short, bandy-legged, yet fear-inspiring, Matho stalked off, beady gaze roving over their fellows.

'Pompous cocksucker,' muttered Gnaeus. A wiry, flame-haired man with wits as sharp as his features, he was the prankster of their tent group.

'Matho's in a mood,' said Antonius. 'Be careful.'

'Aye.' Felix was glad to have his brother's concern. They had their differences, but blood was blood. They looked out for each other, always. He felt the same about Gnaeus and his other comrades, the majority of whom he'd known since his first days in the legion.

Time dragged by. The cloud cleared, allowing the temperature to rise steadily, and with it, the tension. Prayers that had earlier been muttered under men's breaths became audible. The whiff of urine laced the air as nervous bladders were emptied. Felix would have liked a game of dice, but the threat of Matho's vitis put him off. Prayers to Fortuna completed, equipment checked, he craned his neck, trying in vain to see what was going on in front of their position.

Scipio had placed his hastati, the youngest legionaries, in the army's first rank. Principes such as Felix and Antonius composed the second line. Behind them stood the cream of the legions, the *triarii*: Rome's most experienced soldiers. Half as numerous as the soldiers of the first two ranks, they were used only in extremis. Felix didn't like to think about that. If it came to the triarii, he and Antonius would be dead.

Unease gnawed his belly as he watched the mob of *velites*, skirmishers, who filled the large 'corridor' between Matho's century's position and the next grouping of principes. There were similar gaps at regular intervals all along the army's front, running right through the three ranks, but hidden from the enemy by the velites' presence. When the elephants charged, the skirmishers would retreat down the corridors, and according to Scipio, would be followed by the lethal behemoths. Felix was no general, but the tactic seemed laden with risk. If it failed, the men nearest the elephants would die. He tried not to imagine being impaled on a tusk, or trampled to a red pulp. With pricked ears, he listened, but heard no trumpets. Again his guts twisted. He wanted the cursed battle not to begin, but to be already over, leaving him and his comrades alive.

Matho was deep in conversation with the centurion of the next unit to their right; Felix took a chance. He cupped a hand to his mouth. 'Pssst!'

None of the velites heard. Ignoring Antonius' frown, Felix repeated his call, louder. This time, a veles turned. Short, scrawny and bare-cheeked, he couldn't have been a day over sixteen; his shield was old and battered, his spears poor-looking. Even the strip of wolfskin tied around his brow had seen better days, yet he was as cocky as a tribune. 'What?' he called back.

'Can you see anything?' asked Felix.

'Aye. Elephants in front of their army, cavalry on the wings – what you'd expect,' came the untroubled reply. He turned his back.

Felix ground his teeth, but in truth there wasn't much other response that he could have expected. 'Let's get it over with, eh?' he said to no one in particular.

'Aye. Waiting's hard.' Antonius' brow was beaded with sweat.

Later, Felix would think that up above, Fortuna had been listening.

'Here they come!' cried a voice some distance to their front. 'Elephants!'

A chorus of alarmed cries rose; it took a little while for the centurions and other officers to restore calm. Felix listened, but could hear only faint shouts from the enemy lines. Then he felt it – a vibration beneath his feet. Another followed, and another. He exchanged an unhappy look with Antonius. 'D'you feel that?'

A nervous nod.

Matho's appearance was timed to perfection. 'The big grey bastards are coming, brothers, but we know how to face 'em, don't we?' He didn't wait for an answer. 'When they get near enough, the velites will retreat, opening the corridors. We'll face inwards, and the elephants will charge through. Any that don't, well, our javelins will deal with them. Clear?'

'Aye, sir,' rumbled Felix and his comrades.

'Louder!'

'AYE, SIR!'

Matho leered. 'Never tasted elephant before. I plan to change that today.'

The ground began to tremble in earnest. Trumpets sounded from the cavalry positions, and were taken up along the Roman line. This was part of Scipio's plan, to panic the elephants if possible. Sudden bile washed Felix's throat, and he retched. He spat, and was quick to throw his shoulders back, but Matho was on him in a trice, his bloodshot eyes a finger's width from Felix's.

'Ready, maggot?'

Fuck you, thought Felix. 'Yes, sir!'

'I'm watching you.' Matho paced down the side of the century.

Felix threw up another prayer to Jupiter, which made not a bit of difference, so he fixed his gaze on the velites in the corridor, and tried to make sense of the blaring trumpets, shouted orders and the heavy tread approaching their position. It was impossible – everything was confusion – but he was distracted enough not to vomit a second time.

When the velites began loping towards the army's rear, jeering and shouting over their shoulders, a portion of the battlefield was revealed – the space between Matho's century and the next. A quarter of a mile away, the enemy host loomed. Felix could see no elephants, and relief filled him. Perhaps none would come this way. Fighting enemy soldiers was something he was used to, and expected; maybe that was all he'd have to do today.

'ELEPHANT!' screamed a score of voices.

A grey mountain came into sight, some hundred paces away. With flared ears, and trunk bugling a challenge, it was clearly angry *and* scared. High on its back clung its rider, his frantic efforts to direct his beast away from the corridor and at the legionaries coming to naught.

Felix could almost hear Fortuna's mocking laughter.

'Turn to the right!' roared Matho, his voice calm. 'Front four ranks, javelins ready.'

Facing into the corridor, Antonius to one side and Gnaeus the other, Felix gripped his javelin until it hurt. The elephant had covered half the distance to the corridor's 'entrance'. It veered wildly out of sight for a few heartbeats, only to return, tail flicking, ears billowing. Continuing to ignore its rider's commands, the beast lumbered closer to the gap.

'There's a second one coming, and another!' bellowed an hastatus, his voice cracking. 'Three of them!'

Felix, he thought. What a name. I should have been called Infelix. Unlucky.

'Stupidest thing I ever did was to join the fucking army,' Gnaeus muttered.

'Steady, brothers!' cried Matho. 'Release on my command, and not before.'

Felix watched the first elephant with horrified fascination. Rather than make a clean entry into the gap, it barged into some hastati, sending them flying like children's dolls. A vicious flick of its trunk, and two more were swept sideways, into their fellows. It trumpeted its rage and passed into the corridor. A handspan taller than the largest of men, with gleaming tusks and its head encased in leather armour, it was a terrifying vision.

Several heartbeats pattered by before the centurions among the hastati regained their wits. Commands rang out. Volley after volley of javelins rained in from left and right. Most missed, others flew too far and landed among the soldiers on the opposite side, but perhaps a score found their target.

Pierced through legs, chest and belly, its rider slain, the elephant resembled a massive, bloody porcupine. Despite its grievous wounds, it did not die, let alone fall. Stumbling and weaving, it headed straight for Felix and his comrades.

'Ready javelins!' For the first time, Matho's voice held a note of fear.

Fresh volleys showered in, striking the elephant over and again. Still it came on. Piggy eyes almost closed, it collided with a century of hastati twenty paces from Felix's position. Picking up a screaming legionary with its trunk, it flung him high in the air. It gored another to death and maimed several as the hastati swarmed to the attack, stabbing and thrusting with javelins and swords. At last, with an almighty groan, the elephant crumpled onto its forelegs, then its back legs – but it did not fall. Not until javelins had sunk into both eyes, and half its trunk had been hacked away, did it collapse onto its side. A ragged cheer went up from the hastati.

There was no time for Felix and his companions to enjoy this success. Two elephants, one following the other, now came rampaging into the corridor. Men panicked and broke formation; some were trampled by the great beasts, others by their own kind. Crimson sprayed high in the air as a legionary had his head ripped off. Shields were riven by ivory tusks and the men behind impaled. The ragged volleys that followed did not injure either elephant badly enough to halt its progress.

On they came, one making a beeline down the centre, the other lurching towards the far side of the corridor. They're going to miss us, thought Felix with overwhelming relief. Thank the gods.

The elephant came alongside their position.

He never saw the fool who panicked and threw his javelin. So close, he couldn't miss. The elephant squealed with rage and spun, lightning fast, to face its attacker. Its rider was injured; nonetheless, he urged his mount towards the principes with loud cries. This is it, thought Felix, terror battering him. Jupiter's gaze had turned away; in his place, Pluto beckoned.

Matho ordered a swift volley, and for his men to assume close order; they almost managed it before the elephant reached them. Trunk swinging like an enormous club, feet high-stepping to strike anything in its path, the great beast smashed into their midst. The two men to the left of Gnaeus were there one instant, and then they were gone. Gnaeus himself was thrown sideways into Felix, who did well not to fall.

His vision was filled with the elephant; he'd never been this near to something so massive. Blood ran from its myriad wounds; javelins hung down its sides, held in place by their barbed heads. *Thwack.* Its trunk flicked a legionary head over heels, into the men several ranks back. A meaty impact and an agonised shriek followed as it used its tusks on another victim. Every instinct screamed at Felix to run from this unstoppable monster, but he stood fast. Death was preferable to abandoning his comrades.

Setting Gnaeus back on his feet, he drew his sword. 'With me?'

Gnaeus' face was grey with fear, but he nodded.

'Antonius?' Felix called.

'I'm here.'

'Come on,' said Felix.

The elephant had moved deeper into the midst of the principes. A mixture of Matho's men and those from other centuries pressed in around its head. The ground to its left, nearest Felix, was heaped high with bodies, dead and living. He winced at the cries of pain his passage caused, but he couldn't stop to help, even to send someone to the other side. The elephant had to be brought down. Jupiter, let it not see me, he prayed, his sandals slipping on blood and gore.

Felix thought the god had answered his plea. Ten paces he stole towards the elephant, Gnaeus and Antonius on his heels, and it didn't notice. Where the beast's weakest spot might be, he had no idea. Between the ribs, just behind the left leg, seemed as good a place as any – that was the best spot for bringing down a deer with an arrow.

'Stick it behind the elbow,' he hissed.

'Aye,' came the replies.

The elephant couldn't have heard: the din of battle was incredible, but whatever the reason, it turned its head. Where its right eye should have been, an oozing red socket gaped, but its left, nearest Felix, burned with palpable rage. There was no question that it had seen him.

'Quick!' he shouted.

If it presented them with its invulnerable front, they were dead men.

Time slowed. Gnaeus shouted something. A princeps stabbed the elephant in the trunk. With a bugle of pain, it swung back and stamped him into oblivion. Felix got three paces nearer. Sword raised, he fixed his gaze on the elephant's left foreleg. Ichor coated it to the height of a man's knee, and his stomach turned. Back went his right arm. Jupiter, guide my blade, he thought.

He was almost deafened by the elephant's trumpet, saw little other than a wall of leathery, grey skin as it turned, right on top of him. Smacked in the head by the lower part of its chest, Felix was driven groundwards. Landing by some miracle on one knee, he managed to keep hold of his sword. His shield was gone, smashed into firewood by a mighty foot. Worse, he was *under* the fucking elephant. He looked up, panic tearing at him. Making a blind stab was pointless – the javelins in the first elephant had been proof of that.

Marking the ribs at last, he aimed for the left side of the chest. Sure that it would be his final act, Felix gripped his sword with both fists and drove it up, into the elephant's flesh. Sharp enough to slice meat off the bone, the blade ran in hilt-deep without stopping. A mighty shudder, and the elephant let out an odd, sighing cough. Its front knees trembled, and the sword was forced down with immense force. Letting go, Felix fell on all fours. Extra energy flooded his veins at the thought of being crushed, and he scrambled towards the daylight.

He almost made it.

A vast weight dropped from above, trapping his legs. The aftershock slammed his face into the ground; dirt filled his mouth. Everything went black.

Slowly, Felix came to. Pain filled his body. There was grit on his tongue; loud noises filled his ears. Men were shouting, cursing, screaming. Further off, weapons clashed; a trumpet sounded. This can't be the underworld, he thought, feeling the crushing heaviness on his lower half. Twisting his head, he made out the immobile mass of the elephant on top of him.

He made a vain attempt to free himself. Nausea clawed the back of his throat as he realised there was no sensation in his legs, let alone his feet. Perhaps his spine had been snapped. Felix had seen men who'd been injured in that way before – half-creatures who relied on others to wipe their arses. Death was better than that. Don't abandon me now, Jupiter, he thought. Please.

At length, the sounds of fighting dimmed and then died away. Roman voices drew nearer, and Felix began to shout for help. Joy filled him as friendly faces came into sight, clambering over the slain – Antonius among them.

'Brother!' Face spattered with blood, but hale otherwise, Antonius dropped down beside Felix. He heaved at the elephant with an awed expression. 'Did you kill it?'

'Maybe. I think so. Where's Gnaeus?'

A grim shake of the head.

'And the others in our *contubernium*?'

'Most of them are alive, I think.' Antonius pushed at the elephant, and cursed. 'Are you hurt?'

'I can't feel anything below my waist.'

'We'll get it off you in no time. You'll be fine.'

Felix prayed his brother wasn't just trying to make him feel better. The news that one of their own was trapped flashed through the nearest legionaries at lightning speed. Ropes were fastened to its legs, which luckily faced in the opposite direction, and scores of men gathered around Felix, ready to push as their comrades on the far side pulled. A scowling Antonius directed operations, and ensured that there were men kneeling to his left and right.

'The instant the elephant rises,' he ordered, 'shove in those shields, front uppermost, as many as you can. If the fools on the ropes let go, I don't want him crushed again.'

Fresh fear bathed Felix as, with loud shouts of effort, the carcase was heaved off him. Antonius dragged him free at once; he called out, and the legionaries on the elephant's far side released their grip. The enormous body fell back into position with a resounding thump. Felix winced, oblivious to the cheers rising to the skies.

Antonius was by his side. 'Can you stand?'

'No!' He reached down and squeezed his thigh, hard. Pain darted up his body, and he felt a spark of hope. 'Pinch my calf.'

Understanding, Antonius obeyed. 'Can you feel it?'

'Aye.' Felix's voice was hoarse. 'Go lower.' Giddy with excitement as the toes of his left foot began tingling, he looked down. 'Try the other one.' Antonius obeyed, and Felix exulted as discomfort radiated from his right foot. Pins and needles followed as, aided by his brother, he massaged his legs. Little by little, blood and sensation flowed back into his limbs. He beamed at Antonius. 'I'm all right. I'm all right.'

'The gods be thanked. Come on.'

Antonius helped him up, which set their comrades to cheering again.

Matho appeared, putting an end to their jubilation. Antonius explained what had happened, and Matho threw a dour look at Felix. 'The elephant fell on you, eh?'

'Yes, sir. After I stabbed it in the chest.' Felix jiggled one leg, and the other, glad of the darts still radiating through his flesh.

Matho grunted. 'Where's your sword?'

'Under the elephant, sir.'

Antonius and those who heard grinned, but Matho was unimpressed. 'Find another – and a shield.' He cupped a hand to his lips, addressing the rest. 'Pick up any javelins you can find, then back into formation, you maggots. Make it quick! The advance will sound any time.'

Discovering Gnaeus' mangled body close by, Felix took his sword and shield. There was no time to grieve his friend's death, only to accept the javelin Antonius handed him and face the enemy again. Casualties had been heavy – ten men from the century were dead, and another half a dozen injured too badly to fight – and the slaughter was just beginning.

Matho didn't dwell on their losses. Pacing up and down the front rank, and along the century's sides, he told his men what a fine job they had done with the elephants.

'Apart from the fool who threw that javelin, mind,' he snarled. 'If I ever find him . . .'

Most of the monsters were slain or vanished out the end of the corridors, never to return, Matho went on. Some had turned and run in panic at their own side. Reports were that the enemy cavalry had been driven from the field. When the trumpets sounded, the principes would march to the attack behind the hastati. Matho leered. 'We'll show those mongrel Carthaginians what legionaries can do, brothers!'

Still marvelling at his lucky escape, Felix bayed his enthusiasm with the rest.

Matho's prediction came true not long after. Messengers arrived from Scipio, ordering the advance. Shrill trumpet blasts echoed along the army's front, and the earth reverberated to the tread of thousands of hobnailed sandals. Although Felix was at the front of the century, he was blind to the enemy's position thanks to the hastati before them. Since his promotion to the principes, he had never been comfortable with this arrangement and so by way of distraction, he kept count of his steps. One hundred paces they went. Matho, wise to the importance of the coming fight, positioned himself in the centre of the front rank, from where he continued to bawl encouragement. At the back, the optio repeated the chant.

Two hundred paces.

Yells and shouts could be heard from their front now – the enemy's war cries. Matho's vigorous response was endless repetitions of 'ROMA!', while clattering his sword off his shield. Felix and his comrades copied him, and in that rousing fashion, they covered another hundred and fifty paces. They have to be close, thought Felix. Very close.

The hastati charged a moment later, screaming at the top of their lungs.

Matho and the other centurions had their soldiers follow, at the walk, ten wide, and as deep as there were men to fill the ranks. The second century in each maniple came behind the first. They came to a halt some thirty paces behind the massed hastati, who had met the enemy with a clash loud enough to wake the dead. 'Hold the line, brothers!' Matho cried, breaking ranks to face them. 'Ground your shields. Take a piss. Have a quick drink. Our time will soon come.'

'Legs working?' Antonius asked Felix.

'Getting there.'

'A lucky escape.'

'Aye.' Accept the elephant as my offering, Jupiter, Felix asked. If I make it through the day, you'll have a ram too.

Grim-faced, they waited as the hastati did their best against the Carthaginians. Nothing could be seen of the enemy apart from their spears, which arced up to fall amid the hastati. The ranks before Felix swayed and rippled as the fortunes of those at the front ebbed and flowed. Optiones stood ready with their long staffs, on occasion battering men back into formation.

Instinct made Felix unsheathe Gnaeus' sword. He cursed its pitted, nicked blade, but wasn't surprised. His comrade had never been the best with a whetstone. Propping his shield against his earth-stabbed javelin, Felix rummaged in his purse for his own. With careful strokes, he ran the bluish-purple stone up and down the iron, over and over. The comforting rhythm distracted him from the chaos and bloodshed. Testing the edge with his thumb, he nodded with satisfaction. It would do for now.

'Give it here.' Antonius held out his hand.

Felix watched as his brother sharpened his own weapon. 'Hand it over,' he ordered as Antonius finished.

'Don't you trust me?'

'No.'

They both chuckled. It was a standing joke. Felix's Gaulish whetstone was of the finest quality, and Antonius had long coveted it.

Their laughter died away as they spied an optio from the troops in front coming to confer with Matho.

'Prepare yourselves, brothers!' bellowed Matho a moment later. 'The hastati are about to withdraw.'

Felix quickly retrieved his shield and javelin.

Under the watchful eyes of their optiones, the hastati began to retreat, a century at a time. The withdrawal of each unit opened a gap in the battle line, and Matho led his men into the first available space. The remaining hastati should have held until the principes were in place, when the gap left by *their* withdrawal would be filled by the next century of principes, and so on. To Felix's surprise, he and his comrades were still twenty paces from the front when some of these last hastati began breaking away. Gore-spattered, many with wounds, they looked spent, and uncaring of the huge hole now created in the Roman line.

Eagle-eyed, Matho saw what was happening. 'Quicker, you maggots!' he screamed, and broke into a run.

Every man copied Matho; their line reformed just as they reached the hastati. Chests heaving, they assumed close formation: shields a man's pace apart, held at eye height, javelins ready.

'The enemy aren't ready to attack. They're reorganising,' said Antonius in delight.

Twenty-five paces away, across a ground littered with corpses, wounded and discarded weapons, stood their opponents, a ragged mass of Ligurians, Gauls and Balearic slingers, Carthaginian and African infantry. Officers and chieftains strode to and fro, barking orders and shoving men into position.

'With so many different troops, that must be their first *and* second line,' said Felix. He cast a glance to his left and right, and the gaps that had not yet been filled. 'It's good they're not ready. If they attacked us now, we'd be screwed.'

Despite their own disorganisation, some of the enemy sensed an opportunity. Balearic slingers began advancing towards the principes. Slings whirling around their heads, they released their bullets with vicious cracks. Most legionaries raised their shields, but not all. A couple of men went down, stunned by the impact of the stones off their helmets. Noticing the slingers' success, the Gauls chanted and banged their swords off their shield bosses.

Still there was no sign of the holes in the Roman line being closed.

In the stomach-churning moments that followed, Matho came into his own. Stalking along the front rank, he screamed in man after man's face, 'Ready?' With each 'Yes, sir!' he clapped the princeps on the shoulder and moved on. He kept his back to the enemy the entire time.

'He has balls bigger than Priapus,' muttered Felix.

Antonius and his comrades chuckled.

'Hammer your shields,' Matho shouted. 'Loud as those savages yonder!'

Clash, clash, clash, went Felix and his comrades. 'ROMA! ROMA!'

The din they made checked the Gauls long enough for the remainder of the principes to arrive. Everyone cheered as the gaps vanished.

'A volley first, then we advance. At the signal, brothers!' Matho raised his right arm.

Blood pounded in Felix's ears, dimming the clamour. His left forearm ached with the effort of holding up his shield. Under his mail and *subarmalis*, his sweat-soaked tunic clung to his body. A dull ache radiated from the base of his spine, and he wondered if the elephant had done him permanent damage. It didn't matter much, he decided. Death was beckoning.

Trumpets rang. Officers shouted.

'LOOSE!' roared Matho.

Taking a deep breath, Felix threw.

A time later – Felix had no idea how long – the recall was sounded. Savage fighting, with no give or take on either side, had seen heavy casualties. Hundreds of bodies, Roman and Carthaginian, lay entangled in death's cold embrace. Countless discarded weapons and shields were scattered around, on top of, beneath them. With the ground thus obstructed, the fighting had fragmented into smaller, vicious contests that were impossible to control or monitor. During one spell, Felix and Antonius had ended up with just their tent mates, and been lucky to survive.

The century had suffered more losses – six dead, and the same number of wounded. A comrade of Felix and Antonius was among the latter, while the brothers had come through unscathed. Matho had a slash along his sword arm; it wasn't life-threatening, but he'd had to change places with their optio Paullinus, a saturnine individual with a bulbous nose and a deep love of the wineskin. Although Paullinus was more likeable than Matho, he wasn't the same leader, and the signal to withdraw had come as a relief to all.

Their respite was brief, just enough to see the wounded given basic treatment and sent to the rear. Scipio's orders, relayed by fast-moving riders, were to regroup into their usual units, and then to intersperse themselves with the triarii, who were being deployed at last.

'This is it, brothers,' said Matho. White-faced but as combative as ever, he had a rough bandage on his injured arm. 'It's come to the triarii – you know what that means.'

'Things are fucking bad,' said a voice from the ranks.

Felix and Antonius exchanged a loaded glance. The triarii had only been used in one of the battles they had fought in; that victory had come at a high cost.

Matho's chuckle was unpleasant. 'Aye, you're right. The guggas are more stubborn than I'd have thought. The hastati couldn't break them. We gave it our best effort, and still they held. Before we hit them again, we'll have to listen to the triarii giving us shit. Useless maggots, they'll call you. Cocksuckers. Yellow-livered sons of whores. Goatfuckers. Pillow biters – every one of us a *molles* of the worst kind.'

Felix and the rest snarled their anger.

Matho's smile would have made a baby cry.

'Don't like that? Good.'

They bayed like hungry wolves.

'Forget about the triarii. They're old men compared to you fine specimens.' He let them cheer, then went on, smiling, 'The glory of Rome, you are! You're better soldiers than any of the child-murdering gugga scum with Hannibal. Better than arse-humping Gaulish savages, or half-naked brutes from the Balearic Islands. You're even better than those Libyan bastards with the long spears.'

From Matho, this was unexpected, rare praise. The principes lapped it up, cheering until they were hoarse. By the time a unit of triarii had lined up on either side, they barely gave them a look.

'I should be with you in the coming fight, but I can't, worse luck.' Scowling, Matho raised his injured arm. 'Make me proud, brothers. Do your century and your maniple proud. Your legion proud! Make Scipio proud!'

They needed every last bit of grit in the fight that followed. It wasn't as if all the enemy were fighting for their homeland – most weren't even Carthaginian, Felix knew – but something had fuelled their courage the way Matho had roused his principes. Whether it was good leaders, the knowledge that prisoners would receive short shrift, or just love of Hannibal, he didn't know. The struggle was titanic, more brutal than anything he had experienced during seven years of war.

Neither side retreated a single step. When a man was slain or injured, another moved forward to take his place. If a shield was damaged or a sword cracked, those in the rank behind were quick to pass theirs forward. Twice, enemy warriors came close to taking Matho's century's standard, but the principes' brutal determination won through. Rising to the occasion, Paullinus fought like a demon. He hurled abuse at the enemy, using insults that rivalled Matho's, and it was this that saw him singled out in one of the final clashes.

'Paullinus is down!'

The news rattled through the century like a winter gale loosening roof tiles.

His death created more than a hole in the front rank. Morale, that ethereal emotion, sank several degrees. Men's shoulders dropped, and the insults and snarls that had met every enemy attack died away. At the back, Matho could not see, had no way of reacting. The gap left by Paullinus had already been filled by the snarling, bare-chested Gaul who had slain him. Behind came half a dozen warriors, emboldened by their friend's success.

Felix was in the second rank – he'd changed places not long since to have a breather. It was close enough to see the danger they were all in. With a strength born of desperation, he pushed past their startled comrades, urging Antonius to follow.

Lucky for Felix, the first Gaul was busy trampling on the princeps he'd just killed. Felix's sword slid between his ribs, in and out, and he fell, maggot food before he knew it. The warrior behind let out a cry of rage and twisted to face Felix, who rammed his blade into the man's mouth. Teeth splintered, blood sprayed. Felix's sword came to a jarring halt in his spine.

Struggling to free his weapon, Felix would have died if Antonius hadn't appeared at his left shoulder. Even as a third warrior drew back his spear, Antonius stabbed him in the armpit. A precise thrust, it left him ready to face the next Gaul. Felix had a pair of warriors on him by that stage, but the principes around them had been rallied by their ferocity. They closed like a pack of feral dogs on a carcase, and the warriors went down beneath a flurry of blades.

'Reform the line!' bawled Felix. 'Close the gap!'

With their defences shored up, he, Antonius and the rest faced a heavy attack from the dead Gauls' companions. All his efforts were about to be undone. Felix spat in warriors' faces, called them sheep-fucking animals in their own tongue, used every trick he knew. Two warriors took the bait, and died. Stamping on bare feet worked with one man, and another – the pain enough to drag their eyes away from his sword. The old-fashioned powerful slam with the shield boss, followed by a swift blade, proved useful on a smooth-cheeked youth.

Oblivious to their losses, the enemy pressed home the assault. The Gauls were reinforced by a group of Libyans, who used their long spears to great effect. Four principes died one after another, and more were injured. A massive, united spear heave, and the Libyans advanced several steps. Muscles screaming, breath catching in his dry throat, Felix bent his knees and wormed his way in between the spear shafts. Somehow managing to hold his encumbering shield, somehow not being stabbed, he shuffled towards the Libyans. Close in, the soldiers were defenceless. One thrust with his sword, then a second, and he'd slain two men. 'Come on!' Felix roared over his shoulder. He couldn't do it alone.

Next instant, Antonius was there, four others at his back. Together, they forced their way into the Libyan formation. Their daring worked well: the next rank also had their spears levelled, and were unable to defend themselves at close quarters. Soon, however, the Libyans let go of their spears and dragged free their swords. A dozen heartbeats, and every man nearby had wrenched his shield around to face the intruders.

Felix and his companions were now hemmed in on three sides, and in the frantic struggle that followed, they were slain one by one. Drained of strength, hope ebbing away, Felix cursed his rashness. He fought on, sure that he would die, but hoping that Antonius might somehow survive.

'Listen!' Antonius' breath was hot in his ear.

Felix took an enemy's sword on his shield, a blow that sent waves of agony shooting up his left arm. He barged back in reflex, and thrust at the Libyan with his own weapon, granting a tiny reprieve. 'What?'

Antonius was too busy fighting to answer.

Still trading blows with his enemy, Felix listened. The din of battle was overwhelming: screams, shouts and the clash of weapons mixed with trumpets, the whinny of injured horses, and far off, elephants bugling. He had no idea what Antonius had heard. Another massive thrust came in from the Libyan, and Felix ducked behind his shield.

Tremble. Beneath his feet, the earth moved. *Tremble.*

The Libyan froze.

Tremble.

He felt it too, thought Felix.

The earth shook and shook again. Hooves pounded, thousands of them from the Carthaginians' rear. Confused shouting followed, and cries of fear.

Understanding flared. 'It's our cavalry!' Felix roared. 'Our cavalry has returned!'

The Libyan paled; he understood Felix's meaning, even if Latin wasn't his mother tongue. Pinned between the legionaries and the Numidian cavalry, he and his companions faced complete slaughter. Its rumour was already spreading – a blind man could sense the spearmen's ranks wavering. More principes shouldered forward to join Felix and Antonius, and they pressed on, jabbing, thrusting, shouting their defiance at the Libyans, who fell back.

With a fierce cry, Felix's opponent launched a final attack. Over-reaching with his sword, he exposed his armpit. Felix struck. The tip of the blade went in, just enough to slice the Libyan's lung. Coughing pink froth, he stumbled and fell. With a quick lunge, Felix pithed him through the spine. When he looked up, the rest of the spearmen had broken. Many had already succumbed to blind panic. Unarmed, unmanned, they elbowed and shoved at one another in their eagerness to flee the battlefield.

Baying their bloodlust, Felix and his comrades took up the pursuit.

CHAPTER V

Philip had come with his thirteen-year-old son Perseus and a group of bodyguards to survey the wreckage of Kios. A pall of smoke still hung over the town, last remnants of the fires that had burned during his soldiers' rampage. Ruined buildings smouldered; now and again a crash and a cloud of sparks announced the fall of a roof beam. Bodies littered the streets: men, women, children. There were too many for Philip's liking: corpses were no use to anyone, and he said as much to Perseus.

'The next time a city is taken,' Philip declared, 'I'll have the officers keep better control.' He noted Perseus averting his gaze from the corpses. 'War is terrible – but it's necessary, and this–' Philip swung an arm around at the destruction '–is what happens.'

'These people are not barbarians, Father,' protested Perseus. Tall for his age, he had Philip's slim build and sharp eyes; he also possessed the same confidence. Like his father, he was garbed in bronze breastplate and greaves, although Philip's red-crested helmet was the more ornate of the two. A fine sword hung by Perseus' side. He gestured at the body of a man in a fine chiton. 'They're freeborn Greeks.'

'That's right,' said Philip. 'Allied to Aitolia. Need I remind you how the Aitolians have been a thorn in my side for years?'

Perseus shook his head. 'They went to Rome, seeking help against us.'

'They are as treacherous as jackals, and do not forget it.'

'Why was Kios allied to Aitolia, Father?'

Philip shrugged. 'Like as not, the Aitolians aided them once against an aggressor. That, or a ruler's son from here was educated in Aitolia, and became friends with a leading noble's son. Allegiances are strange things, but it explains why so many towns along the Propontis answer to different powers: Macedon, Aitolia, Egypt.'

'Better they all looked to you, Father.' Perseus' face shone.

Philip gave his son a smile. 'Despite Kios' alliance with Aitolia, I would have been benevolence personified if the people had welcomed me, their rightful king. No one need have died, except perhaps a few mule-headed members of the assembly who objected to my rule. Even if they had surrendered after a short fight, I would have spared most of them.'

'Alexander used to do that.'

'Even so.' Philip was delighted by the comment. For years, his purpose had been to take back first the territories taken by Alexander's father, his namesake Philip, and after, the empire won by the Lion of Macedon. 'Instead of submitting, though, they shut their gates in my face. They put up stiff resistance too.' Philip gestured coldly at a greybeard whose throat had been slit from ear to ear. 'This is their reward.'

'Help! Help me!'

A woman's voice echoed from the courtyard of a building to their left. Once a fine two-storey structure, it had mostly burned down or collapsed.

As Philip made to walk towards the sound, the captain of his bodyguard stepped into his path. 'It could be a trap, sire.'

He raised an eyebrow. Wise to the risk, however small, he did not object as the officer sent three men through the doorway before him. Philip followed, a hand on the ornate hilt of his kopis. Perseus was on his heels. The porch led to an entrance hall. A strong odour of burned grain and olives came from the first opening on his left. Philip glanced in; fallen shelves and broken pots lay everywhere: the chamber had been a storeroom. Beyond the hall was a rectangular courtyard, its long end running parallel to the front of the house. On Philip's right stood a small covered area with an altar – the family's place of worship. The rest of the building was little more than piles of roof tiles, bricks and broken ends of timber.

'Over here, sire.' The three bodyguards were at the far end of the courtyard, by what looked to have been the back hallway. A woman crouched nearby, alternately digging and exhorting them to help her.

Close up, Philip saw the dust-covered hand protruding from the rubble. The fingers twitched, and he understood her desperation.

'Help me!' cried the woman to the bodyguards.

Tears had formed runnels down her soot-covered cheeks, and her eyes were red with exhaustion and terror. A fine-looking woman, her chiton was torn and filthy. Suddenly, she saw Philip and took in his fine raiment, if not his exact status. 'Please, sir,' she begged. 'I've been trying for hours to free my son. He's still alive, but he is getting weaker.'

She stood, her bloodied hands held out in entreaty. At once the nearest bodyguard moved in front of Philip.

'Father,' implored Perseus. 'Please.'

It was time for his son to learn more about kingship, thought Philip. 'What are you waiting for?' he cried. 'Do as the poor creature asks.'

His surprised bodyguards hurried to obey. Philip summoned more from the street, and soon enough masonry had been moved, allowing the unconscious youth to be freed. Perhaps eighteen, he had no obvious injuries apart from a heavily bruised leg. A little water poured onto his face from a bodyguard's water flask brought him, coughing, to the land of the living. His eyes flickered open, focused on his mother, who was kneeling by him. She cried out with joy, 'Thank all the gods!'

'Thank the king, more like,' muttered a bodyguard.

The shocked woman twisted to look at Philip. 'Sire, I had no idea. Forgive me.'

Philip smiled. 'No matter.'

'A thousand thanks, sire,' she said, tears welling.

'Is your son well?' he asked.

She glanced down. 'Are you hurt?'

'It feels as if a mule has walked over me – twice,' replied her son, grimacing. He raised one arm, then the other, and did the same with his legs. 'But everything seems to work.'

The woman's eyes filled with fresh tears as her son managed to sit up. 'Zeus Soter bless and keep you, sire,' she said to Philip.

His replying smile was thin. 'Take them to the rest,' he commanded.

The bodyguards' expressions, which had been pleased – the scene was heart-warming, Philip had to admit – registered surprise, before hardening. 'Sire!'

Beside Philip, Perseus looked on in dismay.

'On your feet!' a bodyguard ordered the woman and her son.

Her happiness faded. 'Where are you taking us?'

'To the ships,' answered the bodyguard.

'I don't understand. Why?'

Confined to her house, the woman had seen nothing of her fellow residents' fate, thought Philip.

'You are the king's slaves now,' said the bodyguard, not unkindly. 'Where he will sell you, I don't know.'

Striding off, Philip ignored the wails that followed this pronouncement.

'Father!'

He had been expecting Perseus to object. 'What?'

His son's open face was full of dismay. 'You saved her son only to enslave them both?'

'I did.' Philip made for the street.

'Why?' Perseus lowered his voice. 'It would have been better to leave well alone, for her to weep over his body, than to curse them to slavery.'

'Dead, he is worth nothing. Left here, she is worth nothing,' said Philip harshly. 'In the hold of one of my ships, they are two slaves, worth between them hundreds of *drachmae*.'

Perseus' face twisted with revulsion. 'They're Greeks, Father.'

'This is not something I take pleasure in, nor is my ruthlessness without reason,' Philip explained. 'You would be king after me, no?'

Perseus grinned. 'Of course, Father – if you should wish it.'

'I do,' replied Philip. 'Know then that the ravening beast of war needs constant feeding. Where do you think the grain for our soldiers comes from?'

'From Macedon and Thrace,' began Perseus. 'And from the farms along the Propontis.'

'It vanishes faster than you could believe. Have you any idea how many bull's heads of grain ten thousand men will eat in a day?' said Philip, referring to the shaped lead weights used by Macedonian traders. He smiled to leaven his snapped question. 'Of course you don't, any more than you know how much hay three thousand horses need daily. But I do. Knowing these things are a king's duty. Macedon and Thessaly cannot supply the whole army for a summer's campaign, nor can the farms on the Propontis. Always we need more, and it can't all be taken at the point of a sword. Oft-times it must be bought, and to do that, I need coin. Sad to say, my coffers do not magically fill themselves.'

Understanding bloomed on Perseus' face. 'The money raised from selling the Cianians will buy grain for the army.'

'It will. Which would you rather, then – to leave the woman and her son, ensuring that some of our men go hungry, or to take them and the rest as slaves?'

Perseus stuck out his jaw. 'I see now, Father. Do what you must.'

Philip clapped him on the shoulder. 'This will not be the fate of every town I take. If the campaign continues in the same rich vein, control of the Propontis will soon be mine. Imagine the tolls from the grain ships that beat up and down the waterway. Hundreds pass through yearly, on their way to and from Athens, Aitolia and Sparta – all of Greece relies on the farms north of the Euxine Sea.'

Perseus nodded, and Philip thought, he's a clever lad. Good head on his shoulders too. One day he will make a fine king.

Philip was still in fine humour the following morning, when a head-count was made of the slaves. Numerous ships had been beached to facilitate loading, and the king stood nearby, listening to the tallies.

'Four hundred and sixty-eight able-bodied men, sire,' said the officer in charge. 'There are another three score or so, but they are injured, or old.'

'They're of no use. Kill them.' It was distasteful but necessary, Philip decided. His stepfather Antigonus' advice, given not long before his death, returned to haunt him:

'Some things you will enjoy as king. Leading your army to war. Seeing your enemies vanquished. Accepting the loyalty of new subjects, and rewarding those faithful to you. Other things are more difficult, even unpleasant. Never being able to set aside your responsibilities. Ordering the execution of former friends or allies. Telling your soldiers to massacre every inhabitant of a village that has defied you.'

Or in this case, murdering the injured and infirm, thought Philip darkly.

'These last are the true badges of kingship,' Antigonus had said. 'You cannot turn aside from such tasks, or you will topple from power faster than Ikaros fell to earth.'

The officer said something, and Philip came back to the present. 'Eh?'

'I'll see it's done, sire.'

'How many women and children are there?'

'Eight hundred and twenty-nine, sire, about half of whom are children.'

The numbers were healthier than Philip had feared after his tour of the charnel house that was Kios. He nodded, hardening his heart. 'How many useless ones?'

The officer hesitated.

The man is only human, thought Philip. Like me. 'The army needs all the grain. Would you have your soldiers go hungry that these wretches might live? With no shelter and no food, winter will take them anyway. This is a mercy we do them.'

'I understand, sire,' replied the officer. 'There are about fifty who are hurt, or would be impossible to sell.'

'You know what to do.' Philip was glad that Perseus was at his lessons. Although the boy had accepted the fate of the woman and her son the previous day, he wasn't sure his son would see the logic behind these executions. He will one day, thought Philip. He will have to.

'Yes, sire.' The officer saluted and withdrew.

'Sails!'

The shout drew Philip's attention. His eyes roved the waterway, soon coming to rest on three triremes approaching from the south-west. Their sails were bare of design, which meant they were not his. The ships weren't enough to threaten his fleet, and curiosity filled him.

'Signal Herakleides,' he ordered. 'I want those vessels stopped. Bring their captains to me.'

It amused Philip to find out within the hour that the triremes carried emissaries from neutral cities in the area, as well as a Rhodian ambassador. He met first with the latter – Rhodes was weaker than he, but it was a power at least. He had the emissary brought to him on the beach, where the prisoners from Kios were being forced to embark. The wails and cries of the wives and children being separated from their husbands and fathers would serve as a sharp reminder of his capabilities.

The emissary was short and squat – a wrestler, by his cauliflower ears. It was so like the Rhodians, plain speakers, no lovers of royalty, to send him a commoner, thought Philip. The messenger knew well enough to bow low, however.

'King Philip, I bid you good day.'

Philip didn't even pretend to be polite.

'You are?'

'Dorieos of Rhodes, sire. I bring you word from the Prytaneum.'

'Do you indeed?' Philip picked at a fingernail.

Dorieos fixed his smile. 'Yes, sire.'

'Get on with it then. I'm busy, in case you hadn't noticed.' Philip waved a hand at the lines of captives.

Dorieos could no longer stop himself from looking. 'Are those inhabitants of Kios, sire?'

'The ones that survived, yes.'

'Can I ask what is to happen to them, sire?'

'Isn't it obvious? They are my slaves.'

Dorieos seemed about to say something, but thought better of it. After a moment, he said politely, 'They are freeborn Greeks, sire.'

'They are.'

'Greek peoples do not enslave their own kind, sire.'

'I am Macedonian,' replied Philip flippantly.

'Greek, Macedonian, we are the same, sire.'

'Do all Rhodians think that, I wonder?' retorted Philip. King he might be, yet the knowledge that the Greeks looked down on him still rankled.

'The members of the Prytaneum hold you in high regard, I can assure you, sire,' said Dorieos, continuing, 'which brings me to my message.'

'Let me guess,' said Philip. 'Rhodes wishes me to cease my attack on Kios, and to forbear from attacking any other cities in the region.'

Dorieos looked pained. 'Yes, sire.'

'It's a little late for the first part of your request,' said Philip, drily indicating the smoking ruins of the town.

'It is, sire.' Dorieos took a deep breath. 'As to the second, however—'

'What business has Rhodes here, so far from home?'

Dorieos puffed out his chest a little. 'Rhodes is the protector of the islands, sire. It keeps the seas clear of pirates as best it may, and—'

'It is a self-appointed protector,' said Philip, cutting across him. 'Not every city wishes Rhodes to be its master, not least those who looked to Macedon in times gone by. I will bear your masters' request in mind.' He raised a hand as Dorieos prepared to answer. 'I will not bandy further with you.'

Dorieos' expression was unhappy. 'And the people of Kios, sire?'

'You test my patience.'

'Do not enslave them, I beg of you,' Dorieos entreated.

'Leave.'

'Sire?'

'Do not think to tell a king what he may or may not do, lest your head part company from your shoulders.' Philip signalled, and a pair of his bodyguards materialised.

'Rhodes is not alone, sire,' called Dorieos as he was led away. 'The emissaries who arrived with me will request the same things of you.'

'And I will give them the same answers,' answered Philip, thinking, did Philip, Alexander's father, or the Lion of Macedon himself consider the wishes of those they sought to conquer? They did not. As it had been theirs, conquering the Propontis and beyond was his birthright.

CHAPTER VI

Fifteen days had passed since the battle at Zama, and the brothers were lying on their blankets outside their goatskin tent, which, with the others in their century, formed three sides of a rectangle. On either side, to the front and behind, in similar, regular patterns, were the tents of their entire legion. Avenues divided the camp; at the central crossroads sat the headquarters, and the senior officers' large pavilions. Around the perimeter, earthworks taller than a man and a deep, V-shaped ditch protected those within. The brothers' camp was one of many covering the plains outside Carthage. Mirroring Scipio's legions' arrival, his ships filled the waters offshore.

Before seeing it, Felix and his comrades had had no idea quite how big the city was. It dwarfed Rome. Even now, days after their arrival, off-duty soldiers liked to stroll along the base of the mighty whitewashed walls that ran deep into the agricultural hinterland. The city's south-eastern edge was even more remarkable, formed in part by twin harbours, one merchant, one military, the latter approachable via a secret entrance from the former. Magnificent temples perched atop Byrsa Hill, the highest point of Carthage; from there, it was said, streets radiated like tributaries down to the *agora*, a vast public space bordered by grand government buildings and imposing temples.

This evening, however, the brothers wanted to take the weight off their feet. Orders from on high had rendered the city out of bounds, and a man could only gawp so many times at its walls.

'One day left of watching the prisoners and supervising the shit wagons,' said Antonius. 'I cannot wait until normal duties resume. I'll never grumble about having to dig a latrine trench again.'

'Eight days lasts an eternity, eh?' Felix chuckled. 'Thank the gods the auctions are almost on us.' The prisoners they had been guarding, thousands of enemy soldiers, were to be sold into slavery; the monies raised would add to the punitive reparations levied on Carthage by Scipio. A little would eventually filter down to the ordinary legionaries – something Felix and every man in the army looked forward to with great anticipation.

'Aye.' Antonius' dissatisfied expression eased. 'Once they're done, life can get back to normal.'

After the slave sales, Felix, Antonius and the rest of the army would wait outside the city for approval of the peace deal that Scipio had forced on the Carthaginians. Felix eyed his brother. 'How long is it since the messengers sailed to Rome?'

'You know as well as I do,' said Antonius. 'Five days.'

Felix sighed. The simple life on the family farm he yearned for wouldn't happen overnight. It would be a month at least until the Senate's reply came, and longer before they were sent back to Italia and discharged from the legions. Scipio hadn't insisted on three months' provisions for his army from the Carthaginians for nothing.

'Ho, brothers, look!' One of their tentmates spoke.

Felix sat up.

Ingenuus, another comrade, had hove into view, a medium-sized amphora under each arm. An affable, trusting type, he was in Felix's mind the least suited among them to army life, and yet he had survived five years thus far. 'Thirsty?' Ingenuus asked.

A clamour of ayes met his question, and the questions rained down.

'Where did you thieve those from?'

'Been bending over for the quartermaster again?'

'Matho know about these, does he?'

Ingenuus set the amphorae down with care, and held up his hands for calm. A reluctant silence fell, and he smiled. 'I'll tell you with a cup in my hand, and not before.'

There was a rush to oblige. Pouring each man a good measure – and himself the largest – from one vessel, Ingenuus laid the second on its side and planted his arse on it. He raised his beaker high.

'To sailing home.'

Everyone cheered. 'Sailing home!'

'Tell us where you got the wine,' urged Felix.

The legions had not been allowed to sack Carthage. Similar protection had not been granted to the unfortunates who dwelt in the outlying villages and farms, but the pickings from these were already slim.

Antonius gave Ingenuus a sly dig. 'Tell us, you filth!'

Ingenuus was revelling in his comrades' curiosity. 'You know the inn at the crossroads, the one we pass with the shit wagons?'

For the previous eight days, Felix and his comrades had not just been charged with guarding the prisoners' stockade; they had also supervised the emptying of the latrine trenches there. Accompanying the dripping, stinking wagons to the emptying area was a deeply unpopular duty.

'That inn is derelict. I checked it myself – it's home to nothing more than rats,' declared Antonius, nodding as several others voiced their agreement.

'So you thought,' said Ingenuus, smirking. He took a deep swallow, and gave his cup an approving look. 'Not a bad vintage, this.'

'Get on with it,' Felix urged.

'There wasn't that much to it, in truth,' admitted Ingenuus. He threw a glance at Antonius. 'A child would have found the wine, if he'd looked.'

Antonius punched Ingenuus none too gently.

'Touch me again, brother,' warned Ingenuus, 'and *you* won't see another drop.'

Antonius glowered as the others hooted with laughter.

'Where was it hidden?' demanded Felix.

Ingenuus' face grew conspiratorial. 'There's a shed behind the inn, a ramshackle thing missing half its roof.'

'I searched it,' growled Antonius.

'It didn't make sense for hay to be stored in there, not with holes in the roof,' said Ingenuus, winking, 'so I moved some of it. Underneath, I found a trapdoor, and below that, a nice little cellar.'

'You clever bastard!' Now Felix clouted Ingenuus so hard that his drink spilled. 'What else is in there?' Chaos reigned as their comrades added their demands to his.

When Ingenuus revealed that there was enough wine – if they were moderate – to supply them until the time came to sail home, they threw him onto their shoulders and bore him around their tent like a statue of a god in a victory parade.

Matho's appearance put an abrupt end to their celebrations. His arm was healing, but that hadn't stopped him being his usual hard taskmaster. To everyone's relief, he seemed content with the explanation that Ingenuus had found just two amphorae; he didn't ask where. After drinking several cups straight off, he cracked a rare smile and announced that rumour had it that they'd be embarking for Italia within the month.

That joyous news made it inevitable that the comrades would bring wine to carry them through their last night on sentry duty. The war was over, the prisoners cowed, and the officers slack about checking on the sentries much past sundown.

What could go wrong?

Four hours into his watch, the biggest thing on Felix's mind was emptying his bladder. He'd gone a long time before needing to piss, but since then, as was always the case, the urge had come on him with ever greater frequency.

'Once the seal's broken,' he whispered to himself, letting a stream of urine arc down towards the ground.

Mightily relieved, he lowered his tunic. With a bleary glance into the compound's darkened interior – no one appeared to be stirring – he trudged towards Antonius, the next sentry along, and importantly, the first amphora's current keeper.

Following Ingenuus' instructions, it was working its way around the four walls. To avoid the possibility of anyone telling tales, a decision had been made early on to let the other sentries – three contubernia strong – in on their supply. Not being found out, Ingenuus had declared, was well worth having less wine per man. They could make up for it the following evening when they were off duty, and could pay another visit to the hidden cellar.

The amphora wasn't quite empty yet, thought Felix as he neared his brother. There had to be a couple of mouthfuls left for him.

A rude surprise awaited.

''S empty,' said Antonius, belching.

'Greedy dog!' Setting his shield and javelin against the rampart, Felix tipped up the amphora and held it to his lips. A few drops was his only reward, and he glared at Antonius. 'Why didn't you save me some?'

Another satisfied belch. 'Bacchus' sweaty balls, what does it matter? Ingenuus has the other amphora.'

Felix peered along the walkway. In the pitch dark, he couldn't see

Ingenuus, who was stationed at the corner some fifty paces distant. 'He'd better not have sent it in the opposite direction.'

'He won't have. Our contubernium first, then the others,' said Antonius. 'Go and fetch it, why don't you?'

'By rights, it should be you.'

'I'm not the thirsty one,' jibed Antonius.

'Because you finished the cursed wine!'

Antonius made an obscene gesture by way of reply.

Felix retrieved his shield and spear and, still grumbling to himself, trudged along the walkway. The two comrades he passed wanted to accompany him. There wasn't anything to be concerned about, one argued: Matho wouldn't appear, having been invited to a celebration with the legion's other centurions, and the junior officer on duty had already been around once. A lover of his blankets, that tended to be his norm until dawn. Felix held his ground, declaring that they were pissed, but not so pissed that three of them should desert their posts. His argument won the pair over, and with their demands for wine ringing in his ears, he weaved his way to Ingenuus.

Felix's return was slowed a good deal by his comrades' thirst. He was unconcerned. Inside the compound, all was quiet, and there wasn't a sign of any officers. It had been the best night on sentry duty ever, he decided, prising the amphora from Antonius' grasp and working his way back to his own position. With the wine to himself, he guzzled half a dozen big mouthfuls. He would have had more, but the next soldier along came to claim his share. Reluctantly, Felix relinquished control of the amphora.

Time passed. The wine didn't return. From the muttering on the opposite wall, it was being enjoyed there. The sliver of moon sank further towards the horizon. Dewdrops formed on Felix's helmet, and he grew cold, despite his cloak. He stamped about for a bit, pacing over to Antonius and back to the next man along, which got the blood flowing. Another piss relieved his bladder. More comfortable, but weary now, he took up a static position in the middle of his patch. Shield set against the rampart, he gripped his javelin shaft with both hands and leaned into it. Years of practice meant this was reasonably comfortable.

His eyelids drooped. He flicked them open. Stay awake, fool, he thought. The penalty for falling asleep on sentry duty is death. His heart thumped a little faster. He straightened his back and studied the compound's interior with fierce determination. His approach succeeded for a time, but the wine-induced weariness came creeping back, warm and inviting. Felix's shoulders bowed, and he leaned down on his javelin. His eyes closed, opened and closed again. The clatter of a comrade's hobnails on the walkway moments later hardly made him stir.

Sleep had him firm in its grip.

Felix's dream of a raucous night in a tavern with his friends kept being interrupted by ever more frequent twinges from his bladder. He was aware that his lower legs were cold, and that his shoulders hurt, but his enjoyment of the carousal was pleasant, so he fought them off.

His comrades' shouts in the dream grew louder, and their tone changed, becoming urgent. Rather than a drinking song, one man was roaring, 'Sound the alarm!' A dim awareness that he was in a dream sank in, and then, with the harsh reality of an unexpected bucket of cold water being dumped on his head, Felix was awake. Gummy-eyed, he jerked upright, shoulder pains and full bladder forgotten.

'Stand to! Prisoners have escaped!' came the cry from somewhere to his right – it was Ingenuus' voice, Felix thought.

I fell asleep, he realised with sinking dread. Someone else must have too. 'Antonius!'

'Aye?'

'Is all well with you?'

'No one has passed me,' said Antonius, but his voice was as sleep-slurred as Felix felt.

The call to arms was echoing on every wall of the compound now. Beyond the defences, men were stirring in their tents. The first claws of panic tore at Felix. When Matho arrived, there would hell to pay. Deal with the matter at hand, he told himself, sprinting towards where he'd heard the first cry. 'Watch my position!' he ordered a startled-looking Antonius.

He found Ingenuus standing over the body of a princeps from one of the other contubernia. Purple-faced, his tongue bulging, the man had been throttled.

'Did you not hear something?' demanded Felix.

'I-I came running soon as I heard,' Ingenuus stammered. 'I speared one of the bastards in the back as he climbed the rampart, but the others got away.'

Felix peered over the edge, spying a body in the ditch. 'How many were there?'

'I don't know.' Ingenuus' voice cracked. 'It's my fault. We should never have drunk the wine.'

'Forget the cursed wine.' Matho would have to have lost his sense of smell not to notice the reek of drink from each and every sentry, thought Felix. If there was to be any chance of dragging themselves back from the abyss, it would be to recapture the escapees, yet to leave their posts now risked the flight of more prisoners. 'Toss that amphora into the compound.'

'Matho—' began Ingenuus.

'Tell him that we all had a drink – shared out between the sentries. He might not see the second amphora. Perhaps this poor fool had a drop more than anyone else.' Felix nudged the corpse with his foot. 'He fell asleep, and some of the prisoners noticed. They strangled him – you heard the struggle, and charged to his defence, killing one. You sounded the alarm, then kept your position, like the rest of us.'

Ingenuus didn't answer.

Felix shoved him, hard. 'D'you understand? We have to have the same story, or Matho will fucking kill us!'

Ingenuus' eyes came back into focus. 'Aye, aye.'

'Repeat what I said.'

The instant he was sure Ingenuus knew what to say, and that he would talk with the next princeps along, Felix went hammering back to Antonius. His brother had already realised the urgency of their situation, and he continued on to their next comrade. By the time Matho appeared inside the gate with the rest of the century, Felix had spread the word to every legionary on the ramparts. He prayed that their story held up to inspection.

Making his way to the dead sentry, Matho spoke to Ingenuus before calling for Felix and Antonius, the most senior principes. Stormy-faced, he listened to their account in silence. When they finished, he paced up and down, slapping his vine stick off his left palm.

Felix couldn't take his eyes off it.

'Let me get this straight. You were *drinking* on duty?' Matho's tone was murderous.

'Yes, sir,' the three answered.

'You cocksucking maggots!' Matho's roving gaze promised dreadful punishment. 'How many got away?'

'We don't know, sir,' muttered Felix, receiving a swingeing blow of Matho's vitis as reward.

'Were they guggas? Libyans? Gauls?'

'Not sure, sir.'

Again the vitis swept in, striking Felix's helmet so hard that he saw stars.

'Useless cunts! Get down into the compound and find out who's escaped. Send a man after me with the numbers.'

'You're pursuing them, sir?' ventured Antonius.

'That's right, maggot. Someone has to clean up your mess, and you're all pissed.' Matho clattered down the nearest steps, and marched out of the gate, with the rest of the century at his heels.

Felix gathered the sentries and ordered a headcount of the different groupings of prisoners. Even with torches, this was a difficult affair, but Matho's threat gave them plenty of zeal. It was full daylight by the time they were done. Comparing numbers against the records kept at the gate, it became clear that fifteen Macedonians were gone, as well as five Gauls and a quartet of Libyans. The grim figure was much higher than expected. They drew lots to decide who would go after Matho with the bad news; it was scant relief that the unfortunate selected was from another contubernium.

'Matho will never believe that just the one man was asleep,' said Felix, shaking his head.

'Matho will have to take some of the responsibility for this,' said Antonius.

'Aye.' Felix had been thinking the same thing. 'He'll have it in for us ten times more than normal.'

'What can we do?' asked Antonius, looking anguished.

'Not a thing,' answered Felix, deep in the grip of resignation. The warm glow imparted by the wine was fast fading, leaving a foul taste in his mouth and a thumping headache. Their ignominy was added to soon after by the arrival of fresh sentries. Explaining that there had been a mass breakout, Felix and his comrades endured a tirade of abuse from the officer in charge, and a wave of snide remarks from his men. Humiliated, they trudged miserably back to their tents and awaited Matho's return.

News of the escape swept the camp. A strong cavalry force was sent after Matho, giving Felix some hope that the prisoners would be recaptured. Whether that would make any difference to the punishment they would receive, he could not be sure. As ever, their fate was in the gods' hands.

He didn't hold out much hope that they would intervene.

CHAPTER VII

Three days had passed since the sack of Kios, and the fleet was well on its way towards the free city of Thasos. The campaign was over, according to rumour, and after reprovisioning – with the population of Kios now slaves and in the ships' bellies, the need for food was much greater than before – Philip would lead them home to Macedon.

Demetrios had not taken Simonides up on his suggestion; he told himself that the phalangist had been playing a joke on him. After the hardships of the previous few years, it seemed too easy that the Fates would drop such a golden opportunity into his lap. Despite Demetrios' refusal to act, nothing could make him forget Simonides' offer. He thought of it on the rowing benches; eating his meals and lying in his blankets at night. It was perhaps inevitable, therefore, that by the fourth day, he had changed his mind.

The fleet was at anchor in a half-moon-shaped bay. A gentle tide rocked the ships; the beach was a mass of tents. Fires blazed, wood crackled, fat from cooking meat sputtered. Glad to be ashore, soldiers ran up and down, loosening muscles. Scores of men were splashing about in the sea. Others wrestled, gambled or drank wine. It was enough for the oarsmen to erect their tents, if they had one, and get a meal cooking. Unlike the troops, they had been labouring all day. This was their time of rest.

Theokritos told Demetrios he was mad even to think of going near the phalangists. 'It's a trick, don't you see? That prick had no more interest in letting you become a soldier than a hungry wolf has in allowing a lamb to walk past its lair. He and his mates will pin you down and take turns with you. You'll be shitting blood for days, like that poor bastard on the ship. Remember?'

Demetrios nodded. It was impossible to forget the lad – they had been much of an age. Unluckily for him, he'd been given Apollo's looks, and his flawless skin and flowing locks had driven the predators among the oarsmen wild. The attacks had begun the same night the crew had embarked at Pella. The oar master hadn't intervened; disgusted, Demetrios had thought about stopping them, but the rapists' companions' ready knives had soon ended his attempt. The same night, he, Onesas and Theokritos had agreed to defend each other.

Five days later, the boy had vanished in the dark before dawn. No one had noticed he was gone until it was time to start rowing. A brief search of the shoreline had revealed his corpse behind a rocky outcrop. He'd slit his wrists. The oar master would have left his corpse for the vultures, but Demetrios and his comrades had insisted on burying him. Nothing was said, but the predators must have been given a warning of some kind, because their attacks on weaker oarsmen grew less sustained, and they left Demetrios, Onesas and Theokritos alone.

Simonides was no rapist, thought Demetrios. 'It wasn't like that. He meant what he said.'

'Those animals love a taste of new flesh. Don't say I didn't warn you.'

'I'll take my knife.'

Theokritos made a contemptuous noise. 'Use that, and they will rape you *and* cut your throat.'

Demetrios waved a dismissive hand as he walked away. Some men liked boys; he'd encountered them on occasion during his childhood, most often at religious festivals, when a lot of wine had been consumed. He had learned fast not to stray too near such men, and to bite and shout if their hands strayed. Simonides' eyes had held none of that desire. Theokritos' warning stayed with him, however, and Demetrios' walk was slower than it might have been.

The phalangists' tents were arranged in orderly fashion. In front of each, shields lay in piles with stacks of spears, helmets and greaves. Fires blazed by the hundred; bronze pots hung over the flames. The air was rich with the smells of baking bread, meat and herbs, but Demetrios ignored his growling stomach. Instinct told him that if Simonides had meant what he said, a physical test of some kind was in the offing.

Within moments of asking for the phalangist, Demetrios was cursing his lack of foresight. He hadn't thought to ask where Simonides was from, or what *speira* he served in. Scores of these units made up the phalanx, each numbering two hundred and fifty-six men – and Simonides was a common name. The majority seemed amused at the idea of a gangling young oarsman come in search of them; they laughed when Demetrios, disappointed, made his apologies and said he had the wrong man. More than one listened to his description of Simonides and shook their heads, no, they didn't know him. A few gave Demetrios a lewd wink and said they'd be the Simonides he sought. One patted the blanket he was sitting on and offered Demetrios a cup of wine. Eager not to cause offence, but with his cheeks burning, each time he retreated amid a chorus of laughter and ribald comments. The phalangists didn't seem to care that he refused their attentions; in the army, it seemed, male relationships were consenting, not the brutal things they were aboard ship.

Demetrios soon lost count of the number of tents he'd asked at – it was more than thirty – and the sun was an orange-red orb on the western horizon. Striated lines of cloud high above presaged a calm night. Light was fading, and with it, his hopes of success. Many phalangists were eating, and the appeal of the food Theokritos would keep aside for him was growing by the moment. Six more fires, Demetrios decided, and I'll return to the ship.

He had no luck at the first, second or third. There was a Simonides polishing a breastplate at the fourth, but he wasn't the right man. Frustrated and hungry, Demetrios continued to the next fire out of stubbornness. Expecting yet another disappointment, he asked for Simonides and without waiting for an answer, took a step towards the sixth. Last one, he thought with relief, and then I can head back.

'Simonides, you say?'

Demetrios turned. The phalangist who'd spoken was not much older than he. Tousled black hair framed a friendly face. 'Aye,' said Demetrios. 'He has a short beard. Stocky, maybe thirty.'

'There's a Simonides in the speira that stands to our right in the phalanx. He's about that age and has a cropped beard.' The young phalangist stopped cleaning his nails with his dagger and pointed. 'Their tents are yonder. Half a stadion, no more.'

'My thanks.' Demetrios' step was lighter as he threaded his way between some tents and crossed a dirt avenue. Seeing Simonides – *the* Simonides – feeding a branch into the fire, his heart leaped, and then he wavered. I've come this far, Demetrios thought. There was no way to tell if the phalangist's offer had been genuine other than to continue. He plunged forward into the ruddy orange glow cast by the flames. Half a dozen faces turned to regard him.

'Lost your way?' asked a man with a straight nose and blue eyes.

'I don't think so,' said Simonides, giving Demetrios a nod. 'He's the lad I told you about.'

'The oarsman?' This from a sturdy-framed man with wavy black hair.

'Aye.' Simonides beckoned to Demetrios, who, trying to conceal his nerves, came closer to the fire.

'He doesn't look like much to me,' declared Straight Nose.

A *phhhh* of contempt from the man with wavy hair. 'The boy isn't even shaving yet. He's not fit for the phalanx.'

'You can't be sure, Empedokles,' challenged Simonides. 'This boy has balls. He saved that officer from having his brains smeared along the ground, remember? And the storm of bronze has a different effect on each man – *you* should know that.' A titter went around the group, and Empedokles – the one with wavy hair – glowered.

Demetrios missed the joke, but Empedokles' instant dislike of him was clear. Not wanting to inflame the situation, he averted his eyes.

'It took you long enough to appear,' said Simonides. 'Lose your courage?'

Demetrios tried to make his shrug nonchalant. 'I wasn't sure if you meant what you said.'

'Simonides says so little, he could almost be a Spartan.' As Simonides half-smiled, Straight Nose continued, 'When he does speak, each word has been weighed and measured.'

'Meaning . . .' Demetrios hesitated. 'Meaning you *were* serious.'

'I was.' Simonides' gaze roved over his comrades. 'The boy told me his father had him train at pankration, wrestling and boxing. He wanted – wants – to become a phalangist, like us.'

'Hera's tits! If he was supposed to join the army, how does he find himself an oarsman? He's obviously lying,' sneered Empedokles. 'Do we really want the scrapings of Pella in our ranks?'

The insult stung like salt water in a cut. If Empedokles had been another oarsman, Demetrios would have leaped on him, but his future was at stake. He stitched his lip.

'Tell them, boy.' Simonides gestured. 'Repeat what you told me.'

Demetrios glanced at the hard faces around the fire, and saw a mixture of curiosity, disinterest and plain dislike. Simonides was his only friend here, if he could even be called that.

'Are you going to keep us all night?' demanded a phalangist who hadn't yet spoken. Seated, it was impossible to judge his height, but he looked to stand a head taller than most men. With arms as thick as Demetrios' thighs, legs like small tree trunks and a shiny burn scar on the inside of his left forearm, he resembled an earthly version of Hephaistos, the blacksmith god. 'Eh?'

'Your pardon.' Demetrios dipped his chin respectfully at the huge phalangist, and was comforted by a tiny nod of acknowledgement. He threw up a quick prayer to Hermes, messenger of the gods, and a deity revered by shepherds, and wished that he had offered him a libation before setting out. Taking a deep breath, Demetrios began.

His tale didn't take long. The phalangists listened in silence for the most part. Wine was passed around – not to Demetrios – and Empedokles farted his contempt once or twice. When Demetrios mentioned his father's murder, no one reacted. It didn't surprise him. Life was brutal – everyone had a tragic episode to relate. Wary of seeming boastful, he passed quickly over the rescuing of the officer outside Kios, and described instead how he had speared the man inside the walls, and met Simonides. Finishing, Demetrios realised that the back of his chiton was soaked in sweat. 'That's it,' he said, feeling like a fool.

No one spoke, but Empedokles' lip curled.

Demetrios dared not break the silence. He was the one on trial here, as it were.

'He's modest at least – I would have spoken at length about how I had saved a phalangist officer's life,' said Straight Nose, who Demetrios now knew to be called Andriskos. He cast a look at Simonides. 'You saw him do it, didn't you?'

'Aye. You would have too, if you hadn't been preening yourself as usual,' said Simonides.

A ripple of amusement went around the fire, and Andriskos lifted a rueful hand in acknowledgement.

'Some of you others would have seen as well,' Simonides continued. He eyed the man who looked like a blacksmith. 'Philippos?'

'Aye, it could have been him,' admitted Philippos. 'If you vouch for the lad, I'm happy enough.'

'*I* saw an oarsman heaving an officer about like a bag of wheat right enough,' said Empedokles. 'But I'm not sure – not sure at all – that it was this streak of misery.'

'I am.' Simonides' voice was curt. 'And that should be good enough for every man here.'

'It is, brother, which is why we have sat listening. We believe the boy's tale – in theory,' said Andriskos. Heads nodded, even, reluctantly, that of Empedokles, and he continued, 'Can we get on with it?'

Fresh sweat slicked down Demetrios' back. It, he thought. A fight. That's what this meeting was always going to come to.

'Aye,' said Simonides. 'Who wants to go first?'

First, thought Demetrios, his bowels turning to water. Tartaros, am I to fight two of them?

'I will.'

Empedokles stood, cracking his knuckles. He took off his sandals and undressed, handing his dagger to Andriskos. Demetrios also stripped, laying his blade on top of his clothes.

Using a spear butt, Simonides drew a rough circle in the dirt, about twenty paces in diameter. Empedokles moved inside it at once; Demetrios did the same.

'Empedokles prefers boxing – you done much of that?' asked Simonides.

'No. Pankration was what I practised most.' Years ago, thought Demetrios with dread.

Simonides glanced at Empedokles. 'Happy with pankration?'

'Doesn't matter to me,' came the casual reply.

'Pankration it is. The loser is the first to be knocked down or pinned three times. Stepping outside the circle also counts as a defeat.' Simonides' hand chopped the air. 'Begin.'

Demetrios had thought there'd be a short period of moving around, gauging one another. He couldn't have been more wrong. Empedokles came at him like a charging bull, fast, graceful and dangerous. Punch, kick. Punch, kick. His fists and feet moved in frightening unison. Demetrios backed away, blocking as best he could, taking painful blows on his shins and his forearms. Empedokles followed fast, and only a quick glance over his shoulder prevented Demetrios from placing a foot outside the circle. He dodged to his left, taking a nasty kick to the thigh as reward.

'What's wrong, boy?' jibed Empedokles. 'Forgotten everything you learned? Or did you never learn pankration in the first place, eh?'

Stung, Demetrios launched a counter-attack. Punch, punch. Kick. Punch. As Empedokles jabbed fiercely back, Demetrios seized his left fist with *his* left hand, and swung forward to grip Empedokles' left elbow with his right hand. His hope was to wrench back his opponent's arm and break it, but Empedokles anticipated the move. With a powerful twist of his hips and torso, he ripped free. He drove forward, under Demetrios' raised arm, and instead of ending the contest, Demetrios managed only a punch to Empedokles' ribs.

'The pup knows one trick at least,' said Philippos.

'Ha! Not well enough,' cried Empedokles.

He swarmed forward at Demetrios, kicking high, driving him backwards. Again Demetrios retreated, taking hits to his arms and legs, and Andriskos said, 'Fight, curse you!'

Demetrios was struggling not to despair. The phalangists cared nothing for him, nor would they take into account that Empedokles was the better fighter. If there was to be any chance of being admitted to their ranks, he *had* to impress them somehow. He threw a double kick combination that briefly halted Empedokles. Throwing caution to the winds, Demetrios pivoted on one foot like a Minoan bull dancer and leaped onto the phalangist's back. Wrapping both arms around his throat, Demetrios used his legs to pin Empedokles' arms by his sides.

He hung on for dear life as Empedokles bucked and hopped like a maddened mule. When this attempt failed, he fell backwards deliberately, landing on top of Demetrios. The ground was hard, and hurt like Tartaros, but he retained his grip. They rolled about in the dirt, and still Empedokles could not break free. Ten heartbeats hammered by.

'Yield,' Demetrios hissed.

Empedokles writhed like a serpent, to no avail.

Demetrios tightened his grip on the phalangist's neck. Empedokles' struggles began to weaken. He repeated his demand, and this time, the phalangist's head moved up and down a little. Distrustful, Demetrios asked a third time, 'Do you yield?'

Again Empedokles' head moved, and Demetrios risked slackening his hold. The phalangist took in a shuddering breath, and wrenched himself to the side, away from Demetrios.

'Who would have thought it, Empedokles?' boomed Philippos. 'A wet-behind-the-ears boy pulled "the ladder" on you!'

Empedokles muttered a hair-whitening obscenity.

As Demetrios got up, chest heaving, Simonides caught his eye. 'That was well done.'

Delighted, Demetrios drank in the others' approval. Too late, he remembered that the contest could resume once both opponents were up. Too late, he heard the rush of feet. He turned, and instead of catching him on the side of the head, Empedokles' forearm struck him a mighty blow on the temple. Stars burst across Demetrios' vision, and he stumbled, tripping over Empedokles' outstretched right leg. Down he went, with the phalangist on top. It was Demetrios' turn to be wrapped in a stranglehold this time. Empedokles used all his strength. Demetrios felt himself going faint almost at once; he pounded the earth in submission, but Empedokles did not let go. It took a demand from Simonides for him to release his grip. He gave Demetrios a contemptuous shove in the back as he did.

Head spinning, Demetrios spat out bits of dirt. His ears were ringing, and nausea bathed him – he needed time to recover. To protest at the illegal move would look weak, so he put as much distance between himself and Empedokles as the circle allowed.

'That was a soft defeat, boy,' said Simonides. Heads nodded.

Ashamed, Demetrios said nothing.

'It's no fault of mine the fool wasn't ready,' crowed Empedokles.

'True enough,' replied Simonides. 'One fall each. Begin.'

Seeing that Demetrios was dazed, Empedokles closed fast. He rushed a snap kick at Demetrios' left knee, which part-connected, and converted the movement into a lunge forward. He planted his right foot behind Demetrios' feet and tried to sweep him backwards with his right arm. Desperate, Demetrios swung his hips and turned on his left leg – agony lanced up from the knee, but he moved through it. His solid right hook split Empedokles' bottom lip.

Empedokles shook his head; droplets of blood flew in every direction. Demetrios went on the attack, seizing Empedokles by the throat. He blocked the phalangist's first attempt to do the same to him, but not the second. They stared at each other, pop-eyed, unable to breathe, their free arms tangling as they both tried to loosen the other's grip. Empedokles' sharp fingernails bit into Demetrios' flesh; his eyes shone with a murderous delight. He was stronger, and knew it.

Weakening fast, Demetrios could hear in his head Simonides announcing, 'Two falls for the boy, one for Empedokles.' Furious, Demetrios aimed a knee at Empedokles' groin. The Fates were smiling. Rather than strike his opponent on the thigh, or just a glancing blow, his knee made full contact with the soft mass of the phalangist's prick and balls.

Empedokles' eyes bulged with pain and surprise, and his hand fell away from Demetrios' throat. He staggered back one step, two. Demetrios kicked before he was out of range. Again the Fates humoured him. He caught Empedokles' left kneecap, front-on. An animal scream rent the air. Empedokles' leg folded, and Demetrios swept in on that side, sliding his left leg behind the phalangist. Empedokles managed to punch him in the head, but it was a glancing blow, and didn't stop Demetrios twisting and reaching around with his right arm. He swept Empedokles to the ground, over his left leg, and threw himself on top of the stunned phalangist.

Right knee on Empedokles' left arm, right hand in a choke hold on his throat, and left hand gripping the phalangist's other arm, Demetrios held on for dear life.

Within ten heartbeats, Empedokles' lips formed the words, 'I yield.'

Wise to the other's guile now, Demetrios waited until he was sure before letting go. Never taking his eyes off those of Empedokles, he got to his feet.

'Two victories each. This is proving to be a more even contest than I expected.' Simonides sounded pleased. 'D'you need a breather, Empedokles?'

'Screw you, Simonides.' Empedokles threw a furious glance at Philippos and the others, who were chuckling.

The phalangists' enjoyment of their comrade's discomfiture lit a spark of hope in Demetrios' heart. Perhaps he could win the final bout. Overcome Empedokles, and he would surely be admitted into their ranks.

'Begin,' said Simonides.

Both wary, the two circled each other, fists raised. Empedokles feinted, then threw a vicious jab at Demetrios' stomach. Demetrios twisted, and the blow struck his ribs. He elbowed Empedokles in the side of the head, or tried to – but the phalangist ducked out of the way. Kick. Lunge. Grab. They snapped kicks at each other's shins and thighs, and attempted to throw one another.

They closed and grappled. Empedokles used a leg sweep, which failed, then managed to heave Demetrios over his right hip. Rather than fight the move, Demetrios rolled. Empedokles would fall on him next – and so, desperate, he continued rolling to try and get beyond the phalangist's reach. He failed. Empedokles was on top of him like a pouncing lion. Demetrios struggled, but two heartbeats later, his right arm was twisted back behind his shoulder and the phalangist's fingers were poised to gouge both his eyes.

'Easy. We're not fucking Spartans,' said Simonides.

'As you say, Simonides.' Empedokles removed his hand from Demetrios' forehead; with a laugh, he slammed his face into the dirt. 'Yield, filth,' Empedokles muttered.

Demetrios banged his left palm off the ground.

'Empedokles wins,' said Simonides.

Demetrios climbed to his feet, hurting, trying to conceal his disappointment. Empedokles sneered, and Demetrios flicked his hands at him in a 'Let's fight again' kind of way. It was pleasing that the phalangist's face coloured.

Demetrios' pleasure didn't last.

Simonides motioned he should stay in the circle.

'You have boxed?' he asked.

'A little,' replied Demetrios.

'Philippos,' said Simonides, and the huge phalangist lumbered forward.

Demetrios' guts lurched, but he met Philippos' eyes. 'I'll go easy on you.'

Philippos' belly laugh would have woken the dead. He winked. 'That's kind.'

'Same rules as before,' said Simonides. 'First to fall three times loses.'

The pair advanced towards each other, Philippos with a slow, confident tread, Demetrios with what he hoped was the same. He had no idea what to do. Even his heaviest punch wouldn't knock down Philippos.

In the event, he didn't get to choose a tactic. As he raised his fists,

Philippos' right paw came in, faster than he could have imagined. It connected with Demetrios' chin, and the world went black. The contents of a bucket of water brought him to his senses, but when he managed to stand, his knees would barely hold him up. He heard Simonides say 'Begin' from the other end of a long tunnel. Demetrios didn't even see Philippos' from-the-waist hook, which hit him in the solar plexus.

He was unconscious before he hit the ground.

When Demetrios came to, lying on his back, it hurt to breathe. His head was a throbbing ball of agony; so too was his belly. He opened his eyes, and with difficulty, focused on the sky above, which was full of stars. Men were talking nearby. He could smell garlic, and cooking meat. The smells, usually pleasant, made him retch. When his stomach had finished emptying itself, Demetrios wiped away the drool and sat up. He was still in the circle, and the phalangists were seated around their fire, eating and drinking.

'Look who's back with us,' said Simonides.

'I— uhhh,' mumbled Demetrios.

The phalangists laughed, but there was no cruelty in it, save perhaps in that of Empedokles, whose gaze reminded Demetrios of a vulture waiting for its moment to approach a corpse.

'I didn't finish with Philippos,' said Demetrios, clambering to one knee. His head spun, but he managed not to fall. 'We need to fight again.'

'No third bout. Philippos would kill you.' Simonides' tone was final.

'I'm not scared,' Demetrios lied. He stood, swaying a little. 'I'm ready.'

'Go on, Philippos,' goaded Empedokles. 'The pup needs another lesson.'

'The boy has done enough.' Philippos stared at Empedokles. 'How about you and I fight instead?'

Demetrios watched, not understanding, as Empedokles glowered and the other phalangists jibed at him for refusing to box against Philippos. There was an easy familiarity to their banter that hurt Demetrios more than the pulsing in his skull or the darts of pain from his bruised belly and ribs. He hadn't felt a similar kinship with anyone since his father's death, and this comradeship would not be his now, or perhaps, forever. Crushed, he turned to go.

'Hey!' Simonides' voice.

It didn't register in Demetrios' addled mind that it was he who was being addressed. He walked five or six miserable steps.

'Boy!' Simonides cried.

Demetrios glanced over his shoulder. To his surprise, all the phalangists were staring in his direction. They were preparing to humiliate him further, said his inner demon. 'Aye?'

'Where are you going?' asked Simonides.

'Back to my ship.'

'Sit with us. Share our wine.'

'But I lost. Empedokles beat me. Philippos beat me.'

'No matter. You bettered Empedokles twice, and you showed willing against Philippos.' Simonides beckoned. 'Come.'

To Demetrios' surprise, every face bar Empedokles' was open. Still hard, but friendly. Demetrios' cynicism won out, however. 'I don't want your sympathy,' he muttered.

Simonides threw back his head and laughed.

Confused, Demetrios looked from one phalangist to another.

Philippos took pity. 'A soldier sits with his comrades.'

'Comrades?' Demetrios repeated like a fool.

'Aye,' rumbled Philippos 'That is, unless you don't want to be a soldier?'

Demetrios' throat worked. 'I do. I do, more than anything.'

'Let's drink to that,' said Simonides, holding out a brimming cup.

CHAPTER VIII

Matho didn't return for two days. During that time, Felix and every man who'd been on duty were confined to the legions' prison stockade. A smaller affair than the compound holding the captured enemy troops, it was just as grim, and home to scores of deserters handed back to Scipio by the Carthaginians after Zama. The fate of these men – crucifixion or beheading – drove home the magnitude of what might face them. Stripped of their soldiers' belts, fed on barley normally reserved for the mules, Felix and his comrades slept in the open, without blankets.

Despite their isolation, news filtered through from sympathetic sentries. It seemed the escapees had parted company the moment they'd cleared the ditch. The Gauls hadn't got far. Brought to bay only a few miles south, they had been butchered by the cavalry. One of the Libyans, injured, had been abandoned by his comrades and slain, but used to the terrain, the rest were still at large. Eleven Macedonians had been caught and killed, but four others had evaded capture.

Matho's arrival into the stockade on the second evening had the principes on their feet in a heartbeat. Dust- and blood-caked, face grey with exhaustion, he was a fearsome sight. There were no prisoners with him. He sneered at the principes' salutes, and stalked up and down before them. *Slap* went his vitis off his palm. *Slap. Slap.*

'Twenty-four prisoners escaped.'

No one dared reply. Felix's heart hammered out a frenetic, painful beat.

Slap. Slap.

'Two dozen got away, and I'm supposed to think that only one of you useless turds fell asleep?' Matho was shouting now, the veins bulging in his neck.

Silence.

Matho rammed his vitis under Antonius' chin, forcing it up. 'Are you deaf?'

'N-no, sir.'

The vitis cracked down on Antonius' shoulders, his neck, his up-stretched arm. Groaning in pain, he somehow remained standing.

Skilful as a juggler, Matho spun the vitis sideways, to Felix's jaw. He stared down the length of it. 'And you – lost your hearing?'

'No, sir.'

'Ah, maybe it's your sight that's gone.' Matho raised an eyebrow.

'I can see, sir.'

'In that case, your brother's the blind one!' cried Matho, giving Antonius several more whacks.

'No, sir.'

Felix flinched as the vitis came swinging at his head. An explosion of pain burst in his head as it landed. Vision blurred, he dropped to his knees. A flurry of blows followed, driving Felix to the ground. Agony radiated from his back, his arms, his shoulders. Matho stamped on him, once, twice, the sharpened hobs of his sandal ripping Felix's tunic and raking the flesh underneath. Sensing that if he cried out, Matho would redouble his efforts, Felix kept silent.

And then Matho was gone, repeating his questions up and down the line. Every man gave the same answers. Two received a beating worse than Felix, and another was clubbed into unconsciousness.

'Attention!' roared Matho.

Everyone snapped upright except the insensible man. His comrade on either side dragged his limp frame up and held him, head lolling, in a semblance of their posture.

Slap, slap went the vitis. Matho prowled about like a caged beast. 'You're lying pieces of shit!'

Stertorous breathing, that made by men in great pain, was the only sound.

'I'm of half a mind to execute every one of you. Be a good way to draw a line under this shameful episode. Thirty years I have been in harness, and not once seen the likes of this. You've brought disgrace not just on me, your century and maniple, but the legion! The *entire fucking army* is laughing at us. I've been ordered to report to Scipio himself.' Matho pointed his vitis at Felix, at Antonius, at the next man along. 'Someone has to pay.'

'The fault was mine, sir,' muttered Ingenuus.

Keep quiet, you fool, thought Felix, but it was too late. Matho was already by Ingenuus' side.

'What's that?'

'It was my wine, sir. If it hadn't been for me, we would have been more alert. The escape wouldn't have succeeded.'

'Well done. You're not altogether spineless.'

Fooled by Matho's approving nod, Ingenuus' eyes filled with relief.

Matho pounced. 'Step forward, maggot!'

Terrified, Ingenuus obeyed.

'It's the *fustuarium* for you,' snarled Matho, cold gaze lingering over the rest. 'But you won't be alone.' He raised high a leather pouch. 'Inside are a score of white pebbles, and four black ones. Four contubernia – four deaths. Decimation would be too good for you drunken whoresons, see?'

He rummaged in the bag until he found a black stone. With a sarcastic flourish, he handed it to Ingenuus. That done, Matho glared at the rest. 'Step up, one at a time.'

Felix stole a look at Antonius, whose face was as stricken as his own.

Fortuna, Felix prayed, don't make me have to beat my own brother to death. Please.

'MOVE!' Spittle sprayed from Matho's mouth.

Felix was closest. He shoved his hand into the pouch. Cold and smooth, every stone within felt tainted with death. Throat closed with fear, he glanced at Matho.

'TAKE A FUCKING PEBBLE!'

Felix delved to the bottom, and made his choice. As his trembling fingers emerged, Matho laughed. 'What colour is it?'

Felix peered at it from between half-closed eyelids. He could have wept: the stone was white. Matho scowled when he held it up. A clout from the vitis moved him on.

'Next!'

Three of Felix's tentmates followed, all picking a white stone. The next, a princeps from another contubernium, was unluckier, producing a black. Matho sent him to stand with Ingenuus, and ordered the lottery to continue. On and on it went. Five white stones, and a black, thankfully not for one of the brothers' tentmates. When Antonius' turn came, a grinning Matho had him move back down the line. The cruelty brought out a killing rage in Felix. If he'd had a weapon at that moment, he would have thrown himself at Matho, uncaring.

The wily centurion sensed his fury. 'Did you really think your horse-shit story about one man falling asleep would fool me, maggot?'

'No, sir.' I'm a fool, thought Felix, despairing.

By the time Antonius approached Matho for the second time, there was still one black stone left in the pouch – and only two men behind him. Bile, hot and sour, filled the back of Felix's throat. His brother had a one in three chance of being beaten to death. Offering to take Antonius' place would shame him; attacking Matho would guarantee their deaths.

Felix squeezed his eyes shut and prayed: Fortuna, be kind. And then, to show solidarity with his brother, he looked up again.

Ignoring Matho's leer, Antonius shoved his hand into the bag and pulled out a pebble. 'It's white,' he said in a thick voice. His eyes flickered to Felix, who gave him a fierce, emotional nod.

Visibly disappointed, Matho shouted a command at the next man. He too picked a white stone. The final man blanched, but held out his hand firmly enough as Matho upended the bag and let the black pebble fall. 'Hard luck, maggot,' he said with an evil grin.

Felix couldn't look at Ingenuus as he and the three others had their hands bound. The brothers stood together as the contubernia were formed into a line and marched out of the prison with the condemned men at the front. Sunk in misery at what was to come, no one spoke.

Matho led the procession around the wide space inside the walls of the legion's camp. He did an entire perimeter, stopping at intervals to announce the principes' crime, and the punishment to be meted out. A few soldiers threw insults, but most looked sympathetic, even angry. Rare indeed was the sentry who hadn't drifted off on occasion, if only for a moment. Yet no one protested: this was the army's way, and questioning it risked a similar fate.

The column came to a halt by the main gate. Scores of men crowded around, drawn to the macabre scene like moths to a flame. The guards – their own comrades – formed a hollow square around the prisoners. Matho cut the ropes binding the four principes, laughing off one's request to be slain with his sword.

'You can have my pay, sir. I've hardly spent a *denarius* of it this two years.'

'Even if I wanted your miserable savings, maggot, I wouldn't take them,' sneered Matho. 'If you don't want to wander the underworld forever, take your punishment like a man.'

The princeps began to sob.

Each of the condemned men was ordered to stand near one of the square's corners, and his comrades to take up positions around him. Felix did this with dragging steps, praying that a senior officer would appear and put a stop to the savagery. Any hope he had was dashed when a tribune came through the gate. He watched long enough to discern what was unfolding before curling his lip and riding away.

At this point, Ingenuus managed to catch Felix's eye.

'Make it quick, brother,' he whispered. 'Please.'

Felix nodded, his heart heavy. This 'mercy' was all he and his comrades could offer their friend – it *had* to be done well.

'What are you waiting for?' roared Matho. 'Kill them!'

Felix and the rest stared at each other in confusion.

'Where are the sticks, sir?' asked Antonius. It was normal to use cudgels in the fustuarium.

'Use your bare hands!' Matho entered the square, shoving principes towards their wretched comrades. 'Get to it!'

The man who'd asked to be executed began to wail. 'Mercy! Mercy, in Jupiter's name!'

Matho kicked the man in the balls. He dropped to his hands and knees, whimpering. Matho drew his sword and levelled it at the nearest principes. 'Kill this useless piece of shit now, or gods help me, I'll finish every last one of you myself.' He took a step towards one soldier, who flinched, then advanced on the condemned man. The rest followed, kicking at their comrade as if he were a ball used in a game of harpastum, the brutal ball game played by legionaries.

Matho did the same with two more groups; he left Felix and his comrades until last. 'What are you waiting for, whoresons?' With jabs of his sword, he drove them at Ingenuus, who closed his eyes in acceptance of his end. A desperate momentum took over. No one wanted to be the first to land a blow, but they all wanted to minimise their friend's suffering. Punches and kicks rained in.

Felix would have given a year's pay to have had a stick, but his fists were his only weapon. He hammered a blow into Ingenuus' solar plexus. As he fell, the principes closed in, their studded sandals rising and falling with a terrible unity. Blood spurted as Felix's hobs raked Ingenuus' cheek. He shrieked, and Felix cursed himself for not delivering a better blow. He lunged in again, and was rewarded with only a dull crack as one of Ingenuus' arms broke. The jostling was so great that Felix was pushed backwards a step. He felt wetness on his cheeks, and realised he was crying. In front of him, he could make out Ingenuus thrashing to and fro, screaming for his mother, any trace of dignity gone.

Felix realised that, eager to end Ingenuus' suffering, no one was thinking straight. Half a dozen heartbeats went by, and still the wretch squirmed and wailed beneath their hobnails. Felix elbowed Antonius aside and stood over Ingenuus' head. Framed by strands of sticky red hair, a bloodshot, terrified eye stared up at him. Felix hesitated, and then praying that Ingenuus would forgive him, he slammed his heel down between his friend's eye socket and ear. The skull crunched; Ingenuus' limbs jerked like a puppet whose master has lost his reason, and stopped.

He was dead.

Chest heaving, sweat running down his face, Felix stepped away from the mangled shape that had been his comrade. What they had just done didn't seem real, but the terrible proof lay before them. He could not take his eyes off it. It, he thought bitterly. Ingenuus was a man, not a hunk of meat. Beside him, someone vomited. Antonius was praying out loud. No one could look at anyone else.

Matho arrived. He poked Ingenuus' back with his sword, and for good measure, slid the blade into his abdomen. There was no response, and he turned, smiling, cold-eyed. 'You killed him a bit fast for my liking.'

Felix's rage burst its banks. 'That was me, sir.' At that moment, he wanted Matho to beat *him* to death. It was the only thing that could wash away his guilt.

Matho came so close that every pockmark and blackhead was visible. His breath stank. 'Is that right, maggot?'

'He deserved a quick end, sir,' Felix snarled, expecting Matho to stab him.

To his surprise, grudging respect twisted Matho's lined face. 'You've got balls, I'll give you that, which is more than I can say for some of your friends.' He stepped back, giving each surviving man a hard stare.

Relief filled Felix, and he realised that despite his shame, he didn't want to die. The fustuarium was over; perhaps life could now return to a semblance of normality. He was unaware that high above, Fortuna was cackling.

'Listen to me, filth!' shouted Matho. 'Your comrades have paid with their lives for your crime, but do not think you have escaped further punishment! You are to be dishonourably discharged from the legion.' As Felix exchanged a horrified look with his brother, Matho continued, 'Any weapons and equipment not fully paid for are to be turned in to the quartermaster. Collect any pay owed to you, and leave the camp before sundown. If I catch any of you inside the walls after that, I'll fucking kill you!'

There was a collective, stunned silence.

'What are you waiting for?' bellowed Matho, raising his sword. 'Get out of my sight!'

Blood pounded in Felix's ears, and if Antonius hadn't taken his arm, he would have thrown himself at Matho.

'He's not worth it,' muttered Antonius, dragging him away. 'You'd only go the same way as Ingenuus.'

Felix threw a hate-filled look at Matho. You spared my life, Fortuna, and for that I am grateful, he thought. I have another request. Before I die, give me one chance for revenge on Matho.

Just one.

PART TWO

CHAPTER IX

Rome, autumn 201 BC

Flamininus was striding along a narrow street on the Quirinal Hill, deep in thought. His secretary Pasion scurried beside him; a hulking bodyguard followed two paces behind. The hoods of all three men's cloaks were up. If it hadn't been a miserable day, Flamininus might have worried about attracting attention, but the heavy rain meant that half the passers-by looked the same as he and his servants. The rest – those without cloaks or hoods – walked by with hunched shoulders, their gaze fixed on the muddy and uneven surface underfoot. Even the shopkeepers were subdued; almost none stood in their doorways to their premises, shouting for custom.

It wasn't an hour that Flamininus would have chosen to be abroad – the sun had not long risen, and tendrils of mist yet clung to the taller buildings – but needs must. The meeting he was hurrying to was of vital importance. Since his failed attempt to help the Aetolians and further his own career, he had spent large sums to ensure that news of every type reached him fast. If war with Macedonia and his election as consul were to become a reality, Flamininus needed his finger on the Republic's pulse, and to be aware of what was going on in the world beyond its borders. His spies were in Rome, Athens, Corinth and beyond. He even had one in Pella, the capital of Macedonia.

Flamininus had been excited when word had come a month before that Rhodes and Pergamum, two minor but important powers, were sending a joint delegation to seek the aid of the Senate. Since the capture of the towns on the Propontis – the attacks that had brought the Aetolians to Rome on their failed embassy – Philip had brought fire and sword to settlements all down the western coastline of Asia Minor. In Flamininus' mind, this was more proof that the Macedonian king was a danger to the Republic.

Philip's motives were clear. He was seeking to recapture the lands taken by Alexander's father, which was no surprise. No doubt he had dreams of emulating Alexander too, a leader Flamininus also held in high regard. Accounts of the boy king's campaigns into Persia, Sogdia and the borders of India held pride of place on his shelves. In Flamininus' mind, the conqueror of Macedonia and the birthplace of democracy, Greece, would surely be remembered like the others.

Flamininus' path to those glorious heights was still winding and precipitous. The emissaries of Rhodes and Pergamum had reached Rome, but changing the Senate's prevailing anti-war stance would be difficult. Flamininus' fervent hope was that by meeting the emissaries in advance, he could place the right words in their mouths. See the senators vote for war with Macedonia, and the first major obstacle in his path would have been removed. After that, he had only to win election as consul, a task that he hoped would prove less tricky.

'We're here, master.' Pasion pointed.

Flamininus looked at the painted sign hanging over the doorway they had stopped outside. 'The Charioteer's Rest,' he said. 'Hardly a good place to meet, eh?'

'There are no races today, master, nor will it be busy at this hour. It's also where the–' Pasion lowered his voice '–emissaries insisted on meeting. They say there are quiet cubicles at the back.'

'Very well. Thrax, take a look.'

Flamininus jerked his head at the Thracian, who lumbered inside. He emerged again soon after, declaring the inn safe. 'Two foreigners–' Thrax stumbled over the Latin '–sitting at back.'

'Follow me.' Flamininus practised his most winning face, and crossed the threshold. After a moment to adjust to the dim light, he made out a wooden counter along the side wall; it was manned by a surly-faced, stick-thin man. Tables and stools, the majority unoccupied, filled the rest of the dirt-floored room. At the back were several cubicles separated by slatted partitions. In one of these last sat a pair of cloaked men.

This was no time for hesitation, thought Flamininus, running his tongue around a dry mouth. He threw back his hood and ordered a jug of wine and three beakers for his table. 'Make sure it's drinkable!' he barked.

Awed by his new customer's evident nobility, the fawning innkeeper began rummaging below the counter.

Flamininus studied the emissaries as he approached. One had a swarthy complexion, and a Persian cut to his clothing – he had to be the Pergamene – while the other wore a chiton that wouldn't have been out of place in a shipbuilder's yard.

A typical Rhodian, thought Flamininus. He'll dress well for no man. 'You gentlemen are the emissaries?' he asked quietly.

'We are,' replied the Pergamene. 'I am Eumenes of Pergamum. This is Dorieos of Rhodes. You are Titus Quinctius Flamininus?'

'I am.'

Both men dipped their chins in acknowledgement. 'Do not think us rude, I beg you,' said Eumenes. 'We would stand and bow, but we have eyes enough on us already.'

Flamininus turned as if to speak with Pasion, and let his gaze rove the room. The other customers, a mix of comatose drunks and men with the need for an early drink, were paying them no heed. It was the surly-faced innkeeper Eumenes meant: the man could scarce look away from them. Flamininus motioned to Thrax.

'Tell that fool at the counter to bring the wine before we die of thirst. Tell him also that he's never seen any of us, and won't remember our visit – no matter who asks. If he does that, his legs will remain unbroken. If his tongue flaps . . .'

'I tell him,' said Thrax, beaming.

Flamininus took a stool at the table's end, facing the back wall so he could look at both emissaries and not be seen by the other customers. 'Well met,' he said warmly. 'I am grateful that you have come.'

'Your secretary was most persuasive,' replied Eumenes. 'You are a friend to Rhodes and Pergamum both, he said.'

'I am, and I want to help you. Philip of Macedonia has brought you both here, in a manner of speaking. Tell me everything he has done of recent months to your peoples.'

There was a brief pause as the chastened innkeeper delivered wine and beakers to the table, then Flamininus listened as the two emissaries laid out their tales of woe. Both powers had seen cities and territory lost, on Asia Minor and in the islands off its shores. There had been two naval battles, with one victory to Philip and the other to the Rhodians and Pergamenes.

Philip's transgressions did not end there. He had added insult to injury by supporting the Cretan pirates, with whom the Rhodians were at war, and then by attempting to take the city of Pergamum. By the time Eumenes and Dorieos had finished, both were visibly angry. The only good news was that of recent days, Dorieos reported, their combined navies had blockaded Philip and his fleet into a bay near the Asia Minor town of Bargylia. 'We intend to starve the bastard into submission.'

'If you are sure of that, why are you here?' demanded Flamininus.

Dorieos looked awkward. 'Philip is as wily as a fox. It's not impossible that he will find a way to escape. With Rome's help, however, victory would be certain.'

Even the prospect of a captive Philip, ready for the taking, might not persuade the Senate, thought Flamininus. He needed more. Leaning over the table, he said, 'I hear whispers of an alliance between Philip and Antiochus of Syria. What can you tell me of that?'

'It's true,' said Dorieos, thumping the table. 'Each seeks to wrest as much territory as he can – from Egypt, from Rhodes or Pergamum; their agreement means that neither obstructs the other.'

It would be easy to exaggerate the two kings' secret alliance, Flamininus decided with delight. This information gave him just the fuel to ignite the senators' rage. 'You both desire Rome's aid against Philip.'

'More than anything,' said Eumenes. Dorieos nodded.

'Then you must make light of the wrongs inflicted on your peoples by the brigand Philip.' Their faces darkened, and he made a placatory gesture. 'Hear me out. I am unusual among Romans in holding you in high regard; most senators think only of themselves and the Republic. Emphasise how strong Philip's navy is, therefore, and the ease with which his ships could sail to Italia, and you will send a shiver down every senator's spine. Tell them of Antiochus' recent victories in the east, of his desire to emulate Alexander's exploits. He and Philip are thick as thieves, you will say – it matters not if this isn't the case. Paint an image in the senators' minds that a combined Syrian and Macedonian fleet could land on our shores as early as next spring. Memories of Hannibal are still strong: the idea of foreign armies on Italian soil will have the senators on their feet, baying for Philip's blood.'

Flamininus' eyes flickered from Dorieos, whom he judged to be the more hot-blooded, to Eumenes, the calculating one of the pair. Neither said anything immediately, and Flamininus' guts rolled. The Rhodian and Pergamene were proud men – no doubt they had taken offence at his disregard for the injuries and losses inflicted on them by Philip. 'Perhaps I should explain further—' he began.

'No need,' said Dorieos, cutting him off. 'We remember how the Aitolians were treated last year. Our chief concern has ever been that our mission would fail. I care not how the Republic is persuaded to aid us.'

'Nor I,' added Eumenes. 'Your words had my heart racing.' He placed a hand on his own chest, and said without a hint of embarrassment, 'Know that I am the finest orator in Pergamum – Attalus himself chose me. And Dorieos maintains he can charm the Sirens from their rocks.'

'Not quite, perhaps,' demurred Dorieos, 'but I *am* persuasive.'

Delighted, Flamininus raised his cup. 'War with Macedonia!'

Flamininus accepted another senator's pledge with a broad smile, and a firm handshake. He was inside the Curia, where the consular elections were about to take place. Tireless to the last, he continued to move through the senators, targeting those whose allegiance wasn't yet certain. A month had passed since his secretive meeting with the Rhodian and Pergamene emissaries. Soon after, Eumenes and Dorieos had delivered their speeches with actors' flair, enraging and horrifying the senators by turn. Their descriptions of torn-down temples, violated women and murdered babies – all acts committed by Philip's troops – had seen the motion for war with Macedonia carried by a huge majority.

Flamininus' voice had been one of the first to support Eumenes and Dorieos; he had announced his candidacy for the upcoming consular elections soon after. His co-candidate was Sextus Aelius Paetus Catus. An excellent jurist and lawmaker with scant interest in party politics, he had been horrified by the notion of prosecuting a war with Macedonia. Win the contest, therefore, and the task of defeating Philip would be Flamininus' alone. His rivals were to be Quintus Minucius Rufus and Caius Cornelius Cethegus, and their co-candidates – all four, men who could be beaten. Galba, who had not won election as magistrate in Hispania, appeared to have lost interest.

Flamininus had spent the time since the emissaries' visit assiduously courting senators. Numerous dinner parties had followed; he plied his guests with fine food and wine. Ignoring his wife's protests, Flamininus had also laid on high-class prostitutes of both sexes. He had visited scores of senators, bringing bulging purses of coin and pots of hard-to-find spices such as pepper, cinnamon and coriander. When, during one dinner party, a senator had expressed an appreciation of one of Flamininus' slaves – a willowy female slave from Egypt – he had called on his guest the very next day to deliver her in person.

Flamininus didn't know how every senator would vote, of course. Some wouldn't commit, no matter how handsome his gifts. Not all who said they'd support him would do so either. He hoped that there were senators among his rivals' supporters who would act in the same way. All told, Flamininus had ninety-four votes he was sure of, including his own, and another dozen that seemed probable. By his reckoning Quintus Minucius Rufus could count on eighty-five, with perhaps another ten possibles. Caius Cornelius Cethegus, the third candidate, had sixty-five solid votes, and the potential for five more. Six senators were away, or too ill to attend the election. That left a body of twenty-three senators whose votes would carry the day, for the paired candidates with the greatest number of ballots were elected.

Flamininus had spoken with almost all of the twenty-three. He had spent a wine-soaked morning at the baths with two, and bought an expensive Iberian mount for a third. One had had his gambling debts settled, and another had seen a sudden approval by the city magistrates of his thus far stalled application to rebuild his Aventine mansion. Flamininus had guaranteed places in his army staff to the sons of three senators, and promised to sort out several land disputes.

Despite these Herculean efforts, Flamininus remained unsure if he would emerge victorious. His numbers were hopeful, but Minucius Rufus and Cethegus had also been courting support, and like as not, offering their own sweeteners. Now Flamininus' stomach was tight with nerves, and only surreptitious wipes of his hands on his toga kept his handshake dry, not slick with sweat.

Spotting another of the 'not sures', he put on his solicitous face and asked after the man's ill wife. 'I'll have my surgeon visit. He's one of the best in Rome. Fee? There'll be no fee. It would be my honour if he can help your wife,' said Flamininus, accepting the senator's effusive thanks as another probable vote.

A moment later, another senator who hadn't yet promised to vote for anyone greeted him like a long-lost son. 'Philip must be dealt with, and soon,' said the florid-faced man. 'You're youthful to be consul, but it's young blood that gets things done quickest sometimes. Minucius Rufus, well, he's a hothead. Always has been. And Cethegus is a dullard. Nothing wrong with that, but Philip is shrewd. Rome will need a clever mind to defeat him.' Clasping Flamininus' hand, he moved on.

A couple of other 'not sures' smiled and nodded at Flamininus, and he thought with rising excitement, I'm going to do it. After so long, he could *taste* victory.

When the lictores rapped their staffs on the floor, and the senators hurried to stand in their customary spots, Flamininus felt confident enough to stride down the central passage. Before an election, this was something only the incumbent consuls did, resplendent in their official robes. He felt the weight of men's stares, heard the surprised mutters, but paid no heed. This is my hour, he decided.

A tense wait followed as, surrounded by their lictores, Claudius and Servilius entered the Curia and walked to the low dais at the end of the chamber. The usual ritual prayers were uttered, and confirmation received from soothsayers that the omens for the election were good. Throwing up a last prayer to the gods, Flamininus watched his rivals sidelong. Minucius was impassive-faced, as a man who still had a good chance of winning, but Cethegus' expression was morose, that of someone who has conceded defeat in his head.

'Senators of Rome.' Claudius was on his feet, his tone solemn. 'My time as consul is coming to an end, as it is for my colleague Servilius. It has been our honour to serve the Republic, as it is today to officiate at the election of our successors.'

'Candidates, present yourselves,' commanded Servilius, moving to stand beside Claudius.

Flamininus smoothed down his toga, accepted the encouraging mutters of those around him, and stepped up onto the dais with Aelius Paetus. He was joined by Minucius Rufus and a mournful-looking Cethegus, and their prospective co-consular colleagues. Flamininus' gaze roved the massed senators. Everywhere he could see smiles, nods and men who appeared to support him. Exhilaration gripped him; his long-held hopes seemed about to become real.

Claudius and Servilius greeted each candidate, before Servilius turned to the senators again. 'I have before me three men who would be your senior consuls, and their colleagues.' He listed the names.

'Following the usual protocol, I shall announce each man in turn. Those who support that candidate will raise their right arm, and the lictores will walk through the room, counting. Thrice I shall do that—'

'Four times!' A loud voice cut across Servilius.

As shocked as everyone else, Flamininus strained to see who had spoken.

'Present yourself.' Servilius' lips were thin with disapproval.

'My apologies, consul.' Galba climbed to the dais. 'I wish to stand for election. Caius Aurelius Cotta shall be my co-consul.'

Horror gripped Flamininus. 'You can't!'

Galba gave him a brief, contemptuous glance. 'A senator wishing to be consul may stand forth at any time until the voting has begun.' He looked to Claudius and Servilius, who conferred and announced that as far as they knew, this was correct. Despite the late hour, there was no reason for Galba's or Cotta's candidacy to be refused.

'We must *do* something,' Flamininus whispered to Minucius Rufus and Cethegus. 'He can't be allowed to get away with it.'

'It appears he just has,' replied Minucius Rufus drily.

'Galba has years more experience than any of us. He was consul once before, during the war with Hannibal. The man has also been dictator,' said Cethegus. 'In case you can't remember, he also commanded Rome's forces in the first war against Philip. That's good enough for me.' He raised his voice. 'I wish to withdraw.'

Flamininus gave himself a vicious pinch, but the nightmare continued – indeed, it worsened. He watched, dazed, as Cethegus thanked his supporters, and asked them to vote for Galba, 'the best candidate'.

Numb, Flamininus watched the lictores counting the senators who declared for Minucius Rufus – forty-two – and then those who still supported him. Fifty-five votes, he thought, struggling to take it in. The fact that he had saved more of his ballot than Minucius Rufus was no consolation whatsoever.

Flamininus had calculated Galba's vote long before the senior lictor announced it to the consuls. The margin of victory – stolen from him at the last moment – was bitterer than hemlock.

'One hundred and ninety-seven votes for the last candidate. The result is clear,' declared Servilius. 'All hail the new consuls, Publius Sulpicius Galba and Caius Aurelius Cotta!'

Flamininus didn't think it possible to feel worse, but Galba's triumphant wink made him wish the floor could have opened to swallow him up.

Not only had he failed to win election as consul: he would not be the man to conquer Macedonia. Shunning the senators who crowded onto the dais to congratulate Galba and Cotta, Flamininus made for the door. His father's sour advice repeated itself in his head, over and over.

'History never recalls those who came second in a race.'

CHAPTER X

The Gulf of Bargylia, south-western coast of
Asia Minor, late winter, 201/200 BC

Sitting on a hill above the town and wrapped in a simple cloak, Philip of Macedon stared westward, brooding. His sharp features were softened by a thick beard. At thirty-five, he was in the prime of life, although thinner than normal. His richly worked armour and a purple tunic had seen better days too, but his haughty expression and confident manner would have made a man think he was in the royal palace at Pella.

The blood-red sun was sinking into the Aegean, obscuring the islands that lay in the direction of Macedon. The ships barricading his fleet into the bay were still visible, however, sleek black shapes holding a line between Bargylia and the open sea. Philip's jaw bunched. Rhodes and Pergamum were mortal enemies of his now.

The cowards will not attack me for fear of defeat, he thought. Instead they blockade us, and wait for hunger and deprivation to do their job.

Philip ran again through the events of the summer, wondering how this outcome could have been avoided. His outlook that spring had been worlds apart from that which faced him now. With the Propontis under his control, he had decided to regain more lands that had been Macedonian in the time of Alexander. His new fleet of two hundred vessels had crossed to the eastern Aegean, where Philip had raided the Kyklades Islands, seizing many, both Rhodian and Pergamene. He had been careful not to annex the isle of Samos, however, because of its allegiance to Ptolemaic Egypt. Only a fool picked a fight with every man in the street.

Philip's next intention had been to invade Ionia, part of Asia Minor's western coastline, but before he could land his army, the Rhodians, eager for vengeance, had sailed to meet him. Between Samos and the island of Lade, the two fleets had clashed. He had been victorious, but after their defeat, the Rhodians had gone running to Attalus, the king of Pergamum, who until that point had been neutral. News of his ships joining the Rhodians had caused an enraged Philip to attack Pergamum itself.

A wry smile twisted his lips. It might have been wiser to have controlled my temper, and confined myself to the coast and the islands, he thought.

And yet his surprise assault on Attalus' inland capital had so nearly come off. The scratch force sent to meet him had been routed; it was only the swift closure of the gates that had prevented Philip from seizing the city. It was from this point, he decided sourly, that the Fates had turned against him.

Ill-prepared for a siege – lacking catapults, towers and plentiful supplies – he and his troops had been forced to scavenge the surrounding countryside. Warned by Attalus, the locals had taken in the harvest early and retreated into their towns. Hither and thither Philip had marched with his hungry soldiers, but he had been baulked at every turn. In the end, he'd had to ask his erstwhile ally Antiokhus for assistance, but the help offered by the Syrian king's local governor had paid no more than lip service to their alliance. Four days' food, thought Philip. One day I'll make you pay for that, Antiokhus.

Reunited with his fleet, yet determined to continue his campaign, Philip had decided to blockade Khios. Before he could subjugate the town, the combined Rhodian and Pergamene fleet had arrived. Islands attacked or threatened by Philip had sent ships as well, making the two sides equally matched. The second naval battle of the summer had been a catastrophic disaster, however. Attalus' flagship had been captured – the Pergamene king barely escaping – but almost half of Philip's fifty-odd quinqueremes and quadriremes had been sunk. Three thousand soldiers and twice that number of sailors had gone down with their vessels; three thousand more infantry had been taken prisoner, making his losses the worst since he'd taken the throne. It was as well, he decided, that Perseus had been left in Pella. A campaign under arms would have served the lad well, but not if the price had been drowning at Khios.

Attalus had taken his fleet home after the battle; the Rhodians had also retreated to lick their wounds. Assuming their retreat to be a reluctance for further hostilities, an emboldened Philip had sailed south-east, now attacking the Karian coast where his stepfather Antigonus Doson had campaigned a generation before. Success had followed success: it had been particularly satisfying to subjugate Rhodes' only mainland territory, the Perea. Philip had thought then his enemies lacked unity, yet the news of his continuing campaign had brought them together again soon after. He had known none of this, and with his ships safely beached in the Gulf of Bargylia, he had set about capturing towns in the hinterland.

It wasn't kingly to shake a fist, so he cursed the Rhodians and Pergamenes in the bay instead. Long and hard he cursed them, to be dragged down into Poseidon's watery kingdom, to burn in Tartaros' depths, or to be chained forever to rocks as Prometheus had been, and have their ever-renewed livers torn out by vultures daily. Philip felt only a little better when he was done. By the time he'd known about the enemy fleet's arrival, the blockade had been complete. That hadn't stopped him from marching his army back in haste, but it had been for naught. Shaped like a sideways-facing cup, with the open mouth emptying into the Aegean, the Gulf of Bargylia lent itself to entrapment. Here he and his men had been since. Months of deprivation and hunger had followed – and continued to this day. It took all his leadership to hold his army together.

He cast a look at the dozen Companions who had accompanied him to the hilltop: they could be relied on. Despite their gaunt faces and ragged cloaks, they looked ready for battle, and their comrades in the camp were the same. The rest of his army was in worse spirits, however. Despite sharing the same hardships as his men, Philip was losing men to desertion. If he didn't break the fleet out soon, more would follow. Mutiny might even rear its ugly head.

Falling morale wasn't his only reason for needing to act. Of recent days, his spies – landing in small craft north and south of the bay – had brought word that both Rhodes and Pergamum had gone crying to Rome for help. Although he doubted that the Republic's declared disinterest in Greek affairs, so loudly declared in the Senate the previous year, would change, Philip needed to return to Pella. A king could not afford to be too long away from his throne. He glanced again at the ships in the bay. To have any chance of extricating his entire fleet, still more than one hundred vessels strong, he needed the gods' help – something that had been in short supply these past months.

He clambered to his feet and signalled to the Companions that they should return. His belly rumbled, a reminder that he hadn't eaten since dawn. 'What's for dinner?'

'Bread, sire, and a little roast boar. There's some wine as well – poor quality, I'm sorry to say.'

Philip grunted. The portion sizes of recent months had been tiny. He ate the same rations as his soldiers, and when there wasn't enough, he also went hungry.

Not for much longer, he decided. Like Hannibal, he would find a way, or make one.

Dawn brought the discovery that more than a hundred peltasts, wild men from the mountains of Thrace, had slipped away. Philip's first inclination was to send the Companions after them, but common sense prevailed. The way to win back the loyalty of those soldiers who remained was to give them belief, he decided, not to execute deserters.

'They leave more food for us,' he joked to his gathered troops, although few laughed. 'Soon we will leave this shithole,' he declared. 'Back in Pella, I shall have hundreds of sheep butchered to celebrate our safe return. Wine will flow as if poured by Dionysos' hand!'

The obligatory cheers that followed were thin and unconvinced, and clambering down from the dais, Philip avoided his officers' gaze.

He went to the hilltop alone that afternoon, fiercely ordering back the Companions who tried to follow. How he would find inspiration from the same ships he had stared at for months, Philip had no idea, but he was determined to come up with an idea. For hours he sat there, immune to cold and hunger. Gulls wheeled and cried overhead, but he did not hear. An officer of the Companions who came to check on him got shouted at, and retreated. Despair, an alien emotion, trickled into Philip's mind, like rain seeping through a leaking roof. He cursed it away, and prayed again to the gods. Hermes, the messenger god, and also favoured by those who travelled, would receive half a dozen bulls by way of gratitude if he intervened. So too would Ares, the unpredictable god of war. I'll give you all half a dozen bulls, if only you'll help, thought Philip in desperation.

No bolt of lightning came from the heavens, no flash of inspiration struck. The sun began to set. Refusing to let his hopes fade, Philip decided he would return the following day. In the end, a way to spirit his fleet past the enemy blockade *would* appear. He cast a last, infuriated glance at the ships in the bay.

The answer came, its simplicity infuriating.

Philip studied the ship that formed the blockade's centre, as he had countless times before. During daylight hours, it had neighbours to left and right, but each afternoon as the light faded, it was left alone as the others rowed to shore. Attalus and his Rhodian allies were like most men, thought Philip, and assumed he was too. No one in his right mind voyaged at night. It wasn't something that Philip would have entertained under normal circumstances, but his options were scant.

Silence the sentries on the central ship, he thought, pray that the sleeping crew remained unaware, and the entire width of the bay would offer itself to his fleet. He decided to send one of his trusted servants, an Egyptian, to the enemy camp the next day. Pretending to be a deserter, he would beg an audience with Attalus. Philip was running out of supplies, he would say, and morale among his troops was plummeting. Accordingly, Philip's fleet would seek battle the day after.

It was a huge gamble – who knew if Attalus would be lulled into a false sense of security by the Egyptian, or whether the central trireme could be put out of action? – but Philip was prepared to risk all.

He would be caged no longer.

In the darkest hour of the night that followed, Philip waited on the beach of Bargylia by a small fisherman's craft. Open to the elements, with a single sail, the round-bellied boat could hold a dozen men and the crusty local who owned it. Philip commanded; eleven of his best Companions waited around him. Every man's face and hands had been blackened with ash; so too had their chitons. They wore no armour or helmets, and each carried only a dagger. The task of attacking the trireme could have been led by any number of his best officers, but six months of frustration meant he would suffer no other to do it. Perhaps it was foolish, thought Philip, to risk his life like this, but by the gods, he felt alive. He was doing something at last, and if the Fates willed it, he would be a good way towards Macedon before the enemy realised. If, on the other hand, the old bitches wanted to play with him – despite the cloud cover, this was an equally likely outcome – he and his men would soon be dead, and his fleet doomed.

The boat's owner, a fisherman with a face wrinkled enough to be

Philip's grandfather, limped to his side. 'The tide is on the turn,' he whispered. 'We must go.'

'I hear you, old one.'

Philip had been prepared to kill the families of any fishermen who wouldn't take them out to the anchored trireme, but it hadn't come to that. To his surprise, the ancient had offered the instant the demand had been made. 'Death is coming for me soon,' he'd said with a wink. 'I can't think of a better way to go than with the king of Macedon as he tries to escape this bay.' His entire lack of reverence and surety that they would fail had tickled Philip's humour, and so, against his officers' wishes, he had chosen him.

Philip signalled, and once the fisherman had clambered in, the Companions pushed the boat into the shallows. Two more craft and another twenty-four soldiers on the beach would follow close behind. Next Philip and his men heaved themselves aboard. A pair of Companions laid their backs to the oars. Down the blades went, entering the water with almost no sound. Faint splashes rose as they came up into the air. Philip, crouched in the prow and peering towards the trireme, pricked his ears. He heard only the low screech of night birds skimming over the waves; this relieved the knot of tension in his belly not at all. Never in his life had he been so rash, he thought with a thrill, but there was no going back now.

They had set out from a secluded spot on the south-eastern edge of the beach – the closest point to the anchored trireme. Distance was impossible to judge in the darkness, but Philip knew from the day's practice efforts that the oarsmen could slowly row four stadia as a man's heart beat half a thousand times. The tension would make keeping this tally difficult, so he had ordered every Companion to do it. At three hundred and fifty, Philip could feel cold sweat trickling down his neck. He placed his lips against the ear of the man next to him, and whispered, 'Your count?'

The Companion leaned close. 'Three hundred and ninety-six, sire.'

Philip's eyes shot to the water in front of the boat. He could see nothing still. Then timbers creaked dead ahead, and he almost cried out. With relief, with fear – he wasn't sure. Signalling the Companion to tell the oarsmen to slow their pace further, he began to count his heartbeats again. At four hundred and fifty, the glow of a lamp was visible by the base of the trireme's mast, and he had their little craft come to a halt. The risks of taking it alongside the enemy ship were too great – from here, he and his men would swim.

Philip had no idea how many sentries there were. This was the point his senior officers had made over and again. 'Miss even one, sire, and it won't matter that all the others died without a sound. Noise carries across water. His shouts will wake every enemy crew on the shore.' The officer's point had been valid, but he and his comrades had had no answer when Philip had demanded another way out of their predicament.

'Into the water,' he whispered, giving the old man a nod of thanks before slipping over the side. The Companions joined him. Philip didn't linger. They would succeed, or they would fail. With gentle strokes, he swam and prayed. Prayed and swam.

If the commander of the trireme was worth his salt, thought Philip for the hundredth time, he would be resting his crew before the 'battle' in the morning. There might be four sentries, or as few as two. The rest aboard would be fast asleep, the oarsmen lying by their benches, and the soldiers wherever a space offered itself. Keeping them quiet after the sentries had been slain would be another matter . . .

Stop it, he told himself. Ten paces out from the trireme's prow, he looked up. One sentry was clearly visible, leaning on his spear. He gave no sign of seeing them. Dangerous though it was, Philip waited, treading water; a short time later, a second man appeared beside the first.

'Seen anything?' he murmured.

'Course not.' The reply was sleepy.

'Gods, but this night is dragging by.' The second sentry moved in front of his comrade, and tugged underneath his chiton. A stream of urine arced out, spattering the water close to Philip, who closed his eyes in disgust.

When the second man had finished, he elbowed his fellow. 'It's your turn to walk the ship. Last time I was there, Solon was awake, but Greybeard was snoring. Give him a kick from me.'

'I don't blame the poor old bastard – he should be in his blankets like the rest of the crew,' said the first man. 'Posting four sentries every night is fucking stupid. That mongrel Philip and his yellow-livered followers would never attack us.' Muttering to himself, he set off down the planking that ran from prow to stern.

Four sentries, thought Philip. It was more than he'd hoped for.

He motioned that he and five others would swim along the trireme. At his signal, they would deal with Greybeard, Solon and the man walking towards them; the remaining Companions were to clamber up via the bronze ram, kill the lone sentry and whistle to the waiting boats. Then it would be a mad scramble from both ends of the ship to threaten, gag and murder enough of the crew so that none tried to raise the alarm.

Using the planking of the hull as concealment – only someone leaning right out would see them – Philip swam to the stern. He reached it just as the grumbling sentry did. The complaints as the promised kicks were delivered to a groggy Greybeard provided enough noise for Philip to swarm up one of the steering oars with a dagger gripped in his teeth. A Companion who had climbed the second oar appeared atop the rail at the same moment he did; the four others were following close behind. Greybeard saw Philip, who was only an arm's length away, and his mouth opened. The complaining sentry, who was facing towards the open sea, thought he was about to protest again, and sneered. The third man spotted both Philip and the Companion, and grabbed for his sword. Philip knifed the grumbler in the lungs, twice for good measure, then shoved him, dying, into his sword-wielding comrade. As that man stumbled backwards, the beginnings of a shout leaving his mouth, Philip caught him with a backslash across the throat. Blood showered the deck, and before Philip could prevent it, the swordsman fell backwards into the sea.

Philip lowered himself down to the rowing deck a heartbeat after the resulting splash. Sleeping bodies lay as far as he could see, but woken by the noise, one man sat up.

'What's going on?' he mumbled.

Dagger behind his back, Philip replied in his best Pergamene accent, 'That fool Greybeard only went and fell in.'

With a snort, the man lay back down.

Philip reached down and covered the man's mouth with one hand, and sliced him open from ear to ear. The next oarsman along stirred, and Philip cut his throat too. When he stood upright, he found a third rower regarding him with utter horror.

'Keep your mouth shut, and live,' hissed Philip. The soldiers aboard would be loyal to Attalus, but if the men who pulled on the oars were like most, they would care less for their king than the coin they were paid. 'Say a single fucking word, and you'll go the same way as your mates.'

The oarsman lay back down like a child scolded back to bed by an angry parent.

Like silent wraiths, Philip and his Companions stole along the rowing deck, by times threatening, by times ending protest in a flurry of dagger thrusts. The six Companions who had boarded at the prow were at work too. When they were joined by the two other boats – called in with an owl call – the trireme was soon in their hands. Apart from the man who'd fallen into the sea, the only noise had been a couple of stifled cries from those crewmen foolhardy enough to challenge men standing over them with ready blades.

Nonetheless, the commotion had been more than should be expected aboard a ship in the dead of night. Philip's nerves were in tatters as he listened for any indication of alarm from the shoreline to the north and south.

Time slipped by, slower than he had ever known it, but no shouts, no call to arms reached them. Finally, his anxiety eased into sheer, unadulterated delight. The danger had not gone – his entire fleet had to row out of the bay unseen and unheard – but in the skies above, the Fates were smiling.

By the following day, Philip's escape was complete. The Pergamene and Rhodian fleet had given pursuit at dawn, when the bay was seen to be empty of his ships. Despite their head start, it had been a close-run affair. The enemy's lead vessels had closed to within ten stadia of the rearmost Macedonian ones; lacking crew members, three of Philip's lembi had been caught and taken. The rest had rowed for their lives, and pulled away. After months of virtual imprisonment, these were trifling losses.

Now Philip stood at his ship's prow alone, tasting in the salty air a freedom he hadn't had for too long. Inevitably, thoughts of home filled his mind; they soured his mood a little. He'd be glad to have Macedonian earth beneath his feet once more, but there would be little time to take his ease with his wife, or to go hunting boar in the hills. Odds were that on his northern and eastern frontiers, the Thracians or Dardani would have invaded. The Greek states would be causing trouble too. Sparta, Aitolia, Athens – all had reason to resent his kingship.

If the fools would recognise Macedon's pre-eminence, thought Philip, life would be easy. They will learn to do so, one way or another.

Of less concern were the Rhodian and Pergamene embassies who had been sent to Rome – they would try their hardest, but Philip could not imagine the Senate reversing its decision of the previous year. Having been involved with Greece before, the Republic's attention might well return in the future, but after the gruelling war with Hannibal, Rome currently had no stomach for another war. So reasoned Philip. Spotting a dolphin in the ship's bow wave, he smiled. Two more joined the first, the trio slicing through the water with consummate ease, the picture of power and grace. Mesmerised, sure they were proof of Poseidon's favour, he watched until they tired of their sport and vanished again into the depths.

CHAPTER XI

The army's camp outside Pella, Macedon

D awn was breaking. The air was crisp and cool, and laden with the smell of wet grass. Birds chattered from the nearby woods, delighted with spring's arrival. Trickles of smoke rose from fires that had lasted the night. Most men were still in their blankets, dreaming, but Demetrios was outside the tent he shared with five other men. After a few stretches, he was going to run the perimeter of the great camp. Fitness, he had learned, was vital to being a good soldier.

More than a year had passed since the fateful evening when Demetrios had fought Empedokles and Philippos. Not a single day went past when he didn't give thanks to Hermes and Ares for the beatings he'd received. Well, not the beatings, but the way events had unfolded. Demetrios was gut-sure that both gods had been watching, and smiling on him. How else could he have won the two vital bouts against Empedokles, or been admitted to one of the most prestigious speirai in the phalanx?

To show the gods his gratitude, Demetrios made it his business once a month to visit a shrine to Hermes which lay close to the city walls, and the army's camp. There he poured a libation of the best wine he could afford, sometimes bringing a hen for the priests to sacrifice. Next he gave thanks for his good fortune, and prayed. With Ares, he was a little more circumspect. If Demetrios was truthful, the mysterious war god in his crested helmet scared him. Simonides, already like a father figure to him, said that Ares reaped men in battle the way a farmer cut wheat with a sickle. Demetrios prayed to him, but he was a deity to be feared.

The envy of men in other files had been evident from the first day. Demetrios didn't understand the ugly looks until Simonides had explained that the lowliest phalangist in his file had been slain at Kios. But for that unfortunate death, and the need for a replacement, Simonides would never have offered him a place. After that, Demetrios added Hades, the god of the underworld, to his prayers.

The day after the fights with Empedokles and Philippos, realising that Demetrios knew little of army life, Simonides had set him to learn the phalanx's structure. He could repeat it in his sleep now, but at the time it had been confusing. Philip's phalanx was made up of two five-thousand-men-strong *strategiai*, the white shields and the brazen shields. Each strategia consisted of five chiliarchies, each containing one thousand and twenty-four men. The chiliarchies were ranked in order of importance, one to five, and in each were four speirai. Simonides and his comrades – and Demetrios – served in the first speira of the second *chiliarchy* of the brazen shields.

Every speira had two hundred and fifty-six phalangists, made of up of sixteen files of sixteen men. Each file had eleven phalangists and five officers: a file-leader, a half- and two quarter-file leaders, and a file-closer. Simonides was the file-leader; his friends were front-rankers, and stood behind him. As the newest recruit, Demetrios stood at the back, with only the file-closer Zotikos to his rear.

He smiled. Since that momentous evening, the army had become his life; it was becoming hard to think of any other existence. Sorting through the pile of stacked shields outside the tent, Demetrios pulled out his own. Small, round, and a little dished, the aspis was eight times the width of a man's palm. On the front, against a brazen background, the royal Macedonian star had been painted in black. Demetrios' aspis was old and battered; it had belonged to the dead youth he'd replaced, but he was inordinately proud of it. Along with the dagger he'd owned since he was a boy, a simple helmet and his long *sarissa* spear, the shield was the only equipment he possessed.

Of course he longed for more. Soon after joining, he had expressed this desire to Philippos, the friendliest of the veteran phalangists. Philippos had laughed his great belly laugh.

'Listen to you! First off, you stand right at the back of the phalanx, so you don't need armour or a sword. Second, this kit–' Philippos had flicked a finger off his padded linen cuirass '–is expensive. You can't afford it. Save your pay, boy, and in a year or two, you'll have enough coin. Or you might be lucky and kill a man wearing one, and take it for your own.'

'What if the enemy attacks the rear of the phalanx?' Demetrios had demanded. 'I'll need armour then.' At the time, he had never seen the speirai drilling on the plain beside the camp.

Philippos had laughed again. 'Patience. We're trained to wheel about and reform with the front-rankers facing the enemy. If that happens, you'll be at the back again.' He had smiled at Demetrios' glare. 'Standing at the front of the phalanx is unpleasant and dangerous. Only a madman would choose to be there.'

'Simonides does it! So do you and the others.'

Philippos' face had grown serious. 'Sliding your spear into a man's eye socket takes its toll. Hearing your mate drowning in his own blood, and being able to do nothing for him, is horrific. During a battle some men lose control of themselves – the air is laced with the smell of shit and piss and puke. You can feel the terror – almost touch it. Everyone is afraid, bar a few insane fuckers on both sides.'

'If it's so bad, why are you in the army?' Demetrios had challenged.

'My father was a phalangist, and so was his before him. I couldn't think of any other life. Then there's the comradeship – you already know what that's like. And by the gods, because there's nothing quite like breaking an enemy phalanx. Your heart sings. Ares' strength flows into you, I swear it, and you *know* that no one can stop you.'

Demetrios had liked that part best.

'Live long enough, and you'll work your way up the file. I was a rear ranker when I joined up.' Philippos had clapped him on the back, like an equal.

Demetrios had relived the conversation many times since. He didn't know how long it would take – years, like as not – but one day he *would* stand near the front with Simonides and Philippos. He slipped on his felt and wool arming cap, which already smelt as if he'd worn it his whole life, and after, his plain bronze helmet. Aspis slung over one shoulder, he picked up his sarissa.

'Practising for the *hoplitodromos*?'

He turned, seeing Empedokles' head poking out of his tent. Demetrios uttered a self-conscious, truthful but not-knowing-what-else-to-say, 'No.'

Empedokles curled his lip. 'It's good to practise running, boy, because that's what you will do the first time we fight.'

Demetrios flushed with anger and shame. Perhaps the malevolent phalangist was right – how could he know? He took off at a lope, Empedokles' mocking laughter ringing in his ears.

Demetrios returned from his run, Empedokles forgotten, belly snarling with hunger. Kimon, another rear-ranker and one of the men he shared a tent with, had the barley porridge cooking. Open-faced, with longish brown hair, he had an impressively sized nose. About a year older than Demetrios and about the same height and build, Kimon was interested in everything, and more fair-minded than Demetrios ever cared to be. The two had been friends from the first moment they'd met.

'Is it ready?' demanded Demetrios.

Kimon grinned and spooned in a little honey. 'Hungry?'

'Fucking starving.' Demetrios set down his sarissa and shield with the rest, and sat down by the fire.

'Good run?'

'Aye. You should come along some morning.'

Kimon shook his head. 'I get enough exercise on the training ground.'

He opened his mouth to argue, but thought better of it. Kimon was fonder of drinking and cooking than anything else, and it seemed nothing would change that. Demetrios concentrated instead on wolfing down his porridge. It was a smaller portion than he'd have liked, but for good reason. Soon after joining the phalanx, with memories of the hungry times at the rowing bench still vivid, he had ignored Kimon's advice and gorged himself before the morning's drill. An hour into training, Demetrios had broken ranks to vomit. Everyone had laughed, even Kimon. Everyone apart from Simonides, that is. His measured dressing-down had humiliated Demetrios more than a beating. Now he always held back at the morning meal. Evenings were a different matter – he filled his belly then until it could hold no more.

'A bottomless pit, you are,' Kimon was prone to saying, but his eyes would twinkle as he spooned food into Demetrios' bowl for the third or fourth time.

'Time to move, brothers!' Simonides' voice carried from his tent.

Kimon rolled his eyes. 'Here we go again.'

Demetrios exchanged a look with Antileon, another tentmate who'd become a good friend.

'It wouldn't be the same if Kimon didn't complain,' said Antileon.

Tall, burly, and curly-haired, he liked nothing more than to argue. He disagreed with everyone, even if his opinion was the same as theirs.

'Says the man who would quarrel with himself,' retorted Kimon.

Antileon shrugged. 'I like a good discussion, that's all.'

'Move it, dusty feet.' Empedokles had appeared, as was his wont. 'We don't have time to stand around gossiping like women.'

'I'm not a farmer any more,' said Antileon, glowering. 'I've been in the army for two years, as well you know.'

'Once a dusty foot, always a dusty foot,' said Empedokles with a sneer. 'I had hopes you might change, but here you are, choosing to associate with the sheep-humper.' He gestured at Demetrios. 'And you, Kimon: I thought you'd know better.'

Kimon muttered something under his breath.

'What's that?' demanded Empedokles. Although he wasn't a file-leader like Simonides, he was a front-ranker, which meant his status in the speira was a deal higher than that of Demetrios and his friends. Empedokles liked nothing better than to lord it over the lower-ranked men. In consequence, he was loathed by all except his front-rank comrades, who – for reasons Demetrios could not understand – did not seem to recognise him for what he really was.

'Piss off and annoy someone else, why don't you?' said Antileon.

Lip curling, Empedokles took a step towards Antileon, but Demetrios and Kimon silently placed themselves on either side of their friend. Empedokles looked the three up and down with contempt, and spat on the ground right by Antileon's feet. 'I'm glad you yellow-livers stand ten men behind me.'

Just as well you aren't closer, thought Demetrios. The temptation to stab Empedokles in the back during a battle would be hard to resist.

The confrontation was brought to an end by Simonides' voice, telling his men that if they weren't ready to march by the time he counted to one hundred, any latecomers would feel the point of his foot up their arse.

On the great training ground near the army's camp, Demetrios was standing in file, with Zotikos behind him. In front of Demetrios stood Kimon. After him came the quarter-file leader, and then Antileon. The file then ran all the way to Simonides, at the front. Each man's shield hung by its carrying strap over his left shoulder; every sarissa was grounded butt first, its point aimed straight at the sky. Two paces separated the sixteen men from those in the files on either side; the same distance was repeated across the assembled speira.

'Phalangists, prepare yourselves!' shouted Kryton, the speira commander.

There was a stirring in the ranks.

'On my orders, file-leaders!' Short but barrel-chested, Kryton made up for his lack of stature with a larger than life persona. Possessed of a voice that would rival that of Zeus in a rage, he had killed his first boar – a rite of passage for Macedonian men – at the tender age of fifteen. He also knew the king.

Demetrios had never had occasion to speak with Kryton; he was happy with that state of affairs. There was enough to worry about with Simonides and his officers breathing down his neck, something they were rather practised at.

'File – ready!' cried Simonides.

'Now!' bellowed Kryton.

'Close order!' Simonides' voice mixed with those of the other file-leaders.

Acutely aware of Zotikos' eyes on his back, Demetrios stepped to his right, reducing the distance to the next file by one pace. He swung his shield forward to his front. Slipping his left hand through the arm strap, he used it to grasp the shaft of his sarissa at head height.

'Level spears,' ordered Simonides.

Demetrios straightened his right arm, which had continued to grip the wooden shaft, and lowered the sarissa about fifteen degrees. In every file, the rearmost eight men were doing the same. The five front-rankers in each file were lowering their spears until they were parallel to the ground, facing an imaginary enemy, while those in ranks six to eight lowered theirs by varying degrees. Part protection from arrows, they could also be dropped to face the enemy.

'Not that low!' hissed Zotikos.

Demetrios hastily pulled his sarissa up.

'Forward, slow march.' Again, the file-leaders spoke almost in unison.

They tramped half a dozen paces, nice and steady. Demetrios was so close to Kimon that his shield was touching his friend's back. Zotikos' shield behind Demetrios was a reminder that the only way to go was forward. In a battle, he would shove Demetrios, who would push Kimon, and so on. The strength of sixteen men multiplied all along the phalanx's front provided great momentum – that much was clear, even to the inexperienced Demetrios. They would smash any enemy, Simonides often told them around their fires: 'Battles like Gaugamela, Marathon and Plataea prove it.'

'Tell us!' men would invariably shout. 'Tell us of one!' Most often, Simonides ignored these demands, but on occasion he would accede, holding out his hand for a cup of wine, 'to keep his throat wet' while he talked. Although Macedonians had not fought in the battle of Marathon, it was his favourite story to recount.

'Not quite two centuries ago, before the heyday of Athens, and long before the glories brought to Macedon by Alexander, the gods bless his name–' here Simonides always raised his cup in toast, prompting a loud shout of 'Alexander!' '–a battle was fought on the shore of the bay of Marathon. A marshy place by the sea, it was where the Persian invaders landed, their plan to lay waste to Attika, and after it, Athens and all of Greece. The army was mobilised in haste, but religious scruples prevented the Spartans – a vital part of the force – from joining the Athenians and their Plataean allies. The Persians' numerical superiority – at least two to one – meant that the Athenian leader Kallimachos ought to have waited for the Spartans to arrive, but politics got in the way. None of you dusty-footed turds would understand, but know that it's easier to stand in the phalanx and fight an enemy face to face than it is to have rivals – members of other factions – at home who'll stab you in the back.'

At this point men would growl with impatience, and demand that Simonides tell how the Athenian and Plataean hoplites had won eternal glory on the plain of Marathon. Faces would light up when, smiling, he gave in and began. Everyone knew how, in an effort to reduce casualties, the massed lines of Greeks had charged when the Persian volleys of arrows began to fall. How the weakened Athenian centre had broken before the enemy onslaught, while on the flanks, their comrades had emerged triumphant. How the hoplites on the flanks had turned to aid the men in the centre, and how, combined, they had crushed the Persians, driving them in panic to their ships. There the slaughter had continued.

Now Simonides' voice would be drowned out by chants of 'Six

thousand four hundred!' The number of Persian dead was still a source of continued pride, even among Macedonians. Just one hundred and ninety-two Athenians and Plataeans had fallen.

How Demetrios loved such stories. They made him long to stand further forward in the line than his current lowly position, which granted no view but the shoulders of the nearest men in the next couple of ranks, and with the file-closer's constant orders filling his ears. Zotikos had a nasal voice that he found irritating: 'Don't stop.' 'You're shifting position – move half a step to the right.' 'Keep that sarissa up.' Demetrios never answered back; he just gritted his teeth and obeyed.

These were minor quibbles. Demetrios was content with his lot. He had left the misery of the rowing benches behind. He had firm friends, in Kimon and Antileon, and an incredible leader in Simonides. Empedokles was an enemy, it was true, but the rest of the file were solid, good men. The reality of his dream was not as glorious as he'd imagined it, but he *was* a phalangist. One day, he would stand near the front of the file, and gods willing, prove himself a man in a victory that would, like Marathon, go down in history.

CHAPTER XII

Rome, spring 200 BC

The punch came out of nowhere, and connected with Felix's jaw. Its power spun him to one side, blurring his vision. A heartbeat later, the world went dark. He didn't feel his knees buckle. An impact to the back of his head – the ground – pushed him over the edge, and he fell into the abyss.

Felix had a rude reintroduction to the world of the living. He had no idea how long he'd been unconscious, but someone kicked him into wakefulness. From a long way off, his name was shouted.

'Felix! Up! Get up!'

He groaned. An insane smith was pounding away in his skull, and his jaw felt as if it'd been hit by an iron bar. Whoever was yelling nudged him in the ribs again, hard. It hurt. 'Fuck off,' Felix mumbled through swollen lips. 'Leave me alone.'

'Up!'

Antonius, the bastard, thought Felix dimly. Why is he kicking me?

Feet shuffled nearby. A meaty sound, as a fist makes when it meets flesh, followed. Another chased on its heels. Someone yelped; another person laughed. 'There's plenty more where that came from, filth,' said a deep voice.

'Help me, brother!'

Antonius sounded alarmed, and Felix opened his eyes. Above him, he saw the rough-hewn planks of the ceiling, and reality crashed in like a breaking wave. He rolled onto his side, and then, grunting with pain, got to his knees. No one came to his aid. The tavern's customers had formed a rough ring within which he lay. Some had even moved the nearest tables out of the way, creating a larger space. A few paces from Felix stood Antonius, facing their opponent, a man-mountain whose very presence had screamed trouble when he had darkened the threshold.

We should have stopped him at the door, thought Felix, heaving himself upright.

The giant threw a wild combination of ox-dropping blows at Antonius. He ducked beneath them, landing one of his own in his opponent's midriff, but the giant's only reaction was a frown. He turned, cursing, as Antonius tried a snap kick at his right knee, and missed.

'Do something!' The innkeeper was a diminutive figure with a silver beard. 'Call yourself legionaries?' he screeched. 'Scrapings of the sewer, more like!'

A rush of anger swept Felix. Still struggling to focus, his eyes swept the floor for his cudgel, or that of Antonius. He spied one, snapped into kindling – by the giant, no doubt. Of the other there was no sign. Felix was in no state to begin a slugging match with the giant, but all he had were his fists.

'Are you going to stand there gaping like a fool, brother, or fucking help me?' Antonius had danced backwards, away from the giant. His breath was hot in Felix's ear.

'The whoreson knocked me out cold,' Felix growled. 'In case you hadn't noticed.'

'Oh, I noticed. I took this while you were dozing.' Antonius twisted, revealing a closed, swollen eye. 'Best come up with a bright idea, or we're going to get the hiding of our lives.'

Further conversation was prevented by the giant, who lumbered in, aiming punches at both brothers. They scrambled past him to left and right, Felix landing a weak blow that produced no discernible effect. Safe for a moment at the far edge of the improvised fighting circle, and ignoring the crowd's jeers, they prepared to face the giant again.

'What I'd give for a blade,' whispered Antonius.

Felix rumbled his agreement. Neither brother had owned a sword since the army; thanks to the severe punishments for possession of an edged weapon inside the city walls, their daggers were hidden in the stable.

'You go left, I'll go right. If we attack him from two sides, we might get lucky.' Antonius didn't sound sure.

'Remember harpastum?'

'Eh?' Antonius looked at him as if he'd taken leave of his senses.

'Harpastum,' bellowed Felix. Praying that his brother would understand, he approached the giant, who grinned evilly.

Within reach of those ham fists, thought Felix, he risked being knocked out again, or worse. There was nothing for it, however. 'Harpastum,' he threw over his shoulder, and then, glaring at the giant, asked, 'Your mother still plying her trade by the tombs?'

Laughter rose from those watching; only the cheapest whores worked in the shadows cast by the mausolea that lined the roads out of Rome. The giant's face purpled, and he took a step forward. 'I'll fucking kill you!' Enraged, off guard as Felix had hoped, he didn't see what was coming.

Felix threw himself down and forward, wrapping both arms around the giant's hairy knees, just as he had done to hundreds of opponents during bouts of harpastum. The tackle was far from Felix's best – he was still weak – but he had just enough momentum. With a cry of fury, the giant toppled. If Antonius isn't there when he hits the floor, thought Felix, tightening his grip, I'm a dead man. Hobs pounded past his ear. Grunts rang out, as a man makes when expending his maximal effort. The giant cried out, swore that he'd rip the brothers to shreds. He cried out again, and his legs thrashed about. Felix held on for dear life. Antonius *was* there – kicking and stamping on the big bastard. Perhaps a dozen heartbeats went by, and Felix wasn't sent to oblivion by a mighty punch. The giant's frame relaxed a little, and he dared to hope.

'You'll kill him!' The innkeeper's voice was close. 'Stop!'

'The bastard would have done for us,' retorted Antonius, raking the giant's head with his hobs again.

'If he dies, the justices will come. There'll be an inquiry, and gods know what other trouble. Leave him be!' ordered the innkeeper.

With a snort of contempt, Antonius moved to stand over Felix. He looked down. 'You can let go, brother. The dog will be keeping Morpheus company for a while.'

Despite Antonius' assurance, Felix slackened his grasp a little at a time. Only when he was sure for himself that the giant was unconscious did he let go and stand up. There was time for a pleased glance with Antonius, and then the innkeeper launched an attack of his own, labelling the brothers drunkards, wastrels, unfit to be doormen of his tavern. Keen for the spectacle to go on, perhaps resentful of previous heavy handling by the pair, several customers egged him on.

'Were you even legionaries?' the innkeeper cried. 'It didn't much look like it.'

The cooler head of the two, Antonius did not react, but the insult had cut Felix to the quick. He stuck his face into the innkeeper's, relishing the fear that blossomed in the man's eyes. 'I was at Zama,' grated Felix, 'and so was my brother. I slew a fucking elephant there.' Noting the innkeeper's blank expression, he added with venom, 'Not that a limp prick like you would know what an elephant was.' He made a sudden movement, and laughed as the terrified man took several steps backwards.

'Felix.' Antonius' hand was on his shoulder.

'Out of my tavern!' Spittle flew from the innkeeper's lips. 'Cowards!'

Sensing a second fight, the customers bayed like a pack of hounds.

A red mist descended over Felix, and he bared his teeth. The innkeeper quickly put a table between them.

'He's not worth it, brother,' said Antonius.

Felix could see only the enemy line at Zama, just when the fighting had been at its bitterest. His ears rang with the ring of iron on iron, and men's screams. He could smell piss and shit, and blood. Antonius was on his right, and another comrade on his left. When Matho gave the order, he would advance, and gods help anyone in his way.

'Felix.'

He jerked back to the warm fuggy air of the tavern, to the ring of cruel, eager-for-blood faces around them, to the battered, prone figure at his feet. Ingenuus, thought Felix.

'Let's get our things from the stable.' Antonius pointed outside.

'Aye.' Harrowed, Felix put Ingenuus from his mind. 'Aye.'

Halfway across the room, he halted by an abandoned table. 'Thirsty?'

'I'm parched,' said Antonius, smiling.

'Consider this our final wages,' Felix cried to the innkeeper as he picked up a brimming jug of wine and two cups.

Still cowed, their former employer made no protest. A little disappointed by this, Felix led the way onto the street. A sense of freedom, such as he hadn't felt in many months, lightened his step.

An hour later, with the jug empty and the reality of their situation sinking in, Felix's new-found optimism was fast disappearing. Their victory in the brawl had come at a heavy price. Not only were they jobless and homeless, his jaw hurt enough for it to be broken. He had an egg-sized, oozing lump on the back of his head, and the mad smith was still hammering away inside. Antonius was no better: his left eye was swollen so badly he couldn't see out of it; he also had cracked ribs.

They sat by a fountain, soaking up the last of the afternoon sunlight and ignoring the curious and sometimes disapproving glances from the matrons filling their water containers. Small boys peered wide-eyed at the two bruised, tough-looking men. Inside a nearby temple to Mars, priests chanted. A baker stood at the door of his premises on the far side of the street, offering the last of his bread at bargain prices – the brothers had already eaten two loaves each. Ox-carts trundled by, wheels creaking under their heavy loads. Watched by a couple of bored passers-by, a soothsayer promised to read the future for anyone who would cross his palm with a coin.

The question of what they would do next hung heavy in the air, but neither Felix nor Antonius brought it up. Melancholy from the wine and the humiliation of their ejection from the inn, in discomfort from their injuries, they fell to brooding.

During his years in the legions, Felix's purpose had been clear. Survive the war, and he would return to the family farm with Antonius. They'd had many plans for its future, and their saved army pay was to have provided the means. The brutal circumstances of their discharge had intensified both brothers' desire to go home; their journey from Africa could not have gone fast enough.

The shock of their homecoming, thought Felix, would live with him to the end of his days. The memory of the empty, tumbledown farmhouse made his heart twinge. He'd gone to war, young and full of bravado, never imagining that the last sight of his mother and father would be as he and Antonius walked to the town of Ferentinum to enlist. According to the closest neighbour, a friend of the family, their father had been the first to die, taken by a fever the winter after the brothers had left. Their mother had battled on with the help of their slave, but when he too had succumbed to a flux four years before, strength and purpose had left her.

'It was your letters that kept her alive,' the neighbour had said. 'It's a pity she died just before word came of your return from Africa. She would have gone to the next world a happier soul.'

I should have written more often, Felix told himself: penned at least a few lines. Many messages wouldn't have got through – communication to and from soldiers in the field was an uncertain process – but some might have, giving their mother and father hope. The bitter truth of it was that Antonius was a better hand with a stylus, so Felix had tended to leave communications with their parents to him.

The unpleasant homecoming hadn't ended with the revelation of their parents' deaths and the discovery of the falling-down farmhouse. Weeds had filled the fields, the sheds all had collapsed roofs, and the livestock were stolen or gone. Full of determination, the brothers had pooled their savings and bought tools, building materials, a mule and a plough. All winter long, they had laboured to make the farm what it had once been. Things had gone well until the death of their mule in the spring, just before the crops needed to be sown. The brothers had borrowed a beast from a kindly neighbour, but the wheat and barley failed to thrive. It truly seemed that the gods had turned their faces away.

With their coin almost spent, they'd had to decide between labouring on a rich man's farm, brigandage, and seeing if their fortunes would improve in Rome. Seeing the capital for the first time had won out. Weary of the backbreaking toil, and sure their luck would never change on the farm, the brothers had abandoned their childhood home.

Felix glanced up at the three-, four- and five-storey blocks of apartments around the fountain. He didn't tend to notice them now, but the first time he'd set foot inside Rome's walls, the towering structures had amazed him. So too had the fountains like the one at his back, and the public baths in every quarter. The temples were also grander than any he'd seen before, but most impressive had been the covered markets and huge buildings of the forum, with the enormous shrine to Jupiter lowering from the top of the Capitoline Hill.

Columns and statues wouldn't feed them, thought Felix sourly. 'What should we do?'

'We need coin,' said Antonius. 'Our purses are light. They won't fill themselves either. We could get work in another tavern, I suppose.'

Felix snorted in contempt. 'Doormen are badly paid. How much have we saved in a month and a half?'

'Four denarii,' said Antonius. 'We don't exactly look employable right now, but our bruises will soon go. We can get by until another innkeeper takes us on.'

'Get by? We'll be sleeping on the streets,' Felix shot back.

'Some of the places we slept in during the war weren't any better.'

'Aye, but no one would have cut our throats while we slumbered in the legions. We'll have to take turns staying awake,' said Felix, resentful that they already faced at least one night without shelter.

'So be it,' said Antonius. 'If we find work soon, and spend little, we might have enough to go back to the farm and start again.'

Felix stared at his brother in disbelief. 'The farm?'

'Aye. Where else?'

'I am not going back there without a bulging purse, maybe even a slave.'

'And where in Hades are you going to magic those from?'

They glared at one another.

'I'm telling you, the people's centuries *will* vote against conflict with Macedonia.' The loud voice belonged to a balding, middle-aged merchant with a drinker's blotched face and red nose. 'Everyone says it.'

The wine-lover was with a companion of similar age. The two drank their fill at the fountain, and then, as people often did, paused to continue their conversation.

Intrigued, for the recent street gossip had been of a similar vein, the brothers listened in.

'The people don't understand that the Republic is in mortal danger. King Philip is mad for war,' declared the second man, a sturdy type with the weather-beaten features of a farmer.

'How would you know?' scoffed the wine-lover. 'Have you been drinking with him?'

'Piss off. Since Philip's naval victories over Rhodes and Pergamum – I take it you heard about those?' The farmer smirked at his companion's irritated mutter of agreement. 'Good. With the seas east of Macedonia now clear of his enemies, Philip is free to send his ships to Italia. Why would he do that, I hear you ask? Simple. When his fleet is joined by that of the Seleucid Antiochus, whose lust for fresh conquests rivals that of Alexander, they will have enough vessels to threaten every town on the east coast.'

'That will never happen,' said the wine-lover. 'Antiochus' realm is half a world from here.'

'I seem to remember you saying many years since that Hannibal would never invade Italia,' retorted the farmer. 'Why do you think the new consul, Publius Sulpicius Galba, was given Macedonia as his province?'

'He was consul before, in the fight against Hannibal,' said the wine-lover, looking thoughtful.

Felix glanced at Antonius; they had paraded before Galba once. He had given a stirring speech about how vital it was that Hannibal be defeated. It seemed the old politician was not just ready for another fight, thought Felix, but wanted to lead Rome's legions into it.

'Galba's appointment *proves* the Senate believes the threat from Philip to be real,' declared the farmer.

'Maybe so,' replied the wine-lover in a truculent tone, 'but I'm telling you: the Centuriate will *not* vote for war. Too many citizens – all of us, for Jupiter's sake – lost sons to that gugga bastard's army over the past decade and a half. Men are tired of war without end.'

The farmer would not give in. 'It will come to fighting, one way or another. May the gods grant our first experience of it isn't when Philip's fleet is spotted off our eastern coast.'

Still arguing, the pair walked away, leaving Felix and Antonius to stare at each other.

'Are you thinking the same thing I am?' cried Felix, feeling his gloom lift. 'If there's a war—'

Antonius shook his head violently. 'You – we – can't join the legions again. D'you not remember what happened?'

'Only too well, brother. But Matho's not here, and the prick won't be the recruiting officer when we stand in line either. I'll give a false name. If asked about military service, I'll say that I fought against Hannibal in a different legion to the one we were in.'

'They'll catch you out—'

'They won't.' Sick to his back teeth of their ill fortune, Felix refused to consider the mortal dangers.

Antonius tapped his head. 'The fight has curdled your brains.'

'Maybe,' said Felix, uncaring. 'I agree that we should find another job – working as doormen will keep the wolf from the door. Then we bide our time. If that man is right, the members of the Centuriate will be persuaded to change their minds.'

'And if they don't?' challenged Antonius. 'Have you thought about that?'

'That bridge can be crossed when we come to it.' Felix was determined to hold onto his new-found hope. 'When war is declared, it will be time to re-enlist. What say you, brother?'

Antonius stared into space without answering. It was his brother's way to take his time before making up his mind, a trait that Felix had always found supremely irritating. With their future in the balance, he took even longer. Long moments dragged by, and fear began to gnaw Felix's guts. Antonius would return to the farm, and leave him here in Rome, he decided.

Screw him, thought Felix. He can starve at the farm on his own. I'm staying here until war breaks out.

'Fuck it, why not?'

Felix couldn't believe his ears. 'You'll come?'

Antonius grinned. 'Aye.'

Felix whooped.

Just like that, it felt as if their fortunes had taken a turn for the better.

CHAPTER XIII

Pella, Macedon, spring/summer 200 BC

Philip and a group of his courtiers were standing around a table, upon which a large number of documents were spread. The doors of the meeting room in which they had spent the morning had been flung wide, letting in warm sunshine and a view of the colonnaded courtyard beyond. Noises carried from beyond the walls: the creak of wagons, street vendors' cries, gulls screeching from the harbour. Rich aromas laced the air: sun-baked thyme, sage and lemon blossom from the palace gardens, a trace of cypress from the nearby hills.

Among many magnificent rooms in the vast complex, the chamber stood out. Squares of white on the walls were separated by bars of ochre and red, and topped by successive lines of white and ochre rectangles. Fake columns sat along the top of this 'wall', the gaps between part-filled with red 'bricks'. Above, the spaces between the columns had been painted blue, mimicking the sky. Pebble mosaic covered the floor, with small images of various gods around the room's periphery, and a grand centrepiece depicting the general Krateros saving Alexander from the jaws of a ravening lion.

Bored by the meeting's length, Philip's attention strayed to the mosaic. 'It's said they're one of the hardest beasts to kill.'

'Sire?' Herakleides' gaze followed Philip's. Fox-faced and bright-eyed, the skinny Tarentine had served him for some years. His current position was admiral of the Macedonian fleet. 'Ah, the lion. You would slay such a creature with ease.'

Philip knew Herakleides was flattering him, but he liked it. 'There's been word of a lion in the mountains of recent days. What I'd give for a couple of days to track it down.'

'A fine idea, sire,' said Herakleides. 'Mayhap we could go, you and I – tomorrow?'

'It would give me no greater pleasure than to accompany you also, sire,' interrupted Menander, a heavy-set nobleman in late middle age. He sported a black beard, flecked through with silver. Contrasting with the others' rich clothing, he wore a simple belted tunic and on his head, a Macedonian white *kausia*. 'Yet more pressing matters than lions demand our attention.' In a pointed gesture, he turned back to the documents.

Menander was solid, dependable – like a man's preferred horse, thought Philip. What you saw with Menander was what you got, which was boring. Herakleides was a different prospect, alive to every possibility, dangerous or no. Philip knew his dubious history – betraying his home city of Tarentum to the Romans, and then again to Hannibal – but he paid Herakleides so much that it didn't worry him. The man seemed to understand what it meant to be king; he knew how much Philip wanted to restore Macedon to its former glories. Two years prior, it was he who had urged the king to attack the Kyklades and Asia Minor.

Next around the table was Alexander, the king's aged, stoop-shouldered chamberlain. A spent force, he could still could come up with wise words on occasion. Servants aside, the last man present was Kassander, an angular-faced senior commander of the Companion cavalry. Not the best of Philip's generals – they were all in the field – he was nonetheless brave and steadfast.

Menander coughed.

'You're nagging me,' said Philip, but he returned his gaze to the documents, a good number of which were from his commanders throughout his kingdom and overseas territories.

'Forgive me, sire,' said Menander.

'It doesn't matter.'

Philip ignored the cold look that Menander exchanged with Herakleides. A degree of rivalry was healthy among his courtiers, and reduced the likelihood of a plot against him. His stepfather Antigonus had been fond of saying, 'Trust no one entirely. Not the captain of your bodyguard, nor your chamberlain. Not your generals. Not your oldest friend. Not even your wife.'

Of the men around the table, Philip trusted Herakleides most, and Menander second – yet he always kept Antigonus' words at the back of his mind. His stepfather's advice had served him well before, and would again.

'Tell us how the land lies again,' Philip ordered.

'You'll remember that after your return from Bargylia, sire, the Akarnanians requested your help against Athens,' said Menander. Small, isolated Akarnania lay on the western coast of Greece, south of Epirus and west of Aitolia. It had long been a loyal ally of Macedon. 'With the help of the auxiliaries you sent, the Akarnanians put the countryside of Attika to the torch. At the same time, your fleet captured four warships at the Piraeus.'

'It was a sweet victory,' said Philip, remembering his joy at the news that the lands around Athens had been burned, and the city's port attacked. 'If brief.' The triremes had been retaken mere days after seizing them.

'We weren't to know that Attalus and the cursed Rhodians would appear from nowhere, sire.' Herakleides' tone was defensive.

'Perhaps not,' said Philip. He arched an eyebrow. 'But then again, were the sentries alert, or even manning their posts? A little bird told me that not all was as it should have been on our ships.'

'I acted the instant the enemy was seen, sire. I—'

The loss of the triremes mattered less than the continuing loyalty of the Akarnanians. Philip raised a hand, cutting the Tarentine off. 'You told me. It matters not now. Menander, continue.'

'The embassy sent by Rome while you were still trapped in Bargylia has reached Athens, sire. Attalus is also in the city; he and the Romans seem to be as thick as thieves.'

'And so, thanks to Attalus – and perhaps Rome – Athens has declared war with Macedon,' said Philip irritably. He had already had this news from his spies. 'I'm quivering with fear.'

A rumble of polite amusement went around the table, but the king didn't join in. While he made light of the situation, it did not serve him well to be at odds with Rhodes, Pergamum *and* Athens. Concerning too was the involvement of the Roman embassy. If the Senate did not wish to be involved in Greece, why were its agents here?

'Curse the Romans for interfering. Curse Attalus for a meddling dog. Neither of them have any business poking their noses into Greek affairs!' Philip glared at Herakleides. 'What of his skulking Rhodian friends? Are the rumours true?'

'It seems so, sire. Merchants arriving from the east say that they are retaking the Kyklades.' Herakleides made a helpless gesture. The islands off the south-west coast of Asia Minor – taken by Philip only the year before – were far from Pella. 'I cannot be sure, however: the enemy ships make it too dangerous for ours to leave port.'

Philip had spent years trying to achieve supremacy on the seas around Greece; the new Pergamene blockade along his own coastline was a painful reminder of his abject failure to do so, and also of his incarceration at Bargylia. There was little to do about it for the moment, however, and plenty of other matters that could be addressed, most important of which was Athens.

'What of Nikanor and Philokles?' Incensed by the Athenians' recent declaration of war, Philip had sent two of his best commanders south with a strong force of troops.

'Philokles has established himself as governor of Euboea, sire,' said Alexander. The large island to the north of Athens was vital to Philip – from it, the Greek mainland could be raided at will. At this moment, it meant he could threaten Athens. 'Word arrived this morning that all is well there. Good numbers of locals have been recruited into the army.'

'Some welcome news at last. And Nikanor? The last I heard he had come close to Athens,' said Philip, wishing to have been there as well, wishing even more that he could have seized the city and punished its people for daring to ally themselves with Rhodes and Pergamum.

'That's correct, sire. There's been no word since,' said Menander.

This was nothing to worry about, thought Philip. Nikanor was a reliable commander; he wouldn't send messengers with trivial news. 'Are the northern borders still quiet?'

'Word of your return has reached the savages, sire,' said Kassander. 'The rumours of unrest have died away.'

Philip allowed himself a thin smile. 'They'll be back. Troublesome bastards.'

'The garrisons are well prepared, sire. The frontier is patrolled daily. Any attacks will meet stiff resistance,' said Kassander.

'Good. What are the Aitolians plotting?' asked Philip, running through the list of his enemies, who lay to the east, west, north and south. It was exhausting, and yet he had never known any different.

'I've heard nothing, sire,' said Herakleides. Aitolia lay south-west of Macedon and north of the Peloponnese, the hand-shaped island joined to the mainland by a narrow isthmus. Aitolia had been a bitter enemy of Philip's for years. 'Since Rome rejected their appeal for aid, they haven't had the stomach for a fight. It's my guess that they are keeping their heads down.'

Philip agreed – this was what his spies told him. 'And so to the Peloponnese.' Elis, Akhaia, Messenia, Arkadia and Sparta – the five Peloponnesian states – were often at war with one another, or with Macedon, and sometimes both. 'I hear the Spartans have been quarrelling with Akhaia again.'

'Aye, sire,' came the murmured replies.

'Would Akhaia join me, I wonder, if I crushed Sparta on its behalf? It would be easily done.'

He watched his courtiers' reactions: Menander unhappy, Kassander reserved and Alexander wary. Only Herakleides seemed keen.

'Sparta's glory days are gone, sire, but they would defend their homeland to the death,' said Menander, ever the cautious one.

'My army would sweep them aside. Imagine if, by way of thanks, the Akhaians provided troops to garrison Chalkis, Demetrias and Akrokorinth,' countered Philip. For many decades, the three fortresses – Chalkis on the island of Euboea, Demetrias on the Pagasean Gulf, and Akrokorinth at the neck of the Peloponnese – had protected Macedon's southern borders. Necessary, they were also a drain on his most precious resource: manpower.

'That *would* be useful, sire,' admitted Menander. Kassander nodded his agreement. 'You would then have more troops to attack Athens, sire.'

Philip glanced at his chamberlain. 'Alexander?'

'I suppose it would do no harm to approach the Akhaians, sire.'

'Herakleides?'

'The Akhaians stand to gain more than you from this potential alliance, sire.'

'Unless Rome changes its mind, and invades,' said Philip, devilment making him tempt the Fates. 'Then Akhaian troops in my forts would earn their salt.'

Herakleides made a dismissive gesture. 'It won't come to that, sire, gods willing.'

'Let us hope not, but if it does–' Philip's gaze moved from man to man '–we will fight.'

It angered him that doubt, quickly masked, registered in everyone's eyes. Everyone apart from Herakleides, that was. Philip's pride was stung by their lack of belief. While he had no great wish to add yet another enemy to his already long list, Rome was not invincible. Yes, it had just defeated Carthage, and its legions outnumbered his army, but the Persian hordes had been defeated by a small force of Greeks at Marathon, and again at Plataea. Alexander had smashed huge Persian armies at the Issus and Gaugamela. Similar victories could easily be his.

Rome and Macedon were not at war, Philip reminded himself. Athens was more of a thorn in his side. Formidable defences made it impossible to take by siege, but there were other ways to strike at the city. 'Remember my campaign on the Propontis two years past? Without the grain ships that sail through it, the mongrel Athenians would starve.'

'They would, sire,' said Herakleides. The grain provided by Greek settlements on the shores of the Euxine Sea had sustained Athens for over a century; access to those supplies was limited by whoever controlled the narrow Propontis waterway. 'What are your thoughts?'

'Every town north of the straits pays homage to Egypt,' said Philip. Recent news from Alexandria made it clear that the bloody infighting in the royal court meant that its foreign territories were of little concern. His previous restraint could be discarded. 'They're soft targets. Most will surrender the moment we appear outside the walls.'

'With Egypt in turmoil, they will have little other choice, sire.' Herakleides' expression sharpened. 'The nearby Pergamene settlements would fall easily too.'

'That would give me great pleasure.' Since failing to take Pergamum, and the humiliation of his time at Bargylia, Philip had burned for revenge. 'And grant almost total control of the waterway.'

'Athens will be at your mercy then, sire,' Herakleides continued. 'They will sue for peace. Offer the right terms – the free passage of some of their grain ships, say – and they might be persuaded to ally themselves with Macedon. That would be a fine result, eh?'

Philip's lips twitched. The concept wasn't impossible. In the muddy waters of Greek politics, states often changed sides. Force Athens to join with him by part-releasing his stranglehold on their grain, he thought, and other states might follow suit. The sun would fall from the sky before his old enemy Aitolia did the same, but its isolation would serve Philip almost as well. 'I shall take two thousand infantry and ten score Companions,' he decided. 'Herakleides, you will support us with the fleet.'

The Tarentine beamed. 'Sire.'

'Kassander, you shall go north, and ensure the savages remain behind their borders. You are to remain here in Pella, Alexander, and keep things in order until my return.'

Menander raised an eyebrow. 'What would you have me do, sire?'

'You will be regent while I am gone. Protector of my wife and sons, and the commander of the army.'

Menander looked surprised, then pleased. He bowed deep. 'You leave Macedon in safe hands, sire.'

I hope so, thought Philip, smiling. He clicked his fingers. 'Wine.'

A magnificent silver *krater* was soon borne in by servants. Another followed with a tray of silver goblets. When everyone had been served, Philip raised his cup high. 'Ares, grant us victory!' He poured a generous measure on the floor.

'Ares!' The others copied his libation.

He had much to be pleased about, Philip decided, taking a drink. War with Rome was not inevitable. The Greek states were weak, and more interested in squabbling between themselves than with opposing Macedon. A golden opportunity to dominate Athens, and to fill his coffers at the same time, awaited him at the Propontis.

He would seize it with both hands.

CHAPTER XIV

Rome, summer 200 BC

It was early, but Flamininus had been up for hours. Seated at the desk in his office, he was reading a message from his spy in Pella. Pasion hovered in the background with more letters. Warm air eased through the open door, carrying from the courtyard the scent of thyme and rosemary, and from the ovens, baking bread. Water pattered in the decorative fountain; a slave brushed the mosaic floor of the covered walkway. Pots and pans rattled in the kitchen. On the street outside, a carter shouted at his mules to get a cursed move on.

Mornings were the best time to get business done during the hot months. Not that Flamininus had had to be roused: he had lain awake much of the night. Darkness could not quieten his racing thoughts, nor exhaustion. If he drank heavily, he slept, but then the next day was lost to the ill effects of the wine. Work doesn't get done by itself, thought Flamininus, so best get on with it. He could sleep when he was dead.

Tracing a finger along the lines, he reread the letter in his hand, but try as he might, his mind wandered again. After Galba's stunning victory the previous autumn, it had been inevitable that he should be awarded Macedonia as his province. With winter coming, the new consul had proposed and enacted the sending of a commission to Greece, its mission to win allies for Rome among the city states, and to discover Antiochus' real intentions. Here in Italia, Galba had spent the time preparing his army. The thwarted Flamininus had been busy too.

'Finished, master?' ventured Pasion.

Flamininus glanced at the letter again and realised he'd been staring at the same line: 'Philip is well aware of the Roman embassy, and its demand that he should cease his warmongering against other Greek states. His recent aggression against Athens is proof of his continued hostility towards the Republic.'

Pasion cleared his throat.

Flamininus handed over the letter. 'Burn it.'

'Will there be a reply, master?' Pasion knew the name of Flamininus' spy, but knew better than to speak it.

Flamininus did not mention it either. He nodded. 'Tell him that I want all the news – every last detail – to do with Philip. Where he is, what he is doing, who he is meeting. I want to know where his navy is, and his army.'

Pasion's stylus moved back and forth over his writing tablet. Unprepossessing to look at, he was excellent at his job. 'I would think your . . . informant will require more funds, master.'

'He shall have double his present fee. The coin will be made available in the usual way.' Flamininus had an arrangement with one of the richest moneylenders in Rome, a man with offices in Pella, Athens and Alexandria. 'Any new information is to be sent at once.'

'Master.' Pasion's stylus came to a halt. He indicated the bundle of documents he'd set on the desk. 'Would you like the next letter?'

'Who's it from?'

'Your brother, master.'

'Give it here.'

The month before, Flamininus had sent Lucius to Illyria with one of his equestrian followers, ostensibly to investigate the possibility of buying land suitable for growing vines – a profitable crop on his estates in Italia. Their real mission was to decide the best place to land an army, and from there to launch an attack on Macedonia. This was Lucius' first communication since he'd left. Flamininus snapped the wax seal and opened the tablet. His eyes moved fast over the words. Anger coursed through him. Rather than do his bidding, Lucius seemed to be enjoying the delights of every vineyard in Illyria. There was *some* useful information: Apollonia was a natural choice for an army to land. Galba already had officials there, buying supplies for his legions.

Flamininus' focus moved from his feckless brother back to Galba, whom he had grown to hate since losing the election. The man was being overconfident, thought Flamininus. The invasion was by no means certain. His furious behind the scenes lobbying and bribing of delegates had seen the first motion for war rejected by the Centuriate. Without its support, the Senate could not order the legions to sail for

Illyria and Macedonia. Only a ballot that overturned the first result would allow Galba to set his plans in motion. To prevent him from doing that – thereby stymying his term of office as consul – was what had driven Flamininus these past months. His spies, augmented by scores of ex-soldiers, worked from dawn to dusk. Through a combination of persuasion, bribery and intimidation, they kept the majority of the Centuriate in the anti-war camp.

The all-important second vote was two days off. If the motion for war was again defeated, Galba would become a toothless consul. This was Flamininus' heartfelt desire. He wanted his rival humiliated and deprived of his chance to defeat Macedonia. Come the next winter, Flamininus – with the gods' blessing, the new consul – would ensure that the threat of Macedonia was reignited, that the need for immediate military action became imperative. With their palms well greased by his coin, the Centuriate's members would at last vote for war. The glorious task of defeating Philip – of laying down a legacy not unlike Alexander's – would be his.

If only it were that simple, thought Flamininus. Galba's men were also hard at work among the tribes of the Centuriate. Not a day went by without reports reaching him of bigger bribes than he had paid. Galba's heavies weren't averse to intimidation either – several assembly members loyal to Flamininus had been badly beaten.

'Shall I reply to your brother, master?' Pasion's voice.

'Aye. Tell him to stop drinking, and to do what I fucking told him. I want more information, and not about vineyards. Or boys.'

A raised eyebrow was the extent of Pasion's comment. 'As you say, master.'

'Men at door.' Thrax, his unimaginatively named Thracian bodyguard, had come through from the front of the house.

'What?' demanded Flamininus.

'Some veterans here.'

It was hours before Flamininus would deign to let his agents in to report. 'Let them wait,' he said, glowering.

Thrax shuffled his feet. 'They unhappy.'

'The sun is hot. There's no shade. What do I care?' snapped Flamininus.

'Not that. They say comrade dead. Murdered.' Thrax mangled the last word, but it was still intelligible.

Hades, thought Flamininus, pushing back the chair. 'Enough of paperwork.'

'There are many more letters, master,' said Pasion.

'Later.' He headed for the front entrance, with Thrax at his heels. In the *atrium*, he made a brief obeisance to the death masks of his ancestors. Whatever he was about to hear wasn't good, and any help would be welcome. 'How many are outside?'

Thrax counted on his fingers. 'Six.'

Flamininus had a good deal more men working for him; these would be the leaders. He let the Thracian glance outside before emerging into the sunlight. Spying him, the veterans scrambled to their feet from the waiting bench outside his door. He acknowledged their greetings, but noted at once that Cyclops, a talkative type with only one eye, was absent. Holding in his questions, Flamininus led the way to the shade of the atrium; behind him, Thrax shut and bolted the door. The veterans' hobs rang off the mosaic floor. Entering his office, he took a seat on his grandfather's iron military folding stool. Flamininus had taken it from the family home; it kept fresh his dreams of leading an army to war.

He arched an eyebrow at his men, who had formed an awkward semicircle around him. 'Where's Cyclops?'

The veterans looked at one another. One elbowed the oldest, a scrawny type with flaking skin.

'Cyclops, sir? Well, he—'

Realising, Flamininus swore. 'He's the one who was murdered.'

The veteran with flaky skin stared at the floor. 'Aye, sir.'

'Was anyone else hurt?'

'Aye, sir. His mate was attacked too. He's alive, but the poor bastard shouldn't be. Looks as if his skull's been staved in.'

Flamininus swallowed his next question. Men like these didn't have the coin for a pot to piss in, let alone for a surgeon. 'I'll have him looked at.'

Grateful nods.

'What in Jupiter's name happened?' Flamininus thought he knew the answer, but he wanted to hear it from the veterans' lips.

'We ain't sure, sir–' Flaky Skin glanced at his companions for confirmation '–but we think it was Galba's men. We've come across the bastards in the taverns, regular like, us spreading your word and coin, and them doing the same for Galba.'

'You've come to blows with them before too.' Flamininus remembered warning his men to avoid trouble after an incident a month before.

'Not since you told us to lay off, sir. Cyclops wasn't one to look for a fight either, what with his one eye and all. When we found him and his mate last night, we thought they'd been attacked by cutpurses. But we passed a group of Galba's thugs soon after, and they was laughing and making comments. That we shouldn't go about in pairs and such like.' The veteran managed at last to meet Flamininus' gaze. 'They said more of us would die, sir.'

'What did you do?'

'Walked away, sir. We was outnumbered, and they had clubs.'

'Arm yourselves,' said Flamininus, thinking, I'll beat you at your own game, Galba.

In the pit of his belly, however, he wasn't quite so sure.

Two days later, thousands of Rome's citizens had gathered on the Plain of Mars, outside the city. Flamininus was there with his brother, watching – like everyone else – a great crowd of men separated from the spectators by a large, fenced-off area. These were the representatives of the Republic's thirty-five tribes, organised into three hundred and seventy-three centuries, and selected according to the size of their properties. The members were debating among themselves first; Galba's speech would follow, and then the men in every century would vote on whether Rome should go to war with Macedonia or not. Each century's decision counted as one vote in the tally of all three hundred and seventy-three centuries.

It was baking hot, the sun high overhead in a brilliant blue sky. No shelter was available. More nervous than he cared to admit, Flamininus took frequent advantage of the wine sellers who worked the crowd. Lucius did too, and in the end, it was he rather than Flamininus who broached the subject weighing heavy on both their minds. 'How will the vote go, brother?'

'Only the gods know,' muttered Flamininus. His veterans had got the better of several violent clashes with Galba's men, but whether that would stem the tide of Centuriate members intent on voting for war, he could not be sure. Talk of foreign armies on Italian soil, of mothers and sisters raped, and temples destroyed, was nigh on impossible to combat. After the dark years of constant threat from Hannibal, the population remained wary, and easy to panic.

Time passed, and the temperature climbed further. Hot and uncomfortable, Flamininus was growing impatient when, overseen by lictores, the centuries separated into their own groupings. Sensing that this presaged Galba's arrival, loud cheering broke out. The consul came into sight not long after, accompanied by many senatorial colleagues, priests and more lictores.

Jealousy pricked Flamininus. If things had gone differently, he would have been the one arriving to the acclaim of the crowd. It was heartening to hear shouts about a war being unnecessary hurled in Galba's direction. Not everyone has been won over, thought Flamininus.

An expectant hush fell as Galba and his train reached the curule chair, the dedicated place for the consul to address the assembly. The priests spoke first, declaring that the omens for today's gathering had been taken, and were good. The gods approved. Muted applause met this announcement: everyone wanted to hear what Galba had to say, not least Flamininus. On this speech, like as not, hinged the war with Macedonia.

At last the consul stood forth. Total silence fell. In contrast to his gaunt appearance, his voice was powerful and harmonious, and drew men's attention. Galba first thanked the gods and honoured the assembly members as proud citizens of Rome, valiant men who had fought for long years against Hannibal. He, Galba, understood that after the many sacrifices of this recent conflict, they had felt reluctant to lead the Republic into another one. At this, many heads nodded, and again Flamininus' hopes rose, only for them to be dashed soon after.

'It seems to me, citizens,' Galba cried, 'that you do not realise that the question is not whether you will have peace or war – Philip will not leave that matter to you to decide, seeing that he is preparing for war on both land and sea. No, the question before you is whether to send your legions to Macedonia, or keep them here in Italia to meet the enemy. What a difference that makes; you found that out in the recent Punic war. Who among you doubts that if, when the Saguntines were besieged and calling for our protection, we had promptly sent aid to them, as our fathers did to the Mamertines, we should have diverted the whole war to Hispania? Instead, by our delay, we admitted it to Italia, with innumerable losses to ourselves.'

It wasn't as black and white as Galba said, thought Flamininus in frustration. At the war's outset, Hannibal had attacked Saguntum in the full knowledge that the Republic's legions were in Illyria. Even if the Senate had diverted the army to Iberia, it would not have arrived before Saguntum's fall. It was also disingenuous to suggest that these legions would have prevented Hannibal from his march on Italia.

Few ordinary citizens had such insight, however. Around Flamininus, men were agreeing with Galba, shouting that the shame of leaving Saguntum to its fate must not happen again, that Rome's allies in Greece had to be protected from Philip at any cost. Being further away, it was harder to see how the assembly members were reacting, but, thought Flamininus, they were as open to suggestion as the next man.

Galba continued, 'Do we hesitate now, as we did when Hannibal was fighting in Italia? Let us permit Philip by the recent attack on Athens, as we permitted Hannibal by the capture of Saguntum, to see how slow we are to act: not in five months, as when Hannibal came from Saguntum over the Alps, but in five days. For that is how short the voyage is. Five days, and Philip could arrive in Italia!'

'With perhaps a hundred ships,' said Flamininus to Lucius. 'Maybe two. Not enough for a meaningful threat to the Republic.'

The crowd rippled with unease, however. Men were muttering, 'Remember Hannibal?' and 'Seventeen years it took to beat the guggas.'

'War! War! War!'

The chant began somewhere behind the brothers, and was taken up with gusto. Smiling, Galba paused, letting the noise sweep over the Campus Martius, towards the walls of Rome. When he raised his hands, the effect was magical – again quiet fell.

The bastard has them, thought Flamininus.

Lucius was of the same mind. 'Keep talking like that, and the Centuriate *will* vote with him,' he said.

Flamininus listened with mounting fury as Galba compared Philip to Pyrrhus of Epirus, told the crowd that in fact he was far worse, with greater forces at his disposal. Frequent mention was made of the Greek-speaking peoples of southern Italia who had risen to fight with Hannibal. Never would these populations fail to revolt unless there was no enemy at hand for them to join, Galba declared with passion.

'Let Macedonia, not Italia, have war; let it be the enemy's farms and cities that are laid waste with fire and sword. We already know that our legions are more fortunate and powerful abroad than at home. Go to vote, then, with the blessing of the gods, and ratify what the senate has proposed. It is not the consul alone who supports this opinion before you: the immortal gods themselves favour it, for when I offered sacrifice and prayer that this war should turn out successfully for me, the senate and for you, for the allies and the Latin confederacy, and for our fleets and armies, they gave all favourable and propitious signs.' Galba raised a fist to the sky, and shouted, 'War!'

The crowd went wild. 'WAR! WAR! WAR!'

'That's it,' said Flamininus bitterly.

'I think you're right, brother.' Lucius hailed a wine seller and topped up both their cups.

They had downed several by the time the votes of the Centuriate had been counted. Being half-pissed did not soften the blow that three hundred and fifty-four had backed the Senate's motion for war. Flamininus was glad to be hidden in the crowd where Galba could not see him. To have his rival gloat as he had at the consular elections would have been too much to bear.

They joined the crowds leaving the Plain of Mars. While Lucius talked about drowning their sorrows, Flamininus was deep in thought. Galba was consul, and the Republic would go to war with Macedonia, but neither of these things meant *he* could not continue to work against his enemy. He thought of Cyclops and his comrade, who had since died. You were the first to shed blood, Galba, and you may have scared the fools of the Centuriate into voting the way you wanted. That doesn't mean you will succeed. The beginnings of a smile worked its way onto Flamininus' face. It was time to put his network of spies in Greece to work.

He would stop at nothing to hinder Galba.

Even treason.

CHAPTER XV

Outside the town of Abydos,
southern shore of the Hellespont

Dressed in an ordinary soldier's chiton, Philip slipped through his army's camp. Night had fallen; he had escaped from his large, stuffy tent, and for a time, his responsibilities. It was much cooler in the open air, and the mosquitoes, a plague at Pella, were kept away by the light sea breeze. When the time came, the king decided, he would sleep under the stars, as many soldiers were doing.

Things were going well, he reflected, better than they had been since the loss of his hard-won conquests in the Kyklades. Almost a score of towns had fallen during his lightning-quick advance into first south-eastern Thrake, and then the long, narrow peninsula that formed the northern shore of the Hellespont. Egyptian for the most part, the towns increased his stranglehold on the waterway. Seeking further success, Philip had led his army across to Asia Minor some ten days before.

His mood soured a little as he stared at the walls of Abydos, which lay half a dozen stadia away. The town's refusal to capitulate had not been particularly surprising; what had been unexpected was its thus far successful defence. Philip's initial assault by sea had been repulsed by a vicious catapult barrage and the arrival, from nowhere, it seemed, of two enemy warships. One Macedonian vessel had been sunk, a pair taken, and more damaged. The loss of life had been high. *Herakleides is an indecisive fool,* thought Philip, not for the first time. His admiral couldn't be blamed for the bad news that had followed, however. Abydos had not just been sent ships: its garrison had been reinforced by Rhodian and Pergamene troops.

Undeterred, Philip had set his men to digging beneath the town's walls, and that had gone well. Three days had passed, and his engineers had undermined a large enough section of Abydos' defences for it to collapse. It came as no surprise that the defenders had erected a second wall behind the first, but poorly constructed, it would fall to the next strong assault, which would take place at dawn. Tonight, the king had granted his soldiers an evening off duty and a good ration of wine.

Which brought him to his purpose. Moving between the camp fires until the moon was high in the sky, Philip told his men that Abydos would be theirs by the following sunset. 'There'll be plunder for all!' Faces reddened by wine and the heat, the soldiers cheered and sang. Content that morale was high, Philip spent time drinking with some of his phalangists. After several cups, he made his excuses and retired. Tomorrow was an important day.

Philip slept like a baby, rising before the sun. A pleasant breakfast of bread, cheese and figs was interrupted by one of the bodyguards on guard outside. A messenger had come from Abydos. The king hid his surprise. Barefoot, clad only in his chiton, he strode from the tent to find his guards circled around a proud-faced, middle-aged man in well-used armour. Dents in his breastplate and helmet proved he wasn't shy of fighting, and there was a bandage on his lower right arm.

Philip looked him up and down, and sniffed. 'You are?'

The man bowed. 'Philokrates, sire, the commander of Abydos' garrison.'

'Come to surrender?'

'I have, sire, if you will grant our terms.'

'You want terms?' Philip couldn't keep the incredulity from his voice.

'We do, sire.' Philokrates' gaze was level.

'They are?'

'That our allies' ships should have safe passage from the harbour. The Pergamenes and Rhodians in the garrison are to receive the same guarantee. Our women are not to be violated, and our soldiers are to be allowed to keep their weapons.'

Philip's intention had been to release at least some of the enemy troops; mindful of the harm his troops' behaviour at Kios had done, he would have prevented raping and pillaging as well, but Philokrates' effrontery was staggering. The man might have courage, but was acting as if he were the victor.

Philip raised an eyebrow. 'Anything else?'

Philokrates coloured a little. 'No, sire.'

'And if your terms are unacceptable?'

Philokrates stood a little straighter. 'We will fight on, sire.'

'Your wall will be breached again soon.'

'Before that, we will kill our women and children, sire, and destroy our valuables. We men will fight to the death.'

'I reject your terms utterly,' said Philip.

Philokrates looked startled, but his jaw set. 'Can I ask why?'

'Your pisspot town is about to fall, and you come here telling *me* how you will be treated? Get out of my sight.' Without a backward glance, Philip returned to his breakfast. Despite his confident manner, frustration gnawed at him. Abydos would be the last action of the year. Autumn was coming, and he didn't have enough soldiers or cavalry to take more of Asia Minor. Consolidating his forces on either side of the Hellespont would be his best policy, ensuring they didn't fall straight back into his enemies' hands as the Kyklades had.

There was much to be grateful for, Philip decided. The rewards of this short campaign would become evident before long. Deprived of this season's harvest – much of it had yet to pass through the straits – Athens would come crawling to the peace table. That, or their population would starve in the coming winter.

Either way, he would win.

Two days later, Abydos continued to teeter on the edge. Prolonged assaults by Philip's men the previous day had met with fierce resistance, but poorly trained yokels and a few Rhodians and Pergamenes had no chance against the king's crack troops. The casualties among the defenders had been immense: by late afternoon, Philip's senior officers had estimated three-quarters of the garrison were dead. Still the inhabitants would not surrender. Hurling lumps of roof tile, some fighting with agricultural implements, they had held out until the light leached from the western sky.

Furious with his men's failure, Philip had given the order to pull back. To prevent any attempt to escape, he'd had watchfires lit around the town while his ships had anchored at the harbour mouth. Philokrates had emerged from the town after sunset, a herald's olive branch in his hand. A humbler man than before, now bloodied and beaten-looking, he had fallen to his knees and begged for mercy. Angered by the defenders' stubbornness, Philip had offered nothing more than he would 'think on it'. Sure in his mind that he would spare the Abydians – he had been impressed by their courage – he said not a word to Philokrates. Let them stew overnight, he had thought.

Sunrise had arrived an hour since, and Philip's troops were ready to launch their final assault. Before the order was given, the king had come to survey Abydos from close quarters. His eyes roved the ramparts and the gaping hole caused by his engineers. There were almost no defenders visible – perhaps a man every twenty-five paces. He smiled. His soldiers had only to scale the wall and the town would be his at last.

'Trumpeters,' said Philip.

His musicians, waiting nearby, placed their instruments to their lips.

Sudden uproar broke out among his soldiers by the shore. Philip frowned. A ship was rowing up the straits, from the Aegean. Oars plashed every few heartbeats – it was in a hurry. Concerned that it was one of his, sent with urgent news from either Macedon or one of his forts on Asia Minor, he had the trumpeters stand down.

'Find out what's going on,' he ordered.

To Philip's astonishment, word came that a Roman ship – Roman! – had arrived. On board was a representative of the Senate, who was demanding an audience.

Philip's fury was reaching volcanic levels; he barely saw the unfortunate messenger. His general, Nikanor, had given him the Romans' ultimatum several months before. Palpably unjust and based on no kind of legal right, Philip had entirely ignored the demands. Busy with his campaign on the Propontis and Asia Minor, he had given it little thought since. What possible purpose, he wondered, could they have to deliver it to him in person? The pleasing idea of sending the emissary's head to the Senate by way of reply came to mind. Philip wouldn't do that – he was a king, not a savage, but by the gods it would show that he was not to be trifled with.

'Bring him to me.' Let the dog see what I am capable of, he thought, staring at the ruins of Abydos' walls.

The emissary arrived not long after, accompanied by four legionaries, and around them, twenty of Philip's Companions. He was a short man with tousled hair; despite the heat and the grime, his white toga was immaculate. Perhaps thirty years old, he had the typical confident manner of the Roman senatorial class. Striding from between his men and the startled Companions, he reached Philip. There was no respectful bow – not even a dip of his chin.

'You are Philip?'

'I am,' said Philip icily. Gods, how abrupt these people are. 'Who might you be?'

'My name is Marcus Aemilius Lepidus. I—'

'Who?'

'Marcus Aemilius Lepidus. I am a member of the embassy who spoke with your general Nikanor some months since.'

Philip made a vague gesture, and was pleased when Lepidus' mouth tightened.

'Do you recall the message we gave him?'

'I do. You were interfering with Macedonian business, so I paid it no regard.'

'Your troops attacked Attica straight away – that was answer enough.'

Philip gave Lepidus a 'What did you expect?' look. 'You are here to tell me face to face.'

'That's correct.'

'You had best repeat the demands – I've forgotten the detail,' said Philip carelessly. He was lying, and they both knew it, but his remark irritated Lepidus further, which was his purpose.

'You are henceforth to make no war on any Greek state. The injuries you have done to King Attalus of Pergamum are to be assessed by an independent tribunal, which will calculate the necessary reparations.' Lepidus paused, then added, 'Failure to do so will mean that a state of war exists between Rome and Macedon.'

Philip wanted to strike Lepidus' head from his shoulders. Instead, he grated, 'You come here to tell the king of Macedon how he shall conduct his business?'

'I do so with the full authority of the Senate.'

'Since when did Rome have jurisdiction over Macedon?'

'You might have thought of that possibility before you entered into an alliance with Hannibal fifteen years ago.'

Tartaros, but how Philip wished that more had come of his treaty with the Carthaginian general. Together, they might have turned the tide of war, and defeated the Republic. He glared at Lepidus.

'There is more.'

'More?' cried Philip, losing control for a heartbeat.

Lepidus indicated the walls of Abydos. 'You are to cease attacking Ptolemy of Egypt's possessions at once, and to return the territory and towns seized from him. The previously mentioned tribunal shall also investigate the damages done by you to Rhodes.'

Telling a king – *him* – what he could and could not do showed staggering pride, and confidence. A bitter taste filled Philip's mouth. He was unafraid of confrontation, but behind the Senate stood its legions, battle-hardened from the long war with Carthage. With these hostilities ended, the Republic's entire military might could be sent his way. Such odds were daunting. It would be prudent to avoid a war, thought Philip, yet Lepidus' boorish, overbearing manner was hard to stomach.

Philip threw the dice again. 'Our peoples have been at peace for years.'

'Your hostile actions are unacceptable.'

What he had done impacted on the Republic not at all, thought Philip. The Romans were showing complete disregard for the terms of the treaty between them. 'The Rhodians were the aggressors,' he said. 'They attacked my territory first.'

'And what about the Athenians? What about the Cianians, and what about the Abydians now? Did these peoples attack you first?'

Taken aback, Philip demanded, 'So now Rome is the protector of Greece, independent of any previous alliances or treaties? Rome decides what is right and what is wrong?'

Lepidus' lips twitched. 'Something like that.'

Philip's overpowering rage was replaced by an odd calm. There was no question of degrading himself by agreeing to these outrageous demands. Rome was the interloper here, not he. 'I will forgive your haughtiness because of your youth and obvious inexperience at diplomacy, but most of all, because you are a Roman. I have learned to expect nothing more from your kind. I ask that the Republic does not violate its treaty with me, and that it will not make war on Macedon. If it does, you will find no foe more bitter.'

Lepidus nodded, as if unsurprised. 'Are these your final words?'

'They are.'

'Then I bid you farewell.' Lepidus made a faint impression of a bow and withdrew to his men. Flanked by the Companions, they walked back to their ship.

Philip cast his eyes skywards. Zeus Soter, I will need your help in the months and years to come. There was no answer, but he did not despair. Since the start of his reign, war had been his entire existence. He wasn't about to walk away from a fight now.

CHAPTER XVI

Via Appia, south-eastern Italia,
summer 200 BC

Footsore, sunburned, and covered in dust, Felix and Antonius trudged along the road, two figures amid the throng. Around them were scores of pedestrians, merchants' wagons, farmer's carts and horsemen. The way to Brundisium had been busy for days – it seemed half of Italia wanted to reach the large port that would serve as the assembly point for the attack on Macedon. Official messengers rode in both directions, carrying instruction from Rome, and back again with the replies of those in charge at Brundisium. At least three times a day, trumpet blasts cleared the road so military units – sometimes a maniple of legionaries, at other times, considerably more – could march past.

The brothers were careful to keep their gaze averted until the last men had gone by. Doing the same wasn't as important with squad-rons of cavalry – noblemen paid no attention to lowly travellers – yet they adopted the same policy. As Antonius had declared at the start of their long journey from Rome, there was no point tempting Fortuna any more than they already were. All soldiers and cavalry were to be avoided unless there was no alternative. Felix hadn't argued.

On the Via Appia itself, it wasn't hard, but each evening, their tactic became more problematic. Most roadside inns were full to bursting with ex-soldiers like themselves, heading to re-enlist. Concerned they would be recognised, Felix had insisted they spend their first nights in the open. Cold and wet after a prolonged downpour early the second morning, he had given in to Antonius' argument that when the time came each day to seek lodgings, one could take an unobtrusive walk around the chosen tavern and stables before paying for a quiet sleeping spot, away from other travellers.

'Drink little, and keep ourselves to ourselves, and it should be all right,' Felix had muttered, throwing up yet another prayer to Fortuna.

He cast a casual glance around. In front, a squint-eyed farmer with a cartload of vegetables whistled the same out-of-tune ditty he'd been subjecting them to for miles. Behind, a shaven-headed brute with a club strode along at the head of a line of miserable-looking slaves, bound together at the neck by ropes. Three companions, equally as unsavoury, took up the end of the file. Beside the brothers walked a lanky figure in a threadbare robe. His greasy, blunt-peaked hat marked him as a soothsayer; he supped often from a leather wineskin, and belched almost as much. He was accompanied by the skinniest boy Felix had ever seen, an assortment of bony limbs and angular joints topped by a mass of curly black hair.

The urchin caught his eye and grinned. 'You a soldier?'

Felix scowled and looked away, but it was too late. The soothsayer had heard. Despite his florid drinker's complexion and a breath foul enough to turn the stomach, he had sharp weasel eyes. 'Going to join the legions, boys?'

Felix exchanged a look with Antonius, who gave a minute shrug. Lying would be too obvious – they were two healthy young men journeying to Brundisium. 'Aye, if they'll have us,' he acknowledged.

'Big strong fellows like you are prime soldier material,' fawned the soothsayer. 'You must have served before, in the war against Hannibal?'

'Aye.' This was not information Felix wished to disclose to the world at large, but their sandals and daggers were a clear giveaway. He could already sense the attention of the slave trader behind them; the farmer had stopped whistling, to eavesdrop. 'For a few years.'

'And now you're re-enlisting,' cried the soothsayer, warming to his task.

'We don't need our futures read,' said Felix.

The soothsayer hadn't even noticed. 'An *as* each, and I'll see what the gods have in store for you – which legion you will join, whether your officers will be bastards or no.'

'They'll all be whoresons – everyone knows that,' snapped Antonius, raising a laugh from the slave trader and the farmer.

'Six asses, and I'll determine the perils you will face in Illyria and Macedon,' said the soothsayer, moving to walk in front of the brothers, his back towards Brundisium.

The boy bobbed about, swearing how accurate his father's predictions were. 'They say so in every town,' he piped.

'Buy a hen at the next farm we pass, and I'll see from its liver if you will both survive the war. A denarius it will cost, for both. You'll not find a better offer!'

'If we had money, we wouldn't be going back into the fucking army.' Felix waved his arm. 'Leave us be.' The charlatan could no more read the future than Felix could fly, but his relentless chatter rammed home again the danger they'd be in – not just from the enemy, but from their own kind.

The soothsayer took note of the brothers' grim expressions. 'Of course, sirs. If you change your minds, you need only ask.'

Antonius nudged Felix, who managed to bite back an angry retort.

'Don't give him a reason to remember us,' muttered Antonius.

'Aye, aye.' Relief filled Felix as the soothsayer noticed a stall selling wine and hurried to replenish his sagging leather skin.

Fresh concerns about the risks they were taking gnawed at Felix for the rest of the day; the same worries were mirrored in Antonius' eyes. The soothsayer's curiosity would be as nothing compared to the interest a centurion might take when they presented themselves to re-enlist. Say the wrong thing inadvertently – name a unit in a legion the centurion knew, for example, or let someone hear Felix crying out Ingenuus' or Matho's names, as he often did when the nightmare came – and they could be found out at once. The fustuarium, crucifixion, being torn to pieces by wild beasts in the arena – any one of these dreadful fates would be their end. A troubled silence replaced their previous banter.

The walls of Brundisium were in sight when Antonius voiced his anxiety. 'What are we doing? It's madness to join up again.'

Felix felt no better about it, but their other options were worse. 'D'you want to be the doorman of a shithole tavern in Rome for the rest of your life?'

Antonius shook his head.

'The farm's still there. Back-breaking work from dawn to dusk, month in, month out, four seasons a year, for precious little reward. No wonder Mother and Father died before we returned.' In Felix's mind, a life such as the wine grower they had met was one to be envied, and aspired to; working oneself into the grave for a few bushels of wheat at harvest time was not. 'I didn't spend seven years in the legions to end up worse off than a slave. We can make our fortune in this war – fuck the risk.'

The brothers walked on for fifty strides, then a hundred.

'Well?' asked Felix.

Antonius cursed. 'I'm *not* going back to the farm. At least, not without the money for mules and slaves.'

'That's the spirit,' said Felix, delighted.

Early the following day, the brothers walked to the vast tract of land outside Brundisium that had been set aside for the assembling army. Camps sprawled on two sides of the rough square; in the middle, legion standards marked the places to enlist. Felix and Antonius were but two among thousands of potential recruits, and it seemed half the legions in Rome were represented. Spotting their old legions' standards was terrifying; to their good fortune, it was before they had drawn close. Giving the area a wide berth, nervously watching for Matho, the pair made their way to the far end of the line of recruiting tables.

Here, they told themselves, there was no danger.

'Next!' The centurion's voice was quiet, but it carried down the queue.

Perhaps a score of men were ahead of the brothers, but Felix's stomach gave a painful clench nonetheless. The centurion wasn't Matho – they had both checked – but it was difficult not to imagine it *was* him.

The man in front shuffled forward several steps, and the brothers did the same. A barrage of questions fell on the unfortunate before the centurion; neither they nor his answers were discernible, but the result was soon clear. A disconsolate figure, his shoulders bowed, he trudged away from the group who'd been accepted.

'What's wrong with him?' whispered Antonius.

'I can't tell.' Felix couldn't make out any obvious physical infirmity, the commonest reason for refusal. 'Maybe the surgeon noticed he had bad eyes. Perhaps he's too old.'

'Let's hope the centurion doesn't mind a limp.'

The man in front turned and with a grin, indicated a purple scar running from the side of his right knee to halfway down his calf.

'How d'you get that?' asked Felix. 'Fighting Hannibal?'

A wry chuckle. 'Aye. Somewhere near here, funnily. It makes me hobble, but I managed to serve out my time until the war's end.' Short, thin and with wide cheekbones and a friendly smile, the man was about the brothers' age. 'Gaius is my name, but since the injury, everyone calls me "Hopalong".' He stuck out a hand.

'Felix.'

'Antonius.'

The three shook.

'Brothers?'

Felix could never see the resemblance. 'It's that obvious?'

'Your faces are similar,' said Hopalong. 'Been in the legions?'

Here we go, thought Felix, his nerves wire-taut. Antonius' answer was smooth, however. 'Aye, for some years. Which one were you in?'

To the brothers' relief, Hopalong's old unit wasn't the one they had decided upon. For the moment, their story would hold. Their shared stories of army life put them at ease; this continued when the man behind joined in. About a decade older, he was tall, with thinning grey hair and stooped shoulders. When asked his name, he muttered, 'Fabius'. Before anyone could say a word, he added with a snarl that he was 'no relation of Fabius the Delayer'.

Amused, Felix mouthed, 'He's heard that a thousand times' at Antonius. Fabius' reluctance to be identified with the Delayer wasn't surprising. Quintus Fabius Maximus' cautious tactics against Hannibal were still despised.

Fabius had been in the legions almost from the start of the conflict with Hannibal, but he didn't ask any probing questions of the brothers. The four talked about where they were from, and what they had done since the war's end. Drinking stories began to surface, as did the best practical jokes they had ever played on comrades. Sooner than they'd expected, the brothers were third and fourth from the front of the queue; Hopalong was second in line. A nervous silence fell. No one enjoyed being interrogated by a centurion.

When Hopalong's time came, his scar was inspected, and he was made to walk up and down in front of the Greek surgeon.

'You'll do,' the centurion said when the surgeon had given him a nod. 'Join the group behind me. Give your details to the optio. Go.'

Next it was Felix's turn. Sweaty-palmed, dry-mouthed, he stood forward. A polished vine stick and crested helmet lay on the table before the centurion; numerous *phalerae* decorated his chest harness. Twin silver torcs hung around his neck on a strap. Perhaps forty years old, he had fair hair and a jutting chin, and like all his kind, an intense gaze. Standing by his shoulder was the surgeon. His job, Felix knew, was to perform a quick physical examination of every suitable recruit.

'Name?' demanded the centurion. His low voice was just as threatening as Matho's had been.

'Felix Cicirrus, sir.' This was the family name the brothers had decided to adopt.

The centurion flicked a finger at Antonius. 'And the fool behind you is your brother.'

'Yes, sir.'

A jerk of the chin at Antonius. 'What do they call you?'

'Antonius, sir.' He sidled to Felix's side. 'Cicirrus, sir.'

The centurion's lips thinned. 'Clowns, are you?'

'No, sir,' the brothers said in nervous unison.

Worried about their discharge from the legions being discovered, they had altogether forgotten how mention of their adopted name would make people think of the well-known stage clowns, Sarmentus and Messius Cicirrus. 'It's just our misfortune to have the same name, sir,' said Felix.

'I'd say.' The centurion looked them up and down. 'Healthy?'

'We are, sir.'

'You've both been legionaries, or I'm no judge.'

'Aye, sir. Seven years we served,' said Felix.

'You know one end of a gladius from the other, then.'

'We do, sir.'

'Which legion?'

'The Twelfth, sir, from near Rome.' Felix could feel a pulse at the base of his throat, and it took great self-control to keep his gaze facing front. If the centurion had been in the Twelfth, or knew someone in it, they could be undone.

'The Twelfth?'

'Yes, sir.' Felix could see Ingenuus' terrified eye staring up at him, could feel breaking bone under his hobnailed sandal. He wanted to vomit. We're dead, he thought. Dead.

'You were principes?'

'We were, sir,' the brothers answered.

'As long as the surgeon's happy, you're in. Once he's done with you, see the optio behind me. He'll measure your height and record any scars, make you swear another oath of allegiance to the Republic—' the centurion half-smiled '—you know the drill.'

'Yes, sir. Thank you, sir.' Felix and Antonius exchanged an incredulous, delighted look

'Move, fools. There's a line of men behind you,' said the centurion.

Muttering their thanks, the pair hurried towards Hopalong and the other new recruits.

The centurion called out a command – although his voice was different to Matho's, Felix's stomach lurched again. They had succeeded, he thought, yet this was the first hurdle of many.

From this day on, they would be in constant, mortal danger.

CHAPTER XVII

Outside Pella, Macedon

The sun had reached its highest point in the autumn sky, and on the plain outside the city, Demetrios was drilling with his speira. All the brazen shields were there, but not the white: the two units trained on alternate days. The phalangists had been at it for hours, the chiliarchies trudging to and fro across the flat ground near their camp, performing half a dozen exercises over and over. The commonest routine was the march in open order, the formation used to approach the enemy when it was impossible or impractical to have the speirai fully arrayed. Watched by an eagle-eyed Kryton, the second file walked behind the first, the third behind the fourth and so on, making each unit only eight files wide. When the order came, the alternate files quickly had to resume their usual position, forming the battle-ready speira.

Demetrios had lost count of how many times they had drilled like this since the army's return from Asia Minor. Still new to the army, it was normal routine to him, but some veterans were muttering that regular training was not something phalangists did. Despite the grumbling, no one made their feelings known to Simonides, less still Kryton. The order had come from the king, whose word was not to be questioned. Overhearing, Simonides cried, 'Philip wants us to practise,' and that is what we shall do. Anyone who disagrees is free to take it up with me.' No one said anything. A champion pankrationist, Simonides was not an opponent whom men wished to go up against.

The men of his file weren't the only ones to complain, however, and Kryton had also noticed. At length he ordered the phalangists to ground their sarissae. He stalked up and down before the front rank, down one side, along the back and up the far side, roaring that they were a crowd of lazy good-for-nothing sheepskin-wearers, and that they would go back to their tents when he fucking told them to. No one was stupid enough to answer back; there were plenty of awkward coughs, and men kept their gaze fixed anywhere but on their fuming commander.

'Seeing as you're such experts at the usual drills, we shall practise something different. Something that might prove useful if you are ambushed on the march with no time to form the phalanx,' announced Kryton.

He bellowed a series of orders at the four-file leaders. The next exercise would see the speira split into four groups of sixty-four men.

'I'll be watching,' he shouted at the ordinary soldiers. 'Any man I see who's not doing his best will be severely punished, as will anyone whose spear tip isn't covered in leather. You're to thrust at men's aspides, remember, not their helmets. I don't want anyone blinded.'

Demetrios could scarcely believe what he'd heard. He twisted to look at Zotikos. 'We're to split the file?'

'That's what he said. Our file will break up into four lines of four men, with a second file positioned the same way beside us. We'll face another two files arrayed in similar fashion.' Zotikos' lips twitched. 'That means you'll be in the third rank, yes. You will have to use your sarissa.'

Demetrios grinned until his face hurt. At last, he thought. At last I will stand near the front.

Chivvied by Simonides, the phalangists formed into smaller lines. The phalangists in the other files did the same, and soon a rank that was eight men wide, four deep, faced another of the same size and width across a distance of perhaps a hundred paces. Quite deliberately, Simonides and the other file-leaders had placed their eight front-rankers together on one side. This meant Demetrios and every phalangist in his 'formation' was at best someone who stood ninth in a file, and at worst, was like him, the fifteenth man.

As this grim realisation sank in, Demetrios stared at the men opposite, trying to ignore the knot twisting in his belly. An exercise it might be, but the reality of combat had never been clearer. Four sarissae protruded from between each of the closely held aspides. Over the shields, he could make out little more than the tops of helmets: *pilos* type, Chalkidian and Thracian.

Soon, he thought, those spear tips will be close enough to kill.

'What are you waiting for?' shouted Kryton. 'Advance!'

Both sets of phalangists moved off. Obvious differences were soon evident: the front-rankers kept an even, solid line. Unused to leading, the quarter-file leaders struggled to keep their less experienced men apace of each other. Curses rang out, and accusations that some were marching too fast.

Twenty-five paces on, and the veterans began to scream war cries. The replies of a few men in Demetrios' formation were drowned out.

'Ready to die?' roared the front-rankers. 'Yellow-livers!'

'This is it,' said Kimon.

Demetrios was scared now – properly scared. Although the neat line of approaching shields was only eight men wide, it rammed home the brutal reality of the storm of bronze. Facing an entire enemy phalanx or thousands of Roman legionaries would be utterly terrifying.

'This is it,' said Kimon again. A tremor had crept into his voice.

The quarter-file leader heard. A dull type, he had nonetheless survived ten years in the brazen shields. 'We're younger than every man in the file opposite,' he said over his shoulder. 'Stronger too. They're trying to scare us. Reach them scared, and we've already lost. That's what they want, so hold your nerve, curse you!'

Demetrios was feeling sick. Sixty paces separated them from the 'enemy' now. The din from their war cries had been added to by trumpeters, blowing from both sides. They had been ordered to sound by Kryton, in an effort to increase the tension, Demetrios decided, and the tactic worked. His guts began to churn as if he'd eaten a bad piece of meat the day before. He wasn't alone in his fear. Kimon was praying out loud. The men two files to the right had lagged behind the rest, causing their file-closers to scream abuse and batter the unfortunates in front of them with their shields.

Zotikos' aspis thumped Demetrios in the back. 'Keep up!'

Demetrios realised he'd fallen a step behind Kimon. 'Sorry,' he muttered.

'Think it's unpleasant at this distance?' Zotikos hissed. 'It's worlds worse close up.'

Demetrios wondered if he'd misheard. 'You were a front-ranker?'

'I was fourth in the file.' Pride throbbed in Zotikos' voice. 'Fourth.'

Demetrios' head spun. 'Then—'

'I beat a file-leader unconscious years ago. Not Simonides – he's a good officer – his predecessor, who was a prick through and through.

He mocked me one night after I'd had a skinful of wine, and I hammered the shit out of him. I was lucky not to be hounded out of the speira. I'll be a file-closer until my dying day.'

Further conversation was prevented by the quarter-file leader's shout. 'Shields together! Lower pikes!'

They were little more than two dozen paces from the 'enemy', and Demetrios obeyed with alacrity. Down came his sarissa, for the first time ever pointing straight ahead. His gaze followed its shaft, the length of three men lying end to end, and at its tip, the leather-covered, leaf-shaped blade. On his stare travelled, through the air to the end of his opponent's spear, and down its shaft, to the man's aspis. Above, a bronze helmet framed a pair of gimlet eyes. Demetrios' heart pounded. It was Simonides. Behind him, he knew, stood Philippos, Andriskos and Empedokles: tough soldiers, used to wielding their sarissae.

Twenty paces. The quarter-file leaders in Demetrios' formation had slowed to allow every phalangist to catch up. Their attempt was successful for the most part, but the line of aspides and projecting sarissae was still more uneven than that of the front-rankers opposite.

'This is it,' said Kimon for the dozenth time.

'Aye,' snarled Demetrios, losing patience. 'Our chance to prove ourselves. All we have to do is hold steady. Not take a single step backwards. Thrust at their shields. Wait until Kryton tells us to stop. D'you hear me?'

A moment's hesitation, and then Kimon said, 'Aye. Hold steady. Stand fast. Thrust. Wait for Kryton's order.'

Fifteen paces. Still the veterans roared their war cries, but now Demetrios could see a little of the tension twisting *their* faces. He could sense that Empedokles, the sometime butt of his comrades' jokes, would feel the same fear in his, Demetrios', belly.

'With me, rear-rankers!' he screamed. Heads half-turned. Eyes bored into him. 'They're men, comrades, same as us! Hold steady. Do *not* give way. MA-CE-DON!'

To Demetrios' utter astonishment, the cry was taken up.

'MA-CE-DON! MA-CE-DON!' Its volume matched that of the front-rankers' shout.

The leading spear tips met and passed each other. The yelling continued unabated from both sides. The ends of the second sarissae went by one another, and those of the third.

'Here we go,' shouted the quarter-file leader. 'STEADY!'

Thump. A spear blade punched into an aspis in front – Demetrios wasn't sure whose. A yelp of pain went up as another smacked by mistake into a nearby man's helmet. In a real battle, he thought, that unfortunate might have just taken a mortal wound. A heartbeat later, Demetrios' gorge rose, and his stomach rebelled. Puke spattered his chiton, but he kept his sarissa levelled, kept his aspis pressed into Kimon's back.

Ares, help me, Demetrios prayed. Give me courage.

'On my call,' called the quarter-file leader. 'D'you hear me?'

Demetrios, Kimon and Zotikos rumbled their assent.

'Aim for their shields,' said the quarter-file leader. 'THRUST!'

Demetrios stared at Simonides' aspis and pushed with all his might. All around him, his comrades grunted with effort. Demetrios felt Zotikos shoving his sarissa forward, saw Kimon's arm in front doing the same. Meaty thumps rose from near and far as the spears on both sides made contact with their opponents' shields. Two struck the quarter-file leader's aspis, and he staggered back into Kimon.

Desperate, knowing that the contest would be over if the front man took a step back, or worse still, went down, Demetrios heaved forward with all his might. 'PUSH!' he roared.

To his immense relief, Kimon reacted, helping the quarter-file leader to regain his footing. Angered and humiliated, *he* was quick to order another shove at their opponents. This time, they pushed Simonides back a pace. A roar of delight left Demetrios' lips; Kimon and the quarter-file leader were shouting too. Even Zotikos joined in.

Three short trumpet blasts signalled the retreat – Kryton was ending the exercise. Exhilarated despite the puke on his chiton, Demetrios took a step backwards with the rest.

'We held our own!' he cried.

As he twisted around to ask Zotikos his opinion, something struck Demetrios a powerful blow on the side of his helmet. Stars burst across his vision, and his head was punched to one side. Unbalanced, he staggered and dropped to one knee, almost dropping his sarissa in the process.

He rose to the sound of Empedokles' laughter.

'You all right?' asked Zotikos.

'Aye,' snarled Demetrios.

'That was Empedokles' idea of a joke,' said Zotikos. 'It can happen in battle. You've got to stay alert, always.'

Demetrios wanted to shout an insult at the watching Empedokles, but the prick would only be pleased he'd reacted. It was better, Demetrios decided, to lie low. Gut instinct told him that Empedokles was capable of worse things than a dunt on the helmet.

Hours later, Demetrios arrived at the tavern in the centre of Pella where Kimon and Antileon were supposed to be. Impatient to start drinking, they had left camp soon after the end of training. Demetrios hadn't intended to linger, but sought out by a full-of-praise Simonides and Philippos, he'd ended up taking a seat by the front-rankers' fire, delighted with himself and the chance to soak up their tales of war. Of Empedokles there had been no sign – according to his comrades, he'd gone to Pella with friends from another file. No one made mention of his sarissa thrust on Demetrios, who therefore reasoned it prudent not to mention it.

Now he was looking forward to an evening with his friends. To his annoyance, however, there was no sign of them in the previously agreed tavern. A conversation with the innkeeper revealed that they had been there, but had gone on somewhere else: he didn't recall when the pair had left, or exactly where they had been bound. Rather than wander the city aimlessly, Demetrios decided to call it a night. He set off at a brisk rate, as he had on his way there. Weapons were prohibited inside in Pella, and lowlifes lurked in many a darkened alley.

Eyes peeled for danger, he made good progress, encountering only a pair of two-*obol* whores. Demetrios laughed off their offer of a knee-trembler he wouldn't forget. Before long, the walls of the royal palace loomed into view. Demetrios had never set foot inside, but he'd heard of the grand gardens and magnificent rooms from men who had served as sentries within. One day, it would be his turn; he looked forward to seeing Philip. The king probably wouldn't recognise him, but he might.

Leaving the palace behind, Demetrios entered another run-down area. The stench of human waste wafted from every alleyway. Rats scurried among the refuse in front of a vegetable shop, but the quarter appeared to be otherwise empty. A dog barked as he passed a larger house, and was answered by one in a neighbouring courtyard.

'Quiet!' The voice came from an alley on the opposite side of the street.

Demetrios' heart thumped. Fast and silent as he could, he moved into the shadows cast by the overhanging eaves of a shop.

'That mongrel was barking at something. Take a look,' muttered the voice. 'Go on.'

Dry-mouthed, Demetrios listened. Cautious footsteps, such as those a man who didn't want to be heard made, approached the corner of the shop, which formed part of the junction with the alley. Demetrios pressed himself against the building's front, kept his gaze averted so the whites of his eyes wouldn't betray him, and prayed he wouldn't be seen.

After what seemed like an eternity, there was a grunt. 'Must have been a cat.' The footsteps retreated.

Every instinct screamed at Demetrios to head in the opposite direction. There were at least two men in the alley. They were up to no good, that was certain; they were probably armed too. Curiosity bettered him, however, and he edged to the corner. Taking a deep breath, he peered around it. Fifteen paces away, a pair of dark figures knelt by a prone shape. He had interrupted a robbery, and a hasty retreat was in order if he wasn't to suffer the same fate as the unfortunate on the ground.

'Well?' hissed one cutpurse.

Coins jingled, and the second man chuckled. 'There's enough in his purse to get us both pissed for a few days.'

'Take his sandals too. Phalangists always have good ones.'

There was a one in two chance that their victim had been in the brazen shields, thought Demetrios, bunching his fists. Even a white shield was a comrade, but if he showed himself, his gut told him, they would murder him too. Walk away, and he would live.

A low groan.

Guilt filled Demetrios. The poor bastard wasn't dead. He looked down. At his feet, as if placed by the Fates themselves, was a loose piece of brick. It fitted neatly into his palm.

'Losing your touch?' sneered the first cutpurse. 'You said he was on his way to Tartaros.'

'He will be in a moment.'

Demetrios moved before fear bettered him. Stepping around the corner, he took aim and hurled the brick. Ares was guiding his hand. A satisfying thunk marked the missile hitting the nearest cutpurse in the head. He dropped like a bull that's had its throat cut. Bellowing like a man possessed, Demetrios ran at the second lowlife, who scrambled up and ran.

Demetrios dropped down by the phalangist, who was lying on his front. Hurry, he told himself. Hurry. The cutpurse struck by the brick was already stirring, and once his friend realised Demetrios was on his own, there was every likelihood he would return.

Demetrios saw no bloodstains on the phalangist's chiton, which he hoped was good news. He rolled the man over, and to his utter shock, recognised Empedokles. He was breathing too, shallow breaths, but regular. A mat of bloodied hair on the side of his head, and under it, a nasty lump on his skull, seemed to be the extent of his injuries. Demetrios hesitated. He had loathed Empedokles since his attempt to prevent *him* joining the phalanx, and Empedokles hated him – the proof of that had been evident not four hours since. Leave the whoreson here, thought Demetrios, and the cutpurses would finish what they'd started. At a single stroke, life would become a lot more pleasant. Better still, no one would know.

Low voices carried from down the alley. Demetrios stared, and made out three figures skulking through the gloom. The man who'd run was back, with company. Demetrios spied a fourth, and his guts twisted. If he didn't flee now, he would die. He got up. Took a step away from Empedokles, and another. Coward, his inner demon shouted. Demetrios hardened his heart. Empedokles was an objectionable prick, who loathed him.

'Demetrios?' croaked Empedokles.

Full of shame, he darted back. 'Are you hurt?'

'Someone hit me with a metal bar.' Empedokles managed to curl his lip. 'How do you fucking think I feel?"

I should have left him to die, thought Demetrios. 'Aye, well, best get up if you don't want them to finish the job.' Finding the brick he'd hurled, Demetrios whacked his victim about the temple, knocking him unconscious again. He also took the man's dagger.

'Finish him.' Empedokles was none too steady, but he was on his feet.

'I can't murder him in cold blood.'

'That's what he would have done to me.'

It's maybe what I should have done to you too, thought Demetrios. 'Take this. You'll need it soon enough.' He handed over the lump of brick.

'Where are they?' asked Empedokles.

Demetrios pointed. He cupped a hand to his mouth. 'Come any closer, you sewer rats, and we'll gut you – same as we did with your friend here.'

The cutpurses' answer was to split up, two on either side of the street. Saving Empedokles would have been for nothing if they didn't move fast. With the dagger in his teeth, Demetrios pulled his comrade's right arm over his shoulder and half-carried him towards the junction.

'You were going to leave me, dusty foot,' Empedokles muttered. 'If I hadn't said something, you would have abandoned me.'

He must have opened his eyes as I was getting up, thought Demetrios. Curse it.

'Well?'

'It's not true,' Demetrios lied. 'I'm helping you now, ain't I?'

He could hear footsteps behind, but didn't dare look. He increased his speed as best he could, and prayed that there would be more bricks where he'd found the first. A barrage of missiles might drive the cutpurses off.

The footsteps behind them grew faster. Mutters flew back and forth across the alley.

'They're getting close,' said Empedokles.

Demetrios took immense pleasure from the note of fear in Empedokles' voice. 'We won't go down without a fight,' he said grimly. 'The junction is close. We'll have a better chance there.'

Figures loomed out of the darkness, and Demetrios' hopes plunged into the abyss. The cutpurse had sent his friends to cut off their escape.

'We're dead,' whispered Empedokles.

I should have gone with Kimon and Antileon, thought Demetrios, or stayed in the camp. I should have walked by, and left Empedokles. Instead I'm going to die for nothing. Furious at the injustice of it all, he shouted, 'Try to murder two phalangists, would you? Come on, you pox-ridden cowards!'

'Who's talking about murder?' answered the figure at the front. Stout, wearing a cheap bronze helmet and carrying a cudgel, he peered suspiciously at Demetrios and Empedokles. 'I have five men of the watch at my back. You'd best explain yourselves, and fast.'

The man's bloated sense of self-importance was laughable, but Demetrios was so happy, he didn't care. A quick explanation and the officer sent his men to look for the cutpurses. Of course they had vanished. Even the lowlife whom Demetrios had hit with the brick was gone.

'That was a lucky escape,' pronounced the officer as he escorted them to the west gate. He glanced at Empedokles. 'Just as well your friend found you, eh?'

'Aye,' said Empedokles, but his eyes were flat and hard.

As soon the pair were alone, he hissed in Demetrios' ear, 'I won't forget this.'

'I saved your fucking life!'

'Only because I called out,' Empedokles spat. 'So much for comradeship, eh?'

'Says the prick who tried to injure me earlier. Two fingers' breadth lower, and you'd have spitted me through the throat, leather cover or no,' Demetrios shot back. 'You took against me from the start, and nothing's changed. Would you have helped me if the situation had been reversed?' He laughed bitterly at Empedokles' expression. 'I didn't think so.'

Empedokles looked so angry that Demetrios thought he was going to attack him. So be it, thought Demetrios, balling his fists. With Empedokles injured, he would have the edge.

'Think I'd fight you now?' Barefoot, Empedokles stalked towards the gate. 'Watch your back!' he hurled over his shoulder.

Demetrios' mood was black as he followed. If he had listened to instinct and crept past the cutpurses, Empedokles would now be dead. Even when Demetrios had entered the alley, he could have turned on his heel the instant he'd recognised Empedokles. Instead he had hesitated, allowing his malevolent comrade to see him walk away.

The opportunistic strike with the leather-covered sarissa blade now seemed trivial. He'd stick a blade in my back given half a chance, thought Demetrios.

It was hard to see how the night could have gone worse.

CHAPTER XVIII

Almost a month passed. Discreet enquiries revealed that Felix's old legion – and Matho with it, presumably – *was* to be part of the force sent to Illyria. It was stationed in another part of the great camp. Although this reduced the chance of encountering Matho, he was never out of Felix's mind. He spent his time looking over his shoulder, or felt as if he did.

For the second time in their lives, the brothers underwent the process of becoming a legionary. They were allocated to the century of Titus Pullo, the stern officer they'd met at the recruiting point, and then to one of the unit's ten contubernia. To their delight, Hopalong and Fabius were to be their tentmates, along with four others, men who had never served. They noted the same policy in the other contubernia. Despite the crowding on the road to Brundisium, not as many veterans as they'd thought had wanted to re-enlist, and Pullo was mixing experienced men with the raw recruits.

The comrades were issued with an eight-man tent and individual equipment at the quartermaster's; as before, they had to sign for each and every piece of it. The costs would be deducted from their pay.

'Lose anything, and the price of it also comes out of your pay,' said the officious clerk with more pleasure than Felix would have liked.

Nothing changed, he grumbled to Antonius, and yet it felt good – so good – to don a mail shirt again, and to have a gladius on his hip. Despite Matho's worst, they were principes once more.

For the first ten days, they were instructed by their new optio, Livius. A more diminutive figure than Pullo, he was already popular thanks to his easy-going manner, but Felix suspected there was iron beneath his friendly exterior. Of slight stature, with brown hair, Livius had a noticeable gap between his front teeth, and scars on the soles of both feet – the last a memento, he was fond of recalling, of Carthaginian torture.

Wearing full kit, the principes marched for days in columns of two, four and six, over varying distances up to twenty miles. At intervals, Livius made them run and jump.

'You'll need stamina to climb the mountains in Illyria, brothers,' he announced with glee.

After ten days, Felix was relieved when, following Pullo's instruction, Livius began to drill the principes at last. First he had them assume close formation, using heavy wooden shields and swords. 'Twelve wide, six deep!' he shouted. 'The odd men form a seventh rank.' He pointed at Felix and Antonius. 'You're the centre of the first rank. Move!'

Felix and Antonius shuffled side by side; men hurried to stand alongside, and behind them. The brothers would have lined up with their entire contubernium, but Livius was wise to that ploy, barking that the newer men needed experienced men on at least one side. Felix ended up with Narcissus, one of the greener recruits in the tent group, on his right. Antonius had another inexperienced man to *his* right. Hopalong and Fabius contrived to be behind the brothers, which was reassuring.

'Shields up! Swords ready!' ordered Livius.

Even if his weapons weren't real, and he had an unproved recruit beside him, it felt good to be standing in a shield wall again, thought Felix. His eyes slid right. Narcissus was four paces away. 'Closer,' hissed Felix.

'Eh?' Narcissus could convey disdain with one word.

'You should be two steps and no further from me,' said Felix.

Narcissus shifted, but not close enough. Felix jerked his chin, encouraging him to move again, but Narcissus pretended not to see. Felix didn't say a word. The fool will learn, he thought.

'Closer!' Livius roared, pointing his long staff of office at an unfortunate in the second rank. Topped by a bronze ball, it was as dangerous a weapon as any centurion's vitis, and he wielded it with fearsome skill. Felix winced as Livius leaned in and brought it crashing down on the man's head.

'Just because you're not facing the enemy doesn't mean you can leave a gap that wide, fool. If the man in front of you goes down, a sheep-humping Macedonian will be in your face before you've drawn breath.

That gap will allow him to kill you with ease!' Livius bawled. 'After that, he'll do for one of your tentmates, perhaps even a second one. D'you want to go to the underworld knowing you caused the death of a comrade?' Satisfied with the humiliated answer he received, Livius came alongside the end of the first rank.

'Remember this?' Veteran though he was, the excitement was palpable in Antonius' whisper.

Felix felt the same way. For a moment, he was back at Zama with his comrades, with Matho readying them for battle. The feeling of a man either side of him, and massed ranks behind him, was exhilarating. When the trumpets sounded, they would advance and defeat the enemy.

'What's this?' cried Livius.

Felix's eyes moved to the right. 'Sir?'

'This new recruit is too far from you.' Livius' eyes bulged. 'Did you not tell him?'

'I did, sir. He wouldn't do what I said.'

Livius shoved his face into that of Narcissus. 'Is that right?'

Narcissus flushed. 'No, sir. I moved, sir.'

'Not as close as I told you,' retorted Felix. You fucking liar, he thought.

Livius' staff hammered off Narcissus' helmet, and again. 'Closer!'

Felix could feel the resentment oozing from Narcissus as he shuffled over, but he didn't care. Life in the legion was tough. A man got used to it, or he died.

His inspection finished, Livius faced the century. 'The Dassaretae are some of the first enemies you'll face when we cross the sea. They're nowhere near as dangerous as the Macedonians, but courageous warriors nonetheless. Any one of them will happily send you to Hades if you give him the whisper of a chance. Behind me stand a hundred of them, maybe more.' In a clearly arranged move, the second century in their maniple tramped to stand facing them.

A surprised murmur rose, and Livius sneered. 'None of you are scared, eh? The veterans among you aren't because this is training, but the rest of you filth *should* be terrified. You fucking would be if we were outnumbered!'

Quick as a flash, he rammed the ball on his staff into a new recruit's shield, driving him back a pace.

'They'll throw spears first. *Your* shield is useless now – what are you going to do?'

Before the startled soldier could reply, Livius shouted, 'You're about to die, because another spear has just hit you between the eyes. To the back, quickly! You, behind him – fill the gap!'

Fast as a man could walk, Livius worked his way along the front of the century, removing three principes who had been 'killed' or seen their shields rendered unusable by the enemy spears. By the time he'd done, a different mood prevailed. Men were tense, ready. The earlier gaps in the line had vanished.

'There'll be no javelins for us today,' Livius announced. 'In the main because you're shit at throwing them. Instead we're going to march towards the enemy, nice and slow. At fifty paces, we charge.' His cold eyes moved over the ranks. 'Ready?'

The principes shouted their assent. Even Narcissus seemed enthusiastic.

Livius signalled to the optio opposite, whose soldiers at once began clamouring and hammering their training swords off their shields. 'Swords ready! Shields up!' cried Livius. 'Advance, at the slow pace!'

Livius kept his back to the enemy so he could watch his men. He bawled orders until they were fifty paces out, when he halted them briefly. 'This is the time for javelins – you'll learn that later. Imagine a dozen of the enemy down, wounded or dying.'

He signalled, and the other optio removed ten or eleven soldiers from his formation. Livius raised his staff, quelling the pleased mutters from the ranks. 'They're still equal in number to us, fools.'

Shoving his way in on Narcissus' left, he gave the order to charge.

Unsurprisingly, Livius wasn't happy with the way the principes closed with the 'enemy'. 'Too many gaps at the front,' he shouted once they had reassembled. 'The second rank was three paces further back than it should have been. You slow down just before you hit the enemy, and that's when you make fucking sure that you're close to the man either side of you, and to the men in front of you.' He let out an unpleasant laugh. 'Don't, and you'll be crow-carrion inside ten heartbeats.'

He made them repeat the charge several times, on occasion standing to one side, at others taking a place in their midst. At no stage did they 'fight' the other legionaries. By the time he let the principes take a brief rest, he wasn't shouting as much as he had been. This, Felix knew from experience, was as close as they would get to any praise.

Next, Livius led the principes to ten wooden posts that had been driven into the ground by the engineers. Each the height of a man, they were, he announced, more enemy warriors.

'Without arms, mind,' he said, and the principes risked a chuckle. 'You're going to practise against them, to learn how to handle yourself in combat. The basics are simple. Shove with your shields, thrust with your swords. Batter the *palus* with your shield if you can. Risk a slash now and again, but remember that in real life, your enemy will skewer you in the armpit most times you try it.' He cocked an eyebrow. 'Questions?'

A voice from the back. 'When do we get to fight real men, sir, with real weapons?'

Low mutters of agreement followed. Felix knew better than to agree out loud, but he too was chafing to use the gladius in his tent.

Livius curled his lip. 'Twenty years I've been doing this, and there's always a know-it-all who doesn't need to learn against the palus. The answer is, "as long as it takes". You get to use the real thing when I'm happy. Not a moment before. Any more questions?'

Cowed by the fierceness of his response, or like Felix and the other veterans, knowing not to speak up, no one answered.

'Break up into contubernia. One tent group to each palus. Work in pairs, one veteran, one new recruit, taking turns. Close with the post, carefully, as you would with a real enemy. Go in fast. Slam your shield into it, hard enough to jar your shoulder.' Livius drove his shield against the palus, making it wobble. 'Use the point of the blade on it, and step back. Thrust again, two or three times, then punch the bastard with the shield again. Assuming that your enemy is now reeling, you can slash the post. Hard – I want you to take your enemy's head off, d'you understand?'

'Yes, sir!' the principes shouted.

'Change with your partner, and when he's done, go to the back of the line and wait your turn to do it again.' Livius gestured at the posts. 'What are you waiting for, maggots?' Arms folded across his chest, staff nestled in the crook of one elbow, he watched as the principes got to work.

To his annoyance, Felix again found himself paired with Narcissus. Tall, bony, and with legs that were more than half his height, his new comrade was immensely fond of physical training as well as polishing his armour and kit. From a well-to-do family, his airs and graces had won him few friends. Happy to talk endlessly about himself, he fitted his mythical name to perfection.

'Copy me,' Felix ordered.

Crouched low so that only his eyes and the brow of his helmet were visible over the top of his shield, he advanced on the post with neat, careful steps. Six paces out, he charged. *Smash* went his shield into the palus. He stabbed it so hard splinters flew, and shuffling back a step, he repeated the rest of the moves Livius had ordered. Panting, he eyed Narcissus.

'See?'

Narcissus' lip twitched. 'Of course.' He stepped up and gently banged his shield into the palus. His subsequent sword thrust could have been bettered by a ten-year-old. 'What was the next move?' he asked.

Felix told him. Narcissus' next efforts were no better. 'Gods above and below,' said Felix in frustration. 'You're a soldier, not a child. Hit the cursed thing like you mean it.'

Narcissus muttered something under his breath, and did as he was told, but his second attempts were only a fraction better than the first. Conscious that the rest of the contubernium was waiting, Felix did not persist. At the back of the line, however, he made his opinions clear. Narcissus made a pretence of paying attention, and at one point even yawned.

Felix ground his teeth. 'Don't listen then. Livius will see soon enough.'

Narcissus ignored him.

When they reached the front of the line, Livius was nowhere near. Again Felix repeated the moves, wishing that Narcissus were the palus.

'Go on then,' he growled when he was done.

Narcissus shuffled forward. *Thump* went his shield against the post, harder than before, but still not hard enough. His sword thrust was also weak. Felix had had enough. He strode forward.

'Like this.' *Crash* went his shield. The palus shook. Thrust. The point of his sword dug into the wood. 'See?'

'That's what I did.' Narcissus' tone was petulant.

'No. It's not.'

'You can't order me about: you're a princeps, same as me.'

'Livius will tell you the same thing, fool.'

'*You* call *me* a fool? Peasant.' Narcissus whirled, and surprising Felix, shoved him in the chest. Unbalanced, he fell onto his arse. To his good fortune, he retained a grip on his shield, and was able to draw it over his head as an enraged Narcissus rained down blows with his wooden sword.

He had underestimated Narcissus, thought Felix. In a real battle, such an error would have cost him his life. Angry at himself, he reached out and raked his hobnails down Narcissus' left shin. With a yelp, Narcissus staggered back. Felix was on his feet in a trice. Furious, he charged Narcissus. An ineffectual thrust went by his cheek, and then Felix was close in. Their shields met, and he drove forward, pushing Narcissus back three, four, six steps. When he did brace himself, Felix stamped on the toes of Narcissus' leading foot, visible below his shield. He bawled in pain, and his guard dropped. Felix rammed his sword in, touching the base of Narcissus' neck once, twice.

'You're dead,' snarled Felix. 'Just like that.'

'You've crushed two of my toes!'

'And stabbed you in the throat, fool.'

'What's going on here?' With the skill of all centurions, Pullo had appeared from nowhere.

'He attacked me, sir,' lied Narcissus. 'Stamped on my toes, for no reason.'

Pullo's flinty gaze bore down on Felix.

'He was hitting the fucking palus like a woman, sir,' said Felix hotly. 'I showed him several times, but he wouldn't do it right.'

'So you hit him?'

'No, sir. He didn't like my tone, and turned on me. Knocked me on my arse, truth be told – I wasn't expecting it. I gave him a good kick, and managed to get up.' Felix shrugged. 'This is the result.'

'Well?' Pullo asked Narcissus. 'Lie to me, and you'll rue the day your bitch of a mother whelped you.'

Pullo's ferocity instantly cowed Narcissus. 'Aye, sir. That's what happened.'

Felix had been expecting Narcissus to lie again, and land him in a world of shit. He was taken even more by surprise when Pullo scooped up Narcissus' shield and sword, and without a word of warning, drove at *him*. Felix did well not to fall; he retreated, not daring to strike back at his centurion.

'Fight, cocksucker, or I'll beat the shit out of you,' Pullo ordered.

Old instincts took over. Felix shoved back with his shield, and aimed his sword tip at Pullo's face, forcing the centurion to duck. At once he launched a powerful attack of his own. Thrust. Stab. Thrust. Stab. Felix pushed forward, so they were chest to chest. Laughing, Pullo dodged his attempted headbutt. He came back at Felix with an intense, savage fury, battering him with shield and sword. Unsurprisingly, he was a skilled, relentless fighter.

Felix's youth and reserves of strength were all that saved him in the blurred time that followed. The pair shoved and barged at one another, their blades seeking weaknesses in the other's defence. The career soldier, Pullo landed more blows than Felix. Pain soon needled from his shoulder, his right elbow, his left foot, where Pullo's sword had landed. The centurion had not escaped unscathed, however. A nasty welt was rising under one eye – in battle, the wound would have blinded him – and he had an angry-looking graze on his left forearm.

'For a piece of shit, you know how to fight,' said Pullo at length.

Despite the hint of respect in the centurion's eyes, Felix didn't let down his guard. 'Thank you, sir.'

'Your old officers taught you well.'

Felix said nothing. Matho's favourite part of training had been weapons skills, and he'd been good at it, yet Felix could only picture his mocking face as he ordered the execution of Ingenuus and the rest.

'Well?' Pullo was frowning.

'Aye, sir, they did.' Fortuna, don't let him ask Matho's name, Felix begged. Belly roiling, pulse racing, he couldn't think of an alternative. If Pullo learned of Matho, and then happened to meet him on campaign, which was by no means impossible . . .

'I can tell. Keep your nose clean, and a promotion isn't impossible. Junior officers are hard to find.' Pullo caught Livius' attention. 'This soldier is to help you instruct the new recruits, optio.' He nodded to a stunned Felix. 'Carry on.'

Narcissus didn't have the sense to keep silent. 'What about me, sir?'

Pullo's lip curled. 'In a real battle, you'd already be crow-carrion. You got taught a lesson just now – I suggest you learn from it, fool.'

'Yes, sir,' mumbled Narcissus, throwing an evil glance at Felix.

Felix was so happy he didn't care. Pullo had seen something in him during their frenetic bout. If he were to become a junior officer, his future could be bright. Along with an increase in pay, he could look forward to further advancement. Bitter reality crashed in a heartbeat later. Promotion would increase the chance of encountering Matho many times over, and if Pullo were to learn the truth of his and Antonius' discharge, he would subject them to the fustuarium as fast as their old centurion ever had.

Their situation, Felix decided, was no better than before.

CHAPTER XIX

Rome

Flamininus was walking the streets of the Esquiline Hill, a rough part of the city. His doorman Thrax strode ahead of him, protection and intimidation in one muscle-bound frame. Pasion scurried a couple of paces to his rear. Flamininus was on secretive business. Under a hooded cloak, he wore a workman's rough tunic and plain sandals. A wide-brimmed straw hat shadowed his face.

He was unfamiliar with this quarter of Rome, and had no intention of getting to know it better. Potholes scarred the street surface; refuse lay everywhere. The city's engineers didn't often visit, he thought with disdain. Human sewage ran from the narrow alleys; a multitude of fullers' premises caused the air to reek of urine. The shops were small and dirty, with shifty proprietors and cheap, ill-made wares. Old and dilapidated, three- and four-storey apartment buildings pressed in from either side. Above the stone ground floors, they were constructed from wood. Knock over a brazier in one of the miserable *cenacula*, thought Flamininus, and half the quarter would burn down. It happened in Rome with monotonous regularity; the most recent conflagration had been the previous month. For the dozenth time since entering the slum, he gave thanks for his life, and his fine house on the Palatine.

'Are we nearly there?' he asked of Pasion, who had set the meeting up.

'It's not much further, master.'

'Why in Jupiter's name does he lodge here? An ambassador has access to . . . *funds*,' said Flamininus in a quiet voice. He answered himself before Pasion could. 'He doesn't want to be seen coming and going.'

'As you say, master. Staying in this quarter attracts little attention. Poor people don't care who their neighbour is, unless perhaps he has something worth stealing.'

Rather him than me, coming and going, thought Flamininus.

Visiting once was unpleasant enough. It was an experience that had to be endured, however. Since Galba's rabble-rousing speech to the Centuriate, the fear in Rome had risen to heights not seen since the nadir of the war against Hannibal. When the call went out for volunteers to the legions, thousands of poor citizens had flocked to the port of Brundisium, where Galba's army was already assembling.

Subterfuge was Flamininus' only option now. The man he was going to meet was an Aetolian emissary, once more sent by his ruling assembly to seek Rome's aid against King Philip. It would look suspicious to be seen together in public – the correct conclusion might be drawn – which explained Flamininus' need for secrecy.

He shook his head, no, at a butcher who proffered him a stringy lump of meat. Lip curling, he stepped around a bandage-wrapped leper who held up his nub-fingered hands in supplication. A beady-eyed urchin slipped in behind Pasion, who didn't notice. Flamininus, glancing around at his secretary, did. Quick as a flash, he dealt the brat a cuff that sent him reeling.

Pasion looked startled.

'He was about to cut your purse,' explained Flamininus, thinking it would have been easier to leave his secretary at home. He wasn't really needed: the Aetolian emissary spoke some Latin. No, Flamininus decided, it *was* better that Pasion was present, even if he had to be watched over like a small child. Their mission today was delicate, and Flamininus didn't want any misunderstandings because of language.

His skin crawled, the way it does when a man realises someone is looking. He turned his head, nice and slow. A trio of tough-looking, unshaven types propped against the wall of a tavern were staring at him and Pasion with an unpleasant degree of interest.

Flamininus pitched his voice low. 'Thrax.'

'I see them, master.' *Rap* went Thrax's cudgel off the road surface. A thick piece of wood, shod in iron at both ends, it looked dangerous to everyone but a halfwit, and in his hands, it promised to be lethal. The lowlifes were quick to look away.

The immature part of Flamininus wanted to make an obscene gesture as they passed, but in such a dangerous area, that would be akin to kicking a wasps' nest. He hid his satisfaction beneath the brim of his straw hat.

Around the next corner, Pasion inclined his head. 'That insula, master.'

Just another run-down apartment building, Flamininus would have walked past without a second glance. The wooden stairs that led up the structure's side were bedecked with half a dozen kohl-eyed women wearing close to nothing. A brothel operated on one floor, thought Flamininus. Perhaps the Aetolian preferred women, unlike so many of his kind.

'Where's his room?'

'At the top, master.'

'Of course it is,' said Flamininus. The rickety staircase looked as if it might fall at any moment. It was the least of his worries, he decided, casting a look back whence they had come. A figure rounding the corner made a sharp turn into an ironmonger's. Flamininus stared, but the man did not re-emerge. He'd been on his own, and the three lowlifes were bound to go everywhere together, Flamininus decided. The man had just been in a hurry.

Flamininus jerked his chin. 'Lead the way, Pasion.'

His secretary eased in front of Thrax, who frowned. 'Better if I knock on his door,' said Pasion. 'You'd frighten him.'

Thrax grinned. His smile grew broader as they ascended, and the whores – who ignored Flamininus – fluttered about him like butterflies, promising extra favours and lower than normal prices.

'Not now,' said Thrax in his poor Latin. 'Working.'

In desperation, one offered a quickie for nothing, if he didn't mind doing it outside. 'The pimp expects his cut, you see,' she simpered. 'But he won't see us in the next alley.'

Flamininus was amused by the tone of regret in Thrax's 'No', and by the fact that the women seemed not even to see Pasion. His secretary, on the other hand, could not take his eyes off their bare flesh; by the time the little group reached the third storey, there was a distinct colour to his cheeks.

'Take a moment, Pasion,' ordered Flamininus, before adding mischievously, 'To catch your breath.'

Pasion assumed a prim expression. 'I'm ready, master.'

Flamininus took off his hat and settled his hair. He checked the heavy purse was still on his belt. 'And I.'

'Trouble.' Thrax's tone was matter-of-fact. 'On the street.'

Flamininus peered over the handrail. The three sewer rats of a few moments before were lounging against a wall opposite the stairs' base. His heart thumped a little. Pasion would be worse than useless in a fight. He, Flamininus, could handle himself, but didn't fancy a struggle with men who'd lived their entire lives on the streets. Thrax would deal with one of the filth, probably two, but three? This meeting had taken days to arrange; to have it compromised by scum of the lowest variety was infuriating. They were also in real danger, thought Flamininus. His life – all their lives – were in Thrax's hands.

He glanced at the Thracian. 'What should we do?'

'You go meeting. I fight fuckers. Meet after.'

Flamininus had not expected that response. His eyes searched the doorman's face; it was serene, as if Thrax had described going for a walk by the Tiber with one of the whores downstairs.

He's not joking, thought Flamininus, with another sly look down at the street. He pondered his options. If he didn't appear, the Aetolian, not knowing about the fight, might panic and refuse another meeting. The cursed Greek could even disappear; that was something Flamininus was not prepared to countenance. Thrax *would* deal with the three lowlifes, he decided.

'Very well,' said Flamininus, giving Thrax an approving nod. 'Pasion and I will go inside, while you . . . fight the fuckers.'

Thrax nodded. Whistling happily, he set off downstairs without a backward glance.

'Right,' said Flamininus, Thrax's confidence making him feel for once like the servant instead of the master. 'Shall we?'

Pasion's face was scared. 'Thrax, master? He . . .?'

'Knows what he's doing,' Flamininus declared. 'Let's talk to the Aetolian.'

'Master.' Pasion's smile was more of a grimace. He led the way inside.

Flamininus followed. He had never been inside an insula before, and it didn't impress. A low-roofed, narrow passageway led into the depths of the building. Every five to six paces, a door marked the entrance to a cenaculum. Many were open, affording a glimpse inside. In the first, a straggle-haired, exhausted-looking woman breastfed a baby while three small children screamed and fought on the floor by her feet. In another, a dog whined at a crone who lay unmoving – dead? – on a straw pallet. Incurious, sunken-cheeked faces stared back at Flamininus from several. The entire place reeked of unwashed humanity, urine and smoke. It was a grim view into the underbelly of Roman life, and he didn't care for it. He focused on Pasion's back.

Remember why you're here, he thought.

His secretary came to a halt at a door near the corridor's end. 'This is it,' he whispered.

Flamininus put on his best nobleman's face. He nodded.

Pasion placed his knuckles on the timber, and rapped, one, two three. One, two.

There was a short delay. Footsteps echoed within the cenaculum beyond. 'Who's there?' called a voice in accented Latin.

Pasion cleared his throat. 'Leonidas, with a friend.'

Flamininus almost laughed. The famed king of Sparta was not the figure he would have picked for Pasion's alter ego.

The door opened, revealing a short, olive-skinned man in a fine himation. Handsome, with neat curls of jet-black hair, a straight nose and even features, he was perhaps thirty-five. 'Well met, Leonidas.' He caught Flamininus' eye, and held out his hand. 'My name is Metrodoros.'

'Horatius.' The lie was obvious, but they shook.

'Please, enter,' said Metrodoros.

Flamininus hesitated. For all he knew, six men with ready swords were waiting inside the apartment.

'I am alone,' said Metrodoros, reading his mind.

Discomfited at being seen through with such ease, Flamininus strode in as if entering his own house. The room was larger than the others he'd glanced into; two cenacula had been knocked into one. A curtain divided the chamber in half; the portion he could see was the living area. Four stools stood around a low table, on which a jug and several beakers sat. A brazier occupied one corner; shelves above held crockery and cooking implements. Flamininus strode to the curtain and, pulse increasing, pulled it back. An unmade bed, a document-covered desk and another stool met his eyes.

— Behind him, Metrodoros chuckled. 'I would do the same.'

Flamininus gave him a stiff nod.

'Please excuse the, shall we say, *simple* furnishings.' Metrodoros picked up the jug and poured. 'The wine is Greek, although it could be better. I couldn't find the finest Aitolian here in Rome, you see, but I think you'll agree this rivals most Italian varieties.' He saluted Flamininus with his cup, and threw back a hearty mouthful.

Just because Metrodoros had drunk didn't mean the wine wasn't poisoned, thought Flamininus. He had heard of men who consumed tiny amounts of toxins daily, thereby making themselves immune. That's not happening here, he told himself. What possible reason could he have to murder me? Selecting a cup, Flamininus returned Metrodoros' salutation and took a swallow. The wine was strong, less diluted than the Roman fashion, with a characteristic earthy flavour. It was delicious, but Flamininus wasn't prepared to admit that.

'It's not bad.'

Metrodoros chuckled, and produced a platter of cheese and bread. 'Can I offer you food?'

'Shall we get down to business?' Flamininus understood that the Greeks liked to talk around an issue before getting to the point, but he was growing annoyed with the Aetolian's confidence. He was the one with the money here, the one with power.

'I always forget what plain speakers you Romans are.' Metrodoros offered Flamininus the stool facing the door, and took the one opposite. Pasion remained standing. Metrodoros fixed his gaze on Flamininus. 'You wish to talk about Aitolia's relations with Macedon.'

'I do. Your people are no friends of Macedonia.' Thanks to his spies, Flamininus knew this was still the case.

'Aitolia and Macedon have an awkward history,' said Metrodoros, with a wry twist of his lips. 'It troubles us that the Republic has now changed its mind, and is to make war on Macedon.'

'Yet here you are,' said Flamininus.

'Indeed.'

Both men knew that despite the brutal snub from the Senate two years before, the Aetolians had no chance of winning a war against Philip on their own. Flamininus decided not to rub Metrodoros' nose in it unless he had to. Better to win the man over.

'The Centuriate and Senate make their decisions in the best interests of the Roman people,' Flamininus declared. He had uttered the lie enough times for it to feel comfortable. 'What did not seem wise in the past can sometimes become a natural choice for the present.'

'As you say,' agreed Metrodoros, his eyes suggesting different.

'You are wondering no doubt why I am here.'

'It has been on my mind. My first thought was that you might offer help . . . so that the Senate would look favourably on Aitolia's request for aid.' Metrodoros meant he imagined Flamininus had come looking for a bribe.

Coin for votes, thought Flamininus. Ha!

Metrodoros saw something in his face, and for the first time, seemed uneasy. 'That is not your reason for meeting.'

Flamininus had decided on his course days before, but uttering it to a Greek, felt awkward – and disloyal. He steeled his resolve. The result for the Republic would be the same. Macedonia would be defeated, just by him, not Galba. He cleared his throat. 'It would be better if Aetolia were to remain neutral . . . for the moment.'

'Neutral, but not for ever.'

'That's correct.'

Metrodoros sipped his wine. 'Most men would think Rome might seek allies in Greece at this time. Aitolia is an obvious choice; our army could open a second front from which to attack Macedon. Without the Aitolian route into Thessaly, Galba will be restricted to two or three mountain valleys. Defending those will be easy for Philip, and the legions will suffer huge casualties.'

'Nevertheless, some . . . important politicians think it best if Aetolia takes no part in the coming war,' lied Flamininus. It was he alone who wished it, of course, to weaken Galba's chances of victory the following spring and summer. Succeed in that, and then in the consular elections, and Macedonia would be *his* ripe apple to pluck.

'I see.' Metrodoros' curious eyes flickered to Pasion, and back to Flamininus, but he held back from asking more. 'What you are asking could prove tricky.'

Metrodoros thinks he can extract a fortune from me now, thought Flamininus. Time to drop the pretence. 'Philip has ever been an aggressive king, and bears nothing but ill will towards Aetolia. It is no wonder that the majority of your assembly wish to enter into an alliance with Rome.'

'You are well informed.' There was a new respect in Metrodoros' voice.

'More than you could know. Like our Senate, your assembly has factions. Secure the support of the largest two, and almost any motion will be passed. Nikomedes and Lykeles are the men who need to be persuaded.' Flamininus chuckled at Metrodoros' continued surprise.

'It is uncommon for a Roman to know so much about our affairs.'

'I am no ordinary Roman,' said Flamininus without a trace of irony.

'You are not,' Metrodoros said, and raised his cup again. 'Nikomedes is a reasonable man. Lykeles, now, he's a different type.'

'By which I presume you mean that Nikomedes is not quite as greedy as Lykeles.'

'Even so.'

Flamininus' purse landed on the table between them. 'That should serve as a preliminary payment for both, plus a little for yourself.'

'May I?'

'Be my guest,' said Flamininus, thinking, every man has his price.

Metrodoros could not conceal his greed as he first weighed the bag in his hand, and then looked inside. 'More funds—'

'Will be available,' said Flamininus. He continued, 'I have agents in Aetolia who will provide you with the monies to win over Nikomedes, Lykeles and anyone else who needs persuading. Should Aetolia remain neutral into next summer, *you* will receive three times the sum in your hands.'

'And if I were to refuse your offer?'

'That would not be wise.'

They stared at one another. Metrodoros was first to look away.

'How shall we communicate?' he muttered.

Flamininus indicated Pasion. 'You can write to Leonidas.'

'And after next summer?'

'Aetolia shall act as it wishes,' answered Flamininus. By the autumn, he thought, I will be consul, gods willing. The Aetolian army can augment my own.

'It's a delay, then, nothing more,' said Metrodoros, looking pleased.

'You could call it that.' The last of Flamininus' guilt about hindering the Republic's foreign policy disappeared.

'I am sure the assembly members will listen to common sense,' said Metrodoros. Something passed across his face and was gone.

The prick imagines he can take my money and disappear, thought Flamininus. Safe in Aetolia, he will have nothing to fear from a politician in Rome.

A heavy rap on the door made everyone jump.

'Who knows you are here?' whispered Metrodoros.

'No one,' said Flamininus, wishing that he had come armed.

'Open. It is Thrax.'

Delighted, Flamininus waved at Pasion.

Thrax tramped in, cudgel in hand. He had a cut under one eye. Blood dripped from a slash along his left forearm. Looking alarmed, Metrodoros made to rise, but Flamininus waved him back down. 'He's my slave.'

Metrodoros obeyed reluctantly.

'You're hurt,' said Flamininus.

'Only scratch. Safe outside now,' Thrax pronounced in a satisfied tone.

'They're gone?' asked Flamininus.

Thrax made a contemptuous noise. 'One dead. Another with broken arm. Third ran away – coward.'

'They were simple cutpurses, nothing else,' Flamininus explained to a startled Metrodoros. 'Scum who followed us along the street.' A memory tickled the back of his mind, and was gone.

Metrodoros looked a little less unhappy. 'If word reached the Senate about this meeting—'

'It's nothing like that, I assure you,' said Flamininus, his skin crawling.

Most senators would view his actions as collaboration with a foreign power. Exile would be the least he could expect, but forced suicide was more likely. You're worrying about nothing, he told himself.

'You have little to fear from men like those. I, on the other hand, have a longer reach than you can imagine. It extends to Athens, to Macedonia and Corinth. Even in little Aetolia, there are men who do my bidding. Steal my money, or fail to do as you have agreed, and Thrax – or someone like him – will come knocking on your door. Understand?'

Face taut with fear, Metrodoros nodded.

Flamininus drained his wine and stood. 'Come, Pasion, Thrax. We had best get that wound looked at.'

The carnage that greeted Flamininus outside was satisfying. One cutpurse's body lay in the middle of the street, a gaggle of onlookers around him. The reason for his demise – an unnatural angle between his head and neck – was clear. Of the other two thugs, there was no sign.

Flamininus glanced at Thrax. 'Excellent work.'

Thrax leered.

The Thracian had done well, thought Flamininus, and not just by ridding him of the lowlifes. His blood-spattered arrival could not have been better timed. Metrodoros *would* do as he'd been paid to. In the spring, Galba's position would be weakened by Aetolia's refusal to join with Rome. Forced to attack Macedonia through the mountains, he would, with the gods' help, be defeated by Philip. That setback would open the way for Flamininus to win election as consul, thereafter taking charge of the war against Macedonia. He felt not the slightest qualm in praying for Philip to emerge victorious from the initial hostilities.

Flamininus was so pleased that he didn't spot the shadowy figure watching from an alleyway opposite.

CHAPTER XX

Illyrian/Macedonian border, autumn 200 BC

Pine-covered hills ran along the valley's sides, their dark green contrasting with the vivid blue of the winding river at its bottom. Little farms occupied the flat ground, connected by a rutted track that ran roughly north-west towards the coast. Stubbled fields – the harvest had not long been taken in – sat beside small, fenced pastures in which flocks of sheep usually grazed. Now the fields were empty, like the farmhouses; rumour of the Romans' approach had sent the area's inhabitants hurrying to the local strongholds. Apart from a few mountain goats, the only living creatures were a pair of eagles, gliding the thermals high above.

The noise came first: the heavy, repetitive tramp of thousands of marching men. Soon after, the army came into sight around a bend in the valley. Mounted scouts – Numidians – rode at the front, followed by the velites. After came the hastati, principes, the wagon train and at the rear, the triarii. The single legion had been on the march for days, leaving the main body of Galba's host by the coast, at the mouth of the River Apsus. With the consul stricken by a sudden fever, Praetor Lucius Apustius had been sent inland with orders to ravage Macedonian territory. Success had followed success, and among his troops, morale was high.

Felix and Antonius were with the principes, and roaring a coarse but popular marching song. The first seeds of comradeship had been sown at the recruiting ground near Brundisium, and the bond had been strengthened since their arrival in Illyria. Victory in each of three small-scale battles had served to cement it further.

What was most important, as Felix often said, was the fact that they had a good centurion. Titus Pullo was every bit the officer that Matho had been, minus the cruelty. Experienced, brave and charismatic, Pullo was tough but fair.

'Follow my rules,' he'd warned on the first day, 'and you'll be all right. Break 'em, and you *will* pay.' Pullo's manner of speaking was the opposite to Matho's shouting, quiet yet terrifying. Despite the difference, hardly a day went by when terror didn't clutch at Felix, thinking his old centurion was close by.

As usual, the instigator of the singing was Hopalong. Finishing the rendition with a rousing verse about a soldier and his favourite whore, Hopalong somehow managed to perform a half-bow as he marched. Cheers, jeers and appreciative wolf whistles rained down.

'Very funny.' Yet again Pullo had appeared close to Felix and his comrades' position.

'Thank you, sir,' replied Hopalong, casting a wary look at Pullo.

Pullo gave him what passed for a smile, and ran his eyes over the rest of the rank. Every man straightened his back and hoped the centurion didn't spot any problems with their kit or weapons. Felix tried to calm his racing heart – Matho was nowhere near, he told himself. Ten uncomfortable paces went by before Pullo moved on without a word. A sigh of relief left every throat.

'How does he do that?' asked Hopalong, his good humour returning.

'My old centurion was just the same,' said Fabius.

'So was ours,' said Felix and Antonius in unison. Dark images of Ingenuus' terrified face flashed before Felix's eyes.

Everyone laughed.

Felix hoped yet again that Pullo never discovered their dark secret. Fair he might be, but rules were rules. To the brothers' relief, the omens thus far were good. They were hale and hearty veterans, and it seemed their centurion cared about little more than that.

Pullo had not been the only hurdle to negotiate, however. The brothers had endured a nervous few days in the century before it became clear that no one had been in the legion they were pretending to have served in. Felix's nervousness had eased a little since, because men tended to talk about the war they were waging, not the one with Carthage.

'How many miles until we set up camp?' enquired Antonius.

'Four,' said Fabius and Narcissus.

'Three,' said Felix and Hopalong.

A prolonged but good-humoured argument followed, which saw almost a mile eaten up. The next mile was taken up by a dispute over whose turn it was to cook the evening meal – in the end, it was determined that Felix was the man – which left one or two miles, depending on who had been correct.

Pullo returned, announcing that the site wasn't far, and that they had the easy duty of standing guard that afternoon while the other half of the legion dug out the fortifications. The principes knew this – they had dug the ditch the day before, but they still cheered.

'Twenty miles is enough for any man,' declared Fabius when Pullo had gone. 'No need to spend two hours digging as well.'

'It was only sixteen miles today, you fool,' said Antonius.

Fabius' protests were drowned out by chants of 'sixteen', reducing the veteran to a glowering silence.

'He never learns,' said Antonius to Felix. 'A man who's bad at figures should keep quiet about it.'

'Fabius is the oldest. In his mind, he knows best.'

'Let him keep thinking that,' said Antonius. 'It keeps Pullo's eyes off the rest of us.'

Dawn came, sunny, dew-laden and cool. A trace of frost marked the high ground above the camp, underlining the fact that the campaign could not continue forever. Winter came fast in the mountains, and supplies would soon become impossible to find. The trumpets had sounded not long before, and in the principes' tentlines, men were cooking breakfast and donning their kit. The talk was the same as it had been around the fires the previous night, of Antipatreia, a nearby stronghold of the Dassaretae, a tribe allied to Macedonia.

The town blocked the legion's path eastward, and Apustius had declared that taking it would be their next objective. This information and little more had been relayed by the centurions to the legionaries. Felix had served long enough to want to know the dangers he was to face, and so after Pullo had retired, he had gone to the Numidian cavalry tentlines with a skin of wine. Within an hour, he had been able to tell his comrades that Antipatreia occupied a strong position on one side of a narrow gorge. A steep mountain sat at the town's back, while a river wound sinuously around more than half its diameter. High walls circled it. From the empty farms and villages round about, the Numidians judged the entire population within a ten mile radius to have taken refuge there.

'Those defences sound fucking impregnable,' said Fabius with a scowl.

'Talking like that doesn't help anyone,' Felix warned. 'Pullo will see us right.'

'I'll do my best,' Pullo muttered in his ear. He leered as Felix jumped. 'Someone stood on your tail?'

'No, sir. You startled me is all,' said Felix.

'An old man shouldn't be able to creep up on a youngster like you. Especially when I'm in armour.' Pullo's quiet voice was terrifying.

'No, sir,' said Felix.

'We've got our orders, you pieces of shit.' Pullo faced the comrades, hands on hips. 'The assault will begin against the front wall at dawn tomorrow. When every sentry's eyes and ears are focused on that, a select number of troops already in place among the trees on the slopes above the back of the town will launch a surprise attack. Gaining the rampart, they will proceed to the front gates and open them.'

Wily bastard. He makes the options sound like a stroll through the woods, thought Felix. Both would prove dangerous in the extreme.

'Will we be part of the frontal attack, sir?' Fabius had asked the question in everyone's mind.

Pullo looked amused. 'No.'

Hope flared in Narcissus' eyes – with limited access to the walls, not every soldier in the legion could participate. Felix shared a wary glance with Antonius, however. Pullo wasn't the type to come with news that they would wait to follow the rest of the army into battle.

'You're to spend the day felling trees, and making ladders,' said Pullo. He grinned as understanding blossomed on the principes' faces. 'You guessed right, fools. Our maniple has been given the honour of taking the rear wall. Are you ready for that?'

The principes hid their apprehension. 'Yes, sir!'

'We leave straight after you've eaten. You should have enough trees knocked by midday, perhaps sooner. Finish the ladders quick enough, and I'll give you the rest of the day off. I'm told the river's warm enough to swim in.'

Their morale boosted by this pleasing prospect, Felix and the rest gave him fierce nods.

*

Felix, Antonius and the rest of Pullo's century were hidden among the last trees above the back wall of Antipatreia, with the other half of the maniple close by. Darkness coated the town still, but above the mountains to the east, the sky was lightening. Their long wait was almost over, and Felix was glad. Late the evening prior, they'd had a hot and sweaty climb up the mountain's opposing face, followed by a precipitous starlit descent towards Antipatreia. One man in the century had died, and another broken a leg. Many had turned their ankles, or torn open their shins. Incandescent at the noise made by the unfortunates who'd fallen, Pullo had ranged to and fro, issuing dire threats to anyone who caused a rockfall, no matter how minor.

Whether it was thanks to his threat, or because Fortuna's mood had changed, Felix didn't know, but the rest of their dangerous journey had passed without incident. Brought by the scouts to a small clearing hidden from Antipatreia's walls, they had settled down in their cloaks. Banned from lighting a fire, guts churning every time Pullo materialised out of the darkness and at the thought of the morrow, Felix had had little sleep. Any time he had dropped off, he relived the fustuarium again, feeling Ingenuus' skull crack beneath his hobs.

Pullo was wise to their stiff muscles and low spirits. Before they had moved a step from the hiding place, he'd had the men stretch out. Producing a wineskin, he had given everyone a slug. The strong, undiluted liquid had tasted to Felix like nectar of the gods; even now, it warmed his belly. Pullo's quiet words of encouragement, muttered to each huddled group, had fallen like spring rain on seedling plants. First they would take the wall, he had whispered, and after, the front gate. Succeed in that, and the town was theirs.

Then would come the opportunity for plunder, thought Felix. Booty was supposed to be shared with everyone, but small valuable items tended to vanish into men's purses. He gave no consideration to Apustius' order to spare only women and children. The Dassaretae inhabiting the town had slain many legionaries in ambushes as the army approached Antipatreia. The men among them deserved to die, and the remainder to be enslaved.

'Listen!' Pullo was a few paces to Felix's right. 'D'you hear that?'

'Aye, sir,' said Felix, grinning at the noise of marching men. Despite their elevated position, the walls hid the approaching legion from the principes' sight.

'It won't be long now. Stay alert.' Pullo vanished into the gloom.

Felix studied the sentries, of which there appeared to be four. It wasn't many for the length of defences they had to watch over, but two hundred paces of open ground separated the walls from the nearest trees, and above that, the steep slope was further protection from attack. Pullo had already told his men that they would be spotted after breaking cover.

'Don't think about it,' he'd warned. 'Four sentries can't stop us. Concentrate on getting your ladder into place, and climbing that fucking wall.'

Trumpets sounded below Antipatreia, and Felix swallowed. There was no mistaking the order to advance. Their own time was drawing near. Three men were to carry each ladder. He, his brother and Narcissus had one; the others in their under-strength contubernium a second. The maniple had thirty ladders in total. When the principes reached the bottom of the walls, one man would hold the ladder steady, leaving the others to climb.

'Ready?' hissed Felix at his brother.

'Aye.' Antonius twisted to look at Narcissus. 'Ready?'

'Yes. Are we—'

A sudden clamour rang out below: shouts, weapons clashing, screams.

Pullo let the fighting go on for the space of five score heartbeats. In that time, two sentries had disappeared, to check what was happening, Felix assumed. The remaining pair had come together far off to the right, on a spot that probably had a view of the front wall. Both had their backs turned to the trees and the slope above.

'*Now!*' ordered Pullo. '*Move!*'

Felix shot to his feet, the ladder in his right hand, shield in his left. A quick check that Antonius and Fabius were ready, and he was moving forward. Great care was needed, for the slope was almost as vertiginous as at the mountain's peak: scree-covered ground, with scrubby bushes and pine saplings dotted here and there. Felix wanted to keep an eye on the sentries, but had to keep his gaze fixed on what was beneath his feet.

Rocks moved behind him, and the ladder jerked.

'You all right?' Felix hissed.

Antonius cursed, long and hard. 'I skinned a knee, that's all.'

Thirty paces they had gone. Felix risked a glance at the top of the defences. The two sentries were in the same position.

Keep them there, Jupiter, he prayed.

At eighty paces, knees trembling with the exertion of their descent, they took a moment to rest. On either side, the slopes were alive with their ladder-bearing comrades. Still the sentries hadn't heard. Down the principes went, skidding and scrambling towards the wall.

With so many on the move, it was inevitable that someone would slip. The lead man on one ladder overreached his step; the rock he stood on shifted as his weight came onto it. Both hands full, he pitched helplessly onto his face, in the process tumbling his comrades and setting off a small rock slide. The ensuing racket would have woken a drunken Bacchus from sleep.

Felix looked up to see a pair of terrified faces peering over the rampart. Estimating the distance to the bottom of the wall to be sixty paces, he took heart. Pullo had been right. Four men couldn't stop two ladders slamming up against the defences, let alone thirty.

Fffffewww. A spear hummed down close to Felix. Sparks flashed as the point struck a boulder, sending the missile skittering to one side.

The whoreson's aiming at me, thought Felix with a lurch of fear. 'Come on!' he cried at Antonius and Narcissus.

They covered another fifteen paces.

Fffffewww. A spear hit the ground halfway between them and the next group over. Felix shot another glance upwards. One sentry was staring right at him, right arm cocked back to throw. Felix's bowels twisted; he could almost feel the barbed iron sinking into his flesh.

What a stupid way to go, he thought. Killed on a stony hillside in Macedonia, outside a shithole settlement that no one's ever heard of.

With that, his left ankle twisted. Knee bending of its own accord, unstable with the loads he was carrying, Felix wobbled and went down. His shin cracked off a rock, and a heartbeat later, he narrowly avoided opening his cheek on a sharp-edged stone. Wheezing with pain, half-winded, he heard a spear whistle through the place his head had been.

'Felix! Are you hurt?' Antonius' voice.

'I'll live.' Pain lashed him, and blood was running from a gash on his shin, but Felix was grinning. If he'd stayed upright, the missile would have skewered him through the head.

'Get up,' urged Antonius. 'The sheep-humper on the rampart isn't done with us.'

Felix clambered to his feet and they started forward again. The sentry's chance had been and gone, he decided. Fortuna had made him stumble, and she'd see him through the attack.

Sure enough, they reached the base of the wall without difficulty. A handful of comrades had been injured by the sentries' spears, but the rest were there. Clambering into the defensive ditch, the trio worked the foot of the ladder into the earth, and swung it into place against the stones. The scouts had estimated the wall's height well: it was the right length.

Felix happened to be at the ladder's base. He licked his lips. The first man up risked the most, but to step away would force either Antonius or the inexperienced Narcissus to go in his place.

'Hold the bastarding thing steady,' he said, and set his foot on the first rung.

CHAPTER XXI

The fortress of Demetrias, on the
Pagasean Gulf, north of Euboea

Philip was standing outside his tent, a terrified messenger before him. His camp sprawled all around; in it were five thousand of his light infantry and three hundred Companions. Since returning from Asia Minor and his campaign to control the Propontis, there had been no rest. Word of Galba's arrival at Apollonia had reached him, but in light of the shortening year, Philip had decided to leave the Romans well alone. Galba would be similarly constrained by the poor weather and lack of supplies. There was time, however, to teach the Athenians a lesson, and so he had marched to Demetrias, one of the three 'Fetters of Greece', fortresses that protected Macedon from invasion to the south. Before his plans could be realised, he'd had unexpected and unwelcome news from the man in front of him. It was galling to learn that he was not the only one who refused to sit on his hands.

'Tell me again,' ordered the king, his lips a thin white line.

The messenger, who had come from Chalkis, another of the 'Fetters of Greece', swallowed.

'Fear not,' said Philip in a gentler tone. 'You will come to no harm.'

A pathetic nod of gratitude. 'Chalkis was attacked two days hence, sire. Unbeknownst to us, the Romans sailed up from Athens by night. Their assault began at dawn, when the gates were being opened. The sentries were overcome; because of the hour, most of the garrison was abed. The fortress fell soon after.' The messenger paused, still wary of the king's temper.

Seething, Philip gestured for him to continue.

'The Romans burned the arsenal and the granaries, sire, and freed several hundred Athenian prisoners. They didn't have enough men to hold the place, thank the gods, so they withdrew to their ships and returned to Athens.'

'And Sopater was killed?'

'Yes, sire.'

The Romans were clever bastards, Philip decided. Situated on the southern coast of Euboea, Chalkis was of vital importance; from it, his forces could launch attacks on Boeotia and Attika with ease. His governor Sopater had been one of his best generals, or so Philip had thought. It was as well, he decided darkly, that Sopater was dead.

'This cannot go unanswered.'

'Sire?' quavered the messenger.

Philip had spoken out loud without realising. 'You did well.' He clasped the messenger's hand, then cast around for a servant. 'See that this valiant man is tended to.'

'What are we to do, sire?' asked one of his staff officers.

'Why, the obvious,' replied Philip, smiling at his officer's confusion. 'We shall attack Athens.'

Philip rode at the forefront of his army with his Companions; at his back marched his five thousand light infantry. Attika lay at his feet; in the middle distance, he could see the walls of Athens, and atop the Acropolis hill, the majestic Parthenon. Less than ten days had passed since the calamitous news about Chalkis had come to him at Demetrias. Sailing at once to Euboea, he had visited the ruined fortress before crossing the narrow waterway to Boeotia.

Its land was some of the best in Greece; Philip had made the most of it, raiding every farm in his path. The few wagons he had brought lumbered far to the rear of his army; they were now laden down with grain, apples and wine. He cared nothing for the peasants whose food had been requisitioned. More than a century had passed since Boeotia and Macedon had been allies: these days, Athens was its master. Let the dusty-footed yokels crawl there to beg for aid, thought Philip. A tight smile played across his lips. His rapid journey – made far quicker than Greek armies were used to – meant that, with a little luck, the Athenians had no idea he was coming. He would do to the city what had been done to Chalkis, and curse the consequences. All thoughts of an alliance with the Athenians were gone – now Philip wanted them to suffer.

The first inkling that his arrival had not gone unnoticed came soon after. Responding to the threat of Macedon some hundred and forty years before, Athens' defences had been strengthened by the construction of outer walls, which protected the ground around the city. Today, the first of these lay abandoned. In rising fury, Philip rode through open gates and past more empty ramparts. Smoke still trickled from barrack roofs; the horse manure outside the stables was fresh and moist. The flowers on some roadside tombs looked to have been picked that very morning. No voices echoed in the prestigious school founded by Aristotle. Someone had seen them on the march, he decided, and ridden to Athens with the news. Every soul outside the city had fled to safety. There would be no glorious surprise attack as the perfidious Romans had done at Chalkis.

Incensed, Philip rode in silence for several stadia. Pride prevented him from considering retreat. To do so would send the message that he feared confrontation, that he was intimidated by Athens' mighty defences. They drew nearer, until the guards' helmets atop the rampart were visible, shining in the sun. Philip could imagine their glee. Given time, he would have wiped the smiles from their faces, but with winter nigh – the lowering rain clouds overhead were a pointed reminder of its approach – a wiser move would be to deliver a short, sharp shock, a lesson for the arrogant, look-down-their-noses Athenians to remember him by.

As the Dipylon, the city's north-western entrance, came into sight, Philip knew exactly what he would do. A large rectangle with towers at each corner, the Dipylon's twin double doors formed the shorter sides. The space between granted the defenders four fields of fire on anyone who sought to enter. The first set of gates was open, and standing inside, in a clear challenge – they might as well have insulted Philip's mother – were hundreds of soldiers and cavalry.

He rode towards the walls until he was at the outer limit of arrow range. Turning his back in contempt on the men watching from the battlements, he faced his Companions. Although many seemed nervous, their ranks were steady. Behind, his soldiers, who had followed Philip the length and breadth of Greece, and over the seas to the Kyklades and Asia Minor, were also ready. He loved them in that moment with a fierce passion that subsumed all else.

'See how the yellow-livered Athenians cower behind their walls?' he thundered. 'They offer battle only where they can rely on archers and catapults!'

His men jeered and hurled insults at the defenders, and the troops waiting in the Dipylon.

There was no response, which frustrated Philip. See if they can resist this, he thought, riding towards one of the many tombs that lay on either side of the road leading from the gate. A common enough depiction – a magnificent sculpture of a naked youth striding forward – it commemorated a young Athenian who had died in battle for his city. He barked an order.

In no time, lengths of rope had been tied to the statue's legs. Philip gestured with his long spear, and a dozen soldiers brought it crashing to the ground. The head broke off and went rolling towards the walls. Cries of dismay carried to Philip, and he smiled. A nod saw his men move to another similar statue. By the time he had watched four fall, there was noticeable disorder among the troops in the Dipylon.

Few men can bear to see their comrades, or even their antecedents, dishonoured so, thought Philip. This was his moment. 'Ready!' he called to his Companions. 'Ready!'

He rode casually to the front of his riders, faced the enemy, and without hesitation, cried, 'Charge!' Philip's well-trained horse went from standing still to the canter within two heartbeats. At his back swarmed three hundred Companions. 'Wedge,' he shouted.

Less than ten score paces separated them from the first set of doors. The enemy troops stood perhaps forty paces further in. Their lines began to waver the instant they saw Philip coming. A mad elation consumed him. No one had expected an attack. He paid no heed to the archers atop the ramparts; he did not hear the artillery officers as they screamed at their men to take aim. His ears were filled with the sound of pounding hoofs; his vision narrowed to the line of infantry – they were Pergamene, he saw with delight, not Athenian – straight in front of him.

Some soldiers are trained to stand against a cavalry charge, but few are ever tested in this regard. Philip's gamble paid off in royal style, for the Pergamenes had done neither. Fifty paces before the Companions closed, their formation fell apart like a poorly built wall struck by a catapult stone. Controlling their horses with their knees, the king and his riders levelled their long *xyston* spears and closed with the crumbling enemy ranks.

In the years since Philip had last led a cavalry charge, he had forgotten the exhilaration, and the fear. He had height, speed and momentum on his side, but was vulnerable to determined opponents who got inside the reach of his xyston. Given the enemy's panic, that would not happen soon, he decided with a devilish glee. Wielding his spear two-handed, he buried the point in a terrified-looking Pergamene's throat. His mount collided with another soldier, smashing him to the ground. Already passing his first victim, Philip ripped his xyston free.

A braver Pergamene rushed in, spear raised high, and Philip whipped the metal-shod butt of the xyston into the man's face, bursting his nose like an overripe plum. The Pergamene fell back and was gone. Someone screamed as he was trampled by Philip's horse. The next two men in his path turned in blind panic and tried to force a way through their comrades. Philip leaned out and stabbed one above the top of his linen cuirass. The other dodged sideways, and the next stroke of the xyston skidded down his armour to sink into the meat of his left thigh. Hamstrung, the soldier went down, crying like a baby.

'Sire!'

The cry, from a Companion to Philip's rear, saved his life. A Pergamene without shield or spear came charging in from his left, a curved dagger in his fist. Philip had just enough time to swing the xyston up in front of him, transfer his grip on the shaft and level its butt. The man tried to go left, and Philip dunted him in the helmet, sending him staggering back a couple of paces. Right went the Pergamene, lower this time. Philip smacked him again with the spear butt, but couldn't prevent the man from closing. He swung a booted foot, and missed.

Back went the dagger, and Philip saw his death in it. There was no time to get his xyston around. He bellowed an order. Battle-trained, his horse turned sharply to the left. Its shoulder struck the Pergamene and bowled him over like a child's doll. Before the man could right himself, Philip's xyston butt had sunk deep into his eye socket, and run on into his brain. A couple of powerful tugs freed the butt from the Pergamene's skull, and panting heavily, Philip returned the xyston to his right side.

There was a little space to breathe, and he cast a look around him. Utter chaos reigned in the confined space. Wails and battle cries competed with the whinnies of injured horses. Dust rose in clouds.

Companions and Pergamenes mingled even as they thrust at one another. High above, the archers could not pick safe targets; nor could the artillerymen. His mad attack had succeeded thus far because they had taken their enemies by surprise. The tables would soon turn, however.

On the Pergamenes' flanks Philip spied files of Athenian hoplites. Seasoned soldiers with good officers, they were moving forward of their panicked comrades. Any moment, they would wheel inwards. They did, and Philip's breath caught in his chest. A barked order, and the hoplites advanced, the first three ranks' spears down. The move was risky – both sets of hoplites were leaving the side of their formations nearest the open gate vulnerable to attack – but the Companions were no longer grouped together. The hoplites had already squeezed them into a smaller space, and every moment that they stayed gave the archers and men on the catapults opportunity to shoot. Arrows were already hissing down; he had seen one horse badly injured.

'Withdraw!' Philip shouted. 'Pull back!'

His men were well disciplined, and responded at once. In threes and fours, in sixes and eights, they rode out of the Dipylon. Mad though it was, Philip stayed behind long enough to skewer one last Pergamene. By the time he urged his mount towards safety, the archers were aiming at *him*. The bolt from a catapult thunked into the ground close by, and he laughed.

Philip laughed all the way back to his infantry, who had remained, by his earlier order, where they were. Bolts shot by frustrated artillerymen fell to earth short of their position; defenders yelled their impotent anger. With his back again to the defences, Philip acted as if he were alone with his troops. The Companions reformed under his eagle eye; within fifty heartbeats of returning, they were assembled in neat ranks, facing the city walls once more. It was impossible to know without a headcount how many had fallen, but it hadn't been more than five or six, he decided, a fraction of the casualties they had inflicted on the cowardly Athenians and their craven Pergamene allies.

Philip was delighted by this, and by his men's bravery. He told them so, and when he asked if they'd attack the walls next, the Companions bayed their assent. Rather than that, he shouted, he would offer them another target. Out of earshot of the defences, he announced they would make for the nearby fortress of Eleusis. Seizing it would deal Athens a grievous blow, and make its leaders realise that allying themselves with Macedon's enemies offered scant protection.

There were either friends, Philip decided, or enemies. Nothing in between.

CHAPTER XXII

Antipatreia

Hobnailed sandals were excellent on soft ground, but treacherous everywhere else. Felix's feet skidded off the rungs, and he slowed his ascent. Fall, and he would hit the next man as well as injuring or killing himself below. He threw caution to the wind only a moment later. The biggest sentry had knocked two ladders off the wall by pulling one sideways into the other. If he chose Felix's next, Hades beckoned.

Somehow he reached the battlements unharmed, and with the help of another princeps, dispatched the big sentry. The second died next, leaving a safe climb for the rest of the maniple. Felix clattered down the nearest set of stairs with Antonius and Narcissus to secure their access into the town. To his surprise, Narcissus had done nothing stupid yet.

Not a soul was in sight; anyone inside the simple mud brick houses that backed up to the wall was keeping well hidden. Soon both centuries had assembled, the principes' faces fierce and eager.

'We have no fucking clue where the main gate is, other than it's down there somewhere,' Pullo announced to his men, pointing south. Loud sounds of fighting bore out his direction. 'Speed is vital, brothers. Our comrades are fighting and dying outside the front wall. They're *relying* on us. We can't stop, for any reason. Fall behind, and you're on your own. Understand, fools?'

'Aye, sir.'

'Felix, Antonius. With me, in the front rank. The rest of you, form up, three wide behind me.'

Pullo took up a position on the right of the column's front. With a nod at the other centurion, who was going to take a different street, he led his men into the nearest gap between the buildings.

The journey that followed would live on in Felix's mind. Thatched and tiled single-storey buildings pressing in from both sides. The mixture of dried mud and shit, both animal and human, beneath his sandals. Tight-shut doors, staring like so many blank eyes. The terrified face of a small boy, peering from a half-open window, and his mother's angry hiss that saw him vanish from view. Smoke eddying from a smithy's chimney, and the shocked expression of the hammer-wielding smith as they tramped past.

Their attack appeared to have caught the defenders off guard. Youths appeared and hurled abuse from a distance, their stones clonking harmlessly off the principes' helmets and shields. Urchins ran along the rooftops, throwing pieces of roof tile. Warriors on their own – messengers, like as not – took one look at the armoured column and fled. Only when they encountered a group of the enemy did Pullo's men have to fight.

The narrow street was easy to defend, and slowed the principes' progress to a crawl. Pushing forward with Felix and Antonius, Pullo shouted that twenty men at the back should break away into side alleys and flank the warriors. Their arrival soon after sowed panic among the enemy. During a short, brutal clash, the defenders were slain, or fled. Leaving five men to protect his wounded – it seemed Pullo wasn't as hard hearted as he maintained – they ran towards the sounds of fighting, which had grown louder.

Taking the gate proved easy. All but a handful of warriors were atop the ramparts, throwing spears and dropping boulders on the Roman attackers. Felix and the rest had merely to hack down the few men in their path, lift the locking bar and heave open the mighty portal. A wave of cheering legionaries swarmed in, eager as hounds that had cornered a wild boar.

'Well done,' said Pullo.

Wild-eyed, blood spatters covering his face, helmet and even the horsehair crest of his helmet, he was an awe-inspiring sight.

'Pul-lo!' Exhilarated at the ease with which their mission had been accomplished, grateful that it wasn't Matho before him, Felix battered his sword off his shield boss. 'Pul-lo!'

His comrades took up the chant, and the centurion's face creased into a brief smile. 'The town hasn't fallen yet, fools.'

'Where next, sir?' asked Antonius.

Every eye swivelled to Pullo, for from this point on, men would be out for booty and women rather than seeking out every last defender.

'Clear the section of rampart over the gate, and then it's up to you.'

Pullo was letting them off the leash, thought Felix as he charged, whooping, for the nearest stairs. He asked Jupiter to save him a pot of coins, or a nice stash of jewellery.

Night had fallen long since, but an ominous orange-red glow hung over Antipatreia. Thatched roofs were an attractive target for a thrown torch; men had held competitions to set houses alight. The blaze had spread in certain quarters, and threatened to get out of control, but the celebrations hadn't stopped. Gangs of marauding, drunk legionaries roamed the town, bloody weapons in hand, their bursts of laughter competing with bawdy renditions of songs and verse. Screams rang out now and again, and were cut short. Somewhere near the front gate, a baby shrieked. No one came.

Corpses filled the streets. Warriors, old men and boys for the most part, they lay where they had fallen: together, alone, trying to defend their comrades or loved ones. Some had gaping wounds in their throats, others neat, single stab wounds to the body. A few had been mutilated until they resembled hunks of badly butchered meat. Here an arm lay, the fingers of the hand still curled around a club, and there a joker had balanced half a dozen severed heads. The three on the ground belonged to youths; on the next row, two warriors grimaced, and perched at the top was the head of a terrified-looking greybeard.

Felix curled his lip. He'd killed his fair share of the enemy that day – four, or was it five? – but abusing the dead wasn't his way. He didn't move the heads, however. There was no point. Bleary-eyed, weary, yet still keen for plunder, he had left Antonius and his comrades drinking wine in the town's agora.

Everyone in his tent group had done better than he during the sack of the town. Narcissus had been luckiest, finding a bag of silver coins in the fist of a shopkeeper he'd killed – he was still crowing about it now. Antonius had won the contest when it came to wine, netting a haul of six middling-sized amphorae that he'd needed help to carry. Fabius had freed a fine sword with a silver-chased scabbard from a dead warrior's grip. Even Hopalong was in a better situation than Felix, who'd come away with nothing but a handful of coppers and a worn silver *fibula* ripped from a cloak. Chances were that anything worth taking was long gone, but he couldn't sit about getting pissed knowing that somewhere in Antipatreia, unfound riches remained.

He didn't bother searching near the front gate – the area had been swamped by legionaries in the aftermath of the gate opening. His best hope would be near the back wall, where he and his comrades had entered the town. Weaving – he was a bit drunk – his way in approximately the right direction, Felix investigated house after house without success. Antipatreia was a poor place, it seemed; most dwellings appeared to have had little worth taking *before* the legion's assault.

Families lived in cramped single-room buildings, reminding Felix of his childhood. Beaten earth floors were the norm, the only furniture stools and rickety tables. Beds were nothing more than straw-filled ticks covered with rough woollen blankets, material possessions the battered bronze pots hanging from walls, and the twig brooms leaning alongside. Tools were old and worn. Every house had a ceramic pot for night soil in one corner.

Felix lost count of the murdered and violated women and girls he found. Apustius would have been angered – each blood-coated, chiton-around-the-waist body was a slave that couldn't be sold for coin – but the legate hadn't been here when the legionaries had kicked in doors, the battle lust in total control. Felix had not partaken in the rapes. His comrades might have, but he hadn't seen them, nor would he ask. Some things were better left unknown.

Frustration growing at his lack of success, he tried several larger houses. All that greeted him were more corpses, smashed crockery and furniture. In one, a still chained-up guard dog whimpered in the hallway. Knowing how dangerous such animals could be, Felix approached with caution. The dog didn't even try to stand. A moment later, he saw the pink-grey loops of bowel hanging from its belly. He didn't hesitate. Even an animal deserved a better fate, he thought, wiping his sword clean on its thick coat.

He found a silver woman's necklace in one of the grand rooms beyond. It had fallen down the side of the bed. From the state of the girl's body on the floor nearby, searching for valuables hadn't been on her attackers' minds. Satisfied with his find, and tiring of the carnage, Felix decided to return to his comrades. A bellyful of wine would help drown the graphic images filling his mind, for tonight at least. With luck, Ingenuus wouldn't haunt him either.

He had walked perhaps halfway to the agora when the sound of running footsteps caught his ear. By the light footfall of the first and the metallic clash of the second, he knew one for a civilian, and the other a soldier. The pair were inside what appeared to be a warehouse. A soft thud, the noise of someone falling to the ground, was followed by a triumphant cry and a heartbeat later, a soon-muffled scream. More clashing footsteps and laughter announced the arrival of the soldier's companions.

Walk on, thought Felix. Walk on.

Instead he traced his way along the building's wall to a great, iron-bound door which lay ajar. Sword ready, eyes peeled, he took a step inside. Shrouded in shadow, the entrance area was empty, apart from a surprised-looking man lying in a pool of his own congealed blood. Felix cast about, listening at each of three doors before picking the central one. Placing his sandals with care, he made little noise as he traversed a darkened storeroom full of stacked lengths of timber, some shaped and planed, others fresh-hewn beech trunks. A work-shop followed. Guttering oil lamps on a stand outlined benches and tools, and in the middle of the floor, the body of a young male slave.

Muffled laughter, the noise of hobs moving about and a rhythmic panting could be heard from the next room. Heart banging off his ribs, Felix approached the doorway and peered in. Four legionaries, hastati from their armour, stood in a half-circle with their backs to him. Between their legs, he could see an oil lamp and two entwined bodies. The open thighs of one and the bunched, moving arse cheeks of the other confirmed his suspicions.

Five to one was poor odds, and Felix had no wish to die without reason. He turned to go.

'No! No!' The voice was high-pitched, female, and that of a young girl.

Felix hesitated.

A slap rang out, and the girl whimpered. 'Put your blade away,' said a voice. 'I want the bitch still to be breathing when I have her.'

The coarse laughter that followed masked the sound of Felix sheathing his sword. With his dagger in his right fist instead, he stole into the room. A short distance separated him from the hastati, and he'd covered most of it before anyone even heard him. By the time three of the men had turned, he had a tight hold on the fourth; his dagger tip rested against his captive's neck.

'What's going on, brother?' demanded the nearest hastatus, hands held palm outwards. 'You're one of us, no?'

'I'm Roman, aye,' snarled Felix. 'But I'm not like you filth.'

'You prefer boys, is that it?' The second hastatus to speak was hard-faced, with thick black stubble. He edged a few steps to Felix's left and sensing his intent, the first man moved in the opposite direction.

Felix shoved with his dagger, and his prisoner cried out. A fat drop of blood rolled down the blade. 'Come any closer, and your friend dies,' he warned.

'Do that, and *you're* dead meat,' retorted Black Stubble.

'Your friend with the wet prick isn't in any state to fight. I'll take at least two of you bastards with me, if not three.'

Black Stubble cast a look at his comrades, and Felix poked again with his dagger, making his captive moan.

'All right, all right,' said Black Stubble. 'What do you want?'

'Release the girl.'

An incredulous laugh. 'She's just a Dassaretae whore.'

'*Do it!*'

The hastatus on top of the girl rolled away, but she didn't move. Eyes closed, chest heaving with silent sobs, she was no more than twelve or thirteen years old.

'Get up.' Felix stumbled over the Greek words: he'd learned some from a merchant as a boy, but not used it since. The three hastati opposite shifted from foot to foot, and his skin tingled. They wouldn't hold back for long. 'Stand up, girl. I take you away.'

Her eyes opened, focused on him and the man he was holding hostage. Understanding dawned, and she sat up, trying to cover her nakedness with the shreds of her chiton.

'Go to the door,' said Felix.

Her bare feet made not a sound as she padded past. Felix's rage, already burning, turned white-hot as he saw the bloody prints she left behind. He wrenched his arm tighter, choking his victim, and pulled him backwards, towards the girl. 'Stay where you are,' he ordered the rest.

'What's your name, princeps?' demanded Black Stubble. 'What century are you in?'

'Screw yourself, cocksucker.' Felix reached the girl, gave her a reassuring nod. 'Make for the street. Keep close.' He shuffled back, forcing his victim to come too. 'Don't move,' he told the hastati. 'I'll let this maggot go when I reach the street.'

'What's to say you won't murder him?' cried the first hastatus.

'Nothing. If you don't obey, however, he *will* die.'

The hastati glowered and cursed, but they did as he said. Knowing that they would soon follow, as he would if one of his comrades had been attacked, Felix moved as fast as he could through the various rooms. The girl helped, directing him when he was close to doorways and other obstacles. At the warehouse's entrance, he let his prisoner go.

'Consider yourself lucky,' he warned.

'Cunt. You had no cause to interfere.' The hastatus' lip curled. 'You probably did it so you can have the girl yourself.'

Felix's fury erupted, and with a flick of his blade, he opened the man's cheek from eye to chin. 'We don't all rape children,' he snarled as the hastatus staggered away, holding his face.

Felix could hear movement within the warehouse – the other hastati weren't far. He took the girl's hand, and whispered in Greek, 'Come.'

'We're in the same legion, cunt!' the hastatus shouted. 'We'll find you!'

Unease tickled Felix's spine every step of the way back to the agora. Having enemies within his own legion was a problem he could do without.

CHAPTER XXIII

The royal palace, Pella,
Macedon, winter 200 BC

Several months had passed since Philip's lightning attack on Athens. Demetrios and his comrades had marched south with the king, and witnessed his daring assault on the Dipylon gate, but to their frustration, had had no chance of joining the fight. With all sides retired to their own territories since, the usual winter routines for soldiers still under arms had taken over. Life was a succession of training, marches and patrols. From time to time, men were selected to stand as sentries in the royal palace, which was where Demetrios now stood after a long night.

Spying the replacements walking up the corridor, he grinned. For hours, no one had passed the pair of grand doors that led into the king's quarters; muted conversation with his taciturn comrade Dion – one of the less welcoming front-rankers – had stuttered and failed several times. Demetrios was bored stupid. He was looking forward to his bed, and after that, a run around the *palaestra* and a bout of pankration, if an opponent could be found. A man had to stay active in winter if he wasn't to thicken around the middle. There was no chance that Dion would join him. One of the veterans in Simonides' file, he preferred to study the bottom of his cup in the city's many hostelries rather than exercise. Demetrios would have to persuade Antileon or Kimon.

Slap, slap went the new arrivals' sandals. One raised a hand in greeting.

Dion scowled. 'You're late.'

'How would you know?' retorted the older, a burly-chested type. 'There's no sundial in here.'

'You're supposed to relieve us at dawn.' Dion glanced at Demetrios for confirmation. 'The cock in the kitchen gardens has been crowing this hour and more.'

Dion was in a foul mood, thought Demetrios, and there was no need for an argument. 'It hasn't been that long.'

'There you are.' Burly Chest shrugged; so did his companion. 'Anything to report?'

Shorn of support, Dion let it go. 'No. The king is still abed.'

'He returned late last night, I heard.' Burly Chest mimed draining a cup, and winked.

Dion half-smiled; his love of wine was exceeded by Philip, who had been carousing since the army's return from Thrace.

Demetrios affected not to notice; in his mind, comments like these were disloyal to the king. 'We'll be off,' he said. 'I'm for my bed.'

Their replacements moved to stand either side of the door, and the pair left them to it. Dion began to yawn as they neared the gate that led into the rest of the palace. 'Gods, I'm weary.'

'Aye,' said Demetrios. 'Me too.'

'Fancy a quick cup before we turn in?'

Here we go, thought Demetrios. 'Not today.'

'Come on – you'll enjoy it once we're there.'

Demetrios had made the mistake of drinking with Dion once. 'It won't be one cup. Never is with you.'

Dion pulled a face. 'All right, so we have a few. What does that matter? We aren't on duty again for two days.'

'You'll still be propping up the bar at midday.'

'Watch your mouth, pup,' snapped Dion. 'I was fighting battles when you were on your mother's tit.'

Demetrios glowered. It was an exaggeration, but his experience paled beside that of Dion. Thirty years old, he'd been a phalangist for more than a decade, and had fought for the king in every part of Greece and beyond.

They walked on in prickly silence, passing through two colonnaded courtyards, each of which was surrounded by dining rooms, grand entertainment chambers and bedrooms for important guests. His belly rumbling, Demetrios eyed the vines that grew up the columns: since returning from the Thracian campaign, he'd been stealing the delicious grapes they'd borne every time he came off sentry duty. The plants were bare, however, and he remembered the harvest had been three days before. A touch of frost in the air had turned the leaves yellow; soon they too would fall.

Closer to the south of the palace, which faced into the city, lay the administrative heart used by Philip's officials. A hive of activity each day, the only people Demetrios saw this early were slaves sweeping the floors and through the open doors of offices, a few clerks at their desks.

Feeling something trail, he looked down. 'A lace has come undone. Don't wait.' Retying a sandal took time, and he and Dion were going to part ways at the main gate anyway.

'Aye.' Dion didn't slow.

Glad to be alone, Demetrios took his time setting his shield and spear against the wall. Kneeling, he partly undid the laces in order to tighten them, then carefully pulled each section taut. How they'd come undone in the first place was odd: he tended to use a double knot.

Low voices murmured in a nearby office. Demetrios paid no heed; desk clerks' gossip held no interest for him. Tired from his night's duty, he fumbled the laces and, cursing under his breath, had to start again.

One of the voices became loud enough to recognise.

Demetrios snapped upright. It was Kryton – he was sure of it. What in all the gods' names was his commander doing here, and so early? Finishing the knot, he crept towards the office. The door was almost closed, allowing him to approach without being seen.

'I shouldn't even be here,' said Kryton. 'I could leave right now.'

Alarmed, Demetrios' eyes shot to his spear and shield, a dozen steps away. It would be difficult to reach them *and* manage to look as if he were just walking along the corridor.

'But you won't,' said a sibilant voice. 'I haven't given you leave.'

Demetrios couldn't believe his ears. Herakleides was the admiral – what need had he of meeting a speira commander like Kryton?

'I should never have borrowed that money from you,' said Kryton.

'Gamble more wisely, and you wouldn't have had to,' replied Herakleides. 'When will the first repayment be?'

An exasperated sigh. 'I've told you a dozen times.'

'When you get paid. Soon, then?'

'Yes, yes.' Kryton paced to and fro. 'Why have you brought me here?'

'It's a delicate subject,' said Herakleides. 'Can I be sure of your discretion?'

Kryton swore. 'If word got out about my debts, my career would be over – you know that. My lips are sealed.'

A silence followed, in which Demetrios could imagine Herakleides smiling and studying Kryton's face. It was common knowledge in the speira that their commander was fond of gambling, but this was a step beyond. Heart thudding, Demetrios edged a step closer.

'Close the door,' ordered Herakleides.

Demetrios panicked. Darting back to his equipment, he snatched up sword and spear and moved as far from the office as he thought possible, before wheeling around to 'resume' his journey. Blank-faced, he walked past just as Kryton peered out. He met his commander's suspicious look with a crisp, 'Morning, sir!' and kept going.

'Stop!'

Demetrios turned, hoping his bland expression revealed none of his nerves. 'Sir?'

'What are you doing here?'

'Coming off sentry duty outside the king's quarters, sir.'

Eyes narrowed, Kryton looked up and down the corridor.

'Sentries work in pairs. Where's your comrade?'

'A little way ahead, sir. One of my laces came undone – I stopped to retie it.' Deciding that saying nothing might raise Kryton's suspicions further, Demetrios said, 'You're here early, sir. Catching up with paperwork?'

Kryton's suspicious expression eased. 'Something like that. On your way.'

'Yes, sir.'

Kryton's gaze weighed heavy on Demetrios' back as he walked off. The click of the office door shutting was a huge relief. Back at the phalangists' barracks, sleep eluded him. He couldn't stop thinking about what he'd seen and heard. It was strange enough for Herakleides to meet Kryton on his own, but to do so early in the morning . . .

Demetrios could make no sense of it, and after an hour of tossing about on his bed, he took his concerns to Simonides. He was older, wiser and utterly loyal to the king. He would know what to do. Demetrios found him breakfasting with the other veterans in the hall adjacent to their barracks. A long, rectangular room filled with tables and long benches, it was packed and full of noise. At one end, slaves served porridge and honey, bread, cheese and olives. An enormous krater of wine and dozens of clay beakers sat on a stand. Men sat with their friends, shovelling down food and engaging in the usual ribaldry.

It would look odd to sit down without breakfast, so he queued up and sought out Simonides with his hands full. There was a space on the bench opposite.

'Join you?' Demetrios asked.

Simonides looked up, munching. 'Aye.'

Demetrios sat, nodding to the others, who acknowledged him – apart from Empedokles, of course.

'Sentry duty all right?' asked Simonides.

'Aye, nothing to report,' lied Demetrios. There were too many men close by to say a word.

He tucked into his porridge. Idle chitchat with Simonides followed: about the training – Kryton was a hard taskmaster, both agreed; about Dion's drinking – Simonides promised to have a word. Eventually, the threat to Macedon from Rome came up.

'Twenty-five thousand legionaries will invade come the spring,' said Simonides, grimacing. 'No laughing matter.'

'It's not,' agreed Demetrios with a thrill of fear.

'Pity that first blood went to the Romans.' News of the razing of Antipatreia, and then the defeat of a small Macedonian cavalry force, had swept through Pella, dampening spirits that had been high after Philip's attack on Athens. 'As soon as the passes are clear of snow, they will march. They won't be alone. Spies in the Roman camp say—'

'I heard.' Demetrios interrupted, keen to show that he knew as much as Simonides. 'The Illyrians were always going to join with Rome, and so were the cursed Dardani. The Athamanians don't matter – they can field, what, a thousand hoplites and a quarter that number of cavalry?' Athamania was a small state between Thessaly and Epirus.

Simonides gave him a look. 'They all add up, boy. The biggest boar in the forest cannot be slain by one hound, nor even four or five. Let a pack of a dozen throw themselves upon it, however, and it will fall.'

Demetrios sucked on the marrow of Simonides' words, and found the taste not to his liking. 'D'you think we'll lose this war?'

'I'm not saying that,' hissed Simonides. 'But it will be a brutal contest. Many of us will die.'

Demetrios set his jaw. 'There's not much to be done about it. We'll follow the king, to whatever end.'

'Listen to the voice of youth.' Simonides wiped his plate clean and popped the crust in his mouth. He shoved back the bench and stood. 'I'm for the palaestra later. Coming?'

This was Demetrios' opportunity. 'Why not?'

The moment they'd exited the hall, he acted. 'I heard something this morning.'

Simonides' chuckle was knowing. 'Had the queen joined the king in his chamber?'

'Nothing like that, no.'

A curious glance. 'What then?'

Demetrios checked that there was no one in earshot, then explained. 'It was really odd,' he said, finishing.

Simonides didn't reply, and Demetrios swallowed his impatience. Let the man think, he told himself.

'You're sure about what you heard?'

Demetrios nodded. 'Certain.'

'Maybe Herakleides was trying to spare Kryton's blushes. Meeting that early ensured no one would overhear their conversation – or so he thought.'

'There's more to it than that.'

'Any other reason for their meeting could be . . .' Looking troubled, Simonides hesitated.

'Treasonous,' whispered Demetrios.

'Aye.'

'What should I do?'

'Nothing,' said Simonides.

'Eh?' Demetrios regarded his comrade with dismay.

'Phalangist you might be, lad, but you're new to the ranks. Zeus, you're barely shaving. Kryton isn't just the speira's commander: he's fought for the king in more campaigns than I care to remember, and Herakleides is the admiral. It'd be your word against theirs – and what you heard doesn't prove anything.'

'They might be plotting against the king!'

'Quiet!' Simonides' eyes darted about. 'You have no evidence, and making false accusations against your betters is a dangerous path to choose.'

'I have to do something,' protested Demetrios.

'You don't. Philip is no fool – he won't be taken unawares easily.'

Simonides clouted him on the shoulder. 'We will keep our eyes and ears peeled, never fear.'

'We?'

'You're not in this alone: phalangists look out for each other. Your mates will help. Me and Philippos will too, and Andriskos. I can't speak for Empedokles, but even that wine sponge Dion will play his part. At the first sign of any evidence that the king is in danger, we go to him.'

'Aye. Good.'

This was real acceptance into the group, Demetrios thought, his spirits lifting. Seven sets of eyes would see far more than one, and if the threat to Philip was real, they would spy it out.

PART THREE

CHAPTER XXIV

Western Macedonia, late spring 199 BC

A month into the new campaign, and Felix and Antonius were patrolling the countryside. Their pleasure at leaving the vast camps on the Illyrian coast, where the army had spent the winter, had not yet dissipated. Although the weather had been pleasant – sunny, and not too cold or damp – months of tent-living in one place was tedious. Pullo might have enjoyed the endless hours of training and weapons drill, leavened only by sentry duty and patrols, but Felix and the rest had had to endure it. Their rare periods off duty – as well as one pay day – had been cherished, and occasions for vast consumption of wine.

The peaks of the mountains to east and west might still be snow-capped, and the rivers running swift and deep with freezing meltwater, but the legionaries had left them behind and descended onto flatter ground. Here, summer was just around the corner. Warm sunshine bathed the landscape. Skylarks trilled from on high; the trees were in full bloom. In the small fields, crops of millet, emmer and spelt stood knee high.

Felix and his comrades weren't alone on their quest for food. Half the legion and ten *turmae* of cavalry had also been deployed. Tens of thousands of soldiers, and similar numbers of horses and mules, needed vast quantities of food daily. Foraging close to the enemy was risky, however, and so after offering Philip battle in vain several times, Galba had marched his legions seven miles north along the plain. Fresh camp had been set up on the lower slopes of the western mountains.

From there, hundreds of legionaries, Felix and his comrades among them, were to scour the land for supplies. The principes emptied barns, gathered up sheep and cattle, and if the crops were ripe, harvested the fields. Farmers stood by in helpless rage as wagons following in the Romans' wake took away not just their means of making a living, but most of their food for the coming year. Any foolish enough to resist received short shrift.

'What do they call this place again?' asked Fabius. 'We've been through so many shitholes in the last month.'

'Ottolobus,' said Felix. He had heard Pullo talking with Livius.

Fabius hawked up a gob of phlegm and spat. 'That for Ottolobus.'

'It's better than the fucking mountains,' said Felix.

Thanks to heavy winter snowfall, the approaches to Macedonia from Illyria had been impassable for half a month later than usual. Impatient to begin the campaign, Galba had ordered the army's departure from Apollonia sooner than might have been wise. Felix and his comrades had endured calf-deep snow and freezing temperatures for days before the worst of the heights had been crossed.

'It wasn't pleasant,' agreed Antonius. 'What must it have been like for Hannibal in the Alps? A month it took his army to cross the mountains, and half of them died.'

'A shame the whoresons didn't all perish, and save us a generation of blood and arse-ache,' said Hopalong, to loud mutters of agreement.

'We could have invaded Macedonia years since,' said Felix, raising a laugh.

'Farm ahead.' Antonius pointed.

Livius had seen it too. 'You dozen, have a look. Break up into groups of four. There's to be no raping, and kill only if you must.'

Felix and Antonius were used to scavenging: the war with Carthage had seen to that. Eyes roving from side to side – it was always possible a hot-blooded youth would try to defend the farm – they entered the small yard with their comrades and searched the buildings. There wasn't much: some vegetables and grain, a couple of hams, and perhaps thirty sheep. Forcing the farmer and his sons to move the foodstuffs to their wagons, they watched the woman of the household with amusement as she cursed her family and them by turns.

When one boy answered her back, she flew into an even greater rage, pounding him with her fists as he carried a bag of grain from the barn.

'Silly bitch,' said Hopalong. 'What's he supposed to do – refuse to do what we tell him?'

There was no question that the peasant woman spoke Latin, but at that moment, she wheeled and gave the principes a hate-filled look.

'She'd cut your throat given half a chance,' said Felix to Hopalong.

'Let her try,' growled Hopalong, tugging his blade a handspan from the scabbard. The metallic snick as it fell back into place sent a clear warning, and the woman's shoulders bowed. She began to weep, and Hopalong laughed.

She and her family would see a lean time after this, thought Felix. Losing their grain stores and their livestock meant that starvation during the winter was a distinct possibility. He felt little sympathy. These were Macedonians, and subjects of the renegade Philip.

'Riders!' Livius, who'd gone to empty his bladder, appeared from behind the southernmost building. 'Riders coming from the south. Form up!'

Felix and his comrades hurried to obey. Livius soon had twelve of them gathered together, but the rest of the century were further away in the fields with Pullo. The drumming of hooves was audible, and coming from several directions. Felix's stomach twisted. They were dangerously far from their comrades.

'Form a square!' bellowed Livius. 'Four men to a side!' Placing himself at the front right corner, he led them towards Pullo's position.

'What shall *we* do, sir?' called the wagon driver.

'Abandon the wagon,' said Livius.

'Sir?' The man's voice was shocked.

'Stay, and you'll be slain, fool! Head for the camp, fast as you can.'

The wagon driver and his companions took to their heels, and the farmer and his family realised that, for now at least, they would keep their property. The development emboldened his wife, and the principes' ears rang with her curses as they marched out of the yard.

Confusion reigned in the fields beyond. The other wagons, which had been tracking legionaries along the rutted tracks between the fields, had ground to a halt. The drivers were milling about, arguing. Questions flew between the scattered troops; officers shouted contradicting commands. Some men were ignoring orders and already retreating; in poor order, they were vulnerable to attack.

Livius headed for a large group of principes, which proved to be Pullo with the rest of the century. Even as the men exchanged pleased greetings and the centurion barked for them to form a larger square, the first enemy riders appeared.

'Companion cavalry!' roared Pullo. 'Form up, six wide, ten deep!'

To Felix's horror, the nearest horsemen, four men with flashing armour and long, dangerous-looking spears, aimed for a pair of isolated hastati. Both were ridden down in what seemed the blink of an eye. The men's comrades panicked. Turning their faces towards the Roman camp, they ran. At once the Companions gave chase. More riders appeared, and darting between them, archers on foot. Stopping every so often to level their bows and shoot, they charged on, a devastating second wave of attack.

'Cretans.' Felix had bad memories of the renowned archers from the war with Hannibal.

'Rear three ranks, face the enemy,' Pullo ordered, taking a place in the centre of the rearmost men. 'Left and right sides, face outwards.'

The principes hurried to obey. Felix made sure he was close to Pullo; Antonius, Hopalong, Fabius and Narcissus joined him. They had to get back to the camp fast, Pullo said in a calm voice, if they weren't to be slaughtered. Everyone had to stay together. Any man who couldn't keep up was to be left behind. The command 'Shields up', was to be obeyed immediately, or they risked an arrow through the eye.

'What are you waiting for, fools?' Pullo asked. 'Move!'

It was strange marching backwards, at risk of tripping or knocking into the man behind, but Pullo called a slow speed, which allowed the principes to grow used to it. They covered five score paces, watching the enemy cavalry and archers devastate the disorganised legionaries. Casualties mounted steadily. Fear spread like wildfire, making any soldiers who had stood to fight think again. They broke, and the Companions wreaked havoc. After came the Cretans, raining in volleys of arrows.

Philip's timing was perfect, thought Felix. Pullo and Livius were almost alone in having gathered their men. If the chaos nearby was being repeated across the valley, the slaughter would be terrible.

Another hundred paces dragged by. Arrows hummed in, but Pullo was ready. Their raised shields prevented any casualties, and the Cretans moved on. Fifteen Companions charged the rear of their square, but the principes' solid line and levelled javelins brought them to a juddering halt before they closed. Two of the more skilled riders each managed to spear a princeps – men in the rank behind Felix – but in return lost their weapons as quick-thinking Pullo and Antonius hacked the shafts apart with their swords. A loud cheer went up as the Companions went in search of easier prey.

'Leave the dead. Keep moving,' ordered Pullo.

After half a mile, they were clear of the fighting. Felix had begun to think that the worst was over when Livius, who was leading the square from the front, cried that he could see more Companions ahead.

Ordering a man to take his place, Pullo headed to see what was happening. He came back, grim-faced. Scores of Companions and hundreds of peltasts, Philip's light infantry, had blocked the road to the Roman camp.

'We hit them hard and fast, brothers. Hang around and we'll be surrounded.' Pullo's voice was as quiet as ever, but there was a mad glitter in his eyes. 'The best way I know to get through an enemy line is the wedge. You with me?'

Pullo's tactic saw the principes punch through the enemy line, with the loss of five men. Pursuit died away in the face of their determination. They arrived at the camp to find all was confusion. Sentries on the walls had seen the fighting, but not realised what was going on, and the few stragglers who had already returned were low-rankers. Pullo went to explain the situation to Galba. While he was gone, Livius doled out gruff praise.

'Be ready to head out there again,' he warned. 'The general won't take this lying down.'

Livius was right. Even as Pullo returned, cavalry units rode out through the front gate. Trumpets sounded everywhere, and soldiers ran pell-mell for their tentlines. Galba's orders, Pullo reported, were to deploy as fast as possible. 'He wants the Macedonians driven back. We'll form a great big hollow square, so the bastard Companions can't get at us.'

They didn't have to wait long. Closest to the gate, his principes were among the first to march out. Part of the square's 'front', they tramped back towards the fighting.

It was a short, unpleasant journey. The dirt track was littered with discarded equipment and weapons, and Roman corpses. There were bodies in the trampled fields of emmer and millet, and the moans of the injured came from every quarter. Clouds of flies hung in swarms over the dead, filled open mouths and settled on staring eyes. Overhead, vultures were gathering.

Things went well from that point. Caught up in their pursuit of the fleeing legionaries, Philip's troops had forgotten how far from their own positions they had come. The Roman square clashed head-on with scattered groups of Companions and foot soldiers, driving them backwards. Two groups of Cretans were cornered and massacred. An attempt by the Companions to charge the legionaries was brought to a bloody halt by a massed javelin volley that sent more than a score of horses crashing to the ground.

Pullo had to hold his principes back at this point – every man wanted to take his revenge on the cavalry who had caused so many casualties – but, cowed by his threats, they kept their formation. By the time they had closed on the injured and dying horses, most of the Companions had fled.

The few who hadn't were trying desperately to help a comrade trapped under his dead mount. As the baying principes closed in, they succeeded in freeing him. There was a frantic scramble as the man was helped onto a horse, and then the doomed Companions turned to fight, sacrificing their lives so their friend might escape.

Felix alone noticed the man's magnificent armour and red-crested helmet with ram's horns. 'It's Philip!' he cried. 'It's their piece-of-shit king!'

None of Felix's comrades heard. He skidded to a halt, knowing he was too far away to catch Philip. It was his javelin or nothing. Planting his left foot forward, Felix closed one eye and took aim. With a mighty heave, he threw. A shallow arc upwards and his javelin thumped into the earth right behind Philip's horse. Alarmed, it bolted, with the king holding on for dear life. Felix cursed. As they closed with the Companions, he lost sight of Philip.

The short, sharp fight that followed saw all the enemy cavalrymen slain. Hopalong was dead too; a wet-lipped wound in his throat leaked rivers of blood into the dirt. Despite the loss of their comrade, there was much for the principes to celebrate. Philip's troops had been mauled, and two hundred of his elite Companions slain. After asking for a truce to bury his dead, he retreated overnight through the mountains.

As Felix told his disbelieving comrades, however, the best opportunity of the day had been his, and he had so nearly taken it.

CHAPTER XXV

Pluinna, western Macedon, summer 199 BC

Midday wasn't far off. The sun occupied a clear blue sky. Swallows banked and dived, their high-pitched calls filling the air. Grey-brown peaks brooded on either side of a narrow, tree-lined valley, at the bottom of which lay a burbling river and a track that led north-south. Boys watched over the sheep that grazed the scrubby lower slopes; terraces of vines surrounded stone farmhouses. On the flatter ground below, wheat and barley were ripening. A quiet scene, it could have been anywhere in Macedon.

Part-way along its length, the valley was almost cut in half by a long, wooded ridge that projected from one side to the other. Among the trees, surrounded by the din of cicadas, Demetrios and the phalangists of two chiliarchies had been waiting since before dawn. Hundreds of Cretan archers were hidden with them. The hours had dragged by. At first it had been chilly; cloaks had been forbidden. As the sun's rays had seeped through the canopy, the soldiers had warmed up, but boredom and hunger soon took over. No one moved from their positions, however – the need for secrecy had been reiterated the previous day by Philip himself.

Demetrios had a partial view of the path as it snaked around the base of the ridge and headed southwards; he'd grown tired of staring down at it and seeing a farmer driving his cattle to fresh pasture, or a greybeard hobbling to the river for water. He nudged Kimon, who was standing in front of him.

'Will they come?'

Kimon gave him a look. 'That's the fifth time you've asked.'

Antileon heard him too. 'Sixth.'

'Aye, well,' said Demetrios. 'Waiting is hard.'

'Hard for everyone,' said Kimon.

Demetrios fell to thinking. In the days after the shock defeat at

Ottolobus, morale in Philip's army had dropped. It hadn't yet climbed again. There was only so much drilling and foraging for food that a man could do with an undefeated enemy in the vicinity. The legions were in Macedon now, thought Demetrios, and they had to be faced sooner rather than later. In fairness to the king, he had tried to ambush Roman patrols on several occasions, but to no avail. This was the latest attempt.

The trouble was that no one knew if the enemy would swallow the bait. It was juicy enough this time: a dozen wagons laden down with some of the season's first-cut wheat. The drivers, a mixture of grief-stricken locals who had lost their womenfolk to the Romans and Cretans whose balls were bigger than their brains, had been directed to travel as close to the nearest enemy scouts as possible, before turning around and pretending to return to their homes. Philip's intention was for the scouts to carry news of the wagon train to Galba, who would then, gods willing, send a strong force in pursuit.

Even if Galba reacted as Philip wanted, the plan was riddled with risk. The wagons could well have been taken long since, thought Demetrios, and the drivers slain. They might be seized before entering the valley. To minimise the risk of the enemy seeing the trap for what it was, just one rider had been designated to carry word to the ambush party when the time came. If unfriendly eyes were watching the valley floors, a lone horseman wouldn't attract much attention – that was the hope, at least.

Demetrios peered down the track again. Even if the Romans chased the wagons, there was no certainty of victory. The enemy would need to march around the end of the ridge without seeing any of the hidden Macedonians. Then and only then would the ambush play out in its entirety. His skin itched at the idea. This might be his first fight – his first experience of the storm of bronze. He prayed that his nerves held. Demetrios had no wish to be given a nickname like 'Tent Sulker', as a phalangist in another file had. It didn't matter that the poor bastard had proved himself since, a chortling Andriskos had explained. Once given, a name could never be taken back.

'Empedokles is a brave man, but he hates being called "Trembler".' Andriskos had eyed his glowering comrade. 'Don't you?'

'Piss off,' Empedokles had muttered, making everyone laugh.

It helped to know that a prick like Empedokles felt fear, thought

Demetrios. It meant he could too, and as long as he played his part when the time came, no one would think worse of him.

'Listen,' said Kimon.

Apart from the cicadas, Demetrios could hear nothing. 'What?'

'A horse,' said Kimon.

Demetrios pricked up his ears. From a long way off came the distinctive beat of galloping hoofs. His stomach did a neat roll.

'Is that our man?' whispered Antileon.

'It's got to be,' said Kimon.

His words were borne out as a dust-covered, sweat-lathered horse hove into sight. Reaching the bottom of the slope, the rider threw himself off and ran into the trees. Excited, nervous mutters rose; Demetrios and his friends exchanged grim looks. Word was soon passed up the line that the wagons were eight stadia away. Close behind was a force of perhaps two thousand legionaries. The gods were smiling too. Only a turma of cavalry – thirty men – accompanied the enemy infantry.

The wait that followed was worse than the hours since dawn. Shafts of sunlight fell on Demetrios, making him sweat. He was thirsty, but didn't dare take a drink. The creak of wheels was audible, yet the slow-moving wagons did not appear. Some men talked in overloud whispers, and were silenced by the officers. Simonides came walking up the slope, pausing for a word with everyone.

Reaching Demetrios, he asked, 'You all right?'

'Aye.' Demetrios' voice was husky.

'Remember to keep breathing.'

Demetrios stared at him.

'Men hold their breaths when they're scared,' said Simonides. 'Breathe into it. Stay near the man in front. Listen to Zotikos.'

'I will,' said Demetrios.

With an approving nod, Simonides returned to his position.

Somehow the wagon drivers had worked out the perfect distance at which to alert the Romans. By the time they passed the end of the ridge and the hidden Macedonians, the enemy cavalry were hot on their heels, but had taken only two wagons. The legionaries, marching at the double pace, were perhaps six stadia behind. The earth shook from their passage. Absorbed in the chase, neither cavalry nor infantry paid any attention to the tree-covered ridge.

Thirty heartbeats after the last Romans had disappeared from sight, the first phalangists began spilling down onto the track. The ground had been carefully measured; between the end of the ridge and the river, there was room for an entire speira – including Simonides' file – to stand abreast. Two speirai would remain behind as reinforcements, while the rest climbed to the other side of the ridge in preparation for the second part of the ambush. Half a hundred Cretans swam one-armed across the river, holding their bows and quivers clear of the water. Like their fellows who remained in the trees, their task would be to prevent any attempt by the Romans to flank the phalangists.

'I hope some of the wagon drivers get away,' muttered Demetrios.

'It would be a shame if all the crazy bastards died,' agreed Kimon.

An odd sense of calm prevailed as the speira took shape. The file-leaders led the call, and the phalangists tramped into position, swinging their shields forward off their left shoulders. 'Close order!' cried Kryton.

'Close order!' repeated Simonides.

This is it, thought Demetrios, sliding his left forearm into the strap. This is fucking it.

He edged forward until his aspis was close to Kimon's back. Zotikos' shield was almost touching him from behind; on either side stood the men of other files, close enough that Demetrios could have tapped their shields with the rim of his. Over their heads, hundreds of sarissae formed a forest of long, deadly points.

'They've seen us!' cried Kryton. 'The whoresons don't look happy!'

A great bellow of laughter went up from the front ranks; it spread through the speira and to the phalangists behind. Demetrios found himself cackling like a fool. It felt briefly wonderful, and then the acid taste of fear filled his mouth.

Trumpets blared from the far side of the ridge.

'What are they doing?' There was a nervous note to Antileon's voice.

'Turning. Forming up. Preparing to attack us,' said Demetrios, gripping his sarissa shaft tight, and wishing he could see something – anything – other than the men in front.

'Level pikes!' Kryton was standing at the very right of the first rank – he'd taken the place of the file-leader.

Smooth as falling rain, the men of the front five ranks lowered their spears.

Demetrios checked himself before he too could do the same. A man three files over wasn't so fortunate. He brought his sarissa back up at once, but that didn't stop good-natured abuse raining down on him.

Kryton started singing the *Paean*, the sacred war chant to Ares, and the front-rankers took it up with gusto, their deep voices roaring out the words. Demetrios had heard the tune as a boy, when the men in the village danced the Pyrrhiche, the dance of war. More recently, he'd sung it with his comrades around their campfires. This was more different than he could have imagined. The hairs on his neck stood on end; his heart raced. Above, Ares was watching – Demetrios had never been surer of something in his life.

Through the singing came the tread of hobnailed sandals. Demetrios' voice faltered. The legionaries were close.

The Paean came to an end. 'Here they come, brothers!' shouted Kryton. 'MA-CE-DON!'

'MA-CE-DON!' cried the men of his speira, and every phalangist to their rear.

'Ready,' said Zotikos, pushing his aspis into Demetrios' back.

'Ready,' echoed the file-closers all along the back of the speira.

'Four score paces,' said Kryton.

Demetrios was far from the front, but his mouth was drier than that of a man after a heavy night's drinking.

'At fifty, they'll throw javelins; then the barbarian fuckers will charge.' Kryton could have been talking about the weather.

On the other side of the river, the Cretan bowmen were already at work. As they loosed, they made high-pitched yips, like a pack of hunting dogs. Demetrios' eyes followed their arrows up into the air, and down again, in front of the speira where he could not see.

'Sixty paces,' said Kryton.

'Look up when the whoresons throw their javelins, and you could be a dead man.' Zotikos' breath was hot in Demetrios' ear. 'Remember that.'

Grateful, Demetrios nodded.

'JAVELINS!' cried Kryton.

Demetrios wanted to puke, as he had during the training exercise against the veterans, but the idea filled him with shame. He stared at the ground, taking deep breaths and willing the nausea away.

Somewhere to his right, a man was praying. Five frenzied heartbeats went by, and Demetrios began to wonder if Kryton had got it wrong. Then, with a terrible whirring sound, the enemy missiles came down. *Clack. Clack. Clack.* Wood met wood. Javelins struck sarissae. Another heartbeat, and the javelins hit the phalangists below. Shorn of much of their penetrative power, most landed at a flattish angle, clattering off helmets. Some still had velocity, however. Men bellowed in pain. A couple of files over, someone screamed like a stuck pig. Demetrios looked, and wished he hadn't. The javelin had shattered the man's right shoulder, but its effect was far greater. Dropping his shield, the injured phalangist thrashed about, trying to rip the barbed head free; in the process, he disrupted the speira's formation.

'Get him out of there!' ordered the file-closer. 'Quickly!'

'ROMA!' bellowed the legionaries. The ground trembled beneath their passage.

'Thirty paces!' shouted Kryton.

They're almost on us, thought Demetrios with a thrill of terror. Two thousand cursed Romans. What if they break through?

Zotikos nudged him with his shield. 'When I say "Push", you fucking push.'

'Aye.' Shoving away his concern as best he could, Demetrios bumped Kimon. 'Ready?'

The back of Kimon's old helmet went up and down.

'Twenty paces!' Kryton's voice was steady. 'Fifteen.'

Demetrios prepared himself the way he'd been taught, left shoulder slightly forward of his right, left leg planted ahead of his right, under his angled shield. He kept his sarissa at the same slant as the rest.

'Pick your man!' came Kryton's cry.

The impact reached Demetrios' ears first. It reached him through the men and shields in front an instant later, rocking him back on his heels. He steadied himself, made sure his aspis stayed in place against Kimon's back. Next came the screams, hideous animal mewls that set Demetrios' teeth on edge. He heard Kryton shout something, but couldn't make it out. Another impact struck – the Romans had not been entirely stopped, he realised.

'PUSH!' roared Kryton. The order was repeated by Simonides and the other file-leaders. The half- and quarter-file leaders were next. 'PUSH!'

'PUSH!' cried Zotikos, shoving his shield into Demetrios.

Demetrios ignored the discomfort and heaved his against Kimon. Everyone edged forward a pace.

Two more steps, and Kryton yelled, 'HOLD! HOLD!'

'HOLD!' echoed all the officers, including Zotikos.

Move beyond the end of the ridge, thought Demetrios, and they would expose their right flank.

Chests heaving, legs braced, the phalangists kept their position for perhaps a hundred heartbeats. There were no further impacts. Next, the Cretans in the trees to the phalangists' right began to shower down arrows. As jeers and insults filled the air, Demetrios twisted his head to look at Zotikos. 'Are they cheering because . . .?'

'Aye. The bastards are retreating,' said Zotikos.

Demetrios nudged Kimon. 'D'you hear that?'

'The battle's not over,' Zotikos warned. 'The Romans aren't beaten.'

'If we hold our position, though, and they don't flank us—' said Demetrios eagerly.

Zotikos was having none of it. 'Who are you – fucking Alexander all of a sudden? Two thousand legionaries won't give up just like that.'

Deflated, Demetrios shut his mouth.

A short break in hostilities followed, during which the Romans presumably licked their wounds and were lambasted by their centurions. Kryton used the time to have the injured removed from the ranks. Thanks to the javelin-caused casualties in his file – none of them Empedokles, unfortunately – Demetrios found himself three ranks further forward. A fraction less nervous than before, he craned his neck to catch glimpses of the legionaries when they next charged. Another javelin volley landed; a few men were hurt, but not him or his friends.

The second attack broke quicker than the first, and the triumphant phalangists advanced a score of steps before Kryton and the file-leaders regained control and had them pace back to the end of the ridge.

'We've won now, surely?' muttered Kimon.

Demetrios was about to agree, but he was again cut off by Zotikos.

'These aren't Greeks, son. They're boneheaded Roman barbarians. They don't understand defeat until they're told to withdraw, or they are lying on their backs, bleeding out.'

Zotikos was right. Twice more the ground shook as the Romans charged the impenetrable wall of Macedonian sarissae, and twice they were brought to a juddering halt. In the midst of the final assault, summoned by Kryton's trumpeter, the rest of the phalangists appeared to the enemy's rear; they were supported by Cretan archers. Caught on an anvil between two hammers, the legionaries were massacred. A few score escaped into the trees, and the cavalry rode north up the valley, but the rest were cut down or taken prisoner.

Demetrios was giddy with relief; he hadn't shamed himself in front of his comrades, and their victory had been total. His mood was improved by the addition of a mail shirt, stripped from a dead Roman. Kimon, Antileon and others were quick to copy his example. Many of the casualties from the enemy javelins had been in the rearmost ranks, where men like them – without armour – stood.

Zotikos, who had his own padded linen corselet, watched with an approving expression.

'Better to look like a Roman than take a javelin in the chest, eh?'

'Aye.' Demetrios couldn't put the poor bastard with the shattered shoulder from his mind.

'You did all right.'

Surprised, for Zotikos was scant with his praise, Demetrios raised his gaze. 'Really?'

'You followed orders. You pushed. You didn't try to run.' Zotikos grinned evilly. 'Oh, and you didn't shit yourself.'

Kimon and Antileon laughed until tears came to their eyes.

Demetrios did too.

CHAPTER XXVI

Rome, late summer 199 BC

Flamininus was admiring the bronze statue which took pride of place in his courtyard garden. A discus thrower cast in bronze by Myron, the famous Athenian sculptor, it stood on a marble plinth, and Flamininus never tired of being in its presence. Around and around the effigy he walked, fingers cupping his chin, deep in thought. The slaves that came and went around the garden's colonnaded walkway knew better than to interrupt.

Flamininus suspected that his interest in all things Greek sprang from his loveless upbringing. Introduced by a tutor to Hellenic culture, he had been enchanted by the musical language, rich history, and its writers and orators. He gazed again at the discus thrower.

Look at me now, he thought, successful and wealthy enough to buy this superb piece of art.

If either of his parents had been alive, it would have pleased him to have them visit, so he could flaunt his good taste, not to say his riches. As magnificent as the statue was, Flamininus would have given it and his entire fortune away to be the general who defeated Philip and went on to subjugate Greece. History could not fail to remember such a man. In the pantheon of military commanders, he would rank alongside Alexander. That, thought Flamininus, would be a fitting epitaph.

Frustratingly, his hopes of achieving such a goal continued to fluctuate from one extreme to the other. A sudden illness had prevented him standing for election as consul not long after his meeting with Metrodoros – at the time, he had cursed his luck, that Publius Villius Tappulus should have won instead. Like Flamininus, Tappulus was also desperate to take over from Galba, but the Senate had chosen to leave the general in command – Galba – in place. Tappulus' loss had been Flamininus' gain.

Now the campaigning season was more than half over; so was Tappulus' term of office. There had been recent good news from Illyria and Macedonia too. Come the autumn, Flamininus decided, it would be time to stand for consul again.

'Staring at his cock?' drawled a familiar voice.

'That's what you do, Lucius, not I.' Flamininus turned as his brother came into the garden. 'I admire this statue for its beauty, its symmetry – its perfect representation of the human form.'

'I like its depiction of the human form too.' Smirking, Lucius placed a hand on the discus thrower's well-muscled arse.

'You'll mark the bronze.' Flamininus glared until his brother stepped away. 'You're late.'

'It was a long night, brother.'

Flamininus pursed his lips. 'I won't ask.'

'Why not?' Lucius leered.

'There's more important business to discuss than where you were whoring.'

Lucius shrugged and followed Flamininus to his office without comment. Opening onto the courtyard, it too paid homage to Greek culture. On the mosaic floor, Icarus flew towards the sun, and niches in the walls held superb examples of both red- and black-figure vases. Another Myron bust, Hercules clad in his Nemean lion skin, stood on a table in one corner.

'Wine?' asked Flamininus.

A smile flickered around Lucius' mouth. 'Of course.'

Flamininus clapped his hands and told the Nubian slave who appeared to bring a jug of Alban. 'Well watered down, mind,' he called after. 'Don't,' he warned Lucius in the same breath. 'No doubt you had enough last night.'

'I wasn't going to say anything.' Lucius' face was as innocent as a babe's.

Flamininus snorted. 'Have you heard the latest news from Greece?'

With the war in full flow since the spring, Flamininus hadn't been the only one receiving word from abroad. Official messengers had worn a path to the door of the Curia.

'I'm aware that Galba marched south rather than face Philip in battle. Laying waste to farms, and towns no one has heard of seems to appeal to him. It's baffling.'

'Galba's a politician, not a general.'

'And you are?'

Flamininus glared.

Lucius snorted with amusement. 'Speak your mind, brother. I am listening.'

'It was Galba's misfortune that his army had to overwinter in Illyria, but only a fool would have risked an attack on Macedonia after the harvest. His campaign in the spring got off to a bad start; heavy snow in the mountains delayed the invasion. Galba missed another opportunity when his men forced their way through the dirty gates, the vital pass leading east. If he had pressed home the advantage, the war might have been ended at one stroke.'

'In fairness to Galba, Philip retreated from the dirty gates to high ground,' countered Lucius. 'Attacking uphill is never a good idea.'

'Yet the legionaries did just that at the dirty gates, and won. Galba should have kept on the offensive. Fortunately for me, he did not.' Flamininus paused as the Nubian poured wine. Testing that it was diluted to his taste, he nodded.

Lucius drained his in one swallow and held it out for a refill. 'Tasty,' he pronounced when that had gone the way of the first. He glanced at the Nubian. 'More.'

'We have much to talk about,' warned Flamininus.

Rolling his eyes, Lucius set down his cup. 'What's happened of recent days?'

'The legate Apustius persuaded the Aetolians to join with Rome. He had help from Attalus of Pergamum,' said Flamininus, laughing inside.

Even Lucius didn't know how, through Metrodoros, *he* had bribed the Aetolian assembly to remain neutral until the summer. Their apparent change of heart was his doing. It would have been better for Flamininus if the Aetolians had stood to one side for longer, denying Galba their troops, but there was only so long they could have been prevented from joining the fight against their old enemy Philip.

'A simultaneous incursion by the Dardani helped, of course, as did our sieges of eastern coastal towns,' Flamininus continued. 'And the Aetolians didn't waste time once their minds were made up. They marched straight into Thessaly, taking several towns. Southern Macedonia was open to attack, but their leaders laid siege to the fortress of Gomphi instead.'

'Whoever holds that has Thessaly at his mercy *and* a chance to enter Macedonia,' observed Lucius.

'Aye. Unluckily for the Aetolians – luckily for me – Philip had had word of their intentions,' said Flamininus. 'Marching south at lightning speed, he fell on them with no warning. Their troops were routed from outside Gomphi with heavy losses.'

Flamininus' spies had sent the pleasing news since that Metrodoros was among the slain. Nikomedes and Lykeles would never reveal their involvement either: their own people would kill them for it. His clandestine deal, thought Flamininus with relief, would remain secret.

'Typical useless Greeks,' said Lucius 'So Macedonia will not fall this campaigning season.'

Flamininus permitted himself a smile. 'Even so. Less than a month remains before Galba will have to pull his legions back – he may already be doing so. Philip will live to fight another day.'

'Excellent news, brother. Galba will soon be replaced by Villius, who will be able to do nothing over the winter. You plan to take *his* place.'

'Correct. Assuming I win the consular elections, I shall lead Rome's forces into Macedonia come the spring. You will be in command of the fleet.'

Lucius looked pleased. 'Villius might have something to say about your plan. He intends to set sail any day.'

'Good luck to him. There won't be much to do during the cold months, and while he's away, we can sow the seeds for my candidacy.'

Lucius wagged a finger. 'Even if you are elected, Villius won't want to give up command.'

'He won't stop me!' said Flamininus with a snort. 'But let's not be hasty. First I must become consul – and that has proved a difficult path before.'

'Men will say the same things they did last time,' declared Lucius. 'You'll be criticised for failing to win before. For jumping from office to office without following due process. "From quaestor to consul," they'll complain. "That shouldn't be allowed." They will also say that you lack political experience.'

'Let the naysayers squawk. I have enough support in the Senate to shout them down.'

'Will you stand with Paetus again?' asked Lucius.

'Aye.'

'Is his head still in a book?' When Flamininus nodded, Lucius added, 'The man will barely notice when he hears you are leaving to fight Philip.'

They both laughed.

Lucius raised his cup to Flamininus. 'Salutations, brother. It is good to see your long-held plans starting to bear fruit. Here's to your victory in the election.'

'It's not a foregone conclusion. Others will also want to be consul.'

'Will Quintus Minucius Rufus stand again? His praetorship in Bruttium will end in time, if he wished it. He's popular too.'

'I'm told that he'll be staying on for a while. There have been thefts from a temple in Locris which need to be investigated.'

Lucius' brows arched. 'Do you have spies in every camp?'

'Most, but not all.'

Lucius' eyebrows rose. 'Who else is there?' He held up a hand, counting off his fingers. 'You say Minucius Rufus is out. Scipio Africanus is censor, and has said he's retiring from politics when his term of office is up. Cethegus is useless, and he's busy fighting tribes in Hispania. Purpureo has his hands full working with Galba. Cato will be consul one day, but he's too young for now.'

'Agreed. Marcus Claudius Marcellus will be the main competition, I think. Rumours are that he's interested.'

'If he's the only one you have to beat, your chances are good, brother.'

Flamininus smiled again. Finally, he could see himself at the head of his victorious legions, riding into Macedonia. *He* would go down in history as the conqueror of Greece.

It was a good feeling.

CHAPTER XXVII

Central Macedon

Philip was alone in the meeting chamber of his vast tent. Bare of furnishings but for a long table and stools to sit around, the space was where he spent his mornings and, sometimes, his evenings. Clad in a simple chiton, he nursed a cup of wine as he paced to and fro. It was early, the best time for meeting with his generals before the heat of the day made it impossible to stay beneath the leather canopy. Even with the sides lifted, the place became an oven.

Philip was brooding. Ottolobus should have been a great victory, he thought. Lack of discipline, pure and simple, had seen the day lost. He could still feel the rush of exaltation as he'd realised the Roman foragers were in full flight, and the order he had given to kill every last one of the bastards – but he should have known better. Indeed, he had been lucky to survive. But for the Companions with him, he wouldn't have. Philip made a mental note to have gold sent to the family of the man who'd given his horse and his life to save his king.

He hadn't felt like a king as the army had skulked away through the hills under cover of darkness, but it was better to live to fight another day than die a glorious fool. Ottolobus had been an ignominious defeat, but by no means a total victory for the Romans. Most of Philip's army remained intact, and he had struck back soon after, at Pluinna. There had been no mistakes made there, he thought with satisfaction. A narrow valley had been the perfect spot to spring an ambush on Galba's column. More than fifteen hundred legionaries had been slain that day. Alexander would have been proud of that skirmish, he decided.

An uncertain time had followed, as Philip guarded the approaches to Macedon, and Galba's scouts and cavalry probed for weaknesses in his position. Philip scowled as he remembered the dirty gates, the mountain pass that straddled two vital routes. One led south into

Eordaea, a mountainous part of Macedon, and the other east to the central Macedonian plain. He'd had to defend it – not to have done so would have allowed Galba to walk straight into his kingdom. Yet the uneven terrain had meant the phalanx could not deploy well. Knowing this, Philip had ordered the construction of walls and ditches, and the felling of trees in the pass. The winding track had been made impassable, or so he'd thought, but the legionaries had made short shrift of it, swarming like rats over the obstacles. Smarting from his losses at Ottolobus, Philip had ordered his troops to withdraw from the dirty gates.

Galba's victory had offered him access to the south, but Philip's army still occupied the heights to the east, and the way to Macedon's heart. A flat valley floor below his position meant that the phalanx could form, which was probably why Galba had chosen to march his legions south. There was satisfaction to be taken from this, thought Philip. Despite the summer's setbacks, the consul was wary of meeting his phalangists face to face.

He could hear his generals beginning to arrive, and a claustrophobic feeling stole over him. An hour or more would go by as they sat around the table and discussed their next move. It had been the same every morning for days, and the outcome had been the same every time. No one could decide what to do next. Today would be different, Philip decided.

He smiled at his generals' surprised expressions as he emerged from the tent. 'Walk with me.' He waved the sentries back. 'Not you.'

Perseus was first to his side. 'Where are we going, Father?'

He had the boundless energy and optimism of youth. Philip was forever having to dampen his enthusiasm, and explain how they couldn't fight the Romans every step of the way. Sometimes he felt old and tired just looking at him, but today Perseus' confidence was infectious.

'You'll see.' Noting the enquiring looks flying between his officers, Philip smiled again.

'You're sick of the planning, sire.' Athenagoras had been one of Philip's first appointments; the pair had been friends for decades. Short, squat and with a bald pate, he was one of the finest riders in Macedon.

'You know me well, Athenagoras.'

'After twenty-five years, I should, sire.'

Philip could remember their childhood like it was yesterday. Part of him would have given anything to have returned to those innocent days, when their only concern was not to be caught stealing apples, or spying on Athenagoras' sisters as they got dressed. Pleasing though the fantasy was, Philip set it aside. He was king now, with all the responsibilities that that entailed.

Bypassing the Companions' tents – he would visit them on his return – the king made his way to the infantry tentlines. Men were up and about, making use of the cooler temperature, so his arrival didn't go unnoticed for long. Pleased cries of 'The king!' and 'Hail, Philip!' rang out.

He felt Perseus' questioning eyes on him. 'Do as I do,' he said in an undertone. Catching the eye of a phalangist with a salt-and-pepper beard, he cried, 'Well met. Kallinikos, isn't it?'

'Yes, sire.' Kallinikos beamed at being recognised. He and his excited comrades bowed to Philip, who spent a few moments enquiring after their well-being.

'Are we to fight the Romans again this summer, sire?' asked Kallinikos.

'If the right opportunity presents itself, we will, but Galba seems wary.'

'The scouts say his legions continue their march south, sire.'

'Indeed. Away from us.'

'They don't want to face the phalanx, sire,' said Kallinikos.

'I think you're right,' said Philip. 'It's no surprise, looking at you fine fellows.'

Kallinikos and his comrades grinned at each other like fools.

'You'll be ready when the time comes,' said Philip.

'Aye, sire!' Kallinikos thumped a fist off his chest.

Philip continued to wander through the camp, acknowledging men's greetings here, stopping to have a word there. He shared bread and olives with a party of Cretan archers, and accepted cups of wine from other soldiers. Everywhere he went, he called men by their names, and remembered their fathers, or brothers, or the battle in which they had distinguished themselves. He listened intently to the few grievances he was presented with, and settled most on the spot. The gripes that could not be dealt with at once he promised to remedy at the soonest opportunity.

Athenagoras and the other generals had moved off among the tents to play their part. Perseus stuck to his father's side.

'Try speaking to the men,' Philip said after a time.

Perseus looked self-conscious, unsure. 'What shall I say?'

'Admire their weapons, or armour. Ask if they have enough food. If a man is injured, ask how he took the wound. Enquire if the surgeons are taking care of him. Try to remember their names – they love that.'

Perseus waved a hand at the tentlines, which sprawled in every direction. 'There are so many men, Father.'

'That's right, and they're all your subjects, or will be.' The tiniest seed of doubt nagged at Philip: that Rome might win the war, and his son be deprived of the throne. He crushed it ruthlessly. 'Where you lead,' he continued, 'they will follow, but you must earn their loyalty. They need to know that you care for them. That you love them. There's no better way to do it than this.' Philip raised a hand to a group of peltasts who were lounging about on animal skins before their tent. 'Well met!'

'Sire!' Dirty-faced, clad in rough tunics, the peltasts resembled bandits of the worst variety, but their faces shone at Philip's recognition.

'What has you here, sire?' asked the oldest, a lanky figure with grey hair and almost no teeth.

'Berisades, you old dog!' cried Philip. 'I thought you had gone to Tartaros long ago.'

Berisades cast a delighted glance at his comrades. 'The bones creak and everything aches, sire, but I'm still alive.'

'You're good for another battle or two?'

'Show me the bastard Romans–' Berisades' companions fell about the place laughing, and he looked a little abashed '–begging your pardon, sire. Line 'em up in front of me, and I'll do my bit.'

'I know you will.' Philip clapped the greybeard on the shoulder, and nodded at his friends. 'You all will, and I thank you for your allegiance. We may have other foes to defeat before the Romans, however.'

Berisades' expression grew hawkish. 'Who, sire?'

'The Dardani and Illyrians have returned.'

'Yellow-livers that they are, sire.' Berisades glanced at Perseus. 'Will you be leading that force, sire?'

Perseus hesitated. The troops sent by Philip against the northern invaders previously had been his to command only in name. He glanced at his father, who gave him an encouraging nod.

'I will,' said Perseus, lifting his chin. 'With Athenagoras' help.'

'It would be our honour to follow you, sire,' said Berisades to Perseus, his companions' cries of assent backing him up.

Perseus grinned.

'You're good men,' said Philip.

'D'you see the use in what we've done?' he asked Perseus as they walked away.

'Yes, Father. The men's faces light up at the sound of your voice. Speaking with them shows them you care.'

'Correct. Those Thracians liked you as well. It's an important part of being king, to let your subjects see you, and to recognise them as real people. Remember that.'

'I will, Father.'

Perseus' eyes shone, and Philip thought, how blessed I am to have such a son, and an army like the one around me.

Truly, they are worth fighting for.

CHAPTER XXVIII

Outside Apollonia, Illyria, autumn 199 BC

A month had passed since Galba's legions had marched down from the mountains, mud-spattered, tired and hungry. Felix, Antonius and their comrades were off duty for only the second time since, and they were thirstier than men who'd crossed a desert with no water. Bathed, wearing their cleanest tunics, they beat an eager path out of the vast camp that housed half the army. The other half resided in an encampment of similar size a mile distant. Their tent was among the closest to Apollonia, Felix had been fond of saying as they stared at the city from the earthen ramparts, or as they marched into the foothills on patrol. At last they could take full advantage of their proximity.

'Thank the gods,' said Fabius. 'The fighting is over until the spring.'

Hostilities ended in or around harvest time, and were taken up again when the warmer weather returned. It was no more likely that Philip would attack before then than the sun would fall from the sky.

'Aye,' said Felix, 'but the rumours are that Galba is to be replaced by Villius.'

'Galba didn't defeat Philip in open battle,' said Antonius. 'That's why.'

'It's not as if it was his first chance,' said Felix. 'If he had arrived from Rome earlier last year, he could have taken the fight to Philip then.'

'We can worry about that in the spring, eh?' said Fabius. 'All that's important tonight is finding a decent inn.'

'And a whorehouse,' added Narcissus.

'You'll need one with a mirror,' said Antonius. Narcissus was alone among them in owning such a trinket. When he wasn't polishing his armour and equipment, he was fond of studying his reflection.

They all fell about, and Narcissus glowered. 'It's not my fault if I'm the best looker here,' he snapped.

More hilarity ensued.

'You and Felix should have a contest,' said Antonius. 'He's quite the lady's man when he sets his mind to it. What say you, brothers? First one of the pair to pull a woman tonight wins. We'll wager a denarius each – and the winner takes all. If neither manages to bed a freeborn Illyrian woman, we spend the money on drink.' He dug in his purse and held up a silver coin.

'I'm in,' said Fabius at once.

'And I,' said Mattheus, the newest addition to their contubernium. Short, gregarious and an excellent runner, he'd been named – as he told everyone – by his insistent Jewish mother. 'Are you willing, Felix? Narcissus?'

Felix wasn't fond of Narcissus. He wouldn't admit it to anyone except Antonius, for it didn't do to badmouth one's comrades, but the man was insufferable. Apart from his obsession with his physical appearance and equipment, he only ever talked about himself. Felix knew where Narcissus was from, his father's profession, how many siblings he had. He even knew Narcissus' favourite wine – Caecuban.

The prick doesn't know the first thing about me, he thought, because he's never asked.

'Felix?' Mattheus' voice again.

Still unsure – downing a bellyful of wine held more appeal than the contest – Felix glanced at Narcissus, whose lip curled as if to say, 'You have no chance.'

Felix's temper flared. 'Five denarii – that's more than half a month's pay. I'll do it.'

'Narcissus?' asked Antonius gleefully.

'It will be like taking a pastry from a child,' Narcissus declared.

The rest of their journey to the town, a gentle stroll along a gravelled road, was taken up with loud discussion about the competition. Antonius backed Felix; so did Mattheus, but Fabius reckoned Narcissus would emerge the victor. Predictably, Narcissus was happy to talk about his previous conquests, which he claimed were many. Felix blocked his ears, and thought about the large prize on offer. A good deal of it would be spent on buying drink for his comrades – that was the nature of wagers made at times like this – but some could be salted away. Since re-enlisting, there had been four paydays, and Felix had been careful to set aside every *as* he didn't need. This was a new experience for him – in the war against Hannibal, he had spent his pay within days, on wine and women. Now he had a purpose for depositing his coins with the dour quartermaster. When the war against Macedonia had been won, Felix was determined that there would be no return to penury, no working the fields until his hands bled. He would be a man of substance, and when he caught the eye of a pretty girl, she would smile.

Two hours later, and Felix had a good feeling in his belly. The still-balmy weather meant the streets of Apollonia were thronged, but he and his comrades had managed to secure a table outside one of the many inns. The streets were crowded with locals and off-duty soldiers. Small children gaped at the legionaries, and were chided by their mothers. Greybeards threw suspicious glances. Women kept their gaze firmly on the ground, or engaged in overloud conversations with their female companions. Dogs moved between the tables, hoping for scraps from the heavy-drinking customers.

While Antonius, Fabius and Mattheus busied themselves with getting drunk, Felix and Narcissus had cast about for potential targets. Narcissus had thrown his net early, and was trying it on with the inn's best-looking serving girl, a fine-figured young thing with long brown hair. Tavern girls tended to be either whores or married in Felix's experience, or immune to customers' attentions. Unless Narcissus was Eros himself, he was destined to fail.

Felix decided his best bet would be with one of the women working in the shops beside the inn. Pretending to stretch his legs, and keeping an eye out for Matho – this situation was just when he might meet his old centurion – he wandered up and down the street. He spotted two pretty girls working inside a baker's, but was put off by their burly father, who glowered at Felix in a 'I know what you're about' kind of way. A thick-waisted woman outside her vegetable shop gave him a bold look, but he passed on by. Beating Narcissus wasn't everything – there had to be desire too.

Felix next spotted an attractive woman with braided hair sweeping between the amphorae on display outside a wine shop. Young enough still to be single, she didn't see him approach.

'You have some good vintages,' he said, studying the prices detailed on the wall.

She jumped.

'My apologies,' said Felix. Seeing her blank face, he said, 'Do you speak Latin?'

'Some.' Her eyes were dark blue, her nose snubbed in an attractive way. 'You scared me.'

'Sorry.' He raised his hands in a placating gesture. 'You have nothing to fear.'

The beginnings of a smile. 'You're a Roman legionary. Mother says I shouldn't speak to any of you. That you all want only one thing.'

'That's harsh,' said Felix, thinking, *her mother has the truth of it*, and feeling a little embarrassed.

A voice spoke in Illyrian, and a middle-aged woman emerged from the shop. Her pleasant face hardened at the sight of Felix. 'You want to buy wine?' Her Latin was strongly accented but good.

'I . . . perhaps.' Felix's eyes flickered to the girl.

'Or are you troubling my daughter? The latter, I think.' Folding her arms, she advanced on Felix.

He backed away a step. 'We were talking, nothing more.'

A contemptuous *phhhh*. 'Do you think I was born yesterday? Young men are the same now as they were when I was a girl. Either buy some wine, or be on your way.'

'I'll head back to my comrades.' Felix put on his winning smile, delivering it first to the mother, who scowled, and then her daughter, who blushed a little. Deciding that he and Narcissus had been set an impossible task, and that valuable drinking time was being wasted, he strode off without a backward glance.

As he got back, Narcissus was on the receiving end of plenty of jibes.

'What happened?' asked Felix.

'The serving girl was having none of his sweet talk,' said Mattheus, grinning.

Felix winked at Narcissus. 'Are you sure you weren't exaggerating your previous conquests?'

'You don't seem to have succeeded either,' muttered Narcissus, burying his nose in his cup.

'Anything to report?' Antonius asked his brother.

'The young women of Apollonia are well guarded,' said Felix with a rueful shake of his head.

'You're not giving up?' Mattheus glanced from Felix to Narcissus and back.

Felix poured himself a large measure of wine. 'Let's just get pissed.'

'We can always visit a whorehouse later,' said Narcissus.

'If you can still get it up by then,' retorted Mattheus, holding out a stiff forefinger and letting it droop.

'Speak for yourself,' snarled Narcissus.

'Settle down, the pair of you. Five denarii will last us all night, and more.' Antonius slapped a pair of dice on the table. Made from sheep tail-bones, they went everywhere with him. 'Who's for a game?' he demanded.

'Wake up.' A hand was shaking Felix's shoulder.

Deep in a pleasant dream about the girl from the wine shop rather than the usual nightmare about Ingenuus, he ignored it.

A slap to the back of his head. 'Stir yourself, brother. We're going home.'

Felix came to, his face planted sideways on rough timber. His mouth was dry, his tongue furry. He sat up, swaying. Darkness blanketed the street. The shops were shut, and the crowds of earlier had vanished. Antonius was standing over him – he looked almost as drunk as Felix felt. Mattheus and Fabius were both under the table, snoring. Felix looked around.

'Where's Narcissus?'

'Gone for a piss.'

'Let's get another drink.' Felix could hear himself slurring the words.

Antonius made an obscene gesture towards the tavern. 'The inn-keeper's shutting up shop. 'S time to go.'

It took a few moments to kick Mattheus and Fabius awake, and longer to find Narcissus, who had collapsed in an alleyway, cock in hand, and fallen asleep. Eventually, however, they had gathered. Draining the last drops from their cups, and the jug, they weaved off down the street. The darkness wasn't total: some premises still had torches burning outside, illuminating their way. Mattheus began to sing a popular ditty, out of tune. Narcissus tried to join in, but couldn't remember more than the first word or two of each line and so gave up in disgust. Spying another tavern, Felix made a beeline for the door. He had just reached the threshold when Antonius pulled him away.

'C'mon. Bed.'

'I'm thirsty,' protested Felix.

'Your head's going to be sore enough in the morning.'

'I'll be fine.'

'Don't give Pullo an excuse to put you on latrine duties.'

Antonius' advice sank in. They wouldn't have to fight tomorrow, nor even parade, but Pullo required his men to be functioning. Grumbling under his breath, Felix turned, and collided with someone exiting the tavern.

'Look where you're going,' Felix growled.

'I could say the same to you,' said the legionary.

The pair glared at each other in the orange-red torchlight. A fresh pink scar ran from the corner of the man's eye to his chin. Recognition tickled Felix's drink-fuddled brain. The same was happening to the hastatus. His face twisted with rage.

'It's you!'

Felix planted his hands on the hastatus' chest and shoved, sending him stumbling backwards into the tavern. 'Antonius!'

'I'm here.'

'Trouble.'

Keeping their faces towards the inn, Felix and Antonius joined their comrades.

'Like to tell me what's going on?' demanded Mattheus as the hastatus and three of his friends spilled onto the street. Black Stubble was one, but Felix didn't recognise the others. All four advanced, murder in their eyes.

'Who are these arseholes?' hissed Antonius.

'They're the ones who were raping the girl in Antipatreia,' said Felix.

'That's quite a mark you left on him.' Narcissus' tone was acid. He didn't back away, however. Nor did the rest.

A comrade was a comrade, no matter what, thought Felix.

'I knew we'd meet again,' said the scar-faced hastatus. 'It was only a matter of time.'

'Raped any children since?' Felix hawked a gob of phlegm, which landed close to his enemy's feet.

'No, but I will again, gods willing.' The hastatus leered. 'Where's the whore you took from us?'

'Screw you.' Revulsion filled Felix, but he could no more stop such atrocities than he could pluck the moon from the night sky. He hoped the girl was safe from harm – the morning after the sack of Antipatreia, he'd given her food for a few days and sent her to find the kin she said lived in a village nearby.

The hastatus had his dagger out. 'You're going to pay for what you did to me.'

'Think again, cocksucker,' said Felix. 'It's five against four.'

'Four men against five yellow-livers,' sneered the hastatus, but his friends didn't look so sure.

He was still leering when Felix snatched a jug from a table and hurled it. Catching the hastatus in the side of the head, it dropped him in a sprawl of limbs on the ground. Felix bared his teeth. 'Five against three, maggots. Still keen?'

Black Stubble waved his two comrades back. 'We know you, whore-son, and now we know your mates. Best sleep with one eye open from now on.'

Felix flung another jug at him; Black Stubble ducked, and the vessel shattered off the tavern wall. The noise brought the doormen outside, and with menacing waves of their clubs, they ordered the legionaries to be gone.

Felix and his comrades headed down the street. Hauling the semi-conscious scar-faced man, the hastati went in the opposite direction. Both groups shouted abuse until they were out of sight of each other.

'Bastards,' growled Fabius. 'We should have beaten the shit out of them.'

'Not worth it,' said Felix. 'If an officer had come along, we'd have been in the shit. Or someone might have been stabbed. Then there would be an official enquiry, and gods knows what else.'

'You should have left well alone in Antipatreia,' said Antonius.

'Don't start with me,' snapped Felix, aware that his brother was right.

CHAPTER XXIX

Pella, Macedon, late autumn 199 BC

Demetrios eyed the sky as he and his comrades from the file joined the crowd which was spilling from the northern gate. It was overcast, and looked to stay that way; there was no promise of rain either. That suited him. The year was coming to a close, but when the sun was out, its heat was still considerable. When it came to the hoplitodromos, the prestigious race in armour, Demetrios would need every advantage on offer to have any chance of winning.

The annual festival to celebrate Zeus' role as wind-roarer and storm-bringer was in full flow, bringing business in the bustling city to a standstill. As they did every year, plays, feasts and athletic contests took place almost every day for a month. Most important deity in the pantheon throughout Greece, Zeus was particularly revered in Macedon. His mood would determine the number and severity of storms that would batter the region through the long, dark winter. Along with thousands of soldiers, each delighted that the fighting was over until the spring, Demetrios had been at the ceremony marking the beginning of Zeus' festival.

A grand affair celebrated outside the city walls, it had seen scores of fine bulls die under the priests' blades. Not one had protested its death, favourable omens that had lifted the cheering to the cloud-filled skies. Men said since that Macedon's Greek enemies, such as Aitolia, might also pray to the wind-roarer, but would every sacrificial beast of theirs go to the god so willingly? They would not – it was rare indeed to hear no bellows of protest when the blood was sheeting to the ground, and heads were rolling – which meant that Zeus favoured Macedon not just over Rome, but over Aitolia too.

Wine laid on by Philip that first day had made the celebrations memorable. The young women of Pella, missing their menfolk during the summer campaign, had been most . . . welcoming, thought Demetrios with a little smile. His luck hadn't been quite as good since, but nor had it been bad. No more a lowly docks labourer who slept on the street, he was a phalangist – a man worthy of admiration. Nor was it just the fair sex who showed respect. Shopkeepers and the proprietors of taverns, even well-to-do merchants, would nod as he and his comrades strode through the streets. Demetrios gave silent thanks, first to Zeus (not to show disrespect), then to Hermes and Ares for the change in his fortunes.

It was pleasant to mix with civilians, to forget army life for a time. Demetrios was reminded of the festivals he'd attended as a boy. The same sights were on offer here. Small children played tag through the throng, their garlands often falling to the ground unnoticed. Their mothers cackled and eyed the groups of well-muscled soldiers and farmers who would take part in the races. Priests and their acolytes observed a dignified silence. An exception were those from far-off Dodona: bearded, and famous for their unwashed feet, they were still haughtier than most noblemen. Snaggle-toothed ancients muttered and nodded, remembering the long-distant days when they had competed against one another. Paunchy, self-important nobles and merchants talked in loud voices about the events they had paid for, and the prizes on offer.

The stadium came into sight not long after. Built by Alexander's father, it stood to the north of the city. A magnificent structure of marble and brick, it accommodated ten thousand people. Demetrios had never competed in it, and the idea of so many spectators was terrifying. His older comrades seemed excited too, in particular Philippos, who was flexing his biceps with every stride.

The hoplitodromos was one of the hardest races. Demetrios' older comrades thought him mad to enter it. As might have been expected, Empedokles' had been the loudest voice of contempt. The veterans didn't know that since their return from the summer campaign, Demetrios had been training in the nearby hills at every opportunity. That didn't mean he would win anything, of course, he thought.

It was as if Kimon had sensed his doubt. 'Look,' he said as they entered the area reserved for athletes, under the banks of seating. A large doorway led to changing rooms, baths and the boxing and wrestling squares. 'Cretans. Those are the ones to beat.'

Demetrios stared. Short, lithe and all seemingly carved from the same stone, the Cretans were archers in the king's army. Their athletic prowess had been clear at Ottolobus, when they had kept up with the Companions' horses.

'Think you can beat them?' Philippos' eyes were dancing.

Demetrios stuck out his chin. 'I'll do my best.'

'That's the spirit.' Philippos gave him a friendly clout, which was like being hit with a plank of wood. 'I'll see you later.'

Wishing Philippos luck, Demetrios and the rest went to watch the initial heats for his race, which were about to begin. The first was between youths who had just finished their warrior training. A contest bursting with young pride, it was conducted at breakneck speed.

'They're running as if this was an Olympic final,' said Kimon. 'Fools. They'll have less wind come the next race.'

The second heat was between phalangists. Demetrios observed with great interest. 'Who's that?' he asked as it finished, the winner two spear lengths ahead of his nearest competitor.

A man in the row behind heard. 'Philonides of Beroea. Fast, isn't he?'

More phalangists raced in the third race, which was won by a long-legged warrior from Pydna. Soon it would be Demetrios' turn. With Kimon's and Antileon's good wishes filling his ears, he made his way to the gathering point under the stands, where time was granted to strip off and have another competitor oil one's muscles, before donning their armour. Demetrios tried not to worry that four of the men he'd be running against were Cretan. The last was a phalangist he recognised but didn't know by name.

Luckily, there was little opportunity to brood. New mail shirt on, his aspis over the back of his left shoulder, and a borrowed sword swinging from a baldric, Demetrios followed the official who guided them to the starting point, which was positioned below the king's box. As they emerged from the tunnel into the light, Demetrios could feel the weight of thousands of eyes. His stomach churned; he didn't dare look at the crowd. The six lined up, their feet crunching the sand.

Cretans were renowned for their physicality, and Demetrios judged this lot to be no different – sly looks aplenty were coming his and the phalangist's way. It was best to run a line close to the inner edge of the track, which was marked at each end by a stone column and in between by black and white stones, but this was also the riskiest area

– and was already occupied by the Cretans. Demetrios opted for the outermost position, beside the phalangist.

They crouched down in readiness.

Herakleides was officiating in Philip's absence. The moment he'd been given the nod by the official on the track, he dropped his arm.

The Cretans took off at a fast lope, and Demetrios and the phalangist followed, jostling for position. The two best Cretans soon broke away, and the second pair spread out a little, blocking an attempt to overtake close in. This had been planned, thought Demetrios, increasing his speed. To have any chance of a place, he needed to pass the Cretan blockers before the turn.

Pain lanced up Demetrios' arm. The phalangist had elbowed him. Illegal in the Olympic Games, such tactics were standard practice here. Rather than retaliate, Demetrios sprinted away, leaving the man trailing in his wake. The lead Cretans were nearing the turning point; fear gave him extra energy. Sneaking up on the right of the outside 'blocker', Demetrios shot past him. He angled in and took the bend nice and tight, his aspis brushing the polished stone of the column. Third place, he thought.

One stadion remained to the finish line – less than ten score paces. The front pair of Cretans had split now, with the taller in the lead, his companion a short way behind. Despite the weight of his armour and shield, Demetrios closed in on the second Cretan, his feet pounding the sand in a frenetic rhythm. Nervous, the Cretan glanced over his shoulder, and Demetrios accelerated, managing to give him a dig as he went by. The Cretan stumbled, leaving the race to Demetrios and the tall man.

The leader sensed what was going on, and sprinted for the finish. Demetrios followed, pumping his arms and legs. Sand flew, air hissed by, his aspis bounced off his back. His mail felt heavy as lead, and the effort of carrying it made his chest rise and fall like a smith's hammer. From what seemed a long way off, people were cheering. Demetrios closed in. Two paces separated him from the Cretan. I can do it, he thought. I can take him.

Stars danced at the edge of Demetrios' vision. Lungs burning, leg muscles screaming, he could taste victory. Thirty paces from the end column, he pulled parallel with the Cretan. Kept pace with him for four. Led by a nose for perhaps five, and then watched in disbelief as his opponent somehow recovered the lead. Demetrios had nothing left – his speed dropped away, almost allowing the Cretan's companion to catch him. He was lucky to finish second.

Pride stinging, Demetrios managed a smile when the tall Cretan clapped him on the back. On his return, his friends were less forgiving.

'That was a stupid run,' said Kimon. 'There was no need to try and win. Second place would have been enough to see you into the final.'

Antileon nodded. 'You'll need that energy.'

Demetrios scowled. 'I know.'

'Pride – that's what it was,' said Kimon. 'Just like those lads earlier.'

He was right, thought Demetrios, hoping that the delay before the final would leave him time to recover.

It did, just. Up against two Cretans, a fleet-footed local farmer and a pair of phalangists, Demetrios struggled to keep up from the start. Finding a hidden reserve of energy close to the turn, he sneaked ahead of the farmer and one of the phalangists. The second soldier – Philonides of Beroea – and one of the Cretans barged into each other coming around the column, offering a chance to tail the Cretan in the lead. Demetrios tried and failed to catch him the entire way home.

'Second place isn't bad,' said Kimon, when he returned to his seat clutching his olive wreath. 'You might have done better if—'

'I know, I know.' Smiling, Demetrios acknowledged the praise of the people around them. 'I shouldn't have tried to beat that first Cretan.'

'That's right.' Antileon offered his wineskin.

Demetrios took a long pull, enjoying the warm sensation as the wine coursed down his throat. He wrapped himself in his cloak lest he get a chill. Eyes wandering over the audience, he noticed Kryton and Herakleides close to the royal box. At once the clandestine meeting he had overheard returned to him. During the summer, Kryton had been with the king, while Herakleides had stayed with the fleet on Macedon's eastern seaboard. For all Demetrios knew, they were talking about the upcoming races, but he couldn't help feeling suspicious. When the pair vanished into one of the passageways that led towards the many entrances, his doubts about them surged.

Telling his puzzled friends that he'd be back soon, Demetrios slipped from his seat and hastened towards the area. There was small chance of being recognised by anyone in the crowd, but he left his wreath behind. To his relief, his worries came to naught. There were plenty of other athletes amid the crowds below the seating; the dim light was also perfect for a man who didn't want to be noticed. Demetrios slipped past a gaggle of young women who were doing a bad job of pretending not to ogle a pair of grinning Cretans. He hesitated, belly rumbling, by the stall of a woman selling skewers of fried mutton, before remembering with a chuckle that he was naked apart from his cloak. His purse was safe with Kimon.

There was no sign of Herakleides and Kryton at the staircase he'd seen them take. Cursing, Demetrios paced up and down either side of it, trying to look inconspicuous while also studying the faces of the passers-by. Inevitably, he was then recognised by a man who'd seen his race. Trying not be rude, Demetrios accepted several slugs of wine and congratulatory back-slaps; he laughed in rueful acceptance when he was told *again* how it was unwise to give one's all in the heats. When those nearby realised he was a winner, they also pressed in, clasping his hand and offering high praise.

By the time Demetrios extricated himself from the well-wishers, he had given up hope of finding Herakleides and Kryton. A prime opportunity had been missed. Regretting that he had not moved faster, he weaved his way in the direction of the stairway nearest his friends. Broken pottery underfoot – a drunk had dropped his cup – made him stop to check his foot for cuts.

'I'm telling you, the time has to be now.'

The voice came from an alcove a few paces away, one of the many that ran around the inside of the stadium directly under the seating above.

'The risks are too great,' said a second man.

Demetrios froze. Kryton boomed, even when he was trying to whisper. Against the odds, thought Demetrios, he had found them. Slipping to the wall, he leaned against it in the nonchalant fashion of a man taking a rest, or a good position to eye up passing women. He listened, but to his frustration, could make out nothing of what was being said in the alcove. Risking discovery, he shuffled sideways one, two steps, until his shoulder was at the very edge of the patterned brick archway.

'It must be done soon,' said another voice.

Demetrios' concerns reached a new pitch. Not only were Herakleides and Kryton with a third person, they were planning something.

'I've never taken orders from an Aitolian, and I don't intend to start now.' Kryton sounded furious.

'You will do what *I* say, and if I agree with the Aitolian . . .' Herakleides paused. 'Do I have to say more?'

Kryton muttered under his breath, and fell silent.

Demetrios couldn't believe that Herakleides was meeting with a representative of one of Macedon's bitterest enemies. He longed to leap on the three with pummelling fists, but the king would be better served with proof that his admiral and one of his speira commanders were plotting against him. Demetrios listened, desperate to hear more.

'I agree that we must act,' said Herakleides.

Before the Tarentine could say another word, Demetrios sneezed. One of those come-out-of-nowhere explosive propulsions of breath, he was powerless to prevent it. At once he ducked his head and strode off. A voice cried out behind him, and with quickening heart, he shoved his way into the crowd, ten paces forward and then half a dozen to his right. Staying low, he wove to and fro in the throng, eventually turning back on himself and walking back past the alcove with his chin up and chest out, playing the triumphant athlete. The recess was empty; Demetrios risked a glance over his shoulder, but could see no sign of the conspirators.

His relief at escaping didn't last. The king was in danger – he felt sure of it.

But with no proof, who could he tell?

CHAPTER XXX

Near Pella, Macedon

High in the hills above the city, Philip was walking with his regent Menander among tall cypress trees. It was a crisp, sunny morning, but underneath the canopy, a man needed a cloak. Needles and cones blanketed the ground, deadening the noise of their passage. Both men carried spears; bows were slung over their shoulders. A pack of hunting dogs ran in front, some sight hounds, others scent. Now and again, a bird alarmed by their passage flew off, but they paid no heed. They were after bigger prey.

Philip's eyes strayed often to his favourite. Mostly grown, and called Peritas after one of Alexander's dogs, it was long-limbed and deep-chested, with the same shaggy brindle coat as the rest. He'd been drawn to it as a pup, when its bravery had far exceeded its size. Smaller than its litter mates, Peritas had fought for its mother's front teats with a determination that had warmed Philip's heart, and reminded him of his struggles against many enemies. His disbelieving huntsman was instructed to ensure Peritas got precedence over the others, and before he'd set off to war, Philip had conjured time in each busy day to visit the pup.

'Will they find us a deer, sire?' asked Menander.

'Artemis grant they do.' Philip pointed. 'Mark Peritas – he's right behind the lead scent hound – it's as if he knows what it can do.'

'He looks to be fast as well, sire.'

'Another year or two, and he could be the best dog I've had.' The irony in his words wasn't lost on Philip. The campaigning season was over, yet this was the first time he'd had a chance to hunt since his return to Pella. Come the spring, the legions would return, and his other enemies, the Illyrians and Dardani, the Rhodians and the Pergamenes, would begin circling like vultures. There would be precious little time to hunt for the foreseeable future.

'Sire?'

Philip didn't reply.

'My apologies, sire. You're preoccupied.'

Philip half-smiled. 'Is it that obvious?'

Menander's gaze was keen. 'You're thinking about Rome, sire.'

'Not just Rome. I have many enemies.'

They both laughed. Fifty paces ahead, Peritas looked back. His tail wagged, then he went back to following the scent hounds.

'Oh, to have such a simple life,' said Philip.

'It would be pleasant, sire.'

Philip sighed. 'Perhaps I could have tried harder to keep the city states on my side.'

Menander gave the king a surprised glance, but didn't speak.

'Thessaly and a couple of other minnows aside, Macedon stands alone when it need not have. If my stepfather's Common Alliance were still alive, things might be different.'

'You are being hard on yourself, sire. Too much blood has been spilt for Aitolia ever to see eye to eye with Macedon, let alone become its ally. Once it appealed to Rome for help, there was never going to be a way back. As for the other states, well, none has an army worth talking about. The Piraeus near Athens offers Rome's fleet shelter that we could do without, it's true, but I doubt the Athenians would have considered setting aside their differences with Macedon, even before your attacks on Attika and at the Propontis. Their city's glory days are long gone, yet they still act as if they're better than everyone.'

Philip nodded. Most Greeks regarded Macedonians as unwashed, sheep-humping savages, and city states like Athens did not *want* friendly relations or alliances with Macedon. 'Keeping the Akhaians loyal would be useful.' Akhaia lay in the north of the Peloponnese, its territory forming the southern shore of the narrow Korinthian Gulf.

'Indeed, sire. Should they ally themselves with Rome, their troops could land close to Thessaly's borders.' Up to this point, Akhaia's small fleet had prevented any such attempt.

'They love to bleat about their towns that I hold.' Philip ruled several settlements in Akhaian territory, remnants of his stepfather's attempts to keep Sparta and Aitolia apart. 'They shall have them back.'

'Not the Akrokorinth, sire?' Menander's voice was alarmed. The fortress dominated the narrow isthmus of land linking the Peloponnese to the mainland of Greece. Noting Philip's raised eyebrows, he smiled with relief. 'It shall remain Macedonian.'

'So will the other "Fetters". Macedon would lie open to the south otherwise.' The king scowled. 'We know to our cost that Chalkis is vulnerable. Demetrias is too. With the Rhodian and Pergamene semi-permanent residents in Greek waters, the Romans can easily send ships to join them, as they did for the attack on Chalkis.' Philip shook his head. 'A wiser man might have left Pergamene and Rhodian territory well alone.'

'You were reclaiming what is Macedonian by right, sire.'

Philip remembered that this was how Herakleides had influenced him. He stared, distrustful, and read in Menander's earnest face that here was no sycophant. 'I was, but perhaps my timing could have been better.'

'You weren't to know when Rome would begin meddling in Greek affairs, sire. If you had sat about on your hands, I'll wager that the Pergamenes would have started preying on *your* territories. The skulking Rhodians would soon have joined in.'

'Better to take the battle to the enemy than the other way around, eh? Conquer or perish,' said Philip, repeating the old adage.

'Even so, sire. A king keen for peace is an idle ruler, they say, with questionable honour. But you were born to war, like your forebears. Born to lead your army.'

Philip smiled. 'Stout-hearted Menander. If I had a score of generals like you, I would have few concerns.'

'You are kind, sire. Ten thousand more phalangists wouldn't go amiss either.'

Their laughter eased the sombre mood.

'Before this fight is over, every man in Macedon who can bear arms will be needed,' said Philip. 'It won't be popular.'

'Your people love you, sire. They will fight for you, old and young.'

'Herakleides is the exception then. He will do anything but fight, it seems.'

'I am no sailor, sire. Naval battles are a thing of mystery to me.'

'There's no need to be diplomatic, Menander. I am no sea captain either, but our ships equal the enemy's in number. If the rumours are true about Attalus' squadron – that it wasn't there for most of the summer – our fleet is actually larger. Our sailors aren't equal to the Rhodians or Romans, but curse it all, Herakleides should have managed some kind of action.'

Menander made to say something, then hesitated.

'Speak.'

'I have never liked the Tarentine, sire. In my mind, a man who can betray his own city twice is not to be trusted.' Menander hesitated again.

'What is it?'

'It's a small thing, sire, like as not.'

The king let the dogs run on. 'Tell me.'

'A phalangist came to me yesterday, sire. He is worried about not just Herakleides, but his speira commander, a man named Kryton.'

'Kryton the boar killer? He has been with me since . . .' Philip's eyes returned to the hounds, who were making excited, whining noises '. . . neither of us needed to shave.'

'I know, sire. The phalangist did too. He begged forgiveness for mentioning Herakleides' and Kryton's names. Months had gone by before he had the courage even to approach me.'

Philip glowered. 'Months?'

'Consider his position, sire. He's a newish recruit, with no evidence. He risked much by coming forward. He saw something at the hoplitodromos, you see.'

'What had he to say?'

'It wasn't much.'

Philip made an impatient gesture. 'Artemis' tits, Menander, tell me!'

'One morning last winter, sire, he was coming off duty outside your quarters. He overheard a conversation between Herakleides and Kryton, about gambling debts.'

'Owing money is no kind of treason. If it was, I'd be guiltier than any man.' The costs of keeping an army in the field were immense, and the booty of recent years had not even come close to filling his war chest. Each winter, Philip spent many hours cultivating Pella's bankers and moneylenders, and he hated it. 'Bloodsucking leeches,' he muttered. 'Go on.'

'You'll know that Kryton is overfond of a wager, sire.'

Philip didn't, but nodded regardless.

'He's been borrowing from Herakleides.'

'Again, hardly a crime.'

'Indeed, sire. Why then the need to meet in secret, at an hour when most men are still abed?'

Menander was right, thought Philip. 'What else did he hear?'

'Nothing, sire. Kryton went to close the door, and the phalangist had to retreat lest he be discovered. He said that Herakleides spoke of a "delicate subject" that needed discussing. That's all.'

'Odd behaviour, that's certain. Has the phalangist—' Philip checked himself. 'What's his name? Come, tell me.'

Menander looked awkward. 'He asked me to keep his identity a secret, sire.'

'I am the king!' thundered Philip.

'He's called Demetrios, sire.'

'Like a thousand others.' Philip cast a glance at the lead scent hound, which had just given tongue. 'Is he loyal?'

'It is my belief he is, sire.' Menander returned Philip's stare.

'Has this Demetrios any further evidence?'

'He has seen Herakleides and Kryton together several times, sire, most recently at the hoplitodromos. He heard them talking to an Aitolian.'

Philip gave him a sharp look. 'About what?'

'He wasn't sure, sire. "The time has to be now," one of them said.'

'That could mean everything and nothing,' said Philip. 'What made him come to you?'

'Fear that if he did nothing, something terrible would happen to your majesty. He said that his life was worth nothing in comparison to yours. It's not much, sire, but I had to tell you.'

They walked in silence for a time.

Philip decided to have Herakleides and Kryton watched. He hadn't considered the Tarentine as a possible traitor before, but the phalangist's information should not be discounted.

Frenzied barking broke out. The scent hounds took off into the trees, followed at once by Peritas and the rest.

Philip broke into a run. 'Ready for a chase?'

'Your legs are younger than mine, sire,' replied Menander with a laugh. 'I'll try to keep up.'

Philip's feet flashed over the needles and cones, but his eyes were fixed on the rearmost dogs. He didn't care if they were following boar or deer. It was a joy to be here, with only Menander for company. To forget the threat of Rome, and whether one of his closest advisers was a traitor.

CHAPTER XXXI

Rome, winter 199/198 BC

Flamininus' party reached their destination, a large residence on the Quirinal Hill. Broken by a pair of large wooden doors, a long, high wall gave onto the street. To either side of the entrance, stone benches – empty now – provided supplicants with a place to sit as they waited for the man of the house to emerge. With a shake of his head, Flamininus indicated that Thrax should not yet use the knocker on Galba's front door. He hadn't sweated much on the walk here, but appearances had to be maintained. That was, he thought, if he was even allowed over the threshold. 'Pasion.'

His secretary materialised by his shoulder. 'Master?'

'How do I look?'

Pasion's eyes roved up and down. Pursing his lips, he rearranged several folds of Flamininus' toga. Standing back, he checked again. 'That's better.' His gaze lifted further. With a 'May I, master?', he patted down the hair on the side of Flamininus' head, and smiled. 'There you are. The very picture of *dignitas*.'

Hinges creaked. Flamininus turned to find Galba's doorman, a hulking Gaul, regarding them with a bemused expression. Embarrassed, Flamininus gave Pasion a meaningful glance.

Pasion cleared his throat. 'Titus Quinctius Flamininus, former tribune, propraetor and aedile; current quaestor, to see your master.'

The Gaul didn't seem impressed. 'Wait,' he said, shutting the door with a loud air of finality.

Pasion hissed with disapproval; Thrax looked annoyed. Flamininus stayed calm. Galba didn't know he was coming, so it was improbable that the doorman had been instructed to be rude. He was merely a savage, who knew no better. Besides, thought Flamininus, *he* had bigger fish to fry. Galba had little reason to allow him in. Their enmity was no longer fresh, but nor had it been resolved. No stone could be left unturned, however, for the consular elections were fast approaching, and things weren't going to Flamininus' plan.

Two of the ten tribunes were conducting a vigorous campaign in the Senate to prevent him from standing. Their supporters numbered less than thirty, but they were gaining support every day. Hearing the news had seen Flamininus' efforts to win votes redouble. Although Galba had not succeeded in Macedonia, he retained the trust of a large number of senators – his backing would be invaluable. If making peace with him was part of the price, thought Flamininus, so be it.

With a screech of unoiled hinges, the door opened again. This time the Gaul was accompanied by a well-groomed slave with a haughty expression. Oiled black locks and light brown skin marked him as a Judaean. His bow was not as deep as Flamininus would have liked.

'My master bids you welcome, Titus Quinctius Flamininus. Enter.'

'I will.' Flamininus strode in, thinking this was but the first hurdle of many. 'Come, Pasion, Thrax.'

Feet scurried as the two joined him. The Gaul shut the rest of Flamininus' retinue onto the street, then resumed his post in an alcove by the door.

Pleased – he had thought Galba might refuse entry to Thrax – Flamininus followed the Judaean into the house. The mosaic patterns were simple yet elegant, and the paving stones underfoot were marble. Even the wall frescoes – typical, dark red 'marble' squares – had been painted by master craftsmen.

They rounded the pool in the centre of the atrium floor, and headed for the courtyard beyond. Light flickered from lamps burning in the household shrine. From above its altar, painted masks of Galba's ancestors stared with what seemed clear distaste. Flamininus offered a silent prayer: I come with respect, to ask help of your descendant. He buried his intention to use Thrax as intimidation if it came to it.

Galba was strolling among the trellised vines and lemon trees. He had his back to them, a quite deliberate ploy, but Flamininus stayed calm. He needed Galba a great deal more than his host needed him.

A few paces away, the Judaean called, 'Your visitor, master.'

At last Galba turned.

'Titus Quinctius Flamininus, quaestor, to see you, master,' said the Judaean.

With a deep bow to Galba and a much smaller one to Flamininus, he retreated to the walkway that led around the garden. In a tiny act of rebellion that pleased Flamininus no end, Pasion and Thrax didn't join him, until with a casual jerk of his head, he indicated they should do so. It was better to begin the encounter in a civil fashion, and Thrax was close enough to summon quickly.

'Welcome, Titus Quinctius Flamininus, *quaestor*.' Galba's repeated tiny emphasis on the last word shouted the difference in their social rankings.

You arrogant prick, thought Flamininus, but he let none of his irritation show. 'I thank you, Sulpicius Galba.'

'Will you have wine?'

Flamininus hesitated. The idea of a drink appealed, but he wanted to remain in full control.

'Politics is thirsty work,' said Galba. 'Wine, Benjamin.' His eyes returned from the Judaean to Flamininus. 'It *is* politics that brings you to my door? Unless you've come to offer recompense for my men who were injured and killed by your thugs the summer before last?'

'If you wish to do the same for the men I lost, we can talk about it,' said Flamininus. They stared at one another, like two boxers gauging each other's strength before a fight.

'I didn't think that was the reason you were here. So it's the former,' said Galba, his tone light. 'My support in the Senate would help your chances of election.'

'You see through me with ease.' Flamininus' embarrassment wasn't all fake. He'd been expecting the usual social niceties, not this direct approach. Galba's gaze weighed down on him and, uncomfortable, Flamininus shifted his feet.

Benjamin reappeared with a jug and two glasses on a silver salver. Setting his burden on a one-legged stone table, he poured wine and padded across to hand a glass first to his master, and then Flamininus.

'I suppose we must toast Villius' victory in Macedonia,' said Galba drily.

'To victory in Macedonia,' said Flamininus.

His wording made Galba's eyes narrow; they drank.

'How lay the land when you left?' asked Flamininus.

'Macedonia is vulnerable,' said Galba. 'The Aetolians have been defeated by Philip, but their hatred for him is bitterer than ever. They will fight with us again. Athens is with us, and Achaea is wavering – a shove in the right direction and it will enter our camp. The other states will do nothing to hinder us, and the Illyrians wait only for word to invade with the legions. The Dardani will attack as soon as the legions march. To the east, the Rhodian and Pergamene fleets are ready for the coming of spring.' Galba paused, then added, 'The general who next leads our forces into Macedonia will in all likelihood defeat Philip. But you know that already, thanks to your spies. No wonder you intend to relieve Villius of his command should you become consul.'

Flamininus spat out his wine in shock.

'I knew it!' crowed Galba.

If he knows about my spies, thought Flamininus, he must have ones of his own. 'You seem confident of knowing my mind. Why would I take over from Villius?'

Galba laughed. 'I remember how furious you were when I was elected. Last winter, you were prevented from standing by illness. To try for a third year in a row is extraordinary – most men who fail to win election as consul wait for a few years, but not you. You have an ulterior motive, and you're a Hellenophile. It stands to reason you want to be the general to conquer Macedonia, to bring Greece under the Republic's control.'

The bastard's toying with me, Flamininus thought furiously, but I'm the one with Thrax here, while he has only Benjamin the Judaean.

'Am I not right?' asked Galba.

'You are,' admitted Flamininus.

'Why in Jupiter's name would I help you to have what *I* cannot?' Galba's voice throbbed with anger.

'Villius thwarted you in order to take the glory for himself. You can do nothing about that,' said Flamininus, adding harshly, 'and the task of defeating Macedonia is no longer yours.'

Galba's face was black. 'Nor is it yours.'

'Support me in the elections, and take your revenge on Villius.'

'Vengeance is overrated. I see no benefit in doing as you ask.'

'Greece's riches will lie at the feet of the general who conquers Macedonia, and some of it shall be yours. I thought a thousand thousand denarii, yearly for the first five years after Philip's defeat, suitable reward.' It was a staggering sum, even to someone of Galba's wealth, and Flamininus was prepared to double it.

'Four thousand thousand denarii, for ten years. I also intend to be one of your legates,' said Galba. 'As you know, the real work will begin after Philip's defeat. Setting in place pro-Roman factions to control the Greek city states, breaking up the more troublesome ones, and so on.'

'That was something I had intended to do alone,' said Flamininus stiffly. Or with men *I* chose, he thought.

'Now I shall be there to help you.' Galba's teeth were brown and crooked.

'Two thousand thousand denarii, for ten years. You shall be a legate, but only for a year.'

'I have stated the terms,' said Galba. 'You will accept them.'

Flamininus bridled. 'You cannot force me!'

'I wonder,' said Galba conversationally, 'what the Senate would make of a man who met in secret with foreign emissaries? Who conspired to keep Aetolia neutral purely for his own gain?'

'What are you talking about?' blustered Flamininus, clasping his hands behind his back so Galba would not see them tremble.

'Others in Rome have spies too.' Galba's voice was mocking. 'The day you met the Aetolian Metrodoros, you were followed not just by the cutpurses that your ox of a bodyguard dealt with, but by my man. Metrodoros slipped away before he could be questioned, but the mere fact that you met with him made me suspicious, and months later, when the Aetolians stayed neutral – a complete about-face – I knew you were behind it.'

Flamininus' world felt as if were crumbling around him. If this information got out, he would face trial for treason. At best, he might expect a lifetime of exile, but more probable would be a forced suicide. 'You can't prove it. No one will believe you.'

'You told the Rhodian and Pergamene emissaries what to say to the Senate. I have written statements from both men to prove it,' revealed Galba. 'How will that sound in public?'

'That was three years ago!' cried Flamininus, reeling. 'Why have you said nothing before?'

'I have learned to keep such gems safe and secret until the right time – which is now,' said Galba. 'To become a legate in Greece, and oversee the running of a city like Athens, say, now that's a prize worth having.'

'You will not breathe a word of my meetings,' threatened Flamininus.

'I will not – as long as you agree to my terms. All of them.'

'Thrax.' It was time, thought Flamininus, for some intimidation. The threat of a few broken bones would keep Galba's tongue from wagging. He would support Flamininus' candidacy in the election, and the payment of a more reasonable sum than the eye-watering amounts he had just demanded. Galba would not be a legate either – the very notion was preposterous.

Galba dipped his chin in Benjamin's direction. Flamininus didn't care. By the time the Judaean fetched the Gaulish doorman, Thrax would have a blade at Galba's throat. The pair of slaves would be powerless to intervene.

Flamininus twisted, looking for Thrax. The Thracian had covered half the distance from the covered walkway. His iron-shod staff was ready in his fist. Flamininus smiled. When Benjamin followed Thrax rather than running for the front door, he thought nothing of it. A stripling less than a third of the Thracian's size, the Judaean was no threat. Then, to his horror, Flamininus noted the long, slim knife in Benjamin's hand.

Flamininus' warning cry made Thrax turn, but he was too slow. Too late. Graceful as a dancer, Benjamin leaped in close. Up rose his arm. Down fell his blade. Twice he stabbed, twice the blood gouted from Thrax's thick neck. Even as he flailed his staff at Benjamin, the Judaean spun a full circle to end up behind him again. Stab. Stab. Fresh crimson spurted onto the vines. Thrax shook his head, and bellowed in rage. He staggered, and went to one knee. Red froth bubbled at his lips. As Benjamin came in for a third time, the Thracian was already toppling onto the stone paving.

Flamininus looked away, but he couldn't block his ears to the wet, meaty sound of Benjamin's dagger, and Thrax's grunts each time the blade slid in.

'You think to threaten me in my own home?' Galba's voice was stony.

Flamininus imagined his hands locked tight around Galba's chicken-scrawny throat – and saw Benjamin killing him next. 'I'm sorry,' Flamininus whispered.

'Indeed you will be. My terms have doubled.'

'I accept them regardless,' said Flamininus, spitting out the words. 'And if by some chance I do not defeat Philip?'

'I shall see to it that the Senate receives every detail of your grubby meetings with foreign emissaries.'

I'll be beggared by Galba if I win, and ruined if I fail, thought Flamininus.

'Very well,' he said.

CHAPTER XXXII

Pella, Macedon

It was a cold day, the wind whistling down from the snow-capped mountains to the north and west to howl through the city's streets. Despite the winter chill, Pella was busy. Carters argued over who had right of way. Smiths toiled at their anvils. Directed by a foreman, labourers rebuilt a collapsed wall. Steam rose from penned sheep in a slaughterhouse yard. Matrons gossiped at their front doors; small children ran about, playing and shrieking, as children do.

Wearing their thickest cloaks, Demetrios, Kimon and Antileon wandered amid the throng. The trio were off duty, and inevitably, they had been drinking. At least, thought Demetrios, he had forced his friends to visit the palaestra first. He'd answered Kimon's suggestion that they visit a tavern straight after breakfast with a flat refusal; a short argument had ensued, but he had won his comrades over. A good run – Demetrios had easily outstripped the other two – had been followed by wrestling, almost every bout of which Antileon had won. Since his fight with Empedokles, Demetrios considered himself not bad at pankration, but during his initial bout, Kimon had surprised him with a scissor hold around the waist. Choked, unable to breathe, Demetrios had quickly had to concede defeat. He'd paid Kimon back in style, beating him twice in succession, but the loss still rankled.

Now, he brooded, his gregarious friend was going to drink him under the table. It wasn't that Demetrios didn't like wine – he did – but the pursuit of drunkenness at every opportunity left him cold. His moderate attitude had begun on the rowing benches. The pounding head and nausea that followed heavy drinking was a thousand times worse when a man had to row from dawn to dusk. It was similar with training and drill, and no doubt, he decided, combat.

'This looks like a fine spot,' declared Kimon, the self-appointed leader of their drinking spree, coming to a halt by a tavern door.

Demetrios looked up at the sign, which had seen better days. Despite the cracked, faded paint, he made out a reclining, smiling Dionysos surrounded by grape-heavy vines. Maenads danced around the god; a fig tree stood in the background. 'It's no worse than anywhere else, I suppose,' he said.

Kimon pulled open the tavern door. A blast of warm air hit their faces, laden with the smell of wine, roasting meat and men's sweat. 'I can see a table,' he declared.

'Lead on,' said Antileon. 'First round's on our champion pankrationist.'

'The champion I beat?' Kimon was smirking.

'One and the same.' Antileon glanced at Demetrios, clearly hoping he'd react.

With a roll of his eyes, Demetrios shoved past. 'Come on then, you pair of dusty feet.'

As time passed, he was forced to agree that Kimon's choice had been a good one. The tavern was old and run-down, but the wine was acceptable, and the food – fresh-baked bread, olives and a nutty, flavoursome sheep's cheese – better than that. A pair of musicians, one playing the lyre, the other a double flute, played tune after merry tune. In the centre of the room, the tables had been cleared away, allowing those who so wished to dance. Kimon and Antileon had been quick to take the floor, drawn by the half-clad whores in the dancers' midst. Demetrios, who was clumsy even when sober, stubbornly resisted every demand to join them, but in the end, could hold out no more.

'This song I love to live and sing, and when I'm dead, put my lyre at my feet and my pipes over my head. Pipe away!' Arm in arm, they roared the words with everyone else.

When the musicians stopped for a rest, the red-faced, perspiring friends were glad to take a seat. They hammered their empty cups on the table to get the serving girls' attention. 'More wine!' roared Antileon at the first one to look in their direction.

She sauntered over, all hips and bosom, and Antileon pulled her onto his lap. She protested, but with a smile. At once Kimon sidled closer.

Here we go, thought Demetrios, jealousy gnawing at him. Rather than join in the flirtation with his friends, he began to eavesdrop on the conversation at the next table, which was occupied by four work-men, carpenters and builders from the look of their weather-beaten faces, calloused hands and grimy chitons.

'Theatre?' The nearest man, who sported a bushy beard, snorted. 'Who wants to sit on his arse for hours, listening to actors spout rubbish?'

'Barbarian,' said his neighbour. 'Life's rich tapestry is all there on the stage. Tragedy and comedy, politics, love, sex and humour.'

'The jokes are awful,' said the bearded man, smiling as the others agreed.

'Some are funny.'

'Not many,' declared the bearded man.

'Drink enough wine, and they're hilarious,' countered the first speaker. 'I hear the old comedy that's on this afternoon is very good. *Frogs* is meant to be one of Aristophanes' best, or so they say.'

Surprise filled Demetrios, whose only experience of theatre had been seeing a production of this exact play in his village, put on by a band of itinerant actors. It had mesmerised him, and his spirits soared at the idea of watching it for a second time.

'Even if we wanted to go, there won't be a spare seat in the place,' said the third man. 'The king is attending today's performance.'

'People don't last the pace. By the afternoon, there are always a few spots up the back,' replied the bearded man.

His companions laughed off his suggestion, but Demetrios' interest quickened. Seeing the comedy appealed hugely; the opportunity to see Philip made it irresistible. Herakleides could also be at the theatre; it might be possible to spy on him. Demetrios leaned towards his friends. Antileon had just released the serving girl, who was loudly declaring that if she didn't get back to work, the landlord would turn her out on the street. Kimon told her to send him over.

'We'll put the dog right, won't we, brothers?' he cried.

'Let's go to the theatre,' said Demetrios. 'There's a comedy on.'

Antileon looked at him as if he'd taken leave of his senses.

'And leave this nice, warm tavern?' Kimon jerked his head at the serving girl, who was glancing in his direction. 'She likes me. Give me a couple of hours . . .' He winked. 'She's got a room.'

Imagining another night where Kimon vanished and Antileon headed back to the camp early, Demetrios decided he wasn't going to take no for an answer. It took him a while – they managed to down another jug of wine – and he had to promise his friends the first round of drinks in whatever hostelry they found after the performance, but he won them over.

Reaching the theatre, the three friends found that the second act of *Frogs* had just ended. Knowing that the musical interlude from the chorus afforded a chance to find a seat, Demetrios beckoned to his comrades and slipped through the corridor that fed into the orchestra, the circular space before the stage. He peered around the corner, soon spotting Philip in the lowest, front row. His pulse quickened as he spied Herakleides sitting right behind. Following convention, Philip's guards were positioned by the entrance where Demetrios stood, and at the one opposite. None were particularly near the king.

'Move along!' hissed the doorman, who had followed them in. 'And make it quick – the chorus won't last much longer.'

Demetrios checked his friends were ready, and then ducked into the orchestra. The best place to sit with a view of Philip would be up and to his right. Ignoring the disapproving looks and hisses from members of the audience – as Antileon had repeatedly told him on the way, it was regarded as the height of bad behaviour to enter a play, comedy or tragedy, in mid-performance – Demetrios took the steps to the back of the theatre two at a time.

The Fates were in fine humour. Close to the top, he found three seats, right beside the stairs. Muttering apologies to those around them, Demetrios settled down with his friends. The third act soon began, and the chorus reintroduced the main characters to the stage. Cheers met Dionysos' arrival, and Demetrios chuckled. The actor portraying the god of wine had a huge paunch; under his stained chiton jutted a massive erect penis. His bearded mask had a huge, lascivious grin. The audience booed the black-clad, evil-faced Hades, and jeered at Euripides and Aiskhylos as they came out last, accompanied by an ironic cacophony from the chorus. Silence fell.

'What's the story?' Kimon asked in a none-too-quiet voice.

A man in the row behind tutted.

Demetrios leaned forward so both his friends could hear, and whispered, 'Dionysos has gone down to the underworld—'

'That's a fucking stupid thing to do,' said Antileon.

Demetrios glowered. 'As I was saying, Dionysos enters Tartaros to bring back Euripides—'

'The famous playwright?' asked Kimon.

'One and the same,' agreed Demetrios.

'Shhhh,' said a voice.

Antileon looked confused. 'What's he doing in Tartaros?'

'The reason isn't important,' said Demetrios from between gritted teeth. 'Euripides is there. So is Aiskhylos. The two are having a poetry competition; the winner will be crowned king of the poets. Dionysos ends up judging the contest, but he can't decide who—'

'Zeus, will you be quiet?' muttered the man who had tutted. 'Some of us came to watch the play.'

A burst of laughter from the audience came to the friends' rescue; Demetrios used the noise to sketch the rest of the plot before settling down to enjoy himself. The production was of a far higher standard than the rough-and-ready version he'd seen as a boy. There were more lines too, and he realised that the itinerant actors probably hadn't known the entire script. The best gags were there, however, and as funny as he'd remembered, and the irreverent music played by the chorus was a perfect foil to the buffoonish Dionysos and the glowering, malevolent Hades.

His friends were enjoying themselves too. For reasons unknown, Kimon had taken a shine to Hades; every time the god spoke, he descended into a fit of giggles. Antileon had become more serious than normal, and was listening to every word with great concentration.

Demetrios kept an eye on Philip, who was in excellent humour, laughing throughout. The cutting political comments, which the play's director had daringly changed to reflect on the king, appeared to amuse him; one satirical comment had him slapping his thigh and sharing the joke with the noblemen on either side. Herakleides remained reserved, his expression implacable, which perturbed Demetrios.

The light had begun to leach from the sky by the time the comedy ended. Deafening applause rained down on the four actors, who capered about the stage, bowing to the audience. Dionysos bared his phallus in thanks, which almost brought down the house. As the cheering and clapping died away, the king beckoned to the actor who had played Euripides. A hush fell – it was he who had made the biting comments about Philip.

'Is he going to reward him or cut his head off?' whispered Kimon.

Antileon sniggered. 'Philip has a good sense of humour. A purse of silver is coming that actor's way, or I'm no judge.'

Antileon was right, thought Demetrios, remembering Philip's generosity of spirit when he'd been caught by the slingers. His mind was turning to which tavern might be best to seek out afterwards, when his gaze drifted to Herakleides. The admiral had a curious expression on his face, like a man who cannot quite decide on something. Abruptly, it changed, hardening. Herakleides' eyes searched the crowd gathering around the king and Euripides, and he nodded.

Demetrios was on his feet and pounding down the steps before he even realised. His friends' confused shouts followed him as he shoved and pushed through. It was impossible to move with any speed – everyone was leaving at the same time – so in frustration he clambered into the central bank of seats and began jumping from row to row. He saw Herakleides already making his way towards the passageway on one side of the orchestra, which cemented his suspicion that the king was in danger. He was about to shout a warning, but thought better of it. The guards, who were strolling towards the king, might take *him* for the assassin. He had to get closer.

Demetrios leaped across two rows and almost fell, but didn't. Confident now, he hurtled down the last half a dozen and landed on the sandy surface of the orchestra. Curious looks were thrown his way, but no one stopped him.

His heart pounding, he studied those closest to the king. Philip was having an animated conversation with the actor who had played Euripides. Most of the surrounding crowd appeared to be nobles – their faces were interested, those of men listening to every word, not bent on murder. Demetrios edged around the circle, but could see no one who looked out of place. He began to wonder if he'd made too much of Herakleides' nod. The whoreson might have been doing nothing more than greeting a friend or ally.

He was about to give up and find his friends again when his attention was taken by a figure close to the king. The man's head was down, and unlike the listening nobles, who were stationary, he was moving towards Philip. Panic seized Demetrios – maybe he hadn't been wrong. The man was perhaps five steps from the king, while he was twice that distance away. Dropping his shoulder, he barged forward. He ignored the startled faces, and the angry comments.

Three paces in, he cried, 'You are in danger, sire!'

His shout brought the creeping figure's head up and around. Cold eyes met Demetrios', who knew at once that he was right. The man spun back towards the king. Desperate now, Demetrios heaved a skinny noble aside. He saw Philip's startled face, and a blade held low by the man's side. Lunging forward, Demetrios seized the assassin around the waist and, with his other hand, grabbed at the weapon.

'Beware, sire!' he managed to shout before they fell to the ground in a tangle of limbs.

His leap had been clumsy; the assassin ripped his knife hand free the instant they landed. Slashing wildly, he cut backwards at Demetrios. Stings, like those made by wasps, erupted along his side, but Demetrios paid them no heed. He tightened his grip on the man's waist and tried to wrap his legs in a pankration move, but the assassin writhed like a serpent, and managed to half-throw him off. The knife flashed above Demetrios, and he thought, I'm a dead man.

Others in the crowd suddenly came to life.

Someone cried, 'Guards!'

Men swarmed in.

Two grabbed the assassin's arm; another ripped the blade from his grasp. A vicious struggle ensued, but within a dozen heartbeats, the would-be killer was lying with a sandal on his neck and a bodyguard's sword point resting just below one of his eyes. Demetrios tried to get up, but a kick to the face sent him sprawling onto his back. Remembering the slingers' beating, he curled into a ball and prepared for the worst.

'Stop, you fools! This is the man who saved me!' The raging voice belonged to Philip.

No more blows landed. Demetrios opened his eyes to find the king bending over him, his handsome face concerned. They stared at one another; recognition flared in Philip's eyes. 'By all that's sacred! It's *you*.'

Demetrios had to spit out a gobbet of crimson phlegm before he could answer. 'Sire.'

Philip extended a hand and heaved him to his feet. His eyes moved down. 'You're hurt.'

Finally, Demetrios felt the pain. He reached down, and his fingers came away sticky with blood. 'It's nothing, sire. I . . .'

He fell away into blackness.

Demetrios floundered to consciousness, as if swimming to the surface from the bottom of a deep pool. Breaking the surface, he gasped in a lungful of air.

'Steady,' said a calm voice.

Demetrios opened his eyes. He was lying in a strange bed. Fine linen met his probing fingertips. Above, a frescoed ceiling told him he was far from his tent. Throbs of sweet agony from his side reminded him he hadn't dreamed the assassination attempt on the king. He turned his head, finding a grey-haired man sitting alongside him.

'Where am I?' he croaked.

'In the palace.'

Confusion filled Demetrios. 'The palace? I . . .'

'Drink this.' The surgeon held a cup to his lips. 'It will ease the pain, and help you sleep.'

Demetrios obediently swallowed a couple of mouthfuls of the bitter liquid. Drained by the small effort, he lay back on the pillow and closed his eyes.

The next time he woke, the king was standing over him. Demetrios struggled to sit upright, to bow.

'Sire. Forgive me . . .'

Philip held up a hand. 'Peace.'

Demetrios sagged back onto the mattress. 'Are you hurt, sire?'

'Me?' Philip smiled. 'No, thanks to you.'

Demetrios couldn't help but grin. 'That's wonderful news, sire.'

'You acted when no one else did. I was surrounded by my courtiers, who saw nothing. I should be dead. Truly, the gods sent you, Demetrios – I am told that is your name?'

'Yes, sire.'

'The shepherd who became an oarsman. The oarsman who became a phalangist. The phalangist who saved a king.'

Demetrios flushed to the roots of his hair.

'Your injuries are not life-threatening, I am glad to say. It's fortunate you leaped on the assassin's back – he couldn't reach to stab you properly. The surgeon has stitched the worst of the cuts. You might lose a front tooth, thanks to the fool who kicked you. The fine I imposed on him – a large sum – is yours.'

'Sire, I—'

'I will have it no other way,' said Philip. 'What else would you have of me?'

Demetrios flailed for words, and found only, 'I need nothing, sire. Serving you in the phalanx is enough reward. It was always my dream.'

'If only all men were so modest,' Philip said, chuckling. 'I'm told you stand near the end of the file, and that you have little equipment.'

Demetrios was filled with shame. 'Yes, sire.'

'My armoury is at your disposal. At the least, you shall have the kit and weapons of a front-ranker.'

'T-thank you, sire,' said Demetrios, delighted. 'I am in your debt.'

'I have sent instruction to your file-leader. When you return to the speira, it shall be as a sixth-ranker. I considered placing you further forward, but you lack combat experience – is that not right?'

'It is, sire.' Demetrios' voice had gone hoarse. 'Your promotion – it's . . . well – I don't know what to say.'

A faint frown. 'Are you displeased?'

'No, sire! This is beyond any reward I could ask, but I . . . I don't feel worthy of the promotion.' He could already hear Empedokles' caustic comments; others in the file would also have something to say, he had no doubt.

A snort. 'There are veterans aplenty who haven't done what you did. I say your reward is merited.'

Demetrios bowed his head, a fierce exultation filling him. He would show himself worthy of the king's trust, no matter the price. 'Thank you, sire.'

'It's incredible that you saw the assassin, when no one else did. You thought Herakleides was behind it?' Philip saw Demetrios' questioning look. 'Menander told me of your suspicions.'

Here it was, thought Demetrios, fear clutching at him. It had been frightening enough approaching Menander. 'I-I think he was, sire.'

'Tell me everything,' Philip ordered.

Demetrios' story tumbled out: how he had overheard Herakleides and Kryton talking; confiding in Simonides; how he'd eavesdropped at the games; bringing his suspicions to Menander at last, and finally, what he had seen in the theatre.

'That's when I got as close to you as I could, sire.' Demetrios hesitated, realising how it must sound to say he'd known that Herakleides' gesture had meant the king was in danger. 'It sounds ridiculous, sire, I know—'

'Your story makes sense to me, and it has been confirmed by the would-be assassin.' Philip's eyes were hooded. 'It seems I must thank you again.'

'I am at your service, sire.' Demetrios hesitated, then asked, 'The assassin, sire – he confessed?'

A merciless smile. 'Before the end, he was singing like a bird.'

It wasn't surprising the man was dead, thought Demetrios with grim satisfaction. Drained of energy, he lay back on the bed.

'Rest now.' Philip rose, lithe as a cat.

Demetrios was wondering what would happen to Herakleides and Kryton when sleep took him.

Two days later, Demetrios was sitting in the courtyard nearest his chamber, still amazed to be quartered in the palace. The surgeon came morning and evening to check on him, and the food and drink was better than he'd ever had, yet he was missing his comrades.

To his surprise, the king appeared again. Philip was dressed in a patterned himation; a dagger in an enamelled sheath hung from his plain leather belt. He looked like one of a thousand nobles, thought Demetrios, apart from his eyes, which gleamed with wit and intelligence. He climbed to his feet, wincing as his wounds protested the sudden movement.

'Sire.' He bowed.

'You are not yet fully healed.'

'I'm almost there, sire.'

'The surgeon is of a different mind–' Philip half-smiled '–but you chafe to be with your friends, do you not?'

'You see through me with ease, sire.'

'You shall return to your speira later today,' said Philip. 'Before that, I would ask you to accompany me.'

'Anywhere, sire,' answered Demetrios.

The king didn't elaborate, but turned on his heel and strode from the courtyard.

He hurried after.

Demetrios' eyes roved down the narrow corridor whence they had come, and back to the low, iron-studded door that Philip had halted in front of. Never before had Demetrios suspected that the palace had its own prison.

The king rapped on the timbers with a fist. 'Open!'

'Who's there?'

'Philip.'

A bolt shot back, and the door was heaved open, revealing a brutish-looking man in a filthy chiton. He bowed low. 'Sire.'

The instant that the pair entered, the jailer – also a torturer, Demetrios quickly decided – slammed shut the portal. Intense heat radiated from a glowing brazier in the middle of the flagged floor. A cloying stench of human ordure filled Demetrios' nostrils; he swallowed down a gag. Oil lamps flickering in wall niches gave off a dim light; he made out two stools, a table upon which lay an array of unpleasant tools – and a pair of shapes slumped against the back wall.

'Have you no greeting for your king, Herakleides?' Philip's tone was light, dancing.

One figure stirred. With an effort, he lifted his head. The matted hair around Herakleides' terrified face could not conceal the weeping, fresh burns; they also marked most of his body. Both wrists were man-acled to the wall above his head, keeping him from collapsing, and the mangled ends of his fingers revealed a bloody story of their own.

'Welcome, sire,' he mumbled.

'He had been plotting against me for months,' said Philip to Demetrios, as if talking about the weather. 'Kryton fell into his grasp early on, thanks to his weakness for gambling.'

Now the other figure – Kryton – looked up. 'I played for time, sire. Made up reasons why we shouldn't act. I delayed Herakleides for months.'

'Do you expect mercy?' cried Philip. 'You had not the spine either to kill Herakleides, or to throw yourself at my feet and confess all.'

'He said that if I harmed him or told a soul, my family would be killed, sire.' Kryton began to sob.

Demetrios was surprised to feel sympathy for his commander's plight. How might he have reacted if his own father had been alive, and used to threaten him like this? He hardened his heart. Philip's life was more important than anyone else's.

'What would you do with them?' asked Philip.

With a start, Demetrios realised the king was talking to him. His eyes flickered of their own accord to the table, and Philip chuckled.

'They've been well tortured, but you're welcome to a turn.'

'No, sire.' Demetrios tried to conceal his distaste. 'I suppose I'd have them executed.' Although the two deserved no other fate, the reality of killing them in this grimmest of chambers repelled him.

'Well for you, o brave phalangist.' Philip's gaze was penetrating. 'The burden of ending these creatures' miserable existence does not fall on your shoulders, but know that one day, you may have to act so. Not every enemy is armed. Not every man who wishes you dead can be slain face to face in battle.'

'No, sire,' muttered Demetrios, remembering how he had almost left Empedokles to his fate.

'Go. Return to your speira,' ordered the king, smiling to show he still favoured Demetrios.

'And you, sire?'

'I will tarry awhile.' Philip's voice was flat and hard.

'My thanks, sire.' Demetrios had never been gladder to leave a room, nor to hear a door shut behind him.

The screams began before he'd gone a dozen steps.

CHAPTER XXXIII

Near Apollonia

The sun sank towards the western horizon, its weakened light flashing off the Aegean. Close to the shore, scores of ships rocked gently at anchor. On the flat farmland between the sea and Apollonia, Roman camps stretched away to left and right. The tracks between were busy. Messengers roved from one legion's headquarters to another, and cavalrymen returned from patrol. Off-duty soldiers sought out comrades in other units, and the new sprawl of whores' tents outside the city walls.

Felix was emerging from the eastern gate of his encampment. Deep in thought, he trudged towards the nearest latrines. Antonius was with him; since the clash with the hastati, they made sure never to be alone. The time away from their comrades also afforded a rare opportunity to talk in private. Living cheek by jowl with the others in their contubernium was part of life, but everything was seen and heard, apart from when a man went to empty his bowels.

There had been trouble of recent days. It had been more than that, thought Felix. It had been a small, but full-scale mutiny. None of Pullo's men had taken part, but the conversation round the fires had been of one thing alone: the mutinous veterans of the Hannibalic war.

Unlike Felix and Antonius, plenty of men had remained in the legions after Zama. Since the war's end, two thousand of these had been moved from Carthage to Sicily and on to Illyria without a chance of seeing their families. After a second campaigning season against Macedonia had failed to produce a conclusive result, the disgruntled soldiers had had enough.

'They were stupid bastards to kill that optio,' said Felix. The shocking news had swept the camps.

'By all accounts, he was worse than Matho, but murdering an officer will only ever end in blood,' said Antonius.

Felix checked no one was near. 'I would take that risk to lay Matho in the mud, the cunt.'

Antonius looked at him askance. 'You'd end up on a cross, and me alongside, just for being your brother.'

Felix grimaced.

'If we were to do it–' Antonius held up a warning finger '–*if*, mind, we would have to plan it out to the last detail.'

'You'd help?' said Felix, delighted.

'Of course I would. Blood's blood.' Antonius spat. 'The best thing, however, would be if we keep out of the prick's sight. If he were to discover that we had re-enlisted . . .'

'I know.' Felix chewed a nail.

They had seen Matho twice since the army's return to Apollonia, once stalking about on the parade ground, drilling his men; and again as they returned from patrol with Pullo. On both occasions, one brother had alerted the other, and they'd had time to look away as the century marched past. The chance of meeting Matho face to face continued, slight but constant – he was in one of the camps. They had always to be on their guard. And then there were the cursed hastati, thought Felix. He cast about again, but the nearest soldiers were the few crouched over the trench, some fifty paces away.

'Let's pray Matho gets it in the first battle next spring. That'd be a fine thing, eh?'

'Don't hold your breath. He's a tough bastard.'

'I remember,' said Felix, images of Matho leading them at Zama bright in his mind. He let out a loud fart. 'That for Matho.'

Antonius laughed.

At the latrine trench, they separated by unspoken consent. Brothers they might be, but neither liked to listen to the other's faecal output. Conversation might continue at a distance, or not. Ribald comments from any neighbours about the noises and smells a man made were to be expected; giving back as good as one got was the most effective reply. Brooding, Felix was in no mood for the usual banter, and was grateful that the approach of nightfall and the threat from the lowering rain clouds had ensured the latrines were sparsely populated. He was able to pick a spot clear of other denizens.

Breathing through his mouth to minimise the stench, he laid his wad of moss and leaves close to hand. At least the smell was less overpowering than in the summer, he thought. At that time, it didn't do to be hung-over at the trenches, or a man could end up empty-ing himself from both ends. Undergarment pulled to his knees, Felix squatted down.

'Who's cooking tonight?' called Antonius.

'Narcissus, I think.'

'Fuck.'

'He's making stew. What could go wrong?'

'With that fool? Everything. At the least, he'll burn the pot black. Charcoal stew, anyone?'

Felix chuckled. His brother was right. Narcissus was as bad at cook-ing as he was adept at polishing his armour and helmet. 'You could offer to do it instead.'

'It was my turn last night. Why don't you volunteer?'

'Because I have to do it tomorrow,' Felix retorted.

'Well, look who it is,' said a mocking voice.

To Felix's horror, the scar-faced hastatus was standing over him, thumbs hooked in his belt. Felix tried to get up, but the hasta-tus kicked him in the face. Hot, salty blood filled his mouth, and he fell onto his arse, lucky not to tumble into the shit-filled trench. Spitting out a tooth, he launched himself in desperation at Scar Face. The second kick landed, but Felix managed to wrap his arms around Scar Face's midriff like a wrestler. He drove forward, unbalancing the hastatus. They landed hard, and the air left Scar Face's lungs with a whoosh.

They both lay there for one heartbeat. Two.

Pain lanced from the jagged stump of the fractured tooth; Felix used it to focus his fuzzy brain. He gouged at Scar Face's eyes with his thumbs. His enemy intuited the move and twisted his head sideways; one of Felix's nails ripped a long, red track parallel to the knife scar. A wild punch from Scar Face connected with Felix's left ear. Stars burst across his vision. Unsteady, he swayed to one side, and with a mighty wrench of his torso, Scar Face threw him off. It was Felix's turn to sprawl back, with the other on top.

Quick as lightning, Scar Face locked his hands around Felix's throat. Acid fear surged through him – he'd seen a man strangled to death in a fight once. It hadn't taken long, and the victim's attempts to break his attacker's hold had entirely failed. Felix grabbed for Scar Face's groin.

Luckily for him, the hastatus' tunic had rucked up. His fingers closed on sweaty fabric, and beneath it, a prick and balls. Felix dug his fingers in deep, and squeezed with all his might.

Scar Face groaned, but his grip tightened.

Felix's vision blurred. His tongue felt too big for his mouth. He could feel the strength leaving him. Somehow he managed to separate a ball from the mass of tissue beneath the fingers of one hand. Cupping it in his palm, he set his thumbnail against the middle and drove it inwards, deep into the testicle.

A high-pitched scream, such as a small boy makes, left Scar Face's lips. His grip on Felix's throat fell away. Things might have gone badly for Felix regardless – he was still underneath – but out of the blue, he heard a meaty thwack. Scar Face's eyes glazed, and he toppled sideways to the ground.

Felix sucked in a ragged breath; he couldn't move. Antonius stooped over him, his face concerned. 'You all right?'

Felix tried to speak, and coughed instead. A paroxysm seized him. He rolled onto his side, retching up his last meal. 'I'll live,' he managed at last.

'It was a fight, nothing more. I stepped in before it went too far,' said Antonius. 'Over a whore, I think.'

Someone in the distance made a crude remark, and Felix realised his brother wasn't talking to him.

Antonius' hand was warm on his shoulder. 'Can you sit up?'

Felix tried, and found he could. 'He jumped me.' His voice was hoarse.

'You were lucky he didn't kill you.'

'Attacking a man while he takes a shit . . .' Felix glanced at Scar Face, who lay unconscious beside him, along with the bloody stone Antonius had struck him with. 'Bastard.'

'We shouldn't linger. He'll wake up before long.'

'How far away was the soldier you were talking to?' croaked Felix, standing with an effort. He rearranged his undergarment, taking surreptitious looks to either side. There was no one close by.

'Twenty paces, maybe a bit more. Why?'

Felix gestured at the darkening air. 'Would he recognise you again?'

Antonius frowned, then glanced at Scar Face. 'You mean to finish him?'

'What better way to end the thing?' Felix picked up the rock. 'Do this, and we stop having to look over our shoulders.'

'That's not completely true,' said Antonius, but he too was selecting a sharp-edged stone. 'His comrades might come looking for him.'

'Even if they find his corpse, they won't know who did it. They might suspect, but it'll be a warning, won't it? Fuck with us, and this is what happens to you.' Felix knelt by Scar Face, and readied his stone. Two or three good cracks on the side of his head, just behind the eyeball, would be enough.

'Wait!'

The tension in Antonius' voice made Felix freeze. He peered in the direction of the camp.

'An officer!' Antonius' rock dropped into the latrine trench with a soft plop.

Panic twisted Felix's guts. He threw his own stone in and, whipping off his *focale*, tied it higher around his neck than normal. Whether this would conceal the marks left by Scar Face's fingers, he had no idea.

'What's going on here?' A *tesserarius* materialised out of the gloom, sponge stick in hand. He loomed over Felix, suspicion writ large on his stubbled face.

'We were doing our business, sir, when my brother here noticed this poor fellow lying in a heap,' said Antonius, smooth as you like. 'I came to help.'

'He's been hit on the back of the head, sir,' said Felix, pointing.

The tesserarius scowled. 'Is he alive?'

'I think so, sir.' Felix laid a finger on Scar Face's throat. 'Aye, sir. His pulse is strong.' More's the pity, he thought.

'You must have seen someone near him,' said the tesserarius.

'No, sir,' said the brothers in unison.

The tesserarius made a dismissive gesture. 'A likely story. Give me your names and unit, and then carry the poor bastard to the hospital and see what the surgeons can do.' The instant they had mumbled their details, he dropped his sponge stick and moved to the trench's edge. 'Go on, clear off. I've got more important business to deal with.'

'Sir.' With sinking heart, Felix helped Antonius to pick up Scar Face's limp form. They shuffled off towards the camp with the tesserarius' gaze heavy on their backs.

'What are we going to do?' hissed Antonius.

'What he told us,' said Felix grimly.

'If he doesn't wake up, fingers will be pointed at us.'

'Aye.' Felix could already picture the trial. The penalty for murdering a comrade was death; the same punishment could be handed down for attempted murder. 'If he does come to, the cunt will say *we* attacked him.'

'It will be our word against his,' said Antonius. 'Two against one.'

'We were the ones caught "in the act". It looked as if we had jumped him, didn't it?'

Antonius didn't reply.

Felix sank into a pit of despair. No matter what happened with the hastatus, they were screwed.

Felix hovered at the hospital entrance, his stomach churning. Four orderlies walked by, carrying a man on a stretcher. From the depths of the huge tent, a surgeon called for bandages. A harassed-looking clerk sat at a table, taking details from the soldiers queuing for treatment. It was early the morning after the fight with Scar Face, and Felix hadn't slept a wink. No one had come to arrest them, which Antonius said meant that the hastatus hadn't woken up yet, or had died. Either way, there was nothing they could do, he'd said. 'It's in the gods' hands.'

Antonius' words might be true, but that hadn't stopped Felix's feet guiding him to the hospital. The century had a rare morning off duty, so he wouldn't be missed for a time. Now that he was here, however, fear wouldn't let him enter. If Scar Face *was* dead, it would only be a matter of hours before the tesserarius found out. An interrogation of the brothers would follow, and even if they managed to withhold the truth, severe punishment would result. How could it not? Felix thought. They had been found at the latrines over the unconscious body of another soldier, with no one else near.

'You going in?'

Felix turned.

'Well?' A short princeps he vaguely recognised stood there, cradling one arm. 'You're blocking the entrance.'

'Apologies.' Felix moved, and the princeps stumped in to join the line in front of the clerk's table.

'Out of the way,' barked a voice.

Felix stepped aside, allowing a pair of cavalrymen who were supporting a comrade between them to pass by. It was time to return to the tentlines, or to brave the hospital interior. He made to leave, but then with a curse, entered. He had to discover what had happened to Scar Face – it was eating him up not knowing.

'You've got the look of a man with the pox, or I'm no judge.' An amused-looking orderly was staring at Felix. 'How long has it hurt to piss?'

'Eh? It doesn't. I'm fine,' Felix replied, flustered.

A knowing chuckle. 'That's what all the men say who hang around the entrance like lost souls. Get in line. The surgeon will sort you out.'

'I haven't got the cursed pox.' Felix glared.

The orderly's smile eased. 'Here to see a mate, then?'

Felix hesitated for a heartbeat. 'Aye, sort of.'

'What's his name? I can search the lists for you.'

'There's the thing – I don't know.' The orderly's eyebrows went up, and Felix added, 'I got into a fight with him, me and a comrade. You know how it is: we were pissed out of our heads. The brawl got broken up by an officer, so every one of us is on a charge. I wanted to check on him, see that he's not too badly hurt.'

'Because the worse his injuries are, the more you'll get punished?' The orderly's tone was knowing.

'Aye.' Felix threw up a prayer: Jupiter, help me now.

'What does he look like – can you remember?'

Thank you, thought Felix. 'He's an hastatus. A big bastard, with a scar on one cheek. He was unconscious when we took him in.'

The orderly scratched his head. 'I haven't seen him, but with a mark like that, he shouldn't be hard to find.' He pointed. 'You'll find the patients with head injuries at the back, on the left. See if you can find him there.'

Muttering his gratitude, Felix worked his way around the ever-lengthening queue, towards the tent's heart. Scores of men lay on blankets, in neat parallel columns. Few had obvious injuries – the wounded from the summer campaign had either died or recovered, he judged – but the stink of faeces revealed many were suffering from the dysentery that had affected some units. Felix held his nose and trod light, hoping that the disease didn't strike him down as well.

He began to pay attention to the patients' faces as he passed the tent's halfway point. Almost no soldiers were familiar, and none had a scar on their cheek. Felix felt sick.

The bastard's died, he thought, and when the tesserarius finds out, we'll be charged with murder.

A man laughed, and Felix's breath caught in his throat. It was Matho – he'd recognise the braying laugh anywhere. A furtive look revealed his old centurion squatting down by a figure on a blanket not a dozen paces away. His back was turned to Felix, but that guaranteed nothing. He cast a frantic glance around. The tent's open interior offered no hiding places. Leaving was his only option. He turned.

'Look after yourself,' said Matho. 'Our village lost enough sons to Hannibal, and your parents will want to see you come home.'

'I'll be fine, sir,' said a voice Felix recognised with shock as Scar Face's. 'Takes more than a blow to the head to get rid of me. Gratitude for visiting.'

'It's the least I could do. Your father and I have known each other since we were knee high to grasshoppers,' said Matho. 'Farewell.'

Shit, thought Felix. The whoreson is going to be right behind me.

He dropped to one knee, pretending to retie a lace. His fingers fumbled with the leather thongs, like a child who hasn't learned his knots. He couldn't look up, for fear of Matho seeing him, so he listened with bated breath as footsteps passed behind him and on, towards the entrance. When a good dozen heartbeats had gone, he dared to look again. Bandy-legged as ever, Matho was far enough away at last. Felix closed his eyes and let out a hissing breath.

His skin tingled, as it does when a man senses he's being watched. He raised his head to find the nearest patient, a grey-haired triarius, looking at him with a knowing expression.

'That your centurion?' whispered the triarius.

The man had seen him avoiding Matho, thought Felix. He was so enmeshed in lies that continuing to utter them seemed the best option. 'Aye.'

'They're all pricks in some way. It doesn't change even in the triarii.' The soldier winked. 'Never fear. He didn't notice you. I'd stake my life on it.'

Felix gave him a grateful nod, and stole a look at Scar Face, who had lain back down, an arm over his eyes. The bastard wasn't dead, which was something. What he would say when the tesserarius came to visit was quite another.

'You here to see a comrade?' asked the triarius.

I can't talk to Scar Face, thought Felix. He'll want to start the fight all over again. I'm not making peace with him either – he attacked me. The best thing to do now is leave, before he sees me.

'Aye,' he muttered. 'But I can't find him.'

The triarius' expression grew curious. Felix wondered about confiding in him – it would be a possible way to monitor Scar Face – but discounted the idea at once. The fewer people who knew what he and Antonius had done, the better, and the longer he tarried, the greater the likelihood that his enemy would notice him. Wishing the triarius well in an undertone, he climbed to his feet, careful to keep his back to Scar Face, and took his leave.

He was on edge every step of the way to the entrance, for fear that Matho had not left the tent. His fears proved unfounded, and he emerged into the sunlight without seeing his former centurion. The only thing he could do now, thought Felix, was hope and pray that Scar Face's account of their fight wasn't believed.

The chance of that seemed infinitesimal, yet Matho hadn't seen him, when by all rights he should. Perhaps Fortuna would grant another lucky throw of the dice. That was the best he could wish for, decided Felix, trying to keep his spirits up.

Antonius was furious when he heard Felix's tale. Dragging him away from their tent, he cried, 'What were you thinking, you fool?'

'I couldn't take not knowing if he was dead,' said Felix.

'So you risked being seen not just by the man we almost sent to Hades, but fucking Matho?'

'How was I to know that he and Matho were from the same stinking village?' Felix retorted. 'That Matho would be visiting him?'

'Brothers falling out with each other? That's not good.' Pullo's quiet voice – iron-hard and even less friendly than normal – silenced the pair quicker than a bucket of water separates two fighting dogs. The crunch of dirt beneath Pullo's sandals stopped – he'd come to within ten steps without them noticing.

'It's nothing, sir,' said Felix. Gods above and below, he prayed, don't let him have heard us. His eyes moved to the figure beside Pullo, and his heart fell further.

'That's the pair, sir,' said the tesserarius.

'Get your arses over here,' ordered Pullo.

Giving each other a brief, horrified look, the brothers hurried to stand before him. They came to attention and saluted.

'Been fighting, eh?' Pullo was slapping his vitis off the palm of his left hand, a crisp, stomach-churning sound.

Neither answered, which was the wrong thing to do. *Crack. Crack.* Pullo's vitis hammered down, one blow each to the side of the head. Felix stumbled, his vision blurring for a moment, but he righted himself as fast as he could. Pullo's face was in his at once. 'I asked you a question!'

'I— We— Yes, sir. We have been.'

'At the latrines?' Contempt dripped from Pullo's voice.

'Yes, sir,' said Antonius.

Another blow each. 'That for brawling!' said Pullo, his tone quieter yet worlds more terrifying than normal. *Crack. Crack.* 'And that. You shitty-arsed pair of cocksuckers!'

Felix's head was ringing, but he came to attention again.

Pullo's breath was hot on his cheek. 'Why were you fighting with an hastatus?'

Felix's eyes shot sideways to Antonius. Down came Pullo's vitis again.

'Did I give you fucking permission to look at him?' Pullo whispered.

'No, sir!'

'Tell me quickly, or I swear to you I will break this fucking vitis across your back. When I'm done, I'll stamp some sense into you.'

'I stopped him and his friends raping a girl in Antipatreia, sir. A child, no more than twelve.' Felix had blurted it out before he'd had time to think. 'There's been an argument since as well, outside an inn in Apollonia – he and his mates started that.'

Even if Pullo believed him, thought Felix, neither story would make any difference to his fate.

'What have you to say, fool?' Pullo was standing in front of Antonius now.

'It's as Felix said, sir. Every word.'

'You saw the child being raped?'

'No, sir, but my brother brought her back to our fire. We fed her before letting her go the next day, with some coin. Ask our tentmates, sir – they'll confirm our story.'

Pullo wheeled. 'Did the injured hastatus mention this?'

The tesserarius looked startled. 'No, sir. He said it was a quarrel over money lost at dice.'

Pullo stalked up and down. *Slap, slap* went his vitis.

Felix's heart was pounding; sweat trickled down his back. He cast a lightning-quick glance at Antonius; his face was white.

'When will the hastatus be discharged?' asked Pullo.

'The surgeon says tomorrow or the next day, sir,' said the tesserarius. 'No lasting damage that he can determine.'

'Good. Dismissed.' Pullo waved his vitis.

'Sir?'

'You brought me the information, which was the correct thing to do. I'll deal with these fools now. Unless you wish to go to a more senior officer?' Pullo took a step towards the tesserarius.

'No, sir. Of course not, sir.' The tesserarius saluted and, clearly happy to remove himself from the equation, marched off.

'How many of them were raping the girl?' demanded Pullo.

'Five in total, sir,' said Felix, remembering how scared he'd been, how nearly he had walked away.

'And you were alone?'

'Yes, sir.'

'Fucking idiot!' Pullo hit him with the vitis again.

'Yes, sir,' muttered Felix, his head pounding.

'Tell me what happened with the girl, and about the fight outside the inn.'

Felix obeyed, not missing out a single detail. When he'd done, Pullo frowned and walked off a few paces, still slapping his vitis. Felix threw a worried, enquiring look at Antonius, who replied with a helpless shrug. He pulled his eyes front as Pullo returned to stand menacingly in front of him.

'To think I considered you for promotion,' said Pullo. 'Poking your nose where it wasn't wanted. Slicing someone open just because you could. Brawling when drunk. Attempting to murder a fellow soldier.' Each accusation came with a shove in the chest from his vitis. 'Two of these offences warrant latrine or sentry duty for a month or more; the last could see you suffer the fustuarium. Your fool of a brother deserves much the same.'

I should have ignored the girl's cries, thought Felix. She's probably been raped again since and murdered after; my interfering made no difference.

'I had a daughter back in Italia.' Pullo's quiet voice sank to a whisper. 'She would have been ten now, if malaria hadn't taken her.'

Felix couldn't believe his ears.

'I saw her soon after she was born and a couple of times after.' Pullo made an angry gesture. 'The war, you know – I hardly ever got leave. The apple of my eye, she was.'

Felix couldn't help himself. 'Sorry, sir.'

Pullo whipped around, his vitis raised high, and Felix flinched.

The blow never landed.

'Go on, piss off,' ordered Pullo, his voice thick.

The brothers exchanged a look of disbelief. 'Sir?' said Felix.

'Are you deaf? Piss off out of my sight.'

'Yes, sir. Thank you, sir,' they said in unison.

Emboldened, Felix asked, 'What about the hastatus' officer, sir? He might—'

'You leave that to me.' Pullo jerked his head. 'Go.'

They had gone perhaps ten steps when the centurion called out. 'If I hear so much as a whisper about an hastatus with a scar on his face being found dead, you'll both be crucified.' Pullo paused, then added in a glacial whisper, 'I will hammer in the fucking nails myself. Understand?'

'Aye, sir.'

Pullo said nothing more, and after a few nervous moments, Felix checked over his shoulder. The centurion was gone.

'I need to sit down.' Antonius was trembling.

'Me too,' said Felix, deciding that an offering of thanks to not just Jupiter, but Fortuna as well, would be a good idea.

PART FOUR

CHAPTER XXXIV

Aous river valley, Epirus, spring 198 BC

Philip's journey here from Pella had been difficult. The high peaks on the army's journey through the mountains were still snow-capped, and the grazing for the cavalry horses sparse. It had been a long winter, but at least the threat posed by Herakleides and Kryton had been dealt with, thought Philip. A wave of arrests had seen their co-conspirators thrown into prison. There they could rot until more pressing concerns, such as the threat posed by Rome, had been dealt with.

This valley was one of the most likely routes for the legions. The weather here was kinder than the higher ground, and on the lower slopes, if the west wind was strong, a trace of the sea could be smelt. The muddy browns that dominated the landscape through the cold months were being replaced by vivid greens, proof of spring's joyous return. Grass was growing, trees were in full bloom, and birds sang from every branch. It was Philip's favourite time of year, when the miserable, dark days could be forgotten and a man could sit outside of an evening with his friends, talking.

The illusion was pleasant, but the coming days would offer Philip precious few opportunities to take his ease. The future of Macedon was at stake, and recent news from Rome had been unwelcome. Not only was Villius to be replaced by the new consul Flamininus – a man whose ambition, said Philip's spies, knew no bounds – but two veteran legions were to accompany him to Illyria. His army would face a host that was larger in size, and more experienced.

Philip felt nothing but defiance. Being outnumbered did not mean that he would be defeated. Xerxes sent a million soldiers to Greece, he thought, and he failed to triumph. Alexander's army was far smaller than the Persian host at the Issus *and* Gaugamela, yet he prevailed. 'Rome can be defeated,' Philip said to himself. If Flamininus was as ambitious as he'd been told, the man would seek a swift victory, and that meant he would take risks. Risks that would offer Philip chances.

He had been surprised to learn from his spies that Flamininus was a lover of all things Hellenic. He spoke and wrote Greek, and his collection of Hellenic art was the finest in Rome. Philip had met few Romans, but to a man, they had been arrogant dogs. Speakers of only Latin, they believed all non-Romans to be savages. If the reports were true, Flamininus was a different creature altogether – and quite possibly, Philip decided, a more dangerous one for it. Despite his wariness, he was intrigued to have a Greek-speaking Roman general for an enemy.

From Philip's vantage point on the north bank of the River Aous, with the gorge leading to Thessaly and central Greece at his back, it was easy to take heart. Flamininus might lead his legions via one of the two other possible routes to Macedon, it was true, but that would avoid Philip's army entirely, and leave the Roman encampments on the coast open to attack. No, he decided, Flamininus would be unable to stop himself swallowing the bait; he would advance up this valley.

Battle would be joined before long. Earlier that day, Philip's cavalry had spotted enemy scouts, and in turn been seen by them. Flamininus would soon know of his arrival.

Covered in black pines, beech and fir trees, the steep valley sides made it almost impossible for an enemy to flank soldiers who were positioned on the flat ground either side of the Aous. The mountain slopes dropped to within a couple of hundred paces of the river on the southern bank; several thousand peltasts and skirmishers could hold that, Philip decided. Here on the northern side, the Aous wound away from the mountains, leaving a large area of level terrain: perfect ground for fortifications manned by more light troops. Behind them, the phalanx would stand. He could picture the legions breaking on his defences like waves striking a harbour wall; whatever remnants made it over would be annihilated by his phalangists.

Guard against flanking parties taking the mountain paths, thought Philip, and they could hold this position until the autumn. Further opportunities to strike at the Romans – raids from the forests, attacking their fleet – would also present themselves. He would bloody Flamininus' nose again and again, and when the opportunity came, as it had for Alexander at the Hydaspes, he would defeat the enemy.

A broad smile creasing his face, he called for his horse.

*

In the ten days that followed, Philip got little sleep. Rising while the eastern sky was dark, he supervised the building of ditches and earth ramparts on both banks of the Aous. Spiked branches that had been dipped in human shit lined the bottoms of the trenches. The ground was laced with caltrops, a Roman invention that Philip had been introduced to by a phalangist who had fought at Zama.

Trees were felled in great numbers and hewn into planks, from which sturdy three-storey towers were built every hundred paces along the defences. Catapults were positioned atop the towers, with bolt throwers on each floor. Thousands of arrowheads were forged in temporary smithies. Soldiers carried boulders from the riverbank and stacked them by each tower – ammunition for the artillery.

From dawn to dusk, Philip walked and rode every stadion of his fortifications. To the amusement of his men, he even swam across the icy, sky-blue river in several places: they didn't realise he was assessing the current's strength and where foot soldiers would be able to cross. Messengers and scouts were brought to him the instant they arrived, ensuring he kept abreast of the enemy's movements and the goings-on in Greece.

It was too early in the campaigning season for much to have happened, but Philip knew that for now, Akhaia remained loyal. His general Philokles stood ready to march wherever he was needed in Boeotia and Attika. Spies had sent word that Flamininus' brother was to command the enemy fleet. Before the month was out, he would have sailed around the Peloponnese to Greece's eastern coastline, where no doubt his purpose was to attack and take as many Macedonian towns as possible.

Afternoon was waning on the tenth day, and Philip was watching the catapults find their range. It wasn't much use having the fearsome weapons, he'd told their crews, if they weren't going to make every shot count when the enemy came. Standing on the ramparts midway between two towers, he bellowed commands and encouragement by turn. It was satisfying work – each catapult could loose a stone every fifteen to twenty heartbeats, and when they were ranged in, hit a target seven times out of ten. After the artillery, the Romans would face the deep ditches, full of spiked branches and caltrops, and volleys of spears from the troops atop the wall. The legionaries would suffer huge casualties.

Unless Flamininus was a complete idiot, he wouldn't waste men on repeated attacks: the defences would be tested only a few times, like as not. Philip was relatively content as he moved from one catapult to another. Spying Demetrios approaching along the walkway, he raised a hand in greeting. The youngster had real balls, first to have won his way into the phalangists' ranks, and then to have saved Philip's life. The king hadn't seen him since he'd recovered from his injuries. What, wondered Philip, was he doing here?

'Sire!' called Demetrios.

Philip cast a critical eye at Demetrios' fine bronze cuirass, padded pteryges and pair of matching, contoured greaves. 'Every part the phalangist,' he said.

Demetrios shuffled his feet. 'Gratitude, sire.'

'You didn't come to show off your armour,' said Philip.

'No, sire. I have news for you.'

Now Philip noticed the slight figure in a ragged tunic and sheepskin jerkin behind Demetrios. The wretch looked terrified. Philip's curiosity rose. 'Who's this?'

'A local shepherd, sire. We came across him on patrol. He tried to run, but didn't get far. I told him about the reward you were offering; I also thought you would want to talk with him.'

'Aye.' Philip's interest quickened. Thus far not a single local had come forward to claim the coin. It was likely, he thought, because of his previous bloody campaigns in the area. He beckoned the middle-aged man forward. Short, brown-skinned, sinewy-muscled and as lean as a hunting dog, he looked to have lived his entire life outdoors. He dropped to one knee and bowed his head.

'Sire.'

'Rise,' commanded Philip. 'What do they call you?'

'Aetos, sire.' The shepherd's voice trembled.

'Be at ease. You are among friends,' said Philip. 'The eagle? That's quite a name.'

Aetos ventured a shy grin. 'It wasn't my birth name, sire. My father gave it to me when I started herding. He said my eyesight was gods-gifted.'

'It's a valuable gift,' agreed Philip. 'Come, are you thirsty? Hungry?'

'A drop of water wouldn't go astray, sire.'

'Try this wine.' Philip pulled free the leather skin hanging from his belt and held it out.

Aetos bobbed his head. 'My thanks, sire.' He took up the skin, he took a long pull. When he lowered the skin, his eyes were full of wonder. 'I've never tasted anything like that, sire.'

'Keep it.' Philip wanted him to feel safe.

'T-thank you, sire,' Aetos stammered.

'The pleasure is mine. You know the mountain tracks around here?' Philip gestured at the slopes above.

A toothless grin. 'Like the back of my hand, sire.'

Philip felt a mixture of pleasure, that Aetos should be in his grasp, and regret, that the man had to die. 'How many shepherds like you are there?'

'In the area? About thirty, sire. When I met your soldier here, he said we'd be paid well to hide away from the Romans. You not wanting them to get around behind your army and all.'

'That's right. You will be rich men,' lied Philip.

Aetos beamed. 'After your man here promised his words were true, I sent my boy to the caves where our families are hiding. The other men will be here by sundown, after they've brought their flocks off the mountain, see.'

'Thirty, you say?' demanded Philip. 'Could it be less? More?'

Aetos looked confused. He thought for a moment.

'Perhaps it's twenty-nine, sire.'

'That's all?' Philip's gaze bore down hard.

'Aye, twenty-nine. I swear it on my ancestors, sire.'

Aetos said no more, because Philip had slashed his throat wide open. He dropped, gouting blood on the king's feet; a few drops even hit a stunned-looking Demetrios.

'You did well,' said Philip, wiping his dagger on Aetos' grubby chiton.

'Y-you killed him, sire.' Demetrios was pasty-faced.

'I did.' Such is the price of kingship, thought Philip. The lives of thirty peasants counted as nothing before the defence of Macedon and the lives of his soldiers. 'At least he died happy, thinking he was rich.'

'I told him he'd be rewarded, sire. He would have kept his word, to hide from the Romans.'

Philip did not tolerate men who questioned his actions, but Demetrios *had* saved his life. 'You can't be sure, boy. Imagine your wife's feet, your child's, your father's, being held in a fire, and what you might do to stop it. That's precisely what the cursed Romans would have done to Aetos. Or, I suppose, they might have paid him more than I would have to show them a path around my army. Brutal though it is–' he nudged Aetos' bloodied corpse with his foot '–this removes that possibility.'

'So the other shepherds must also be slain, sire?'

'They must.' Philip concealed his regret.

'I see, sire.' Demetrios bowed his head.

'War is not all singing the Paean and standing in the phalanx with our comrades. Sometimes it's this.' Philip indicated Aetos again. 'Don't think he would have survived if you hadn't found him. Someone else would have brought him to me.'

'Yes, sire,' said Demetrios miserably.

Philip dismissed him, resolving that the next time he saw Perseus, he would tell him what he'd done. One day his son would have to make similar decisions. Shocked though he'd be, it was better to know about them from his father than be thrust, wide-eyed and inexperienced, into brutal reality.

Kingship came at a heavy price.

CHAPTER XXXV

Mouth of the River Aous, Epirus

Flamininus breathed deep. It wasn't far to Brundisium in Italia – less than two days' voyage – but the air here was different. Somehow fresher, and full of promise. He was on the seashore, and had just disembarked. At his back, scores of troop transports filled the waves as far as a man could see. The air was full of gulls, wheeling and screeching. The beach and the countryside beyond appeared to be one great Roman camp. Once the new legions came ashore, he would have a force more than thirty thousand men strong.

Flamininus smiled. The months of politicking had paid off, but Galba's support was what had swayed the Senate: the protesting tribunes' speeches had fallen on deaf ears. Trying not to think about the price he would have to pay Galba, Flamininus had swiftly put his plans into action, filling every moment of the time since his election in March. There had been meetings with the commanders of his legions; discussions with quartermasters about the army's supply needs; appointments of staff officers who would see his every order carried out. He'd sent letters to the senior officers in Illyria, but had left it to the Senate to inform Villius that he was to be replaced.

Setting in place arrangements for his departure had been far from the only things requiring Flamininus' attention. Every political ally had been visited to ensure their support in his absence. Hands had been shaken, gifts offered, undying friendship sworn. To make doubly sure, plenty of palms had also been greased with silver. Subtle threats had been offered to the less trustworthy; one or two had been warned that switching sides – in particular, returning to Galba's camp – risked much.

Flamininus had managed to persuade Galba to accept a legateship for the year following. 'Men in post have a better understanding of the current situation,' he had lied. He had succeeded in this, but Galba

305

had not relinquished his hold. The night before Flamininus' departure from Brundisium, he had received an unsigned letter that had said simply, 'I will have eyes on you. Do not fail.'

Flamininus put Galba from his mind. I am here at last, he thought. After years of dreaming, I am consul of Rome, and general of a huge army. Macedonia lies over those mountains, and there Philip awaits me. Despite Flamininus' concerns, it was impossible not to be delighted with himself. His path to glory, his future as a modern Alexander, lay open. The next simple step was to relieve Villius of his command.

'Horse!'

Flamininus' steed was brought to him, and the groom waited as his master cast a critical eye over it. A spirited grey mare, she stood taller than most of her kind. Her mane had been combed, harness fittings polished, and the saddle blanket on her back was of the finest weave. Even her hooves had been polished. Flamininus gave the groom an approving look and mounted. His staff officers took his lead and did the same.

'Take me to Villius,' said Flamininus, his anticipation brimming over at last.

'Welcome.'

Publius Villius Tappulus wasn't in full military dress like Flamininus, which accentuated the difference between them. A short, ill-shaped man, Villius had podgy features and a tendency to sweat. He waved a hand, indicating Flamininus should enter the command tent's meeting area. The gaggle of officers who had been attending him gaped at the new arrival, and realising who it was, came smartly to attention.

Flamininus acted as if they didn't even exist. 'Villius, good day.'

If it hadn't been for the grand surroundings, he decided, Villius' wine-spotted tunic could have seen him mistaken for a lower-end tradesman. Poor sense of decorum aside, he had never been someone to warm to, but *was* an effective politician. The man was friendly without being obsequious, and like Flamininus, assiduous at making allies. Where he fell down was in retaining them.

If more of your so-called friends in Rome had stood by you, thought Flamininus, I might not be standing here. He indicated the neat arrangements of coloured stones on the table. 'Discussing your plans?'

Fleeting irritation marked Villius' features. 'I— yes.'

Flamininus strode closer. 'Show me. I want to know how the land lies before I order the legions to march.' The staff officers' muffled whispers gave him immense pleasure.

Villius smoothed down his tousled hair, a clear effort to remain calm. 'You're assuming command at once? I had thought to share the duties for a time—'

'That won't be necessary. Your staff will have all the logistical details to hand. That is, unless . . .?'

'My subordinates know where each and every unit is, and its disposition,' said Villius stiffly.

'Excellent.' Flamininus leaned over the stones, orienting himself. 'Ah. These white ones must be the legions' camps.' He glanced at Villius.

'That's right.' Villius' finger traced a sinuous line eastward. 'This is the path of the River Aous, and this, to the south, is its tributary the Drynos. Both run through narrow valleys, but only the Aous runs east to Thessaly and Macedonia. Philip has built fortifications on both banks of the Aous—' he indicated the lines of black pebbles '–here and here. The mountains on either side of the river are steep, and covered in forest.'

'There must be goat tracks,' said Flamininus, thinking of Thermopylae, when the Persians had outflanked the Spartan king Leonidas and his men.

'Too many to count, and most lead nowhere in particular,' replied Villius. 'The locals have hidden themselves too. It will prove hard to find a way around Philip's army.'

Flamininus pointed to the black stones. 'What of his defences?'

'They are strong. Ramparts run from deep in the treeline to the water's edge, with ditches in front. There are towers on the walls, where he has placed catapults and bolt throwers.' Villius' finger came to rest on a neat square of grey pebbles. 'The phalanx is positioned behind the defences. Taking the place by storm will prove costly.'

Flamininus hoped that Villius' assessment was incorrect. He would see Philip's fortifications with his own eyes at the earliest opportunity, but it seemed that ingenuity would be the key to success, rather than a full-frontal assault. And yet, with Galba's threats hanging over him, it would have to be taken one way or another. 'Is there anything else?'

Villius' eyes flickered from the stones to Flamininus and back again. 'I— Well, yes.'

Flamininus felt a twinge of sympathy for Villius, who resembled a child deprived of a long-expected birthday present. 'Continue.'

'The mountain passes to the north, including the one used by Galba, lie undefended.'

'Yet to use them would leave our camps on the coast vulnerable. Philip would not look such a gift horse in the mouth.'

'Which is why I had thought to attack him here.' Villius' voice had risen.

He *can* make sensible decisions, thought Flamininus.

'Our naval forces are ready to sail. They await only my order.'

'Don't concern yourself with the fleet. My brother is the new commander; he will already have taken charge.'

Villius' mouth was a surprised *O*. After a moment, he said, 'We have local allies.'

'The Epirotes, yes.'

'They're a bunch of brigands for the most part, but there is one chieftain who has proved useful – Charops, they call him.'

'Has he many warriors?'

'A few hundred, but they're a rabble. He's of more use with finding water and supplies, that kind of thing. My staff officers know how to reach him.'

'Very good.' Flamininus made a mental note of the name. 'I think that's about it, eh?'

'Yes, I suppose.' Villius blinked, as if he was waking from a bad dream.

'Dine with me this evening. Any details you've forgotten can be mentioned then. Dress appropriately, won't you?'

This was dismissal – only a fool wouldn't see it. Villius nodded miserably. 'May Jupiter and Fortuna guide you.'

'Gratitude.' Flamininus clicked his fingers at the staff officers. 'I want the details of every unit, cavalry and infantry. Now.'

Absorbed, he didn't see the humiliated Villius leave the room. When he realised, Flamininus felt no remorse. Cream rises to the surface, he thought. The best men succeed, and lesser ones fall by the wayside. Galba was a thorn in his side, it was true, but Flamininus intended to make the best of the situation. Back in Rome, he had paid a dozen of his spies to find out everything they could about Galba. The man would have a weakness – everyone did. All Flamininus needed was to find it.

Flamininus stared at Philip's defences. Two days had passed, and he had a thorough grasp of his army's situation. It was time to understand his enemy, and to that end, he had ridden up the Aous valley with ten maniples of his best principes at his back. Some hundreds of his troops were in place already, to monitor Philip's soldiers, but Flamininus had brought the extra protection regardless. Dying in a surprise attack was not how he intended to leave this world.

'Is there any chance of sending men through the trees to come down on the enemy's flank?' He directed his question at the closest centurion, a bandy-legged type with a beady stare.

'From what I understand, sir, it would be difficult. The incline is steep, and the trees thick. The ground underfoot is treacherous, full of roots and rocks.' The centurion hesitated, then added, 'Fighting on such terrain would be very risky, sir.'

'Your information is from . . .?'

'The scouts, sir. They crept through the forest right to the edge of Philip's ramparts. Both sides of the river are the same.'

The centurion was confident and not intimidated by his rank, thought Flamininus. He liked it. 'What's your name?'

'Matho, sir.'

'You fought against Hannibal?'

A wry look. 'I spent half my life at it, sir.'

'Were you at Zama?'

'I was, sir. A hard fight.' Matho raised his right arm, exposing a scar that ran from elbow to wrist. 'That's my memento of it.'

Matho was a tough one, Flamininus decided. A leader of men. 'Last year, the legions smashed Philip's lines at the dirty gates.'

'Aye, sir. I was there too.' Matho glanced at the enemy positions. 'Those will be harder to break through.'

'Why?'

'They're much better constructed, sir. The enemy marched in before the snows had melted. They've had half a month of building without any interference from us. Villius—' Matho stopped.

'Speak your mind. No harm will come to you.'

'The scouts brought word of Philip's presence here, sir. It would have been easy to send up a force to attack the enemy. Catch them off guard at first light, like we learned to do against Hannibal. Villius lost an opportunity.'

'Perhaps. You wouldn't have stopped the defences being finished,' challenged Flamininus.

'No, sir, but we would have slowed the bastards – beg your pardon – the enemy down. Put the filth on the defensive, made it harder to erect such strong ramparts. Taking them will prove costly, sir. Unless you're of a mind to march up one of the valleys to the north, that is?'

Flamininus' laugh was cold. Ruthless. 'No, centurion. We shall attack Philip, head-on, and smash through his men. If the gods are with us, victory will be ours here in this valley.'

Matho's leer was unpleasant. 'I like the sound of that, sir. Me and my boys will play our part.'

With soldiers like Matho, his destiny would be made real, thought Flamininus. He could see Philip now, kneeling before him. Gods, but he looked forward to that day. It would make his deal with Galba worth the price.

CHAPTER XXXVI

Philip had ordered his peltasts to man the fortifications on both sides of the river. His phalanxes were positioned behind the defences on the northern bank, a further barrier for the Romans to break on if they succeeded in taking the first. The enclosed space there meant his cavalry could not be used, so the king had ordered the horses out of harm's way, letting the Companions form up on foot beside the phalangists.

Upwards of three days had passed since word of Flamininus' arrival had reached the Macedonians; the legions had been marching up the Aous valley from sunrise to sunset each day. Sick of waiting where they could see nothing, Demetrios, with Kimon and Antileon, had asked and received permission from Simonides to join the peltasts on the ramparts. Several skins of wine had seen them offered places on the walkway with a fine view of the Romans and their allies, who were assembling unit by unit. Demetrios and the others pointed and stared, much as the peltasts were doing. Spirits were high, but men were on edge.

Thousands of the enemy were in sight now; they had forded the river and filled the open ground before Philip's defences. Milling about in front were hundreds of warriors who had bound themselves to Rome: swarthy Epirotes, wild Illyrians and a smattering of Dardani. Expendable allies, they would no doubt be in the initial assault. Legionaries with triple-feathered crests formed the first line; Demetrios knew these to be the hastati, young men with some experience in battle. Behind, he saw more of the crests. These were the principes, mail-shirt-wearing veterans who usually finished what the hastati had started. At the back were the triarii, Rome's best infantry. Simonides had said they were kept in reserve unless the need was great.

It was hard to watch the enemy prepare for battle. Demetrios' guts were in constant cramp; he kept having to empty his bladder. Yet it had to be even more unpleasant for the enemy soldiers tasked with attacking their fortifications.

Send fear into their hearts, great Zeus, he asked. Make them tremble as they draw near, and let our artillery reap them like wheat. When they throw their ladders at the wall, give us the strength to hurl every last man into the ditches.

'I'm sick of waiting,' grumbled Antileon. Like Demetrios, he was armed with sarissa and sword; his shield leaned with the others against the rampart. A dozen spears they had procured from the armourers were stacked alongside. 'You?'

Demetrios nodded. 'The sooner the child-rapists come—'

'The sooner we can get it over with,' said Kimon, finishing his sentence. 'We all feel the same.'

Time dragged by. The comrades could determine no reason why the Romans weren't attacking: their lines seemed fully formed. They amused themselves by playing dice – Demetrios lost half the contents of his purse to a grinning Kimon – and wagering who would kill the most enemies. Kimon reckoned a dozen or more; Antileon nine; Demetrios opted for a conservative seven. No one mentioned the possibility of being slain. Despite these attempts at distraction, their eyes often moved beyond the parapet to the massed enemy lines.

Demetrios was having another piss when the Roman trumpets sounded. Heart racing, he bounded back up the ladder and shoved his way between his friends.

The entire enemy front was advancing. A mixture of allied warriors and hastati, they came at a steady pace. The non-Romans cheered and shouted, and hammered their weapons on their shields. Among the legionaries, a grim silence held sway.

'Here they come,' said Kimon, his usual grin absent.

'Let them come,' snarled Antileon.

'I didn't believe it before. Sometimes they march in silence,' said Demetrios, shivering.

'The bastards are as scared as us. They're just trained to keep quiet,' said Kimon with contempt.

The peltasts had no interest in copying the Romans' tactic. Insults and war cries filled the air, and their spears clattered off shields.

Half a thousand paces had separated the enemy from the Macedonian fortifications. At four hundred, the hastati were still in formation, but hotter heads among their allies had broken away from their fellows and charged. Soon the entire contingent of warriors was running towards the Macedonian ditches.

They would come nowhere near Demetrios and his comrades. Fools, he thought. Why rush to your deaths?

His eyes returned to the hastati, who continued to tramp at the same speed. Three hundred and fifty paces separated them from Demetrios' position, while the warriors were a third of the distance closer. The artillery began to shoot. *Twang* went the bolt throwers. The catapults made deeper, ominous *thunks*. In no time, the air was full of missiles and rocks.

Black blurs, the arrows scythed through shields and flesh alike, often cutting two men down. The carnage caused by catapults' stones was mesmerising. Shields and helmets were no defence. Prayer helped not at all. Shredded into chunks of muscle and bone, men ceased to exist. Heads vanished in sprays of crimson and brain matter. Limbs were ripped clean off. Great gaps opened in the warriors' ranks, and still the artillery shot, each weapon loosing every fifteen heartbeats without fail. Ranged in over days of practice, aiming at a massed enemy, the catapults and bolt throwers could not miss.

Perhaps a hundred and fifty paces out, the charge came to a dragging halt. Demetrios estimated that a full quarter of the warriors were down, dead or injured. The rest could take no more. With the defenders' jeers following, they dropped their weapons and fled. No mercy was granted. The artillery rained down yet more volleys, wreaking a fearful slaughter.

'Our turn,' said Kimon, dragging Demetrios' attention to the ground in front of their position.

The hastati were now within range, and the artillery crews facing them were ready. *Twang. Thunk.* Arrows shot up. Stones curved arcs through the air, and among the hastati, men died.

Demetrios studied the nearest catapult crew, who worked almost as one. Using lengths of wood inserted into the ratchet wheels, a man either side of the weapon wound the arm back to its maximum angle. Two men loaded a stone into the leather pouch that hung from its end. The instant they had stepped back, their officer pulled the release rope. Faster than the eye could see, the arm snapped upright. As it collided with the thick wooden upright forming the middle section of the frame, the stone was hurled into the air.

Demetrios followed its passage, a high trajectory that briefly silhouetted it against the azure sky before it plummeted to earth. The stone's power was such that it obliterated an hastatus – one moment he was there, the next he was gone – and killed the two men behind him before breaking the limbs of several in the ranks behind. Officers bawled orders, and the gaping hole in the legionaries' formation closed.

Demetrios' gaze returned to the catapult. It was about to shoot again: the arm was nearly wound down to its fullest extent, and the loaders stood ready with another large rock. There was a terrible beauty to the weapon, he decided, remembering how he'd almost been slain by one at Abydos.

'Ready yourselves!' shouted the nearest peltasts' officer. 'Do not throw until I give the order.'

Demetrios set down his sarissa and selected a spear from the stack. Urged on by their officers, the hastati were running now. Two men in every six to eight were carrying a ladder. Perhaps a hundred and twenty paces separated them from the ditch, and the artillery barrage was relentless. High-pitched screams of agony carried from everywhere beyond the wall. Bodies, and parts of bodies, littered the ground. Demetrios could see pools of blood, and what had to be pieces of skull and brain tissue. His stomach turned.

A spear shot over the rampart, hurled by a young peltast close to their position. Mocking laughter from his fellows went up as it thumped into the dirt well before the hastati.

'Hold!' roared the furious officer. 'Hold, curse you!'

No more spears were thrown, and the hastati passed inside the artillery's killing range. They had suffered as many casualties as the allied warriors, but their attack did not falter. Demetrios could identify faces now. To a man they were grim, lips peeled back with the effort of running. He saw fear, but more than that, he saw determination. Romans were entirely different creatures to their allies, he decided.

'Seventy paces,' shouted the peltasts' officer.

Demetrios' vision had narrowed. All he could see were four or five hastati, right in front of him. He could sense Kimon and Antileon on either side; he knew they too had their right arms cocked back, ready to throw.

'Sixty!' came the officer's cry.

Demetrios ran his tongue over dry lips, and picked an hastatus whose helmet was missing a feather.

'Fifty. LOOSE!'

Demetrios threw. There was no time to see if his shot had been accurate; he picked up another spear.

'Loose at will!' ordered the officer.

Demetrios looked down; the hastatus with the missing feather was no longer there. Taking aim at another Roman, he hurled downwards with all his might.

The four spears they'd had apiece were gone in no time, and the hastati were clambering down into the ditch in their scores. Try as they might to avoid harm, some trod on the caltrops; others fell onto the sharpened spikes. There were so many, however, that ladders were soon being slammed up against the rampart. One appeared in front of Kimon, who seized hold of it and with a mighty shove, sent it tumbling sideways. One of the two hastati who'd been on the ladder landed on his feet, but the other wasn't so fortunate, impaling himself on a wooden stake.

Demetrios snatched up his sarissa. It was if it had been designed for this situation, he thought, leaning over the parapet. A neat thrust, and he skewered an hastatus where his neck met his trunk. Spraying blood, the man dropped off the ladder, taking the comrade below with him. Demetrios repeated the move when the fallen man picked himself up and made a second attempt to climb. He did it again and again, until his arm muscles ached.

A little time passed. Not a single Roman had reached the rampart alive. Corpses now lined the ditch so deep that the hastati reaching it could walk straight across. The uneven flesh and bone footing for their ladders made it hard to ascend, and far easier to unbalance. Stay where they were, however, and the legionaries would die from a spear hurled by a peltast. Death ruled supreme.

Demetrios spied an optio beating men with his long staff, forcing them forward. 'They're wavering!'

He leaned right out over the parapet, and when the staff-bearing optio looked up, Demetrios stabbed him in the eye. In a few fingers' breadth, and out again. The optio dropped like a discarded rag doll, and the hastati nearest him quailed.

'MA-CE-DON!' bellowed Antileon.

The cry was taken up along the rampart, a swelling wave of noise that rose to the skies. It gave the defenders heart, and leached away the last of the legionaries' courage. In ones and two, in larger groups, they broke and fled. Shields and swords dropped on the bloody ground, unwanted. In vain the injured cried to be saved; many were trampled to death in the chaos.

'We did it,' said Demetrios, clapping a grinning Kimon on the shoulder.

Antileon spat over the parapet. 'They'll be back.'

'Not for a while,' said Demetrios, full sure that the scale of the slaughter would give the Roman commander cause to deliberate.

He was wrong.

By the time men had clambered down the far side of the fortifications, their purpose to retrieve spears and kill enemy wounded, and returned, the trumpets had ordered the principes to advance.

The struggle on this occasion was bitterer, and more prolonged. Better armoured than the hastati, fewer principes were slain by arrows. Despite the stones, which reaped swathes of death and destruction, they did not falter. Thanks to the savagery of the first attack, the defenders had fewer spears, so fewer Romans died inside the final fifty paces. With the ditch filled with hastati corpses, the principes who reached the base of the walls could throw up their ladders at once.

Up they came. Down they fell, but thanks to the soft corpse-landing, the casualties were not as severe as before. Tired, drenched in sweat, Demetrios, his comrades and the peltasts used their spears until there were none left, or they had broken. Then it was time for swords, which allowed more principes to climb to the rampart. Not long after, they won a foothold at last. Wounded, but apparently unstoppable, a huge princeps forced his way onto the walkway ten paces from Demetrios. Attacked from left and right, he was soon cut down, but his sacrifice allowed two other principes to follow his example. They killed a pair of peltasts, even as more Roman heads appeared at the parapet.

Demetrios hurled himself forward, cracking his aspis into the nearest princeps' shield. A savage headbutt, and his helmet rim smashed the man's nose. A heartbeat later, he stuck the stunned princeps in the neck. With a great heave, Demetrios sent the body tumbling to the ground behind the fortifications, bringing him nearer to the still-climbing princeps. *He* had one foot on the ladder, one on the walkway. Shield in his left hand, gripping the timbers of the parapet with his left, he was defenceless. Demetrios smacked him in the face with his aspis, and pushed the man backwards, into the ditch. The other princeps on the rampart had been slain by a peltast; together he and Demetrios threw the ladder earthward, toppling yet another legionary onto the piled corpses. The pair exchanged a pleased look, and went back to their positions.

On it went, until the principes could take no more. For every brief, failed foothold that they won, a score died. The haemorrhaging of their strength could not go on, and at length, their commanders realised it. Trumpets sounded the recall, and the principes broke off their assault. In stark contrast to the hastati, they did not run. Some even helped injured comrades to hobble away. One had the courage to stand within spear range, lift his tunic and expose his privates, all the while hurling abuse at the defenders.

Spears were thrown, but the princeps just laughed. In no hurry, he let his tunic fall, picked up his shield and walked away, offering his back to his enemies.

A peltast near the Companions levelled his spear.

'Don't,' said Demetrios.

The peltast gave him an incredulous look. 'Eh?'

'Enough brave men have died today.'

The peltast sneered. Closing an eye, he threw. His shot was daring – the princeps must have been seventy paces from the fortifications. To Demetrios' amazement, the spear drove deep into the meat of the Roman's right thigh. Bellowing like a spitted boar, he dropped to one knee. Delighted cheers rose from the peltasts, and the man who'd thrown grinned at Demetrios. 'Second shot should finish him.'

Demetrios didn't have the energy to argue, but he was glad when the peltast missed. By then, two of the princeps' comrades had come to his aid. The peltast's third spear landed well short, and with a curse, he gave up.

Wiping away sweat, Demetrios surveyed the battlefield. Many hundreds of bodies decorated the ground. Thinner at the limit of the artillery's range, they multiplied in number closer to the defences. At the ramparts' base, they filled the ditch. In some places, they lay the height of a man. Plenty were still alive. Arms moved here; fingers twitched there. Pain-streaked voices cried for their mothers. They moaned unintelligibly, shrieked at the uncaring sky.

Demetrios could look at the carnage no more. A hammer blow of exhaustion hit him, and he sat down, setting his back against the parapet that they had fought so hard to defend. His eyes closed, but all he saw was mangled, bloody corpses.

Tomorrow would be the same.

CHAPTER XXXVII

Felix yawned. The trumpets hadn't yet sounded, signalling the end of his sentry duty, but it wouldn't be long. He peered at the enemy ramparts through the early morning light, and saw nothing of significance. The sentinels there were as bored as he, like as not. More than a month had passed since the first failed assault on Philip's positions, and although Flamininus continued to send troops against the Macedonians, every subsequent attempt had ended the same way. These defeats, and the numerous casualties suffered, had seen Flamininus' tactics change. Attacks now tended to be probing efforts. For most legionaries, therefore, life had entered a kind of routine. Skirmishes and scouting were the norm by day; a pleasant peace held sway each night.

Felix's sentry duty had dragged by, as it always did. The first hour often wasn't too bad: belly full from the evening meal, a man could enjoy the sunset, and feel grateful that he hadn't died in the brutal fighting thus far. During the second and third, it was easy to keep busy, walking along the rampart and having a word with the sentries to either side. In the fourth and fifth, a man tended to grow cold and bored. Thoughts of home, and of family, if a man had one, filled the mind. Frustration that he would remain in this miserable valley, for only the gods knew how long, drove them out.

The anger could be used to keep drowsiness at bay, but not for long, because the sixth hour and onwards were the worst. This was when men fell asleep. Felix no longer had that problem, however. Any time his eyelids drooped, images of Ingenuus' terrified face filled his mind, and he jerked awake again, guilt ravaging him.

A good centurion came to check on his soldiers when they were at their lowest; Pullo was no different. Just a couple of hours before, he had crept from sentry to sentry, placing his hobs with such care that if a man wasn't alert, the first he knew was when Pullo appeared by his shoulder.

Felix had been weary but wide awake when Pullo came to check on him. Despite knowing that Matho was nowhere nearby, Felix's heart had leaped into his mouth. It took a good while after Pullo's departure for his nerves to settle down. This obstacle bypassed, the last period of his watch had been the hardest of all; he'd thought of nothing but Ingenuus until the first rays of sunlight had tinged the eastern horizon. With the end of his watch in sight at last, he had brightened up. It wasn't his turn to cook; a nap would be in order while one of his comrades prepared bread over the fire. Once he'd eaten, Felix decided, a proper sleep was called for.

After that, he would go hunting. The army diet of bread and wine kept a man alive, but by the gods, it was monotonous. The countryside had been emptied of supplies. Luxuries like cheese and meat were available, the quartermaster being the chief source. Prices were extortionate, however, and often beyond the means of ordinary soldiers. Pilferage could be profitable, but a man risked the fustuarium if caught. The best option was to head into the hills with a spear, asking the gods' favour. Felix was a proficient hunter. More often than not, he returned with a rabbit or a hare, and sometimes even a deer or wild boar.

His stomach rumbled at the thought of such providence.

By sunset, Felix was in a foul mood. His hunting trip had been fruitless; he'd returned to the camp sunburned and footsore, and nursing a host of scratches. Rather than offer sympathy, Antonius, who hadn't come with him, led the jokes at his expense.

'You fell into a thorn bush?' he asked for the third time.

'Aye,' muttered Felix. 'I told you.'

'How in Hades did you manage that?' Narcissus was only too happy to join in.

'I tripped.'

Fabius wasn't going to be left out. 'Was this before or after you'd failed to spear the rabbit?'

'Piss off,' Felix snapped. 'I don't see you bastards coming back too often with something for the pot.'

'Maybe not,' jibed Mattheus, 'but none of us have ever fallen in a thorn bush.'

Hoots of laughter.

Felix liked a joke as much as any man, but it wasn't easy to be on the receiving end. 'Next time I bag a deer, you won't get as much as a taste,' he warned. 'I'll sell the meat, you cocksuckers.'

Antonius mimed falling over. 'Gods, the thorns!' he cried, and the others laughed even harder.

Pullo's unexpected arrival saw them scramble to attention. He looked Felix up and down. 'Been fighting with a bush?'

'Something like that, sir,' muttered Felix as his comrades chuckled again.

'Can you fight?'

Felix straightened. 'Of course, sir.'

'Have you eaten?' Pullo's soft question was directed at everyone.

'We were about to, sir.' Antonius pointed at the flat bread baking on the stones around the fire. 'Would you care for some?'

Pullo dipped his head in recognition. 'That's not why I'm here. Fill your bellies, fools, but don't drink much.' He saw their interest rise. 'Our maniple has been chosen for a mission.'

'Tomorrow, sir?' asked Felix.

Pullo bared his teeth. 'Tonight.'

Wary glances were exchanged. As the domain of evil spirits and wild beasts, the hours of darkness were no friends to men. It was easy to lose one's way, to trip and fall. Easy to mistake one's comrade for the enemy. Unsurprisingly, attacks at night were rare indeed, not to mention unpopular.

'What are we to do, sir?' Antonius this time.

'There's no point attacking the enemy fortifications. We'd break our fucking necks before we even climbed the bastarding thing,' said Pullo, relieving them all. 'Scouts who've searched the forests above the Macedonian positions are reporting few sentries. The enemy seems to think no one would be stupid enough to try coming through the dense vegetation.'

Except us, thought Felix. At night. He saw the same doubt in his comrades' eyes, but no one said a word. Pullo was their centurion, and when he ordered them to jump, the answer was 'how high?'.

'We are to make our way through the trees to a position behind the enemy defences. If no one spots us, we launch an attack at dawn. Our task is simple: take the nearest section of rampart, signal to the troops who'll be waiting, and then hold it until they arrive. Sounds easy, eh?' Pullo's smile reminded Felix of a wolf standing over its kill.

'No, sir,' said Felix, firming his chin. 'But we'll follow you.'

As if we had any choice, said Antonius' sidelong look, but he muttered in agreement with the rest.

'Flamininus has promised every man who survives three months' pay.' Pullo leered at the swift change in their faces. 'Nothing like a full purse, eh?'

Felix was grateful for the banks of cloud overhead. No stars and no moon meant the darkness was almost complete. There was no question of being seen by the enemy until, gods willing, it was too late. Given the snail's pace at which they were walking – necessitated by the lack of visibility – there was little chance of being heard either. After blackening exposed flesh with mud, the maniple had marched at the start of the second watch from their camp to the River Aous. The crossing had been made easier by two lines of stakes, ten paces apart, that had been sunk all the way across. Willow branches had been woven between the posts that were nearer to the river's source, creating a barrier that slowed the current considerably.

Met on the far bank by half a dozen Epirote scouts, they had taken a short time to regroup, and to replace the mud that had washed off their legs. Pullo had whispered encouragement and told his men they'd be a lot richer come the following evening. He'd said in Felix's ear, 'I'm relying on men like you', which had made Felix proud enough to burst.

When the order came to move, he was ready and willing. With Pullo in command, he thought, they were sure to succeed. A pair of scouts went off in front, checking for signs of the enemy; the other four each led a column of legionaries. Slow and steady, they headed up into the trees, away from the killing ground before the Macedonian defences where so many of their comrades had fallen. No one carried torches. Total silence was to be maintained. The journey wasn't easy. Stones moved underfoot. Branches whipped into men's faces and tugged at their mail. Barked shins and thorn scratches became the norm. Felix made a mental note to study his comrades' arms and legs in daylight, swearing that any with scratches would receive the merciless ribbing that he'd endured earlier.

Surrounded by cork and holm oaks, and dense evergreen bushes, roofed in by heavy cloud, their world shrank to the winding animal track along which they were being led. Felix soon lost his sense of direction. Up, up the slopes they went, then down and up again, and on occasion, back on themselves. At times he wondered if the guide was lost – were the frequent stops an indication of that, or just the need for secrecy and silence? No information came back down the line. Felix had to dilute his concern with the knowledge that Pullo was at the front with the guide, and that he knew what he was doing.

Their slow progress went on for an age. It was impossible to know how much of the night remained, but Felix judged that sunrise wasn't far off when the order was passed on to ground shields and wait.

He leaned close to Antonius, standing behind him, and whispered, 'We must be near.'

'You'd think so.' Antonius pointed past Felix, down the slope. 'Is that light?'

Felix peered. A faint glow could be seen between the shadowy outlines of two mighty cork oaks. 'It's a sentry's fire. Well spotted.'

Positioned in single file, they leaned on their shields and waited. Nervous bladders could be emptied, but only from where a man stood. Livius patrolled up and down the line, making sure no one spoke. The undergrowth rustled as invisible small animals went about their business. An owl called, its eerie cry unsettling Felix. The bird wasn't perched on a roof, he told himself, so it couldn't be a harbinger of death. He did his best to ignore it. Now and again, sounds carried from below. A man coughing. The crackle of new fuel being added to a fire. Two soldiers greeting each other.

Tension heightened as tinges of pink stained the eastern sky. Pullo beckoned them together in little groups, and explained quietly that they were two hundred paces from the treeline. Emerging into the open, the enemy defences would be a short distance on their right. Apart from the sentries on the fortifications, there were a score or so of tents scattered around, presumably occupied by comrades of the men on duty. When it was light enough, Pullo and the other centurion would lead most of the legionaries to take the defences; the rest, under Livius and the second optio, would take care of the men inside the tents, before joining the main attack.

It seemed clear enough, thought Felix. The gods, and in particular the capricious Fortuna, seemed to be smiling on them.

They waited.

Pullo came back down the line, returning to his position at the front. 'Not long now, brothers,' he whispered.

They waited.

Streaks of orange-pink illuminated the sky over the mountains. Felix could make out Antonius' strained face; the same unease was mirrored in the next man along, Fabius. He shoved down his own nervousness. Pullo was leading them. The attack would succeed.

They had not allowed for any of the men in the tents to have a dog, or for it to accompany him when he went to empty his bladder close to the trees.

A single bark split the air, the kind a dog makes when it's not sure what's out there.

'Shit!' hissed Felix, exchanging a look of utter dismay with Antonius.

The dog barked again, this time with more certainty.

'It's heard us,' said Felix, willing Pullo to sound the attack.

The barking grew louder. A second dog started up from some distance away, and then a man called out. The words were indiscernible, but the urgent tone could not be mistaken.

'We've got to move, or the entire fucking enemy camp will be awake,' muttered Antonius.

Pullo's whistle sounded, three sharp blasts ordering the attack.

Charging in single file down a path they could hardly see wasn't how it was supposed to happen, but the principes didn't have any choice. Down they ran, fast as the treacherous footing would allow, spilling out of the treeline to a scene of pandemonium. Pullo was waiting, sword drawn. The dog that had sounded the alarm stood twenty paces from him, its barking now frenzied. Behind, men were emerging from tents, fully armed and ready to fight – they had gone to bed prepared. Sentries were running to and fro on the fortifications; one was blowing a trumpet.

Felix had a bad feeling in his belly. The chances of success were slipping away before his eyes. Pullo knew it too – Felix could see it in his expression – but Flamininus had ordered the attack, and to return without having even tried risked severe punishment. When Pullo led forty-odd of them towards the enemy defences, Felix ran after, his lips moving in prayer. Great Mars, hold your shield over us. Don't let us all die here, for nothing.

Their first attempt to win a foothold on the walkway atop the fortifications failed. Sensing what was at stake, the sentries put up a heroic defence. Without javelins, Pullo's men had no means of reaching their enemies other than the ladders, which were at thirty-pace intervals. Single men had no hope of fighting their way up.

In what seemed moments, men were crying that the entire enemy camp was awake. Felix glanced to their rear, and cold fear clenched at his throat. Hundreds of Macedonians *were* on the move, charging, running, sprinting towards the defences. They faced annihilation, and the rampart wasn't even close to being taken. To his immense relief, Pullo had seen it too. Sharp blasts of his whistle told Livius at the tents that they were also to withdraw. Wheeling his men around to the left, Pullo headed straight towards the trees. The scouts were there, waiting, as he must have ordered.

'Get them out of here,' Pullo said. 'Fast as you can!'

Using fifteen men, he formed a protective line to defend the principes heading up the slope and away. Felix, Antonius and their comrades were part of it. Knuckles white on sword hilts, they prepared to sell their lives dearly. Juddering breaths of relief were taken as the last men barged past while the nearest of their enemies were some hundred paces away. Pullo made an obscene gesture at the charging Macedonians, which raised a laugh, then set the fifteen to following the rest. Like a hero of old, he took up the rear.

Dawn had arrived, allowing the scouts to make for the Aous a great deal faster than before. No one cared this time about the thorns that ripped their arms, or the branches that lashed their faces. A combination of fear and mad delight filled Felix's heart. The emotion had infected others too: he could hear manic laughter as men tripped and were helped up by comrades. Fabius was cracking jokes about Macedonians being shit at running. At the back, Pullo's encouraging shouts told them that all was well with their centurion.

Their losses had been light – two men in the century had died, and a handful were injured – and things were to get better. Emerging onto the ground by the River Aous, they found several units of cavalry had come to water their horses – the sight of them would surely dismay their pursuers.

The mission had been a failure, thought Felix, but against the odds, they had escaped with their lives.

That was what mattered.

*

Two days after the night attack, Felix was hunting. Eyes fixed on the narrow path, he searched for animal tracks among the evergreen shrubs covering the mountain's lower slopes. Yellow-flowered broom plants and white rock roses dominated, but the rich scents of lavender, rosemary and sage also laced the air. Lone holm oaks stood like sentinels; thick-barked cork oaks thrust their branches at the brilliant blue sky.

'Seen anything?' Antonius was ten paces behind Felix. Although he was no archer, he was armed with a bow. Better to have a shot at a deer than no shot at all, he had said, and Felix hadn't argued.

'Well?' demanded Antonius.

'Only rabbit trails.'

Antonius grunted. They had agreed beforehand to try for bigger game first. One rabbit afforded each man in the contubernium a few mouthfuls; a deer or boar would feed them all for days.

T-t-t-t-t-t. T-t-t-t-t-t. A warbler registered its outrage at Felix's presence. *T-t-t-t-t-t. T-t-t-t-t-t.*

The bird would sound until they had left its territory, so any game nearby would be on the lookout for danger, or vanish. He picked up his pace. A hundred paces on, the call was as strong as ever, but at double the distance, the alarm had died away. Felix stopped. There were other warblers in the trees further up the slope, their happy, trilling song mixing with the loud churring of cicadas. The occasional shout from down in the valley was the only reminder of their purpose in Epirus. He cast a look at Antonius. 'We could almost be in the mountains near home.'

'If we were, you'd be complaining about having no money, and being hungry.'

Felix grinned. 'You'd be moaning as well.'

Antonius shrugged, but he was smiling. He jerked his chin at the track. 'Best get a move on. We don't want to head back empty-handed.'

'Aye.'

After a quick slug from his water bag, Felix set out again, his eyes roving the ground. His spirits rose soon after when he spotted tracks leading across the path, but they proved to be made by a lynx: four-toed, and without impressions from claws, as a wolf would make.

'Pssst.' He pointed at the marks, and Antonius' eyes widened. The graceful, elusive hunters also lived in Italia, but were rarely seen.

326

On they went, the track hugging the slope on its journey towards a saddle that was skylined between two peaks. One faced down into the Aous valley; the other was situated to its north. The brothers had agreed that if they reached the saddle without a kill, looking for rabbits on the return to camp was the best option. To continue further risked an encounter with Macedonian scouts. Several legionaries had failed to come back from hunting trips. The local people, farmers and shepherds, wouldn't be to blame. They had disappeared into the mountains.

Felix found more rabbit trails, and then, to his excitement, a boar's. His hopes came to nothing. The dried sausage-shaped faecal pellets he found next were proof that the track was days old. Telling himself that patience brought success, he resumed his search.

Perhaps a thousand paces later, an unexpected sound stopped him dead. Not a boar snuffling in the dirt, not the rustle of leaves made by a deer pushing through bushes – it was a human voice, of that he was certain. Felix caught Antonius' attention with a look. Using his fingers, he mimed a person walking, then pointed along the trail.

Antonius' lips framed the question, 'Macedonians?'

Felix shrugged an 'I don't know' in reply.

Antonius jerked his thumb down the path, and mouthed, 'Go back?'

Take a look first, Felix signed. Antonius nocked an arrow to his string.

They padded on, treading soft, aware that the slightest sound could betray their presence. At twenty paces, Felix paused to listen. He heard nothing. After another twenty, he stopped again. This time, he made out a low moan. He set his lips against Antonius' ear. 'D'you hear that?'

Antonius nodded.

The moan came again. Surrounded by dense bushes and shrubs, the sound was impossible to localise, but it wasn't far off. Was it an injured shepherd, Felix wondered, or a trap set by Macedonians? His mouth had gone dry, and suddenly his spear and Antonius' bow didn't seem like much protection against an enemy patrol. Skulking away unseen seemed a coward's choice, however – what would Pullo say, if he found out? Felix took a step forward, and another.

'Help me.' A groan followed.

Felix understood: he had learned a few words of the Epirote language from the tribesmen who fought with the legions. If this was a

Macedonian trap, he decided, it was a poor one. The sight that greeted him around the next bend seemed to confirm his opinion. A man clad in a rough woollen tunic was lying on the track, a dog close by. Seeing Felix, it growled.

Felix stopped. His brother came alongside.

'Is it an ambush?' hissed Antonius.

'I'm not sure – I don't think so.' Felix was still wary enough to go no closer.

The man sat up, grunting with effort. He was about their age, but his face was gaunt with exhaustion. He raised a hand, palm outwards. 'Help, please.' His Latin was bad, but intelligible. He pointed to his right ankle. 'Leg. Hurt.'

'Shepherd?' asked Felix.

The man gave him a blank look.

'You . . . sheep?' Felix indicated the slopes above and below, and bleated. 'Goats?'

Understanding bloomed on the man's face. 'Yes. I care . . . sheep.'

'This is no ambush,' said Felix. 'We'd be dead by now if it was. He's a local. I'd wager he twisted an ankle, and he's been up here since it happened.'

'I think you're right,' said Antonius.

Despite their hunch, they kept a firm grip of their weapons as they drew closer, but nothing happened, other than the dog wagging its tail. No Macedonians leaped out of the bushes; no arrows showered in.

'Water?' Felix held out his skin.

The shepherd nodded his thanks. When he handed the bag back, it was almost empty. Felix gave Antonius a glance. 'How long you . . . up here?' he asked.

The shepherd held up two fingers.

'That's a long time,' said Felix. 'Your belly must be clapped to your backbone.'

Another blank look.

Felix rummaged in his pouch and found the hunk of bread he'd brought. He held it out.

The shepherd fell on it as if he'd not eaten in a month. Swallowing the last piece, he gave the brothers a brown-toothed grin.

'What shall we do with him?' muttered Antonius.

They stared at each other, realising the same thing. Every local village was empty, abandoned because of the Roman advance. Farmers wanted to save their crops and livestock from the scouting parties that took everything they could find. Wise heads, Pullo included, had also suggested Philip might have paid the natives, with their expert knowledge of the terrain, to make themselves scarce. That way, it would be impossible for the Romans to find a path around the Macedonian position. Whatever the truth of it, this man might know some of the trails. He might be useful to Flamininus, and was therefore of value to the brothers.

Using his dagger to cut a small, low-hanging branch from a holm oak, Felix trimmed it into a crude but serviceable staff. The shepherd accepted it with effusive thanks in his own tongue. Standing, he pointed up the mountain.

'I . . . go.'

Felix shook his head. 'You come with us,' he said in Latin. The shepherd didn't seem to understand, so he pointed down the valley. 'You come . . . our camp.'

The shepherd looked most unhappy. 'I . . . go . . . family.'

'You can see your family afterwards,' said Felix.

The shepherd tried to hobble away, but Antonius blocked his path. 'We go to the camp,' he said firmly.

The shepherd glanced at Felix, at Antonius, then Felix again. Their implacable expressions changed not an iota, and his shoulders slumped.

'You kill me.'

'We mean you no harm,' said Felix.

'Macedonians murder my friends, my cousins.'

The brothers stared at each other in surprise. 'Why?' asked Felix.

'To stop them showing Romans . . . path around their army.' The shepherd's face was sad. 'I have wife. Children. Not want . . . die.'

'No one's going to kill you,' said Felix. 'I swear it.'

The shepherd looked from brother to brother. They nodded reassurance. He shrugged in resignation.

'You know the mountain paths?' asked Felix.

He nodded.

They both cheered.

CHAPTER XXXVIII

Philip had come to view the enemy. It had become his ritual over the previous month and a half. He visited a different part of the ramparts across the valley each day, allowing plenty of time to survey the battlefield, to hear reports from the officers in charge, and most important of all, to encourage his troops.

As he climbed the ladder, the familiar stomach-churning stink of rotting human flesh wafted from the other side of the defences. He'd allowed the Romans to collect their dead at various times – in the main, so his own men didn't have to live day and night with the stench – but they could never gather every corpse.

'It's safe, sire.' A Companion had gone up the ladder first. Philip found the new routine supremely irritating, but with Herakleides' and Kryton's plot and his near escape at Ottolobus fresh in his mind, had acceded to his generals' repeated requests that bodyguards accompany him everywhere. Revealing none of his smarting pride, he acknowledged the delighted salutes and greetings that met his arrival on the walkway.

'Melankomas, you rogue.'

Philip shook hands with a burly phalangist with cauliflower ears and an oft-broken nose that resembled a misshapen sausage. From Karia in Asia Minor, Melankomas was a recruit from Philip's campaigns there two years prior, and a ferocious fighter. In the king's mind, he was worth five ordinary soldiers.

'It's good to see you, sire.' Melankomas' smile revealed more gaps than teeth.

'Had any time to box of recent days?' asked Philip.

The nearest soldiers roared with laughter, and Melankomas grinned. 'Once or twice, sire.'

'Did you win?'

'He wore them out, sire. As usual!' cried a voice.

It was well known that Melankomas' primary tactic was to wear his opponents down by dodging their blows rather than landing his own, but Philip arched an eyebrow.

'It's not against the rules, sire,' said Melankomas with a chuckle.

'True enough,' said Philip, amused.

Promising that he would try to watch the Karian's next bout, he moved on. Five Companions stayed close.

Philip continued his tour, enjoying the description by an artillery officer of the most recent Roman attack, which had taken place the previous day. Two siege towers used by the enemy lay a short distance before the rampart, shattered by stones from the catapults. Bodies were scattered in and around, and the cries of trapped men inside could be heard.

Philip had decided that Flamininus' readiness to continue throwing troops at his defences showed his lack of experience, and his desire for a speedy end to the war. After forty days and a dozen failed assaults, it should have been clear that the Macedonian positions weren't going to be taken by storm.

Let him waste his men, thought Philip.

It was conceivable that Flamininus had other irons in the fire, and so scouts had been sent to find any surviving locals. As with the unfortunate Aetos, men and older boys were to be killed, and their wives and surviving children threatened. Offerings had been made to Zeus, asking for his favour; the priests had been consulted often. His position was being protected by every means possible.

Thus far his tactics were working, and the longer that continued, the better it was for Philip. Trapped in the narrow confines of the valley, unable to advance, Flamininus' legions' numerical superiority was useless. Keep it up for another forty days, Philip decided, and the harvest would be upon them. Flamininus would have to give serious consideration to abandoning his campaign for the year. His reputation would be damaged, as Galba's had been; the Senate might recall him to Italia. With the Roman campaign in disarray, Philip could utilise the autumn and winter to maximum effect, recruiting more soldiers and reinforcing his relationship with Akhaia. With a little luck, bridges might be built with Sparta and other states.

'A rider comes, sire,' said one of the Companions.

Philip's eyes followed the man's outstretched arm. A rider was fording the Aous. Even at a distance, it was clear that he bore a branch in his hand.

'A herald,' said Philip. 'It comes to this.'

Not everyone had seen the olive branch; an officer barked orders from the nearest tower. His crew hurried to load their catapult.

'Hold!' roared Philip. 'Let him approach.'

His command rippled along the rampart. As the horseman drew near, the air grew tense. Although Philip had had the upper hand in the battles thus far, Roman arrogance knew no bounds. The messenger's demand might be something preposterous, such as he surrender to Flamininus at once.

As the rider entered artillery range, he reined in and held the olive branch high.

'Ha!' said the Companion who had spotted him. 'He's frightened.'

'I would be too,' said Philip. He cupped a hand to his mouth and shouted in Latin, 'Come in peace!'

There was no response, and men on the ramparts began to jeer.

'Silence!' roared Philip. He repeated what he'd said, but louder.

The Roman sat for a short time. Whether he was considering Philip's words – if he'd even heard them – or was waiting to see if the artillery would shoot was unclear, but in the end, he urged his horse towards the defences.

Philip stood forward so his fine armour and red-crested helmet might be seen.

The messenger halted one hundred paces out. 'Flamininus sends word to Philip,' he cried in Latin.

'I am Philip.' There was no reaction, not even a dip of the chin, and anger coursed the king's veins. Even the lowliest of these barbarians was haughty beyond belief.

'Flamininus would meet with you.'

'Does he wish to bend his knee?' asked Philip. The soldiers who understood Latin laughed.

A frown. 'He wishes to treat with you.'

It would be pleasing to send the messenger away empty-handed, thought Philip. Flamininus would be furious, and powerless to retaliate. Curiosity defeated malice, however.

'What does he want?'

'Will you meet him tomorrow morning at the lone holm oak by the river?'

'I will. Just him, mind, and a pair of bodyguards – no one else. I trust you Roman bastards as much as I do snakes.'

The rider nodded, and without another word, turned his horse and rode away.

At once Philip's Latin-speaking soldiers explained to their fellows what had happened. Loud debates about what Flamininus would say began.

'He's lost so many men, he will surrender – there is no other option.'

'Rome will renounce its interests in Greece, and the legions will withdraw.'

'He'll offer an alliance to the king – I know it.'

Their optimism was refreshing, but Philip knew Flamininus would lay no such deals on the table. The campaign had but started. No blows would be struck come the morn, he thought, yet the struggle would be bitterer than that of the previous forty days.

The following morning was glorious. Not a cloud marked the blue sky. A light, refreshing breeze flowed up the valley from the coast. From the bush-covered slopes, cicadas kept up a relentless chorus. A pair of choughs tumbled about in the air overhead, playful as children. On the Macedonian ramparts, soldiers watched their king and his escort ride towards the enemy lines.

Philip looked every part the king. His armour had been burnished until it shone, the feathered crests of his helmet renewed, and his sandals polished. Beard combed, hair oiled, he was mounted on his favourite Thessalian stallion. In a quite deliberate gesture, he waited for some time after Flamininus had arrived at the agreed spot before deigning to appear.

I am the king, he thought, and you the leader of a barbarian army.

Despite his scorn, he was eager to meet the man who so desired to defeat him. Philip had been intrigued by his spies' reports of Flamininus' repeated efforts to become consul, and his love of Greek history and culture.

Flamininus had two companions as agreed, one a cavalryman, the other a senior officer. The trio watched in silence as Philip approached with a pair of Companions at his back. Twenty paces from the river, he halted, giving the Romans a haughty stare.

'King Philip.' Flamininus bent his head.

'How pleasant to be shown some respect at last,' said Philip. 'It seems a quality that most Romans lack.'

'I apologise for any discourtesy shown you,' said Flamininus.

You mean that no more than you shit drachmae, thought Philip. 'You speak Greek.'

'I do. I am a lover of all things Hellenic,' said Flamininus with no trace of irony.

'So I have heard.' Delighting in Flamininus' surprise that he should know this, Philip continued, 'Invading the region is an odd way of showing that regard.'

'I am but the Senate's servant. Where it commands, I must go.'

These barbarians must take lessons in sounding genuine while lying through their teeth, thought Philip. 'Forty days of fighting has seen you gain not a single stadion. Your men's morale must be low.'

Flamininus' eyes glittered. 'They fight for Rome. Their purpose will not waver.'

I annoyed him, Philip decided. Good. 'Do you wish to sue for peace?'

'You are the one who should consider that policy.'

'I'm happy here, and so are my soldiers.' Philip indicated the steep valley sides, and the fast-flowing river. 'What with the magnificent scenery, it's hard not to feel at home. If we have to stay until after the harvest, so be it.'

'You cannot defend every route into Macedonia,' said Flamininus. 'Sooner or later, the legions will reach your kingdom.'

'Ha!' Philip made a dismissive gesture, but the barb had sunk in. The Romans would not lose heart from being held in this pass for months. Next year, Flamininus might attack on two or even three fronts. And if he does, thought Philip defiantly, I will build defences as I have here. A second summer spent camped before my fortifications will wreck his career. I will defeat the general who follows him, and the one after that. Bold as Philip was, he knew the possibility remained that Flamininus was right.

'An unpleasant idea, is it not?' Flamininus' tone was mocking.

'I was enjoying the thought of your losses here being repeated in the valleys to the north,' lied Philip. 'The Senate will not approve; you will be replaced, like Galba and Villius before you.'

Flamininus' lips thinned. 'I am here to deliver terms.'

Philip raised an eyebrow.

'Your garrisons are to be removed from all Greek towns. Reparations must be paid to those whose lands you have ravaged: in particular, Athens, Pergamum and Rhodes.'

Philip was furious, but he kept his face blank.

Chiach, chiach. High above, the choughs called to one another.

Looking disappointed by Philip's lack of reaction, Flamininus continued, 'Any other disputes that you are involved in are to be opened to arbitration by a mutually agreeable third party.'

A third party which will no doubt look to you for guidance, thought Philip. What gives Rome the right to intervene here? he wanted to shout.

They stared at one another.

'Well?' asked Flamininus. There was no denying the annoyance in his voice now. 'What shall your answer be?'

I *will not* roll over and present my belly like a scared pup, Philip decided. And yet, bitter though the medicine was, it was preferable to swallow a little. If he gave in to some of Flamininus' demands, outrageous as they were, Rome might end the war.

'I will renounce control of the lands that I have conquered personally. Those I inherited shall remain Macedonian, for they are mine by right. I will accept mediation on matters outstanding between me and my enemies – including the matter of reparations. The arbiter should be a party with whom neither state is at war.'

Flamininus tutted. 'The unprovoked aggression you have shown to Athens, Pergamum and Rhodes needs no arbitration – you were the one to initiate hostilities, the one who seized territory and destroyed property that did not belong to you. They shall calculate the monies owed.'

'Very well,' said Philip, thinking, if this is the price for peace, so be it.

'As for the Greek towns that must be freed, why not start with those in Thessaly?' suggested Flamininus airily.

Philip was shocked into silence. Thessaly had been under Macedonian control since his namesake, the father of Alexander, had deposed its tyrant more than a century and a half before. Relinquishing it without a murmur would send the message to every Greek state that he was a toothless lion. Powerless, a king without pride or honour.

'No,' Philip muttered.

'No?'

'You heard me! What heavier condition could you impose on a defeated enemy, Flamininus?'

'Rome is merciful, offering to leave you as king of Macedonia.'

'Your idea of mercy and mine differ somewhat.' Despite his best intention, Philip's anger flared. 'You arrogant Roman prick.'

Flamininus' face coloured. 'What did you say?'

'Call yourself a Hellenophile?' sneered Philip, furious at Flamininus' audacity. 'You're a barbarian, no better than the stinking Illyrians and Dardani who slink at your heel.'

Flamininus swore, and ordered his cavalryman to hand over his spear.

'Think you can hit me from there?' Philip jibed, ready for a fight himself. He edged his mount to the water's edge. 'Do your best.'

Knuckles white on the shaft, Flamininus gauged the distance. After a moment, he shook his head angrily. 'It would be a waste of a fine weapon.'

'You would have a better chance of hitting a barn door, more like,' cried Philip. He took the light spear offered by his Companion. 'I, on the other hand . . .'

Flamininus flinched, but did not back away. 'Throw.'

'It will be far sweeter to destroy your legions – if you ever manage to leave this valley, that is.' Philip smirked at the fury that now twisted Flamininus' face, and turned his horse's head towards his camp.

The verbal battle had been his, Philip decided as he rode away, and the physical one would be too. By reacting to his goad, Flamininus had revealed a chink in his armour. Provoke him in the right way, and he would make unforced errors. Ensure that these took place in the right location, and his legions could be beaten.

Philip was sure of it.

CHAPTER XXXIX

The sun was rising over the Aous valley, and Flamininus was at breakfast. Seated on his grandfather's folding camp chair in his personal tent, he regarded the well-stocked table in front of him with relish. He'd already spent hours catching up on paperwork; now his favourite meal of the day was at hand. The fresh bread smelt as good as loaves from the finest bakeries in Rome. Large, plump olives, green and black, glistened in oil. Various cheeses, white, yellow, moist and crumbly, begged to be eaten. Hard-boiled eggs formed a neat circle on a plate. His magician of a cook had even produced honeyed pastries. Flamininus reached for one, making a mental note to thank the cook when next he appeared.

A couple of mouthfuls, and the sweet morsel was gone. At home in Rome, Flamininus would never have been allowed more, but free of his wife's disapproving gaze, he took a second. There were three more on the plate – sore temptation, but there was too much else on offer. He dipped a hunk of bread into the oil around the olives, took care not to let any drops fall on his pristine tunic, and took a large bite. Gods, but that was good, he thought, trying in swift succession two types of cheese, and then a third.

Pace yourself, Flamininus told himself, taking a long swallow from his ornate blue glass. He studied the wine with an affectionate eye. Caecuban, diluted as he liked it. A second mouthful was just as good. So was the next – and then it was back to the cheese and bread. His eyes kept getting drawn to the honeyed pastries. Perhaps he would place one on the side, a morsel for later in the morning. Or else he could have it now. With a reflex glance to make sure his wife wasn't looking, he wolfed down a third. It was divine – better than the pastries in Rome. I shall have them daily, he decided. A smile of satisfaction marked his lips.

There were worse things than going to war.

Culinary delights could only keep reality at bay for a time. His thoughts returned to the stormy meeting with Philip, which had gone less well than he'd hoped. He hadn't imagined the Macedonian king would lie down and accept every demand, but nor had Flamininus intended things to deteriorate the way they had. He felt little regret, though. Despite his army's failure thus far to take the pass, he held the upper hand, and Philip's refusal to acknowledge this had wounded his pride.

King he may be, but I am consul of Rome, thought Flamininus. I am the Senate's voice. The strong arm of its military might. I am the modern Alexander, not Philip.

'When will Rome be victorious?'

Flamininus could already hear the question being asked in the Senate. He could see it written in a letter from Rome, the reply to his news that he had spent more than forty days – nigh on half the campaigning season – encamped in a narrow valley in the arsehole of Epirus. Results remained of vital importance. All the hard work he had put into becoming consul might be wasted if successes didn't start falling into his lap. Fail to achieve as Galba had, and he'd eventually be replaced by the Senate. Soon after that, he would be ruined by Galba's revelations of his murky political dealings with the Aetolians, Rhodians and Pergamenes.

Flamininus wished Galba a slow, painful death, and not for the first time, considered having him murdered. Sadly, it wasn't worth the risk.

'If I should die unexpectedly, by fair means or foul, my lawyers will publish every document in my possession with your name on it,' Galba had said, standing over Thrax's body. Flamininus had to live with the agreement he'd made – and that meant battering the Macedonians into submission, somehow.

The day's end would see if the legions could finally break through the enemy defences: Flamininus had ordered another large-scale attack. He held little hope, however. The assault was as much a message to Philip that Rome's determination would not wane as it was an attempt to force a way up the valley. Flamininus' dilemma was threefold. Direct assaults were doomed to fail. Moving part of his army to the northern passes while he marched south-east was an option, but time was against him. The same applied if he sent troops to join his brother Lucius on the east coast.

A month and a half remained before the harvest; campaigning after that was a daily gamble, and not the way to win a war. Furthermore, Philip was well used to splintering his own troops and sending them in different directions. They could travel at great speeds, meaning Flamininus' smaller forces would risk being isolated.

Fresh frustration stung him. He needed a path through the mountains *here*, yet all attempts to find local tribesmen to serve as guides had failed. It was as if they had vanished with their families and livestock into thin air. Philip was behind it, thought Flamininus. He had to be.

'Master?'

Recognising the voice as Pasion's, Flamininus wanted to groan. As ever, duty beckoned. 'What is it?'

His secretary sloped to the table; his eyes flickered over the food, better fare than he could ever hope to eat, and came to rest on Flamininus. 'An Epirote chieftain wishes to see you, master.'

Flamininus' lips thinned. Roman allies they might be, but he'd found the Epirotes to be bearded, stinking savages clad in fleece jerkins. Their main interests appeared to be hunting, drinking and screwing. To be confronted by one at this early hour would be more than his nostrils could bear, he decided.

'Send him away.'

'Yes, master.' Pasion didn't look surprised.

Flamininus' curiosity raised its head. 'What does he want?'

Annoyance flitted across Pasion's features. 'He wouldn't speak to me, master. I'm a miserable secretary, he said.'

'Rude as well as malodorous, eh?'

'Master?'

'Never mind.' Flamininus reached for a fourth pastry. I really shouldn't, he thought, but they're too good to leave. Pasion will pilfer it otherwise, or the cook.

Pasion spoke from the entrance. 'He was boasting to the sentries, master.'

Flamininus' ears pricked. 'Go on.'

'He said that he'd walk into your tent a poor man, and come out rich.'

339

Flamininus brushed crumbs from his lips and stood. 'You did well to mention that, Pasion. Show him in.'

'Of course, master.' Pasion vanished.

The brute might have something of worth to tell me, thought Flamininus, his interest rising.

He smoothed down his tunic, and checked that no pastry remained on his face. Not wishing to seem eager to the Epirote, he selected a parchment at random from the mounds on his desk and began to walk about, pretending to read.

'With your permission, master,' said Pasion. Framed in the entrance, he had someone behind him.

'Enter.' Flamininus didn't lower the scroll.

Pasion was followed by a wiry-framed figure with long black hair. His sleeveless sheepskin jerkin was belted at the waist; under it, he wore a tunic. Plain leather shoes covered his feet. Two empty scabbards, one for a knife, the other a sword, proved Flamininus' guards were alert. Sharp-featured, with hungry wolf's eyes, the chieftain looked as untrustworthy as a man could be.

'This, master, is Charops, a local Epirote chief.' Pasion dipped his chin and stood aside.

Flamininus said nothing. He'd heard of Charops – the man had served Villius well, apparently. That didn't mean he was to be trusted.

Charops bowed. 'I thank you for this audience, consul.'

His Latin is poor, thought Flamininus. Typical. 'You have information of interest?'

'I do, consul.' Charops' smile was all reddened gums.

Flamininus averted his gaze, and kept silent. I'll be beggared before I ask him to go on, he thought.

Unseen by Flamininus, Charops' eyes moved to the breakfast table. 'A fine spread.'

'Indeed,' replied Flamininus caustically.

'What's that?' Charops was pointing at the last pastry.

'It's a sweetmeat, made with flour and honey,' said Flamininus, growing more irritated.

'*Sweetmeat*. Can I have it?' Charops was already walking towards the table.

'I suppose.' Gods above and below, thought Flamininus. Next he'll be asking to sit in my chair.

Charops ate with an open mouth and great enthusiasm. He smacked his lips when the pastry was gone. 'Good. Are there more?'

'No.' Flamininus' tone was now icy; he was also glad that he'd left only one.

Charops grunted and helped himself to several pieces of cheese.

'I didn't invite you in to dine,' Flamininus snapped. 'Tell me why you're here, or I'll have you thrown out on your arse.'

Charops wiped his mouth with the back of his hand. He belched. 'I want a plate of how you say . . . *sweetmeats*.'

By this point, Flamininus would have had any Roman hauled from the tent and whipped. It was clear, however, that Charops had – or thought he had – information of great importance. Taking a long, deep breath, Flamininus said, 'If our meeting goes well, you shall have as many as you wish.'

Charops repeated his hideous grin. 'Your soldiers fight again today.'

'That's correct.' If Flamininus listened, he could hear the clash of arms from up the valley.

'They lose.'

Flamininus gritted his teeth. 'Perhaps. Perhaps not.'

'They lose. Defences high. Strong. Macedonians love their king. They fight for their homeland.'

'We will break through in the end.' But not this year, unless things change, he thought.

Charops' expression grew sly. 'There is path. In mountains.'

'There are many paths,' said Flamininus dismissively.

'I have shepherd. He knows way around the Macedonians.'

Flamininus came close enough to smell Charops' fetid breath. 'Where is this shepherd?'

'In safe place.'

'Bring him here.'

'I want silver.' Charops' tone had lost any hint of friendliness.

'If the shepherd can do as you say, you shall have a reward, never fear,' said Flamininus.

'Silver. Five hundred coins.'

Flamininus buried his fists in Charops' greasy jerkin and dragged him in, eyeball to eyeball. The nauseating odour from his mouth drove Flamininus' anger to new heights. 'Do not think to lecture a consul of

Rome, filth! You will hand over this shepherd, or I'll have your entire family crucified. Understand?'

'Aye.' For the first time, fear was writ large on Charops' face. 'I bring him.'

'Right now.' Flamininus shoved Charops away and regarded him with disgust. The man ate in the jerkin; it looked as if he blew his nose on it too. 'Pasion, fetch a bowl of water and a drying cloth.'

Truth be told, he wasn't worried about his dirty hands – if the shepherd could do as Charops said, Flamininus wouldn't have a care in the world. The Epirote could have sweetmeats every morning for the rest of his days, he thought, and five hundred silver coins besides.

A path through the mountains would allow some of his soldiers to flank Philip's army. Smoke signals would let him know that they were in place; he could then draw the Macedonians to their defences with a feigned assault, allowing his men at the enemy's rear to attack. This was the chance he'd been waiting all summer for.

'Master.' Pasion again. 'One of the sentries is here.'

Deep in thought, Flamininus hadn't noticed the legionary behind Pasion. 'Speak.'

The princeps, a dependable-looking type, saluted. 'There's a centurion Pullo to see you, sir. Says he has a possible guide through the mountains.'

Flamininus' smile grew broad. Not one guide, but two! Truly, the gods favour me today, he thought. 'Bring him in.'

'Sir.' The princeps wheeled and vanished whence he'd come.

'Philip, you mongrel,' said Flamininus with immense satisfaction. 'I have you now.'

CHAPTER XL

A tide of allied infantry marched towards the Macedonian fortifications. Demetrios, atop the ramparts with his friends in the
place they had come to regard as their own, couldn't understand why
Flamininus was committed to the deaths of yet more men. True, they
were allies, not legionaries, but soldiers were soldiers. Every corpse
below was one enemy less for Philip's army to face. It seemed not to
matter to Flamininus – from the numbers tramping in their direction,
the assault was to be a big one.

The clash began in the usual fashion, with the artillery wreaking a
terrible slaughter among the enemy. Demetrios thought it odd that the
allied troops did not break, as they had before, but with men already
leaping into the ditch, he had no chance to think about it. He and
his friends fought in grim, determined silence, talking only when one
needed another to help throw down a ladder or the like. Philippos,
who had taken to joining them, was a noisy fighter, however. A great
roar left his mouth each time he dispatched an enemy, and he laughed
when ladders toppled sideways, taking the legionaries to their deaths.

As the allied troops began to falter, a wave of hastati began to advance. 'What's Flamininus up to?' cried Demetrios.

'The prick thinks the allies will hold if they see legionaries coming
to help.' Kimon spat over the rampart to show what he thought of that.

'The attack will fail regardless,' pronounced Antileon. 'Flamininus
has too many men, to throw them away so easily.'

It couldn't be that simple, thought Demetrios. Something was going
on, but what it was, he didn't know. He leaned out and with a precise
stab, killed the first man on a ladder. Dodging his comrade's falling
body, the second soldier quailed, which gave Demetrios time to shove
the ladder to the right, unbalancing it. Despairing cries rose; he paid
no heed.

Something made Demetrios glance over his shoulder, back up the valley. Cold fear uncoiled in his belly. Twin lines of smoke were rising from the tree-covered slopes to his left. A short distance behind the army's camp, they were being made by enemies – there could be no other reason. Somehow the Romans had appeared to the rear of their camp. 'Look,' he muttered.

No one answered.

'Kimon, Antileon, fucking look behind us! Philippos!' he shouted.

His friends obeyed. So did Philippos. Demetrios didn't need to say a word. They all swore, and swore again.

'What do we do?' asked Kimon.

'Back to the speira,' said Demetrios. 'Men here will have no chance of escape. Our best hope is with the phalanx.'

Antileon began to argue, but Philippos cut him off. 'He's right.'

Like that, it was settled. Throwing their aspides over their shoulders, they pounded down the nearest ladder. The peltasts were too busy fighting to see them go.

In the short time it took the four to reach their speira's position, total chaos had broken out through the camp. Hundreds of legionaries were spilling from the trees along the side of the valley. Many of Philip's troops weren't under arms – over the forty days previous, it had become accepted that the Roman attacks would fail, obviating the constant need for every soldier to be ready – which added to the confusion. Men scrambled for their weapons and armour, while their officers bellowed at them to move faster.

Simonides already had the phalangists in file, facing the rampart. He greeted the four's arrival with nothing more than a raised eyebrow and an order to join their comrades. Demetrios scrambled into place, nodding at Zotikos. The rest of the speira was also in formation. Stephanos, the man who had replaced Kryton, stood before his men, face set. Demetrios remembered his old commander. Both he and Herakleides were food for the worms now – as they might be soon.

'This is going to be dirty, brothers,' cried Stephanos. 'When the peltasts realise what's happening, they'll be off that wall like rats off a sinking ship. After that, things will go to Tartaros, fast. Many of us will be slain in the next hour, like as not, but we're not going to run. There's a job to do.'

'Apart from die?' Philippos called out.

Plenty of men laughed, and Stephanos grinned. 'Aye, apart from that. We have to hold the Romans back so that our comrades can escape.' He raised a hand at the unhappy muttering. 'Aye, I know the barbarians are in front of us and behind. Two chiliarchies are going to form up, one facing towards the ramparts, the other up the valley.'

'Where are the other chiliarchies?' demanded someone.

'The king has ordered everyone but us to retreat – there's no room to deploy. The honour of holding the barbarians has been left to us,' said Stephanos in a proud tone.

'How long do we have to fight for?' asked a voice – Demetrios thought it might have been Empedokles.

'Until I fucking say so, that's when!' bellowed Stephanos.

'A man's got to die some time,' said Philippos, laughing his great belly laugh.

There were some chuckles, but most men remained silent. No one moved from their position, however. Everyone obeyed as the four speirai spread out, leaving gaps for the retreating soldiers to pass between and up the valley. The second chiliarchy was doing the same, but facing in the opposite direction.

Demetrios thought Stephanos' suggestion insane, but he couldn't abandon his comrades. He shot a glance at the men behind, who were a mixture of stony-faced and nervous but resolute. Demetrios clenched his jaw. They were in this together, for better or worse.

Their position offered a good view of the fortifications; he watched with fascinated horror as the first peltasts came hurrying past, still carrying their shields and spears. What followed had a dreadful inevitability. Ladders soon appeared in the gaps left by the men who'd retreated, and moments after that, hastati scrambled up onto the walkway. The remaining defenders began suffering heavy casualties; that was enough for the less determined among them, who threw away their weapons and ran. Before long, the press at the ladders was so thick that men began leaping to the ground below, uncaring of the height.

The faces of the next peltasts to pass Demetrios and his comrades were terrified, panicked; some were even weeping. None would look at the mass of phalangists standing ready to fight. It was strange, but their fear, their frantic desire to escape, stiffened Demetrios' resolve.

He had heard of the carnage that unfolded when soldiers broke. He and his comrades *had* to hold the enemy if the entire army wasn't to be butchered.

Their test began not long after, when the first hastati clambered down inside the defences. Perhaps fifty strong, they charged in a disorganised mass towards the gap between Demetrios' speira and the next one over. A shouted order from the two commanders had the speirai shuffle towards each other, closing the space. The hastati faltered, and then, mad with battle lust, charged on. They died to a man, impaled on the deadly sarissae.

The centurions were quick to restore discipline, assembling their men by the century at the base of the ladders. Organised, the enemy advanced in a great line, as they had so many times during the previous forty days.

Stephanos began to sing the Paean. Demetrios seized on the tune; it was a way to voice his fear, refusal to retreat, and if it came to it, his willingness to die. He had tapped into a shared emotion. The phalangists' voices soared towards the heavens, a crescendo of defiance that checked the Romans' advance. Angered, their centurions blustered and threatened until the hastati again began to move forward. Their advance was less confident than it had been, however, and it was no surprise to Demetrios when their charge came to a halt before the ends of the sarissae.

'Yellow-livers!' roared Stephanos.

A centurion in the front rank pointed his sword at the phalangists and shouted something. He took a couple of steps forward; a few men followed him, but an instant later, a front-ranker jabbed forward with his pike. His thrust was perfect, spitting the centurion through the throat. Drowning on his own blood, he went down, and the phalangists cheered. The hastati were frozen to the spot, and when the speira moved forward, they retreated. It wasn't until another centurion appeared, and began beating men with the flat of his sword, that they attacked. Even then, their efforts were half-hearted. They died by the dozen, unable to close with the jeering phalangists.

Word of their success moved down the files. Demetrios was delighted, but Zotikos dampened his enthusiasm.

'It won't last – it can't.'

'Their numbers will become overwhelming,' muttered Demetrios, peering over men's heads at a wave of principes scaling the defences. After them would come the deadly triarii, he thought.

'Aye. We can use the valley side and the river as protection on our flanks, but sooner or later, some bright centurion will lead his men into the trees, or into the water.' Zotikos sighed. 'Once they come at our sides, we're like the mouse in the pitch pot. Screwed.'

The speirai commanders were also alive to the danger, and during another lull in the fighting, sent messengers to one another. Not long after, the two chiliarchies moved, awkwardly, but without breaking formation, up the valley. It was hardest for those facing the defences – Stephanos' speira included – because they had to walk backwards. The Romans followed at a safe distance, waiting, Demetrios realised with horror, until the phalangists had to enter the camp and negotiate their way past tents and fires.

'We're going to have to break formation,' the quarter-file leader announced. 'Unless Stephanos commands otherwise, we will move into quarter-files when I say.'

Demetrios didn't like it, but he'd seen the disorganised peltasts being harvested like wheat by the pursuing legionaries. Staying together had to be a better choice. 'What about our sarissae?' he asked Zotikos.

'Lose your pike at your peril,' Zotikos answered. 'This isn't the only battle we will have to fight.'

Trying to ignore the feeling that once broken up, they would be slaughtered like lambs, Demetrios nodded.

Events began to unfold fast. A group of principes led by an optio in a black-crested helmet burst from the trees to their right. Demetrios' file was three in from the speira's right flank; he and his comrades could do nothing but shout a warning. The men on the rightmost file did their best to turn towards the enemy, but the wily optio had already formed his men into a small wedge. They drove at the speira, picking off the phalangists who weren't yet facing them.

Demetrios' quarter-file leader didn't wait. 'Break file!' he roared. 'About turn, and follow me!'

'We should stand and fight,' Demetrios protested.

'We've done our work here,' grated Zotikos. 'If you want to live, follow!'

Demetrios and Kimon slung their aspides over their shoulders, lowered their sarissae and followed. The quarter-file leader was on their heels. Joy filled Demetrios as he glanced over his shoulder, and saw Antileon and the rest haring after them.

The attack from the trees proved to be a blessing in disguise; by breaking away, the phalangists had outrun the main body of legionaries who had scaled the defences. Once they had cleared the camp, the path up the valley was unobstructed by Romans at least. It was clogged with phalangists and other troops, however, and soon the comrades were forced to walk. That was a relief, for the sarissae were incredibly difficult to run with – and dangerous.

After perhaps five stadia, they stopped for a brief rest. Demetrios stared back down towards the position they had held for almost a month and a half. The flat ground behind the wall was dense with legionaries, and more were appearing atop the rampart. The repetitive *thunk* of axes told him that the fortifications would soon fall, allowing Flamininus' entire army through.

'What a fucking mess,' said Kimon sourly.

'We're alive, at least,' said Demetrios.

'Thanks to us, most of the army got away,' said Zotikos. 'That's something to be proud of.'

It felt like a hollow victory to Demetrios.

CHAPTER XLI

Thessaly, central Greece, summer 198 BC

Philip had ridden out from his camp to survey the landscape. Although it was pleasant to have reached the flat Thessalian plain, which spread out south and east before him, he was already missing the cooler temperature of high ground. Waves of baking heat radiated from the bone-dry ground, cracked open by the sun's heat in many places. Golden fields of wheat, barley, spelt and millet rolled away into the distance.

Poor farmhouses were dotted here and there; red-tiled roofs marked their richer neighbours' dwellings. A tiny figure led a mule-drawn wagon along a rutted track, another watched over a flock of grazing sheep and goats. At Philip's back, forming a huge semicircle, were the tall, forest-covered mountains that protected Thessaly's western and northern borders. It was these ranges that he and his army had marched out of that afternoon. Some ten days had passed since the defeat in the Aous valley.

Before him, in a defensive position between a hill and the river Lithaios, lay the town of Trikka. Alerted to his troops' presence by the noise of their arrival, the local leaders had sent messengers with flattering words and offers of food and supplies. These Philip would take – his army was an ever-hungry beast – but he needed more from Trikka. There was every chance that Flamininus would come this way, and soon.

The choices facing Philip were tough. The legions' needs were as rapacious as those of his troops. Leave the towns of Thessaly unharmed, and he would hand Flamininus immeasurable quantities of provisions. If he sacked and burned the settlements, and torched the crops in the fields, he would deprive his enemy of vital rations, making Flamininus' advance a great deal more perilous. Despite this, Philip did not want to destroy his own kingdom. The people of Trikka were his subjects, and the idea of forcing them from their homes before razing the place to the ground was repulsive.

Frustration lashed Philip. He had to decide what to do, if not now, then within a few days. The legions were on the move, sure as death followed life. He threw a bitter glance at the sky, from where the gods were watching, and no doubt laughing. They would have known that his refusal of Flamininus' harsh demands was pointless. Just a few days later, he was effectively ceding Thessaly.

Trikka was dear to Philip's heart. Birthplace of the healing god Asklepios, his temple complex there was revered by Greeks and Macedonians alike. He had visited it once as a boy, on a rare journey with his stepfather Antigonus Doson. They had slept in the shrine for several nights alongside other pilgrims, each morning reporting their dreams to the priests. Philip had vivid memories of waking in the darkness and seeing moonlight streaming through the open window onto the mosaic floor, where two snakes lay entwined. Whether they had been placed in the room by the priests – as his stepfather said later – or sent by the god, he hadn't been sure. The image still brought goosebumps up on his arms.

I cannot burn Trikka, he decided. I should, but I will not.

Many other towns *would* have to be destroyed. He had no choice. Antigonus' advice again returned to haunt him: 'Some things you will enjoy as king. Leading your army to war. Seeing your enemies vanquished. Accepting the loyalty of new subjects, and rewarding those faithful to you. Other things are more difficult, even distasteful. Never being able to set aside your responsibilities. Ordering the execution of former friends or allies. Telling your soldiers to massacre every inhabitant of a village that has defied you.'

Murdering thirty shepherds, thought Philip darkly, knuckles white on his horse's reins. 'The Romans shall not have Thessaly,' he muttered. 'Instead it will burn.'

'Sire.' Amid the clamour, the shouts, the screams, a Companion's voice.

Philip focused. The Companion sat astride his horse, not ten paces away. Black smudges marked him from head to toe. A smear of blood ran the length of his sword arm. Philip didn't ask where it had come from – he knew, and it made him sick to his belly.

'What?'

'Most inhabitants are leaving, sire, but a few are refusing.' The Companion looked troubled. 'The majority are old, or ill. They'd rather die than leave their homes, or so they say. What is your command?'

Philip's face was impassive, but inside, he was wavering. He glanced upwards, almost expecting to spot Ares, the bloodthirsty god of war, laughing as he rode high in his chariot, with his sons, Fear and Terror, by his side. All he saw were plumes of smoke billowing up from the town of Phacium, which lay before him. Some of the houses had already been fired, thought Philip.

'Take me to them.'

'Sire?' The Companion looked taken aback.

'Bring me to every person who will not leave their home.' Philip urged his horse towards the main gate, forcing his startled bodyguards, a dozen Companions, to follow.

Phacium wasn't a big town. Perhaps two thousand souls lived inside its stone walls, with another five hundred or so farming the surrounding countryside. Around half the population had heeded Philip's command the previous day to abandon their homes, but the rest had stayed on, hoping the order wasn't true. Theirs had been an unpleasant awakening that dawn, when his troops had marched in, hammering on doors and ready to evict people by force.

Now, the exodus was in full flow. In family groups, in ones and twos, carrying heavy loads and trailed by servants and slaves even more laden down than they, the inhabitants filled the road leading away from Phacium's main entrance, an arched gateway topped by a section of crenelated rampart. Trying to squeeze past felt like swimming against a river's current; Philip soon had to raise his voice, and then his fist. Some thought about answering back, even blocking his path. They swiftly realised who he was and moved aside, protests dying in their throats.

A stony glare saw the Companions remain at his back. No one is going to attack me here, thought Philip, and if I can't defend myself against a civilian, I don't deserve to be king. He couldn't stop an image of Pyrrhus flashing through his mind. A skilled general from Epirus and famous mercenary, he'd died not by the sword, but from a roof tile hurled by a woman in a town such as this.

'This is one of the dwellings, sire.' The Companion pointed at a ramshackle hovel, the door of which hung on a single hinge. Hens pecked about in the dirt, scuttling into the house when the horses drew close. A black and white cat with purulent eyes watched malevolently from the single windowsill.

'Hail,' said Philip.

No answer.

The Companion pounded his spear tip on the door, which almost came away from its hinge. 'Come out! Your king is here.'

Silence.

The Companion's face darkened. He swung down from his horse and made to enter the hovel.

Feet shuffled within. A hen darted outside, followed by a second malevolent-looking cat with one ear. 'Who's there?' called a quavering voice.

'I am Philip of Macedon.'

Wheezing laughter. 'The king?'

'Aye,' said Philip, reining in his temper. 'Come out, that we may speak.'

A barefoot crone in a ragged dress appeared in the doorway. Possessed of wispy grey hair, and a face more lined than a piece of crumpled parchment, she had to have seen three score summers and ten. Her rheumy eyes regarded Philip with unusual intensity. 'You look like a king.'

The woman owed him nothing; she was no fawning courtier, no arse-licking Herakleides, thought Philip with pleasure, yet she discerned kingship in him. 'What do they call you?'

'Briseis.'

The name of a queen of Troy; in response, snorts of amusement from his Companions. Philip glared, and they averted their gaze. He turned back to Briseis. 'You were a beauty in your father's eyes to be named so.'

Her chin lifted. 'I was. Never found a husband, though.' She opened her right hand, which was little more than a set of stubby claws at the end of her wrist.

Philip sensed rather than saw the Companions' revulsion. Her deformity was unsightly, he thought, but she didn't seem evil, or cursed by the gods. 'Your father loved you indeed.'

Most parents exposed such babies, left them in the open to die. It was considered bad luck not to do so. To have reared Briseis would have required parents, and in particular, a father with real spine.

'He did.' Briseis' gaze went dim with memory. 'I looked after him well into his dotage.'

Smoke filled Philip's nostrils: more buildings were ablaze. 'I must ask you to gather what valuables you have, and make your way to the front gate. My soldiers are burning the town.'

'Why would I go? My place is here; Mother and Father are buried outside the walls. I will join them soon enough.'

'Time is pressing, sire,' said the Companion. 'Shall I deal with the others who will not leave?'

'Aye. Do not harm them. Promise everyone that they will be looked after, by order of the king.'

As the Companion rode away, Briseis shuffled to within a few steps of Philip's horse. 'You care about your subjects.'

'It pains me to destroy their homes, but I have little choice. The Romans will arrive before long, and they will take everything by force. No woman will be safe, not even a greyhair like you.'

Light flashed off a blade Briseis had magicked from the depths of her dress. Philip stiffened. His Companions levelled their spears. She cackled. 'This is not for you, o King. Any Roman who tries to lift my skirts will get this in the neck.'

'Do as I say, and no Roman will threaten you,' said Philip. 'Soldiers will escort you to Macedon, to safety.'

'I'll take my chances.' Briseis retreated to the doorway.

'Stay, and you will burn!' cried Philip.

'You seem a good man, o King. Better that you rule Thessaly than Rome. The gods' blessings on you.' Briseis bowed deep and vanished inside.

Philip was lost for words. He sat astride his horse, the air around him filled with crackling sounds and the groan of collapsing timbers.

'Sire, we must go.' This from the most senior Companion. 'It's not safe.'

'Aye.'

'Shall I send a man inside for the crone, sire?'

'No.'

Briseis was right to remain, thought Philip. Inside Phacium's walls, she had some kind of life. Outside, she would have none.

The Companion didn't argue. Ordering two men to lead the way and another to ride to Philip's left, he placed himself by Philip's right side. 'With your permission, sire?'

Philip nodded.

They rode.

Philip had seen many unpleasant sights in his life. Men slain on summer battlefields, more maggots than flesh, their stench palpable from five stadia. Corpses that had been eaten by wild animals, their bones gnawed clean, eyeballs eaten, picked of every sinew. Criminals thrown from a high place, their crumpled bodies an ugly tangle of awkwardly bent limbs and shattered skulls. He'd seen death at sea, and in rivers, outside town walls and in sacred places. He had ordered plenty of the deaths – had sent thousands of men to die in battle. In the coming days and months, he would see many more.

None would haunt him more than Briseis.

CHAPTER XLII

Outside Phaloria, western Thessaly

More than a month had passed since the battle at the Aous. It was midsummer, and the lack of cloud presaged another scorching day. Together with hundreds of other legionaries, Felix, Antonius and their comrades were waiting to advance on Phaloria, the first decent-sized town they'd seen since crossing the border into Thessaly.

The time since their victory over Philip had been pleasant. Rather than pursue the enemy, they had been in Epirus, where Flamininus had cultivated relationships with the tribes, and purchased vast quantities of supplies and food for his army. No one had been unhappy, least of all Felix and his comrades. Patrols through friendly countryside and accompanying wagons laden with grain was boring work, but worlds better than risking their lives in battle. And yet remaining in Epirus would not bring Philip to heel, or fill the brothers' purses. They were here to win a war, thought Felix, and the sooner that was done, the better. Phaloria was but the next obstacle in their way.

Occupying one slope of a valley that led south-east, the town was home to a strong garrison. Rumours were that Philip had augmented the local troops with two thousand of his own men. It was possible to bypass Phaloria, but Flamininus had no intention of leaving his army open to attack from the rear. Orders had come the evening before that the place was to be taken by storm. As at Antipatreia, Pullo's response had been to have his men fashion ladders from trees felled on the slopes above.

'You should be expert at it now, maggots,' he'd growled as sweating, they wielded axes, saws and adzes under the blistering sun. 'Faster!'

Felix eyed the worst of his blisters, a raw, oozing circle where his right thumb met his hand, caused by hours of gripping tools. If he came away from the impending fight with that as his only wound, he'd be grateful for its constant stinging.

'When will it start?' Narcissus' nasal voice.

It was a question in everyone's mind, but Felix was tired of his self-absorbed comrade. Much of the time they'd been waiting – an hour at least – had been given up to a long-winded explanation of how Narcissus' parents had met, been separated, and then come together again through the gods' favour. The tale had not long come to an end. Felix gave him a withering stare.

'See the artillery? When they start shooting, it begins. Once they've done, the allied troops go in. If they don't succeed, we'll get the order to advance with the hastati. Get it?'

Chuckles from everyone bar Narcissus. 'Very funny,' he said with a sneer.

'You asked. I told you.' Felix fixed his eyes on the lines of bolt throwers, which had been carried to within ten score paces of Phaloria's defences. In order to find the best angle, each machine had loosed a number of ranging shots. Jeers and insults from the defenders had met the first attempts, which had smashed harmlessly into the stone walls, or landed short. Their derision had been silenced by the next volleys, which had caused several casualties on the battlements and from the strangled cries beyond, in the town itself.

The artillery crews stood ready now, weapons loaded, their officers listening for the signal. Felix couldn't see the trumpeters, who were with Flamininus, behind the principes' position. It had to be soon, he thought. The town was encircled, the troops in place. Epirotes, Illyrians and other allies made up the first wave. Hastati and principes like themselves comprised the second. As ever, the triarii were at the back.

Pullo had been at the rear, talking to Livius, but reappeared along the side of the century, vitis slapping its familiar rhythm off his left palm. Felix had done nothing wrong, yet he still dreaded the sound. The expressions of those around him revealed the same truth. Men joked sometimes that many enemies would run from a centurion armed only with a vine stick, but Felix didn't know anyone with the balls to crack it in front of men such as Pullo or Matho.

'Ready, fools?' asked Pullo.

'Yes, sir!' they shouted back.

'You'd fucking better be.' Pullo came to a halt along the middle of the front rank, about ten paces out. His cold eyes raked the principes.

'The savages—' here, a sour smile '—that is to say, our allies, are going in first. They should soften up the enemy nicely.'

'Rather them than us, eh?' Felix muttered to Antonius.

'Silence!' Pullo's low voice was terrifying, as always.

The blaring of trumpets drowned out whatever else Pullo might have been about to say. The noise hadn't died away when the artillery began to shoot. Felix watched the nearest bolt thrower. *Twang*. A bolt shot towards Phaloria's walls. Two hastati sprang into action, winding back the arms. The instant there was room on the groove, a third man laid a new bolt in place. At its maximum draw, the string ran over the final ratchet with a metallic click. A nod from the loader, and the officer pulled the release cord. Off went the bolt, faster than the eye could see.

Over the course of perhaps two hundred heartbeats, the artillery laid down a brutal barrage on the enemy. It was impossible to judge how many casualties had been caused, but there were fewer men on the ramparts. Screams aplenty floated through the air from Phaloria.

Trumpets halted the artillery, then sounded the advance. Roaring fierce battle cries, the allied troops charged at the town walls. Felix watched, fascinated. Nervous archers among the defenders began to loose before it was time. Their arrows fell short, and the allies roared with contempt as they pelted closer. The second volley, less ragged than the first, dropped a few men. The next couple did a little better, but by then, the warriors were scrambling into the ditch at the wall's foot, and throwing up their ladders.

'All we do is scale fucking ramparts,' said Antonius. 'Antipatreia, the Aous valley – now here. Give me a line of enemy soldiers any day.'

'Agreed.' Felix wasn't bothered by heights like his brother, but he didn't enjoy climbing towards men who wanted to kill him.

Savage fighting broke out as the defenders threw down ladders, hurled stones and arrows, and fought with warriors who had succeeded in reaching the walkway. Felix willed on the allied troops. If they took the wall, casualties among the hastati and principes would be light.

His hopes were dashed when scores of soldiers – the town's reserves? – appeared atop the rampart. The balance swung towards the defenders for the first time, and after a bloody struggle, the troops who'd scaled the defences were cut down to a man. The last two were heroes, fighting back to back long after their comrades had been hurled down into the ditch. An audible groan went up from the principes as one, then the second, were slain.

At the end of Felix's ladder, Narcissus began muttering a prayer.

Fabius was rubbing his phallus amulet. Mattheus was whistling under his breath.

'Our turn now.' A faint sheen of sweat marked Antonius' brow.

'Steady, brother,' muttered Felix, although his own stomach was clenching. 'Think about the enemy at the top of the wall.'

'Aye. Aye.'

'Prepare yourselves.' Pullo thrust his vitis into the ground – he'd find it later, or, as he often said, it could be buried with him. 'On my word, pick up your shields.'

Jupiter, Greatest and Best, watch over me and my brother, Felix prayed. Carry us through the fight to come.

'Ready, you filth?' Matho's measured voice was as shocking as if someone had emptied a bucket of ice-cold water over Felix.

Panic battering him, his gaze moved to their immediate right. In front of a century of principes stood their old centurion. Beady-eyed, bandy-legged, no doubt foul-breathed, he was readying his men for battle, just like Pullo. He wasn't looking in Felix's direction, but that didn't stop Felix from wanting to vomit. Never had the danger of their re-enlisting been plainer. Antonius was behind him, but *he* was in the front rank. Thirty paces separated him from a man who, with a single word, could see both of them executed.

'Shields!' ordered Pullo.

As one, the principes obeyed. During their wait, it was permitted to rest their shields on the ground, leaning against their bodies.

'Ladders ready!'

Felix cursed himself for volunteering to be the front man. Matho would see him now for sure. Turn away, and Pullo would notice. He was helpless. 'Antonius!' he hissed.

'What?'

'Matho's here. Look right.'

A muffled gasp. 'If the cocksucker doesn't see us before the wall, we should be safe enough. You know how it is once the fighting starts.'

'Aye.' Felix began to pray again. He asked Jupiter and Mars, even Fortuna, the capricious goddess of luck – his plea was the same to all – not to let Matho spot either him or his brother.

The deities laughed.

The next time he glanced towards Matho, the prick was staring right at him. Felix's every muscle froze. In Matho's expression, he saw astonishment, disbelief and then, calculating rage. 'Felix?' said his lips. 'It is Felix! I see you!'

Felix's knees almost gave way. 'Matho's seen me,' he hissed.

Whether Antonius heard or not, Felix couldn't be sure, because the trumpets shredded the air. Pullo led the way at once, stepping out as if he were on an evening stroll. 'Follow!' he shouted. 'With me, fools!'

Stomach roiling in fear, Felix obeyed. He couldn't stop his gaze from roving towards Matho. The centurion seemed to sense it: he was always glaring at him, and mouthing obscenities. We're dead men, thought Felix, swallowing bile. If the defenders don't get us, fucking Matho will.

Pullo walked the principes for half the distance – until the braver archers started to loose – and then charged. The ladders prevented them from raising their shields against arrows, making every step potentially lethal. It was a case of not looking up, and praying. Not missing one's footing, and hoping that other men were injured or killed.

As Felix ran, his lips repeated over and over, 'Let Matho be hit. Let Matho be hit.'

A choking cry closer to home and a sudden drag on the ladder snapped him back to the present.

'Narcissus is down!' Antonius' voice, terse and sharp.

Felix twisted his head. Narcissus had taken an arrow in the worst spot possible: just above the neck of his mail shirt, at the base of his throat. He'd dropped the ladder, and was clutching at the arrow. Bright red blood poured from around the wooden shaft. Narcissus tried to speak, but emitted a horrible, gagging sound. He coughed, and streams of bloody froth sprayed from his lips. Down he went, to his knees, then toppled back to stare at the sky. He rasped a bubbling breath in and out, and died.

'Felix! Antonius!' Pullo had somehow seen. 'Move!'

Narcissus had a better end than poor Ingenuus, thought Felix. If I am to die, Great Jupiter, let it be like him – anything but the fustuarium.

He snatched up the ladder, exchanged a grim nod with Antonius, and charged on to the ditch, which was full of injured and dying men.

'Mother,' moaned a warrior. Jagged ends of bone glistened white from the red ruin of his left thigh. 'Mother.'

Felix tried not to listen, tried not to feel what was beneath his sandals. He set his shield against the wall. Without Narcissus' help, it was harder to feed the ladder upwards, hand over hand. Vulnerable, balls tight with fear, Felix worked as fast as he could.

It doesn't matter if you survive the attack, a voice in his head said. Matho will have you beaten to death.

Felix's grip slipped. Cursing, he caught hold of the ladder again and brought it in to an angle suitable for climbing. He looked up, but could see no one watching. Rather than elation, despair took him.

'What's the fucking point?' he cried.

Antonius heard. 'Climb, brother. Worry about Matho later.'

Felix set his jaw. He picked up his shield and set his foot on the first rung. Halfway up, he looked to his right, trying to spot Matho. To his horror, the centurion was three ladders over, shouting orders as he ascended. Thoughts of Matho vanished at the parapet. As Felix clambered over, he had to fight for his life against a wild-eyed warrior with a rusty spear. Poorly aimed, the first thrust missed. With no time to draw his sword, Felix barged forward, slamming the warrior with his shield. Heave. Barge. With a wail of fear, his enemy fell off the walkway and was gone.

The next man along the rampart was a comrade from Felix's century, which gave him time to look for Antonius, who had just reached the top of the wall. Despite the threat from Matho, they exchanged a relieved look. Few defenders were in sight. Any sense of where a man's unit was had gone, and Pullo was nowhere to be seen, but they could see allied troops and legionaries down inside Phaloria. Individual fights raged. Bodies lay everywhere, and some defenders were running for their lives.

'The town will fall soon,' said Felix.

Despair filled him. When it did, Matho would have them arrested. Pullo wouldn't stop the fustuarium demanded by Matho – he'd join in, like as not.

The gods were still watching.

'It *is* you.' Matho's voice, out of nowhere.

Felix felt a hand in his back, could not prevent Matho shoving him off the walkway. He let go of his sword and shield, in case the one impaled him and the other broke his wrist on landing. The packed earth rose to meet him with incredible speed. He landed badly, winding himself, and taking a dunt on his helmet from the shield.

Head spinning, Felix peered at the nearest buildings. Men were running in all directions: legionaries, warriors and townsmen. No one paid him any heed. Where was Matho? Felix wondered dully. He was coming, sure as the sun rose in the east, but he had to come down a staircase. Gods willing, he would have to fight his way down.

Move, thought Felix. Move if you want to live.

Sucking in a lungful of air, he rolled onto his side. On his knees next, he pulled his shield closer and with an effort, flipped it over to put his hand in the grip. His sword was lying some dozen paces away. Reach that, he decided, and he had a chance of holding Matho off until Antonius got there. Together they would see that the bastard never left Phaloria. Silencing their former centurion was their only option now.

Felix never saw the blow that sent him sprawling sideways into the dirt again, could do nothing about the hobnails ripping the flesh of his unprotected legs and buttocks. He curled into a ball, protecting his face with his arms. The brutal assault ended as fast as it had begun. A boot nudged him in the back.

'Look at me.' It was Matho's sibilant voice.

Felix could taste bile. He rolled over.

Matho was standing right over him. The point of his sword was aimed at Felix's throat. 'So you joined the legions again, eh?' said Matho. 'I'm not surprised, really – *you* were always a fool. I'd have thought Antonius was smart enough to know better.'

'Bastard,' hissed Felix.

'Me, the bastard?' Matho lost his composure. 'I was demoted because of you and your drunkard friends! If it hadn't been for you cunts, I'd be commanding triarii these past two years. Instead I can expect to end my career as a junior centurion of fucking principes.' He kicked Felix in the balls.

Felix almost passed out from the pain. This is it, he thought, next expecting to feel Matho's blade slide into his flesh. It didn't happen. Wary, terrified, Felix opened his eyes.

'Think I'd let you die without suffering?' Matho's voice oozed malevolence. 'You and your useless brother will die as slow as I can make it. The fustuarium would be too fast, I think. The cross is better. I've heard tell of a strong man – like you, in the prime of life – who lasted four days. Or was it five? A drop of water now and then, and you might last even longer. It will be a joy to watch, to listen to you beg for an end.'

'You'll never hear those words from my lips,' said Felix, hating the obvious fear in his voice. Antonius, where the fuck are you? he wanted to scream.

Matho read his mind. 'Your brother chose the wrong set of stairs. He's stuck halfway down, fighting a warrior twice his size.'

Felix lunged with one foot at Matho, trying to goad him into making a killing blow. He missed, and the chuckling centurion moved out of the way.

'Antonius will kill you,' said Felix from between clenched teeth.

'If he even tries, I'll finish you. No,' said Matho with extreme satisfaction, 'the maggot will lay down his sword. Then he'll tie you up, before I do the same to him. After, your crosses shall face each other. Each of you shall watch his brother die.'

Rage filled Felix, and he reached for the dagger at his belt. It was pathetic, but he could think of nothing else.

Matho didn't try to stop him. When Felix threw, he simply raised his shield, letting the dagger clatter off it to the ground. Matho kicked it behind him. His gaze flickered to the right. 'Your brother's still alive,' he observed drily. 'Holding his own, even. Good. I'd hate for him to die at the enemy's hands rather than mine.'

Now Felix was consumed by hatred. He'd have given his lifetime's army pay – twice over – to have been on his feet with a sword in his hand, rather than sprawled on his back, helpless as a babe. He had to do something: he was *not* going to the underworld without a fight. Throwing caution to the wind, Felix rolled to one side. To his surprise, Matho did nothing, so he stood up.

'You want your sword.' The centurion jerked his chin at the blade, which was to *his* left. It was perhaps six paces from each of them. 'Go on,' said Matho, as pleasant as a man offering another a drink from his water bag. 'See if you can get to it.'

Felix shot a look at where Antonius had been – Matho hadn't been lying, he was disappointed to see. Antonius was fighting for his life against a huge warrior armed with a spear.

I'm on my own, thought Felix.

Matho would maim him, like as not, before he reached his sword, but that was a risk worth taking. If Fortuna smiled on him, he might even take a fatal wound, and thus deprive Matho of his revenge. Felix took a deep breath.

'I'm enjoying this,' said Matho.

Fffffewww. Felix barely registered the distinctive sound of a spear in flight. His gaze shot to Matho, whose mouth opened, but no sound emerged. His eyes bulged, and stumbling, he dropped both sword and shield. Reaching for the back of his neck, his fingers came away red. Down he went, face first into the dirt, a spear jutting from the base of his skull.

Stunned, Felix traced the missile's possible path. Twenty paces away stood a thin figure, a smooth-cheeked youth. Without armour or even a helmet, the spear his only weapon, he was one of the town's defenders. He looked as astonished by his throw as Felix felt. They stared at one another.

Thank you, thought Felix.

He raised a hand, and the youth's face crumpled with terror – he saw no friend, of course, but another legionary. Quick as a flash, he sprinted off down an alleyway.

Felix's immediate concern was for Antonius. To his delight, his brother had bested his opponent, who had fallen off the staircase. Antonius was hammering down to meet him. Worried next that his encounter with Matho had been witnessed by some of his own, Felix looked up at the walkway. Principes were spilling over the parapet, but none appeared to have noticed what had gone on. A wave of relief bathed him. Matho was dead, and no one had seen.

Antonius reached his side, chest heaving, his face covered in sweat. 'You hurt?'

'Not a scratch. What about you?'

'Just my pride,' Antonius replied. 'The brute was useless with a spear, but he had the strength of Hercules. I should have got to you sooner, brother.'

'You did your best, as I would have for you.' They exchanged an emotional look.

Antonius poked Matho's body with his foot. 'The gods are in a good mood, eh? The cunt is dead, and we didn't even have to kill him. I can't think of a better result.'

'Aye,' said Felix, feeling as if the weight of the world had been lifted from his shoulders.

'Come on,' said Antonius. 'Best find Pullo.'

Side by side, they disappeared into the maze of streets, their weapons at the ready.

CHAPTER XLIII

Dawn was breaking over Tempe, and the king had gone for a ride on his own. Not advisable, Menander might have said. Philip's stepfather Antigonus would have gone further, accusing him of recklessness, but he was beyond caring. A few hours by himself – curse it, even a single hour – was worth more than anything. From dawn until dusk, Philip had to deal with the burdens of kingship and the war with Rome. Of recent days, it seemed, all the news had been unpleasant. Slipping out of the rear of his tent, dressed in a plain tunic and hooded cloak, he had made his way to the horse lines without his bodyguards realising. The pages who cared for his mounts had been startled to be woken by the king, but had soon saddled the Thessalian stallion, and sworn not to tell a soul.

No one had been up to see him ride to the camp's perimeter, where the astonished sentries were also sworn to silence. Other than magicking himself into a bird or learning to become invisible, it was impossible to leave without being noticed, thought Philip with some frustration as he headed south-west, into the mountains. While he was king, it would ever be thus.

For now, he could savour his stallion's grace and power. Breathe the crisp air, laden with pine scent, rosemary and sage. Spy the deer watching him from the treeline. Watch the eagle already soaring the currents overhead. Admire the narrow gorge and to his left, the swift-flowing river that bisected it. Let Flamininus come here, thought Philip, and I will slaughter his legions.

The pleasing dream vanished whence it had come. Tempe was just one of the pinch points leading to Macedon; once the location of his army had been determined, Flamininus could choose several other options. If Philip divided his forces to defend more than one route, he risked the Romans being able to force a passage. He had to trick

Flamininus into attacking in a place of his choosing, where the might of the phalanx could be utilised.

Despite his best intentions, Philip fell to considering the news that had reached him the previous day. The threats on land weren't his only concern; those posed from the sea were of almost equal importance. Earlier in the summer, Flamininus' brother, newly appointed to the command of the Roman fleet, had joined with the squadrons led by Attalus of Pergamum and the Rhodians. Before his arrival, these allies had failed to take an important town on Euboea, in the main because of reinforcements sent by Philip's general Philokles.

United now, however, the three fleets were attacking a neighbouring settlement. Philokles' message to Philip had been short and to the point: 'Enemy strength too great. Defeat inevitable. Will fight as long as I am able.'

With the fall of one town imminent, thought Philip, it was hard to see how the other, isolated further down the long island, could withstand another assault. Unless the gods themselves became involved, Euboea, a Macedonian territory for five generations, was about to fall.

I need a new admiral, he thought. A bitter laugh escaped him. He'd needed a suitable replacement for the ineffectual Herakleides since the Tarentine – a mere husk by the end – had been executed, months before. Various ships' commanders had taken temporary charge, but none had the ability to match, say, Philokles or the king himself, on land. It would be one of his primary tasks during the winter, Philip decided. Find a skilled admiral, and the possibility of victory at sea could become a reality. His hope was that if he bloodied the noses of the Pergamenes and Rhodians enough, they would pull out of the conflict.

In the meantime, Philip was left with the task of defeating Flamininus, or at the least, preventing him from reaching Macedon. Thessaly was lost to him, its towns destroyed and crops burned, yet that had not stopped the legions' advance. Shrewdly, Flamininus had bought vast quantities of supplies in Epirus. Worse, his legions would soon be joined by the Aitolians and Athamanians, who were mustering their soldiers. Philip sighed. Unpalatable though Flamininus' demands had been, they were already coming true in part. The Thessalian towns Philip had bridled at giving up were no longer his. Come to an agreement with Flamininus before the start of winter, he thought, and the Macedonian people might escape the brutal attentions of an invading army next spring. The thought of that humiliation stoked Philip's defiance. There was time yet to find the right place, he decided, the location his army *could* beat the legions. Where was it, though?

Rock scraped on rock above and behind him, and he cursed himself for not paying attention to his surroundings. He listened, but the sound was not repeated. His pulse quickened. A deer clambering the steep slope would continue to make a little noise; so too would a boar. A man was watching. Men, more like. The types who hid from sight in a place like this didn't operate alone, and the two light hunting spears lying across Philip's thighs were his only defence. Wry amusement seized him. Here he was, worrying about the dangers facing his kingdom and ignoring lethal ones closer to home.

Bandits were ubiquitous in the mountains. Criminals, murderers, younger sons with no prospects and escaped slaves, they preyed on the unwary traveller, and sometimes, remote farms. Outcasts, enemies to all, they would kill him without a qualm. His best option, therefore, would be to reveal his identity. Philip wasn't wearing royal attire, but the bandits would be well aware of the army a few stadia away. Intimidate them, and they would take him prisoner in the hope of earning a large ransom. He bridled. It seemed cowardly to save his skin by dint of rank.

'I know you're there,' he said, reining in the stallion.

'Kill him and have done,' called a rough voice from the trees to Philip's right. 'Then we can take the stallion and be on our way.'

Two, thought Philip. There are bound to be more. 'I have no coin,' he answered. 'Slaying me will achieve nothing.'

'It'll provide us with sport,' said a deep voice a little way to Philip's left.

A squat, black-haired man with a jutting salt and pepper beard appeared from behind a large boulder on the river bank. He wore no armour, but his pelte shield and spear had a well-cared-for, often-used look. 'What other reason do we need to lay you in the mud? Apart from your stallion, that is.'

The mocking laughter that followed was being made by more than three men, Philip decided. Slow and careful, he turned his head. A skinny youth with a bow was the one who'd been dogging his footsteps, hiding among the plentiful evergreen bushes that covered the valley sides. Watching from the trees was a rangy figure in a wolfskin cloak; a spear was his only weapon. Were there more? Philip wondered.

'Where's your purse?' The youth's voice had barely broken.

'I left it behind,' said Philip, telling the truth.

He spied a fourth man behind the leader. Older than the rest, he had two spears, a shield and cold, killer's eyes.

'That stallion's too good a mount for a piece of filth like you,' said the youth. 'Where d'you steal it?'

Philip hadn't been called such a name, to his face at least, since he was about ten; then it had been a boy in the royal stables at Pella. Although marriage to another man after a husband's death was accepted practice – his mother Chryseis had wedded Antigonus after his father's passing – it hadn't stopped malicious whispers from noblemen's sons at court about his parentage. The mouthy stable lad was but the last one to say it, and hearing the insult, a red mist had descended over Philip's vision. If a groom working in the next stable hadn't intervened, he would have choked the boy to death.

'I said, where did you steal it?' The youth's voice was full of bravado. Philip was back in the royal stables almost twenty years before.

'Your mother's a whore,' said the stable boy.

Overwhelming fury consumed Philip.

'I'm talking to you!'

Philip blinked, coming back to the riverbank. There was no question of pleading for his life, let alone telling the outlaws who he was. 'The stallion is mine,' he said.

'Liar!'

With measured gaze, Philip calculated the distances separating him from each brigand. The youth was closest; in theory, that made him the most dangerous, but he might not be as practised as, say, the leader was with a spear. He was also the hardest to reach, being above and behind Philip's position. The man with the wolfskin cloak was furthest, which, he decided, left the bearded leader and the one with killer eyes as his first targets.

'Yours?' Killer Eyes made a contemptuous noise.

'Aye.' Philip kneed the stallion in the ribs, aiming it towards the two brigands. 'He's the finest horse I've ever owned.'

'Get down,' ordered the leader.

They had avoided killing him thus far for fear of injuring his mount, thought Philip. It was the one tiny advantage he had. 'What's that?'

'Off the fucking horse,' said Killer Eyes.

'Why?'

Philip was only fifteen paces from the pair now; the youth was about three times that distance to his rear. Wolf Skin was walking out of the trees, but he was still a long spear throw away.

'Because I said so.' Killer Eyes' right arm went back, his weapon ready.

'Ha!' Philip shouted, flicking the reins.

The stallion broke into a canter. Philip would have preferred to have slid around to hang off the right side of its chest, with his left leg over its back, but that would have meant discarding his spears. He had to hope that Killer Eyes would miss. Philip lay forward onto the stallion's broad, maned neck, making himself as small as possible.

Air moved; a spear shot over him, close enough to shear a hole in a rucked-up part of his tunic.

Killer Eyes' first spear, thought Philip. They have one left each. He tugged on the reins, and the well-trained stallion came to an abrupt halt. Philip dropped light-footed to the ground, putting the horse between him and the brigands.

'Get the whoreson!' ordered the leader.

'I can't fucking see him,' snarled Killer Eyes.

Philip tried not to think about the youth with the bow. Passing his second spear to his left hand, he ducked under the stallion's belly – prayed they wouldn't see him coming that way – and emerging, levelled his right arm and threw. The spear took Killer Eyes in the belly. Making a horrible mewling noise, he dropped.

Instinct made Philip duck. The movement saved his life; an arrow shot through the space where his head had been. Sparks flew as its iron point struck a rock.

'Try to trick us, would you?' The bearded leader lunged with his spear, and Philip did well not to be spitted as he'd done to Killer Eyes. Stumbling, he went to one knee and the leader closed with a triumphant cry.

So this is how it ends, thought Philip. No glorious death leading my Companions into battle, no single combat with Flamininus. Butchered like an ox in the charnel house. His right hand trailed along the ground; pebbles and gravel moved beneath his fingers. Grabbing what he could, he cried, 'Zeus, help me!'

The leader checked his thrust for a heartbeat.

With all his power, Philip flung the stones, catching the leader full in the face. Part-blinded for a moment, the outlaw roared in pain. The roar became a scream as Philip transferred his second spear back to his right hand and stabbed him in the throat.

Ssshhhewww. The youth must have been waiting to loose. It was a better effort than the first, but the arrow only nicked Philip's right arm. In the time it took him to notch another to his string, Philip had snatched up the leader's pelte shield and finished off Killer Eyes. The next arrow smacked into the shield, its barbed head driving through close to Philip's fist. Three more followed as he retreated to the boulder which the leader and his comrade had hidden behind; just one hit the shield. Protected by the great rock, he snapped off the shafts, rendering the shield usable once more. Stones rattled out of sight. Low voices muttered. The youth and the wolfskin wearer were conferring.

Philip remained in mortal danger. If the man in the cloak was any kind of fighter, he could engage Philip while the youth positioned himself for a fatal shot. He had to plant fear in their hearts, had to force them into something rash.

'Who wants to die next?' he shouted.

'It's you who will go to Tartaros.' The youth's voice cracked. 'That man was my father!'

'He was filth,' Philip yelled, not knowing or caring whether he meant the bearded leader or Killer Eyes. 'A snake in the grass, who deserved what he got!'

'Bastard!' Pebbles rattled as the youth drew closer. A voice counselled caution – the man in the wolfskin cloak – and he stopped.

Philip cursed. Perhaps he could dart from cover to kill one, withdrawing before the other reacted. Spear held overhand, he crept as far as he could around the boulder without being seen.

'Coward! Yellow-liver!' The youth was close.

Zeus Soter, help me again, Philip prayed. He lunged around the great stone, finding the youth half a dozen paces away. An arrow stared him in the eye. Philip ducked behind his shield. The youth loosed. Pain streaked through Philip's skull as sharp iron ripped open his scalp, and the shaft was gone, disappearing with a soft plash into the river. The youth reached frantically for another arrow. Philip tried to reach him, but was stopped by the thrusting spear of the man in the wolfskin cloak.

Philip retreated behind the boulder and pondered his next move.

Nothing happened for perhaps fifty heartbeats. He could hear the two brigands talking in low voices – they appeared to be arguing.

Good, thought Philip. He stole forward for a second time. When he caught the words 'only one arrow', he again darted around the boulder, with another prayer on his lips. Just as he'd hoped, the youth shot and missed, his last shaft vanishing into the fast-flowing water. Again his companion came to his aid. Stepping carefully, Philip walked back whence he'd come, facing the brigands.

'Not much of an archer, are you?' he cried.

'Shut your mouth!'

'Your comrades must do the hunting. If it were down to you, you'd all be long dead of starvation,' taunted Philip.

Losing his head, the youth charged forward, snatching up his father's spear as he came. Cursing, the man in the wolfskin cloak followed, which was Philip's exact hope. The space between the boulder and the river's edge was too narrow for both bandits to stand abreast and use their spears. When they were ten paces away, he converted his retreat into an attack, his target the inexperienced younger brigand.

The youth rushed in, all balls and no brain. His spear skidded off Philip's shield, which was angled just so. He never saw the precise thrust that slid into *his* belly. Screaming like a stuck pig, the youth fell backwards. Rather than tugging free his blade, Philip shoved it deeper, at the same time pushing with his shield. Half behind the stumbling youth, the last brigand couldn't bring his spear around to bear on Philip.

The three tumbled to the ground, Philip on top, the man in the wolfskin cloak on the bottom, and the shrieking youth between. Quick as he could, Philip grabbed a fist-sized rock and smacked Wolf Skin in the side of the head. Another blow, and he felt the skull give. Philip gave him another two cracks for good measure. He finished off the youth with his spear and, leaving the corpses where they had fallen, whistled for his stallion. Used to the sounds of combat, it hadn't moved far.

As Philip rode back down the valley, a better mood than he'd been in for days descended. He had faced insurmountable odds alone and come through victorious. And yet, he thought, it had been a close call. If the youth had had more arrows or been a better shot, the ambush would have had a different outcome. Philip would also have died if the youth hadn't been so callow, so overeager. Two experienced men would have taken their time, splitting up to attack him from front and rear. Instead, he had forced them to come to him in a narrow space, negating their numerical advantage.

An idea came from nowhere, and Philip cried out with excitement. It felt as if Zeus himself had spoken. He laughed: he knew how to beat Flamininus.

CHAPTER XLIV

Near Gomphi, western Thessalian plain

Flamininus was closeted in his command tent with his senior officers. After marching his army from the charred ruins of Phaloria, and bypassing the small but impregnable Macedonian stronghold of Aeginium, they had arrived in Thessaly the day before. The summer was passing, and with it, Flamininus' chances of complete victory this year. Frustration had become his constant companion – and gnawing worry. If more wasn't achieved before the arrival of autumn forced his withdrawal to the safety of Apollonia, Galba would be unhappy, and in that case . . .

Flamininus' gaze roved over the expectant faces around the table, and he wished that Lucius were present. Decadent he might be, but his brother could be confided in. Although these men were reliable enough, they couldn't ever know about Galba's hold over him. Forget about the prick, Flamininus told himself. Focus on the here. The now.

'It is well for us that Gomphi is in friendly hands,' he said, 'but Atrax is only twenty-five miles to the east. What did the scouts say about the garrison?'

'According to what few locals remain in the villages, sir, there are at least two thousand phalangists inside,' replied one of his legates.

'That's too many to leave at our backs if we march towards Tempe,' said Flamininus. Philip and the main body of his troops were encamped fifteen miles further on from Atrax. Reach him, and there was a chance of forcing a battle before their supplies ran out, or autumn weather set in. Despite the allure of fighting Philip, Flamininus could not put his legions at risk. It galled him beyond measure to be so close to the man he had obsessed about for years, and yet so far. The risk could not be denied, however. Whatever Galba might say, a surprise attack in the army's rear from two thousand phalangists might prove disastrous. It was the type of thing Alexander would try, thought Flamininus – and Philip.

'Atrax has to fall, and fast,' said Flamininus.

His officers agreed to a man.

Flamininus' certainty grew. As long as Atrax was taken, it wouldn't be the end of the world if Philip managed to avoid confrontation this campaigning season. The capture of two major fortresses would be enough to keep the Senate – and Galba – happy. Flamininus could march his army back to Apollonia, and renew the conflict in the spring. No forty-day delay in the Aous valley, no wooing of Epirote chieftains would have to be endured. With no fortresses to be besieged either, Philip would either have to face Flamininus' army, or see Macedonia laid to waste.

'Ideas?' demanded Flamininus.

One legate proposed a night attack on Atrax using ladders. Another wanted to lure the garrison out with a small force of allied infantry, with the cavalry ready to sweep in to the enemy's rear and cut them off from the fortress until the legions arrived from their hiding places in the hills. Two others suggested pounding Atrax's walls with artillery until the legionaries could storm in to overwhelm the phalangists.

Flamininus discounted the second idea at once – unless the enemy commander was a fool, he would not fall for such a simple trick. The first appealed more. Syracuse had fallen to a similar assault during the war with Carthage, and an impregnable mountainous Sogdian stronghold had once been taken by the best climbers in Alexander's army. Equipped with ropes and iron spikes, three hundred brave men had scaled a sheer cliff face in the depths of night, appearing far above the dismayed defenders' heads at dawn. How glorious it would be to take Atrax like that, thought Flamininus, deciding with regret that it was unlikely to succeed. Even at night, the fortress's ramparts were thick with sentries – anyone trying to climb up would be heard or seen well before reaching the top of the rampart.

'The simplest option is often the best,' Flamininus pronounced. 'We will use catapults to smash the walls of Atrax to rubble. Two thousand phalangists cannot prevail against four legions.'

He was still enthusing about the glorious victory his legionaries would win at Atrax when a messenger entered the chamber. He was followed a moment later by an unhappy-looking Pasion.

There is always something, thought Flamininus, grinding his teeth. He pinned the messenger with a hard stare. 'What?'

The messenger, a cavalryman by his scale armour, saluted. 'I come from Gomphi, sir.'

'Yes?' Flamininus could not imagine a problem there. Amynander of Athamania, a recent Roman ally, was the new lord of Gomphi. He had taken the fortress in recent days with Flamininus' help, a force of several hundred legionaries.

'The gates have been shut, sir.'

'You mean the fools on sentry duty forgot to open them at dawn?' scoffed Flamininus.

The cavalryman looked awkward. 'No, sir. They opened at sunrise, as you'd expect. It was when one of our patrols made to enter the fortress, to check on the savages, sir, that the gates were slammed in their faces.'

Flamininus saw his surprise mirrored in his officers' expressions. 'Did the patrol leader demand entry?'

'Yes, sir. They told him to go to Hades.'

Flamininus swept his crested helmet from a side table. 'Take me there,' he said to the cavalryman. Next, he barked orders that four troops of cavalry and three maniples of triarii should accompany him. As he strode from the tent, Pasion hurried in alongside.

'This had better be important,' said Flamininus.

'A letter, master.' Pasion proffered a wooden message tablet.

Flamininus gave him a sharp look. 'Who delivered it?'

'I didn't see, master. The sentry said it was a dark-haired man. He spoke Latin like a Roman.'

Fucking Galba, thought Flamininus, snatching the tablet. The wax seal was unstamped, reinforcing his intuition. Wanting to remain anonymous to those who carried his communications, the wily politician never marked his letters.

Flamininus used a thumbnail to slice open the seal. Heart in his mouth, he flipped open the top part of the tablet. His eyes drank in the cursive script scratched into the two small, rectangular patches of wax.

Is it a deliberate ploy that your campaign moves with the speed of a snail? Know that my patience is finite.

The note was unsigned, as ever. Raging, Flamininus crushed the tablet in his fist. 'The whoreson thinks to lecture me? I have done more in three months than he did in a year.'

Realising he had spoken aloud, and that the cavalryman's ears were pricked, Flamininus swallowed his rage. Amynander could bear the brunt of it, he decided.

Flamininus had to admit that Gomphi was an impressive sight, and its position had been well thought out. A rough circle in shape, the massive fortress had high stone walls and a deep defensive ditch. Atop its towers sat catapults of varying size. It was sited close to the mouths of two important westward-leading valleys, one that led to Athamania's heart, and another that wound its way to the sheltered Ambracian Gulf. Whoever held Gomphi could defend both valleys at once, as well as controlling the ground for miles around, which was why Philip held the fortress dear, and why Amynander had coveted it.

And, thought Flamininus, setting aside his anger for a moment, only a handful of Roman lives had been lost in its capture. How fortunate it was that the Greeks were so quarrelsome, that they flocked so readily to Rome's cause. The Italian peoples had often fought one another, but if he recalled his history lessons aright, they hadn't changed sides or back-stabbed with the frequency of the states here. Amynander was less volatile than most Greeks – he had dallied with Philip on occasion, once letting the king march through his territory, and more recently, acting as a peace broker between Macedonia and Rome – but in the main his loyalties lay with Aetolia, and by extension, its ally Rome. Amynander had history with Gomphi too – attacking the place once before, and failing to take it, so when Flamininus had sent word of his success in the Aous valley, Amynander had requested help at once. Rather than attack Philip, or Macedonian territory, he had made straight for Gomphi.

Until the upset with the gate, Flamininus had been content. With the fortress now in friendly hands, he could move men and materials from Illyria to the Ambracian Gulf, and thence to Thessaly. The route was a speedier alternative than transporting supplies along the route of his recent march, or sailing it all the way to the Gulf of Corinth. If Amynander had changed sides – which, given the closure of the gate, was possible – Flamininus would have to besiege Gomphi before Atrax could be dealt with. This potential delay was not something he wanted to contemplate.

The main entrance into Gomphi, reached over a filled-in section of the defensive ditch, drew near. Flamininus noted with displeasure that the cavalryman had not been deluded. The mighty gates were shut. It was hard to draw any conclusion but that Amynander was in bed with Philip. The cavalry in front of Flamininus reached the solid 'bridge' over the ditch, and still the portal remained closed. Impassive-faced sentries watched from the battlements, but to his relief, he could see no archers.

The first riders halted. The cavalry officer glanced back, and Flamininus muttered, 'Say nothing.' Much could be determined from the guards' words and tone.

One of the sentries peered over. 'Who comes to the fortress of Gomphi?' he demanded in Greek.

Most of the Romans present didn't understand. Flamininus did, and his mood soured further. The discourtesy was quite deliberate. It was beneath his dignity to get involved, however, and so he listened as, in heavily accented Greek, the incensed cavalry officer demanded access for Titus Quinctius Flamininus, consul of Rome.

'Is Amynander expecting him?' asked the sentry.

'Open the gate this instant!' In his fury, the cavalry officer spoke in Latin.

The sentry said something under his breath.

To Flamininus' ear, it sounded like 'barbarians'. He showed none of his rage – that would please the sentry. Instead he called out in perfect Greek, 'Amynander answers to me, as well you know, you dusty-footed sheepskin wearer!'

Little could be seen of the sentry's face through the vertical slit of his helmet, but his change in posture revealed his surprise.

Flamininus' breath caught. Was Amynander a traitor, or were some of his men proud fools who thought to challenge Rome?

His answer came a few heartbeats later as the sentry barked a command. After a slight delay, the gates opened, creaking and groaning.

'It could be a trap, sir,' warned the senior cavalry officer as Flamininus urged his mount forward.

'They're not that stupid,' said Flamininus, sure now that his hunch was correct. 'Kill me, and every man in the fortress would end up on a cross.'

He had decided upon his reaction before he'd even cleared the cool shadows cast by the great, arched entrance. Beyond was a courtyard bounded in part by the ramparts and in part by an imposing citadel. The walls were manned by perhaps two score warriors, which lent further credence to Flamininus' theory. The gate had been closed by some cocksure young hotheads – it was possible that Amynander, fond of his wine and, like as not, still abed, didn't even know what they'd done. Flamininus waited until his entire escort had entered before ordering the cavalry off to one side, and the triarii to form a defensive circle around him. The surprised centurions obeyed. He showed no interest in dismounting, or seeing Amynander. He stared, cold-eyed, up at the walkway over the gate, where the insolent sentry, notable by the red horsehair crest on his helmet, still stood.

'Come down!' Flamininus shouted. 'I would speak with you.'

The four sentries glanced at one another. A few words passed between them. 'Which of us?' called a soldier wearing a dented bronze breastplate.

'All four.'

Flamininus rolled his tongue around a dry mouth. If they didn't obey, he would have to send the triarii up, and things would get messy, fast. The result would be the same, however: complete slaughter. The sentries seemed to realise this, and a moment later, the wooden ladders shook beneath their tread. The triarii parted to let them through. At a word from their officers, half the legionaries turned inward, placing scores of swords at the Athamanians' backs.

The sentries – visibly uneasy now – reached Flamininus. The insolent one was the youngest, which didn't surprise him, and his helmet was the best bit of kit he had. His armour was padded linen, and looked old enough to have been used by his grandfather. By their faces, two were brothers, men in their mid-twenties, with good quality weapons and armour. The last was the leader, a straight-backed veteran in his thirties and like as not, the only one who'd seen much fighting. A small state, Athamania didn't go to war as often as its larger neighbours.

'Lay down your arms,' ordered Flamininus, wishing that Galba and his servant Benjamin were among their number.

The sentries exchanged shocked glances.

'Why?' demanded the insolent one.

'We are allies,' protested one of the brothers. 'Athamania and Rome are allies.'

'That's why the gate was shut, is it?' snapped Flamininus.

'Do as he says,' said the leader.

No one moved.

Flamininus threw a look at the nearest centurions that said, if I give the command, fall on them with drawn swords.

'Do it!' shouted the leader.

Spears and swords clattered onto the hard-packed dirt. The brothers had the sense to keep their gaze lowered, but the insolent one couldn't help himself, staring at Flamininus with hate in his eyes.

The fool acted alone, Flamininus decided. I'd wager Amynander knows nothing of this. That was well, for if he had, even more blood would have to be shed. 'Know that I am consul of Rome, and the commander of four legions,' Flamininus said in Greek. 'Every man atop these walls knows of me. Is that not correct?'

The leader looked unhappy. 'It is.'

'Amynander is an ally of Rome. So why was the gate closed?'

An awkward expression came over the leader's face. 'Some of us think Gomphi should be Athamanian.'

Flamininus laughed. 'Gomphi, which *my* troops helped to capture?'

'Aye.' The leader made a helpless gesture. 'Closing the gate was against my wish.'

You were too weak to stop the rest, thought Flamininus. He caught the eye of the nearest centurion, a solid type, and switched to Latin. 'Execute the sentry with the red-horsehair-crested helmet, and the two who look like brothers.'

Flamininus found it easy to picture Galba as the first of the three.

'Sir.' The centurion drew his sword, and without hesitation, stabbed the insolent sentry in the belly. As the man dropped, screaming, the centurion ran him through the neck. He turned side on as the blade came out, letting the blood spatter the ground rather than his legs. The sentry sprawled at his feet, lips still moving in shocked protest. While the brothers died at the hands of the triarii, the leader looked on in horror.

Flamininus regarded him with contempt. 'If you'd had more balls, your comrades would be alive.'

'Flamininus!' Amynander's voice came from the citadel.

'Back to your post,' cried Flamininus.

As the last terrified sentry obeyed, he turned, casual as you like.

Dressed in a wine-stained chiton, Amynander was hurrying down the steps to the courtyard. The triarii opened ranks to let him pass. A portly type, he had an open, amiable face. His thinning black hair stuck out in all directions, and there were deep bags under his eyes. He peered around Flamininus' horse at the three sentries' corpses.

'Tartaros! What happened?'

'The gate was closed when I arrived,' said Flamininus.

Amynander looked confused. 'My orders were for it to be opened at dawn.'

'Your sentries shut it in the face of one of my patrols.'

'My apologies, Flamininus. I was abed – I knew nothing of this.' Amynander gestured at the bodies. 'These are the men?'

'Were they acting on your command?'

'No! Of course not. I would never . . .' Amynander flailed for words.

The Athamanian's shock was unfeigned, Flamininus decided. The sentries had acted alone, but Amynander could not go unpunished. Again imagining that it was Galba standing before him, Flamininus demanded, 'Would Gomphi be in your hands without my help?'

Amynander's eyes flickered to the bodies, and back to Flamininus. 'I— No.'

'I didn't hear you,' grated Flamininus.

'The attack couldn't have succeeded without your soldiers.'

'That's right. The defenders surrendered as my legionaries' scaling ladders slammed up against the walls. If it wasn't for me, you'd still be hiding in Athamania. You occupy the fortress by my leave. Do we understand each other?'

Amynander's throat worked. 'Aye.'

Flamininus looked to his cavalry and triarii. 'We're returning to the camp. Form up!' He urged his horse towards the gate.

Such was Flamininus' pace, Amynander had to run to keep up. 'What about our meeting later? What about Atrax?'

'Consider yourself lucky not to be lying in the dirt with your half-witted sentries,' said Flamininus.

Amynander's mouth closed with a snap.

The fool will keep a tighter rein on his men in future, thought Flamininus with satisfaction.

He rode out of Gomphi without looking back.

CHAPTER XLV

The fortress of Atrax, Thessaly

Demetrios looked out over the battlements, and wished he hadn't. Since the last time he'd looked, not that long before, a great deal more of Flamininus' army had arrived. Atrax was now half-surrounded. Sunset was about two hours off, and by then the encirclement of the fortress would be complete. There seemed no end to the enemy column, which came marching from the direction of Gomphi, to the west. Demetrios picked out hastati, principes and triarii. There were Numidian mounted scouts, Illyrian and Dardanian tribesmen, and hundreds of Epirote warriors. Amid the tramp of feet and creak of wagon axles, he had heard a strange bugling sound; Simonides said it was elephants. Demetrios hadn't seen yet the great grey beasts; that, he decided, was a small mercy.

The enemy's numbers made it hard to see how any of the Macedonian troops within the walls could survive. Two chiliarchies and a few hundred Cretan archers, he thought grimly, against more than twenty-five thousand enemies.

'Incredible view, eh?'

Demetrios jumped. For such a big man, Philippos could move quietly.

'Don't you think?'

'I suppose,' admitted Demetrios, his gaze lifting to the magnificent orange-red sky above the mountains, one he had paid scant attention to.

'A man could die content with a view like that. Mayhap we will, eh?' said Philippos, booming his great belly laugh.

'Why are *you* so happy?' Demetrios found his comrade's happy-go-lucky attitude baffling.

Philippos gave Demetrios an amiable clout, and sent him staggering sideways. 'You're here, pup, and so are your two young mates. Andriskos

382

is here, and Simonides, and Zotikos, and that prick Empedokles. The grumpy bastard Dion is here. So is our entire fucking chiliarchy, because the king picked us – *us* – to defend Atrax. We've got nice dry stables to sleep in, with hay for our beds. There's enough mutton down there–' Philippos indicated the sheep penned in the courtyard below '–to feed all of us for a month.'

'A month isn't long,' said Demetrios, not liking his comrade's meaning.

Philippos laughed again. 'It will be over before then, one way or another. As I was saying, the cellars are full of wine, most of it drinkable. Yes, the whoremongering Romans are here, but there's a great big wall and ditch between them and us. When they climb the defences or batter down the gate, we'll slaughter the bastards. They will overrun us in the end, but we'll die like men. Like the heroes at Thermopylae! What's not to be happy about?'

This was the longest speech Demetrios had ever heard Philippos utter. He had to concede that the big man made a lot of sense. It was a huge honour to have been chosen to defend Atrax, even if the task meant they would die.

He was in the phalanx now, thought Demetrios. Fighting, and if needs be, dying, for Macedon was his duty. He glanced at Philippos. 'Aye. Better to be with you fuckers, I suppose, than anywhere else.'

'That's the attitude,' said Philippos, delivering him another mighty buffet. 'And you, a sixth-ranker and all now. You have a reasonable chance of blooding your sarissa soon.'

Demetrios' nerves jangled, but he smiled. 'You're mad.'

Philippos' laugh shook the air again. 'Says the pup who took on two veteran phalangists.'

Demetrios snorted with amusement. He caught Philippos' eye, and the big man chortled louder. That set Demetrios off. The two of them laughed and laughed until their bellies hurt, and tears ran down their cheeks.

'What's so funny?' Simonides was watching from below.

Demetrios tried to speak, and couldn't. He pointed at Philippos, who boomed his great laugh again.

'Fools,' said Simonides, but he too was grinning.

Even when their laughter came to an end, the good mood remained. It had infected the other sentries; where there had been a grim silence, they were now talking and joking. In the courtyard, where the enemy couldn't be seen, men were drinking, wrestling and oiling their weapons. The rich smell of cooking mutton rose from the fires.

This is home, thought Demetrios, loving the palpable air of comradeship. He remembered the hardship on Pella's streets, and the misery of the rowing benches. Both lives were worlds safer than where he stood, but he wouldn't have gone back to either for every coin in Philip's treasury.

It took Flamininus' crews a full day to assemble their catapults and bolt throwers. Another two days passed while the artillery did its best to reduce Atrax's mighty walls, which were the height of five men and as thick as two lying head to toe. The enemy barrage was a complete failure, because the catapults weren't powerful enough to damage the defences. One sentry had been slain, but as Simonides said, that was because the fool had spent his time watching the artillery. In the end, a stone had taken his head clean off.

The Macedonian catapults atop the walls had fared better, smashing three of their Roman counterparts. A night attack ordered by the fortress's commander was even more successful; a dozen artillery pieces were burned with the loss of just a few soldiers. The move was premature, however. The enemy weapons were heavily guarded thereafter, and over the following days, Demetrios and his comrades watched in dismay as dozens of large tree trunks were hauled by mules from the forests nearby. Hundreds of legionaries toiled from sunrise to nightfall, constructing artillery larger than any Macedonian had ever seen. The ammunition they would use, stones each half the size of a horse, promised to do what the earlier used ones had not.

The pair of great catapults – the fact that Flamininus had only ordered two constructed was disquieting, to say the least – were completed almost at the same time, late in the afternoon of the sixth day since the Romans' arrival. Cheering broke out among the nearest legionaries, while on the walls, a despondent air fell. Antileon, who'd spent days complaining that waiting was worse than what was to come, was uncharacteristically silent. Demetrios asked Zeus to destroy the machines with lightning bolts, but of course he did nothing of the sort. Kimon fell into a black mood.

'Barbarian bastards,' he ranted. 'Roman whoresons.'

'Calling them names won't do any good,' said Simonides, appearing at the top of the nearest ladder.

Kimon muttered a final insult, and fell silent.

Simonides peered at the catapults, which were being loaded. 'The order's been given: one man in every four is to remain on the battlements. The rest are to go down to the courtyard.' He caught Kimon's questioning look. 'We'll suffer fewer casualties up here that way.'

It was a sensible decision, thought Demetrios, who could remember the deadliness of the catapults at Abydos in vivid, bloody detail.

Simonides paced along the walkway, counting and ordering men down. Soon the only ones remaining from the file were Antileon, who was on Demetrios' left, Empedokles standing on his right, and Simonides further on from him. They were manning half the width of the top of the front wall; four phalangists from another file occupied the other half.

Without warning, one of the enemy catapults loosed. Demetrios was taken off guard; he had been expecting more ceremony. He watched the boulder scythe through the air with horrified fascination. It landed short, smacking into the ground fifty paces before the walls and expending the last of its energy bouncing into the defensive ditch. Once, Demetrios would have jeered at the failure, but now he knew it for a test shot. His stomach churned as the second catapult loosed. Its effort also landed short, but not by as much. The stone had enough power to strike the base of the walls and send chunks of brick flying.

A slight delay ensued as the artillery officers ordered adjustments made to the great weapons. The second volley was better: one stone squarely hit the defences, destroying a section of battlements between Demetrios and Empedokles, while the other landed in the courtyard, killing several sheep. Demetrios' heart banged an unhappy pattern off his ribs. Remaining where he was felt like asking the enemy to use him as target practice. He had to remain, however. The command had been given; Antileon was here, and Simonides, and the whoreson Empedokles. They were in this together.

Third time around, both stones hit the wall, although not near the four comrades. Splinters of rock flew high; slabs broke off and slid down into the ditch. To Demetrios' surprise and relief, the barrage ended just like that. He had presumed the fortress would have been pounded until it was too dark to shoot, but as Simonides explained later, delaying further use of the catapults was a deliberate ploy by Flamininus.

'The clever dog wants us to lie in our blankets, worrying about the morrow. Fear leaches a man's courage,' declared Simonides. He glanced at the expectant faces. 'Which is why we have two sheep roasting on that fire, and some good wine. We'll pour a libation to Ares, and then we will fill our bellies, and drink a few cups each – no more, mind. The Paean will lift our hearts, and in the morning, we will take whatever those bastards throw at us.'

Despite Simonides' speech, it was hard to feel enthusiastic about the Roman catapults, and after, the legionaries. Feeling guilty, Demetrios glanced sidelong at his comrades. Philippos looked entirely unconcerned, but that was Philippos. Andriskos was such a good soldier it was impossible to imagine he'd do anything but play his part. Empedokles was chewing his fingernails, while Zotikos was grumbling to another veteran. Kimon and Antileon looked scared, as did most of the rest, but they were nodding their heads at Simonides.

Hold your nerve, Demetrios told himself. Hold your nerve.

Simonides raised his cup high. 'Mighty Ares, guide our spears tomorrow. Let us die like men.' He poured, and the wine sizzled as it hit the fire.

Like that, they were on their feet, making their own libations and asking their own requests of the war god. Demetrios replenished each man's cup from the amphora they had been issued with, and they drank deep. Death seemed certain, but Simonides had made it seem as if Ares was smiling down on them.

A man couldn't ask for more than that, thought Demetrios.

CHAPTER XLVI

Outside Atrax

It had seemed no one witnessed Felix's and Antonius' confrontation with their old centurion in Phaloria – apart from the youth who had stuck Matho with his spear, that was. The chances of him telling a Roman were tiny, but the brothers had hunted for him through the town nonetheless. When they found the youth, his body had been mutilated – they had identified him by his long brown hair. Felix was glad not to have murdered the boy, but he would have done so. Ridding themselves of the malevolent centurion was worth a man's life, and more.

Matho's death did not lay their fear completely to rest. The clash had taken place in the midst of a battle, but that didn't mean no one had seen. In the days following the sack of Phaloria, Felix and Antonius had listened with pricked ears to every conversation. When Pullo interrogated them about what they'd done during the taking of the town, as was his wont after a fight, the brothers had been sick with nerves.

It all seemed in the distant past now, thought Felix, enjoying the warmth of the rising sun on his face. Pullo hadn't pried. Matho was gone; their secret was safe. If he could win Pullo's favour again, a promotion might be possible. Fresh dangers faced the brothers today, but at least it was from the Macedonians. In the Roman lines, morale was high. Not everyone had seen the catapults' ranging shots the day before, but word had spread how they had, with just three attempts each, caused noticeable damage to the fortress wall. Men said that the great weapons would pulverise the fortifications. After that, the defenders would give up hope. A slaughter would follow the attack, as at Phaloria.

Felix suspected the fight might not be quite so easy, but he still had a good feeling in his gut as he stood with Antonius and their comrades, watching the artillery crews prepare their machines. Dozens of helmets marked the Macedonians' positions on the rampart; they were watching, he was sure.

'The poor bastards must know they're about to die.'

'What would you do if we were in there, and I told you to stand on the walkway?' asked Pullo quietly.

'I'd obey, sir,' replied Felix, understanding. 'They're following orders, like we are.'

'Aye.'

'Rather them than us, I'll tell you that for nothing,' Felix muttered when Pullo had moved out of earshot.

Whoosh. The first catapult released. Its stone shot skywards, hung for the blink of an eye at the top of its arc, then hurtled down to strike the top of the wall with terrible force. Wails rose. A section of battlement cracked away, and fell into the ditch, taking several defenders with it. The stone from the second catapult landed a short distance away, causing more damage and casualties.

The barrage became continuous. Every fifteen to twenty heartbeats without fail, the catapults released, always aiming at the same part of the wall. Their purpose was simple: to create a hole large enough for the infantry to enter Atrax. Felix watched, mesmerised. During the war against Hannibal, sieges had been rare; he'd never seen an enemy position pounded in such dramatic, brutal fashion.

Their wait wasn't long. Perhaps two hours later, the catapults' barrage had yielded a decent-sized breach. A great mound of stones and bricks sloped down to the ditch, a rough-and-ready 'ladder' for the attackers to climb. Flamininus was watching; soon after, the artillerymen stood down. The allied troops were sent in first. Screaming fierce war cries, the Epirotes led the charge, scrambling up the heaped rubble. A desultory shower of arrows from bowmen situated on either side of the breach killed or injured perhaps a dozen, and then the foremost warriors were in the gap. There they hesitated a moment, before climbing down into the fortress and vanishing from sight. Their comrades followed by the hundred, until the fallen stones were black with soldiers.

Around Felix, men were jostling, and joking that they wouldn't be needed to win the battle. He began to feel the same certainty. Demoralised, surrounded by overwhelming numbers of the enemy, the defenders would crumble before the courageous Epirotes.

He was taken aback, therefore, when confused shouting broke out among the visible warriors. The attack had just started; a decisive outcome for either side seemed improbable. That was unless, thought Felix with a sickening feeling, the Epirotes were losing.

The shouts soon became cries of fear. Men in the breach pointed, and began to make their way back down towards the outer ditch. Their comrades who were still climbing also stopped, and did the same.

There was a dreadful predictability about what followed. Within fifty heartbeats, the Epirotes' retreat changed from a trickle to a flood. Mad with terror, warriors came flying back through the breach which they had entered with such confidence. Wounded men, or those who fell, were trampled underfoot; no one helped them to their feet.

The tide soon dried up. A last pitiful figure reached the top of the breach from the inside, and was shot by an archer on the rampart above. It was impossible to judge how many warriors had fallen, or been left behind, thought Felix grimly, but it was a sizeable number. Now it was time to see if the Illyrian and Dardanian tribesmen could do any better.

The second attack was doomed to fail before it even began. Everyone had seen the Epirotes running for their lives. Lacking Roman discipline, the Illyrians and Dardani advanced to the breach with clear reluctance. They clambered slowly up the piled stone and brick and, reaching the hole in the wall, came to a dead halt. Their chieftains shouted, and tried to drive them on, but many would not obey, which meant the few warriors who *did* pass through the gap were vulnerable.

Again the sounds of combat rose from inside the fortress. They didn't last long. Moments later, half a dozen tribesmen came straggling back through the breach. The rest of their fellows, who had already descended to the level of the ditch, took one look and ran for the Roman lines.

That was short and sweet, thought Felix sourly. The allied tribesmen had fought well in previous battles; their failure did not bode well.

Flamininus' purpose did not waver. The trumpets blared, ordering the hastati forward.

'Those Macedonians are tough fuckers – you'd have to be blind not to see that from what's happened,' said Pullo, his face grim. 'I don't have a good feeling about the hastati, and if they fail, we are next. You're to stick together inside. Listen for my orders. Do exactly as I say – d'you hear, fools?'

The principes rumbled unhappy agreement at him.

'Pullo's worried,' whispered Felix to Antonius.

'Of course he is,' retorted his brother. 'I'm fucking terrified.' He glanced at Felix. 'I will do my bit – but I don't fucking want to.'

'I will too,' said Felix, his voice suddenly thick. 'Because you're here, and Fabius, and Mattheus. Livius and Pullo too.'

CHAPTER XLVII

Demetrios' heart was still pounding. He was standing with his comrades in the courtyard of the fortress. They remained in close formation – the enemy warriors sent in second by Flamininus had pulled back moments before, and according to the phalangists' officers, a third attack was imminent. Nonetheless, an air of grim satisfaction hung over Atrax. Casualties had been light during the first two assaults – less than a score slain, and barely half as many again injured. No one in Demetrios' file or the one to either side had suffered as much as a scratch.

In contrast, the ground in front of the phalanx was layered with corpses and wounded men. In places, their enemies were piled waist high. Flies settled on staring eyes. Bloodied hands yet clutched shields and spears. Mouths gaped, as if trying to call to a comrade. A man's arm pointed straight up at the blue sky. The mound of stones leading up to the breach bore a similar gruesome covering, and from both areas came the cries of those who had not yet departed for the underworld. Demetrios eyed the peltasts and archers scrambling down from the walkways with ready blades and thought, they'll be on their way before long.

Although he hadn't had to use his sarissa, the initial clashes had been utterly terrifying. At last he had seen the storm of bronze unfold. The enemy's appearance at the breach had made his stomach churn; as they had descended to the courtyard under a hail of arrows and sling bullets from the men on the walkways, Demetrios had wanted to be anywhere else but in Atrax. Shamed by his fear, he had gritted his teeth and stood fast.

The fighting remained a blur of jagged memories. A ragged javelin volley from the enemy. How their war cries had changed to screams as they charged the sarissae. The madness of a few warriors who had squeezed into the narrow space between the bunched spear shafts of every file. How the man with the shortest length of his sarissa extending beyond the shields – the fifth phalangist in each file – had stopped the warrior in his tracks. Demetrios could still hear Dion grunting as he thrust his blade forward, could yet see the rictus of agony on the face of the man he had skewered.

The second time had been easier, but still terrifying. Demetrios tried not to think about the attacks to come.

Trumpets sounded beyond the wall, and a tremor of anticipation rippled through the phalangists.

'Here they come again,' said Simonides, echoing the call that was rolling along the phalanx's front. 'It'll be legionaries this time – a far tougher prospect – but we'll throw them back. Check there are no loose stones beneath your feet. Slip at the wrong moment, see, and you'll hand the enemy a golden opportunity.'

This was something Demetrios had been taught, but had clean forgotten. Mortified to find several stones large enough to unbalance him, he gently moved them to one side – but not as far over as his equivalent, the sixth man in the next file. He looked up to find Philippos twisted around, looking at him.

'Ready?' asked the huge phalangist, who stood third in line after Simonides and Andriskos.

'Aye.' Demetrios was grateful his voice remained steady.

'Keep your aspis in Dion's back. Stand firm, and you'll be all right.' Philippos' wink was encouraging.

Empedokles, fourth in the file and with only Dion between him and Demetrios, turned. His eyes were like a snake's: cold and dead. 'Scared, dusty foot? You should be.'

Demetrios, his stomach roiling, could think of no quick reply.

'We're all in this together, as well you fucking know,' snarled Dion. 'Save your grudges for another time, "Trembler".'

Demetrios knew better than to kick a wasps' nest, but nervous, furious with Empedokles, he couldn't help but join in. '"Trembler",' he repeated.

Empedokles could do no more than mouth a curse in reply, for Roman legionaries – by their helmets and armour, hastati – had appeared in the breach. At once the front five phalangists in each file lowered their sarissae until they were parallel with the ground; the men in ranks six to eight dropped theirs, creating a partial 'roof' of shafts overhead. This, Demetrios knew from experience, would work like the raised sarissae in the eight ranks behind, and break up the enemy javelin volleys.

Several hastati were dropped by the peltasts and slingers, but the rest clambered down the rubble with raised shields, reaching the courtyard with few casualties. They were thirty paces from the phalanx. Rather than rush at the phalangists, as their allies had done, the centurions took the time to reform their centuries. Slings cracked and spears shot down from the men on the walkways, but the Roman formations did not falter.

Gods, they're disciplined, thought Demetrios.

'It'll be javelins next,' said Dion, muttering a prayer. 'Whatever you do, don't look up.'

Demetrios' hands trembled on his sarissa shaft. He clenched them tighter, grateful that facing forward, no one could see the fear in his eyes.

Dion was right. Soon after, the centurions at the front shouted an order. Up shot scores of javelins. Demetrios quickly stared at the back of Dion's cuirass and tried not to think about the death hurtling towards them. Two frenzied beats of his heart later, and the javelins landed. Clatters and bangs rose as they struck first the upraised sarissae and then helmets, aspides and men's shoulders. One smacked off Demetrios' breastplate and thunked point first into the ground between him and the phalangist to his right. His relieved smile vanished as a second hit his helmet, shot off at an angle and joined its mate in the earth. Demetrios felt as if a smith had hit him with the largest hammer in the forge. Only by locking his knees did he manage not to fall. His sarissa swayed like a sapling in a gale before he managed to tighten his grip again. He took a juddering breath, and another.

At last the world stopped moving, and his eyes returned to the front. Demetrios' concern for himself dropped away. Dion was down. He'd dropped his aspis and sarissa, clutching in vain at the Roman javelin that had, by some ill fate, dropped out of the sky at the perfect angle. Even as Demetrios leaned forward, a cry on his lips, Dion's arms fell away. He was dead. The javelin point had gone in where neck met torso, running two handspans and more into his chest.

Whistles blew. Voices cried in Latin. Hobnailed sandals clashed off the stones.

'The bastards are coming,' shouted Simonides. 'Keep those pikes steady!'

'Move forward!' said someone.

Dazed, Demetrios didn't realise he was being addressed until the man behind dunted him with his aspis.

'You're the fifth-ranker now! Move forward, and make it quick!'

Demetrios stepped over Dion, part-propelled by the shield in his back. He pressed his own into Empedokles, who gave no sign of realising what had happened, and lowered his sarissa into place.

'MA-CE-DON!' someone shouted.

'ROMA!' roared another voice.

Demetrios' faint effort was drowned in the crescendo of cries that rose above the courtyard. His gaze was riveted on the lines of hastati, and the elongated oval shields they bore. Black feathers waved atop every helmet, turning each enemy into a giant. Between every ten to twelve men was a centurion, recognisable by his dyed horsehair crest. Above and behind these legionaries hundreds more were descending from the breach, a relentless tide of the enemy. These soldiers, thought Demetrios nervously, were some of the same men who'd smashed through the phalanx at the dirty gates. Maybe they would do so again today. He was glad to be deep in the ranks. There was no choice but to fight.

Wary of the sarissae, the centurions had their hastati walk towards the phalangists, and so the clash began slowly. File-leaders and the second in file – the two whose sarissae protruded forward the most – acted first. Simonides heaved, and with a neat forward flick, shoved his pike over a legionary's shield, and into his eye. Andriskos' target, the man beside Simonides' victim, ducked down, and the sarissa missed, driving into his shield instead. As the hastatus tried desperately to wrench it free, the file-leader beside Simonides stuck him.

Fresh hastati moved into place, closing the gaps. They pressed forward over their friends' corpses. Splinters flew as they hacked at the sarissa shafts. Demetrios felt the first stirrings of panic. Cut the ends off enough pikes, and the hastati could swarm forward to engage the phalangists head-on. Close in, their much larger shields would grant a huge advantage.

'Are you going to use your fucking sarissa, or just hold it like the useless prick you are?' Empedokles shouted.

With a guilty start, Demetrios took aim and rammed his sarissa into the open mouth of a shouting hastatus. In, out, man down. Another legionary appeared at once, and Demetrios killed him too. He had no time to feel pleased as the battle grew more vicious. Wiser heads among the hastati behind the fighting realised they could be of use, and javelins began to shower in thick and fast. Casualties were inevitable, and when a phalangist went down, his file's position was weakened momentarily by his sarissa dropping before the next man in the file could step up to replace it with his.

Watching for these opportunities, the centurions sent men to the attack. Stooping and sliding, they wormed their way towards the line of locked aspides, their faces contorted with determination and fear. For a time, none got more than half a dozen steps before a sarissa punched him into the next world, but in the end, numbers told.

An hastatus attacked the file to Demetrios' right, and somehow reached the front rank. He was either insanely courageous, or protected by the gods. Shield lost, he had two comrades close on his heels, using him to shield themselves from the deadly sarissae. More hastati came piling after.

Demetrios' fear redoubled. If they broke through, the phalanx would split like a block of wood struck by an axe. He didn't know that behind his aspis, Simonides had let go of his sarissa and drawn his kopis. As the hastatus slammed up against the aspides, he leaned out and chopped off the man's sword arm. The next hastatus was just close enough – and so eager to close with the enemy – that Simonides slashed open his jaw with the upstroke of the blade. He fell backwards into the third hastatus, wailing and spraying blood, and the slight increase in the distance from the line of aspides gave Demetrios the chance to skewer hastatus number three in the side of his chest, just to the side of his bronze *pectorale*.

Three comrades slain or maimed in the space of half a dozen heartbeats was enough to make the men following waver. Their hesitation saw two die under Andriskos' and Philippos' sarissae. The rest fled towards their comrades, and despite the centurions' furious shouts, that section of the Roman line edged back a little.

The speira commander had seen. 'Forward, one step!' he shouted.

Demetrios readied himself, and when Empedokles moved, he was right behind him. He took confidence from the aspis pushing into his own back: it was as if Demetrios could feel the ten comrades to his rear. When another order to advance rang out, the Romans retreated before the deadly sarissae. There was fear in most of their faces now, an emotion that hadn't been present moments before.

'Three steps, and PUSH!' came the command.

Demetrios felt as if Ares' hand was guiding his sarissa. It glided forward, taking a Roman officer – not a centurion unfortunately – in the cheek. He rammed it in a little deeper, then wrenched it free. The officer fell from sight. Whether his hideous scream was the reason the hastati broke, Demetrios would never know, but one moment their formation had a semblance of order, and the next, it had disintegrated.

To the centurions' credit, they re-established control fast, preventing their retreat becoming a rout. The cheering phalangists – and Demetrios – didn't care. The enemy had been thoroughly beaten.

Let the next wave come, he thought. We will slaughter them like sheep.

CHAPTER XLVIII

Outside Atrax

F elix was dismayed when the hastati fared only a little better than the allied tribesmen had. A little, in that fewer were slain inside the courtyard. Casualties were still heavy, however, and they made no headway against the Macedonians. In reasonable order, the hastati came tramping back up to the breach, and down the piled stones that had, until a short time before, been part of the defences.

The number of missing and walking wounded made it obvious the encounter had gone badly, but the principes heard more as Pullo cornered a passing centurion. Bloodied, weary-faced, he painted a terrifying scene.

'It's wall to wall fucking spears in there,' he revealed. 'There's no way of getting at the whoresons – none.'

'What about the walkways on either side?' demanded Pullo.

'They're defended by archers, with peltasts behind. I don't envy you, brother.' Without another word, the centurion rejoined his men, who were marching dejectedly by.

It was even worse than he had imagined, thought Felix with growing dread.

The canny Pullo picked up on his men's nervousness. Directing them to empty their bladders, and check their sandal laces, he marched up and down, telling the principes what fine boys they were. They had looked like pieces of shit in Brundisium – they did still, much of the time, he said, which raised a few smiles – but they were good soldiers. Brave men, who followed orders, and stood shoulder to shoulder with one another. They were men who would lay down their lives for their comrades. Pullo came to a halt close to Felix and Antonius. His gaze, usually flinty, was full of emotion.

'I'm proud to lead you, brothers. Proud to call you my comrades.'

Pullo had never called them his brothers before. Felix couldn't help himself. 'PUL-LO!'

'PUL-LO! PUL-LO! PUL-LO!'

Something glinted at the corner of Pullo's eye. He brushed it away, and chopped his hand down, silencing them. 'Enough. Quiet.' He smiled then, and the principes cheered. Under normal circumstances, Pullo would have leaped down their throats for disobeying his order, but instead he smiled again. 'Fools. You're fucking fools, the lot of you.'

Pullo is really worried, thought Felix unhappily. He threw a heart-felt look at the sky. Mars, we need you. Hold your shield in front of us.

The trumpets sounded. Pullo resumed his place in the middle of the front rank. As fortune – or ill luck, many would have said – would have it, his century was one of those standing directly opposite the breach. They would be among the first units to the attack. One of the first to face the Macedonians, who had already stopped three assaults dead. Every step they took towards the brooding mass of Atrax was a step closer to Hades, thought Felix.

At the base of the fallen wall, the centurions of the closest units had a brief conversation. Pullo's century would climb second; more principes would follow behind. An uncomfortable wait followed as the first century began their climb. Arrows skittered off their raised shields now and again. Despite his fear, Felix wanted to attack. The sooner they did, the sooner the unbearable tension would end.

'Ready, brothers?' asked Pullo.

'Yes, sir!'

Felix looked. The first unit was halfway to the breach; the centurion was bellowing orders.

'Climb!' said Pullo. 'Keep your shield in front of you – remember those bastard archers.'

The century broke up within a few paces. It was hard enough for a man to clamber up the stony slope while holding a shield before his face, let alone keep in line with his comrades. It didn't matter overmuch, thought Felix: they could reform at the breach. Foot by exhausting foot, he worked his way upwards. An arrow dinked off his shield. He glanced to either side. There was Antonius, swearing at the knuckles he'd just skinned on a rough piece of masonry. Mattheus was close by too, muttering to himself. Fabius was a little behind, climbing with dogged determination.

Felix cursed under his breath. There was no going back.

'That's it,' called Pullo. Older than most of his men, he had still got to the breach first. An arrow struck his helmet; he paid no heed. 'There's a fine view up here, I tell you!'

Reaching him, Felix wasn't so sure he would agree. Bodies – Epirote, Illyrian, Dardanian and hastati – lay thickly all the way into the courtyard. The first century of principes was edging down towards the enemy, over the gruesome footing. Almost filling the area at the bottom was a massed square of phalangists. A small space had been left for attackers to form up – from the deep layer of corpses, it served, he judged, as containment before the phalanx advanced to annihilate them.

So this is where I will die, Felix decided. He could imagine no other outcome, and if Pullo's drawn face was anything to go by, his centurion thought the same.

'Get your arses up here!' ordered Pullo.

As each contubernium arrived, he sent it to join the first century, who were waiting part-way down the slope. Once half his men had reached the gap, he left Livius to chivvy the rest, and joined the group below. It seemed an eternity, what with arrows hitting their shields and the phalangists roaring abuse in bad Latin, but at last the two centuries were lined up, side by side. It didn't take long for another four centuries of principes to reach them. The Macedonians, who were about thirty paces from the base of the rubble, stood patiently throughout, which was unnerving.

Pullo checked with a look that the other centurions were ready, and pointed at the enemy with his sword. 'FORWARD!'

Felix and his comrades were at the front – he would have given anything not to have been, and even more to have been somewhere else altogether. A thick, bristling line of spears filled his vision. A long way behind the deadly points were the phalangists with their overlapping shields, and behind them, in serried lines, were hundreds of their fellows; their spears pointed at the sky.

Pullo and the other centurion called a halt at twenty paces, and ordered a javelin volley. It was at closer range than usual, but their hope of better success came to nothing. The upraised sarissae broke up the shower of javelins, and few did any harm.

'Close order!' Pullo ordered.

The principes shuffled together until only their blades poked between their shields. No one spoke. A man in the rank behind Felix vomited. He could smell urine too – he badly needed to piss himself. Despite the noise – the screams of the wounded, the phalangist officers' shouts – Felix could hear men panting with fear. His own heart was banging off his ribs so fast it hurt. There seemed no way through. There *was* no way through, he decided. They were walking on the fucking proof of it – the bodies of tribesmen and hastati.

'Steady, brothers,' said Pullo. Despite the danger, his voice was as calm, as quiet as ever. 'At the spears, I want every fourth man from me to break formation. Try to slide your way between the shafts – the spears don't all project the same distance from the enemy's shields, see. Get close enough to the first rank, and we'll have a chance. If they lose a few men, it will break their line, and then we have a chance. Pass it on.'

It sounded like an order to commit suicide, thought Felix. Thanks to their positions, however, neither he nor Antonius would have to follow Pullo's order. The relief Felix felt at this soon vanished. Ten steps from the enemy spears, his whole world shrank to a narrow tunnel. He could see five spear tips, their long shafts running away to a line of painted shields. Over these, he could make out men's faces bracketed by cheek guards and brow pieces. Cold eyes stared back at him. Lips moved in prayer, or curses – or both.

Nausea washed over Felix; sudden drool filled his mouth. He swallowed it. You killed a fucking elephant at Zama, he told himself. The knowledge gave him no relief. In that needing-to-vomit moment, he would have fought such a beast again. Anything not to advance onto the bristling Macedonian spears.

'With me, brothers!' said Pullo, taking a step forward.

Felix copied him. One. Two. Three. Never in his life had the simple act of moving his legs been so difficult. Four, five, six.

Men were shouting in Greek. Around Felix, men were praying, babbling to the gods.

'Mars, guide us. Mars, guide us. Mars, guide us,' repeated someone.

The princeps who'd puked wasn't alone – men were retching throughout the ranks. Their line held, however. Step by terrible step, they closed with the enemy.

No one had faced the phalanx directly; not even Pullo was ready for the Macedonians to strike first. Several steps from the closest spears, a one-word command in Greek rang out. Fast as striking snakes, the phalangists thrust. Their spears shot forward in unison, a lethal tide of sharp iron. Mattheus was run through the eye, dead before he even knew it. The man right behind Felix took a spear through the cheekbone; he died choking on his own blood. Felix was lucky: his shield took the blow meant for him. It was a double-edged blessing; he fought to stay upright as the phalangist wrenched his weapon back and forth. Another sarissa stabbed at his face and another – a sea of keen-edged spear tips filled his vision. Terrified, he ducked, and the point hissed between the feathers atop his helmet.

'Every fourth man – now!' ordered Pullo.

Felix was so busy trying to keep hold of his shield and avoid being stabbed by the jabbing spear tips that he didn't see Pullo break formation, or the man behind Mattheus move forward to do the same. It was all *he* could do to remain standing. Indecision battered him. To let go of his shield would leave him defenceless. Hold on, and he could do nothing.

'Pullo's down!' Antonius' voice cracked.

Sucking in a horrified breath, Felix peered over the top of his shield. Ten steps to his front, Pullo writhed, both hands clutching the shaft of a sarissa that was buried in his throat. A heartbeat later, the centurion's fingers slackened, and he sagged, pulling the spear down with him.

'Pullo's dead!' The news flashed through the ranks; it leached the principes' courage faster than frost melts under the morning sun. 'The centurion's gone!'

Felix was consumed by grief, and fear. Unable to free his shield from the enemy spear, he would join Pullo in the underworld any moment.

Most in the front rank took a step back. Felix did not – he could not.

The phalangists' officers bellowed an order, and the phalanx advanced a pace. Another command, and the sarissas jabbed forward. With a strength born of desperation, Felix hung on to his shield. Principes screamed as they were skewered. Gaps appeared in the front rank, and were not filled. He heard a man behind him drop, and he wrenched again, frantically trying to free his shield.

At the rear, Livius shouted for the men to make an orderly retreat.

'We have to go, brother!' cried Antonius. 'The other centuries are withdrawing too.'

'I can't!' replied Felix. 'Look at my shield!'

'Drop the fucking thing!'

Only cowards or dead men leave their shields on the battlefield, thought Felix.

Heave. As one, the phalangists advanced another step. The move almost toppled Felix, gripping his shield, on his arse. Fall, and he was dead for sure – that much was clear amid the madness. The impenetrable lines of sarissae offered only death.

'Felix!' Antonius was still beside him.

Felix couldn't bear to think of his brother dying for him. That was what would happen next. He let go of his shield. Freed of its weight, naked before the enemy spears, he shuffled backwards, praying not to lose his footing.

The phalangists pushed forward, narrowing the gap. Men screamed and died. More principes dropped their shields. Felix saw a man to his left turn around, presenting his back to the enemy. At once another copied him. The fight was lost, thought Felix, even as an enemy spear drove through the first man's neck, emerging scarlet-tipped beneath his chin.

'Remember Pullo, brothers! Don't let him have died in vain!' Livius roared. 'Face the enemy as you walk!'

Some men heard. Determined to honour Pullo, and armed with the shield he'd stripped from a body, Felix obeyed. Antonius did too. Fabius, who had been wavering, joined them. A couple of men shoved in behind; then it was two more. A solid nucleus, they held shape, spurred by the desperate knowledge that fleeing in panic meant certain death. Ten paces they went back, with the phalangists coming after.

'Pullo,' someone repeated over and over again. 'Pullo.'

Ten more paces. Livius was shouting something – Felix couldn't make out what. Next, his shuffling feet hit the first of the masonry that had fallen inwards from the breach. Unbalanced, he fell down. The phalangist's spear that had been meant for him shot over his head, and back again. Felix's lips parted in a silent, bitter laugh. Never before had his clumsiness saved his life.

'On your feet, brother.' Antonius had stabbed his sword upright in a corpse, and had a hand under Felix's arm. 'That is, if you want to live.'

Somehow Felix got up. Antonius retrieved his blade. With Fabius beside them, the three edged backwards, up the mounds of stone and dead bodies. In ones and twos, their comrades were doing the same. Eager for the kill, the phalangists tramped forward, their sarissae probing forward in a hideous, graceful tide of sharp iron. To the principes' utter surprise, the slope then came to their aid, its steep angle soon making it impossible for the Macedonians to reach them, even with their long spears. The danger wasn't over, however. From the ramparts either side of the breach, bowmen loosed volleys of arrows. Those not quick enough to lift their shields were struck down, or injured.

Afterwards, Felix would look at the breach and calculate that their climb up from the courtyard and down to the outside of the fortress walls could have taken no longer than four hundred fevered heartbeats. At the time, it seemed to last forever. He would remember parts of it to his dying day. Bodies, some still living, underfoot. Screams and cries for help from those left behind rising into the clear blue sky. Arrows dinking off armour and stones. Livius, bellowing orders, doing his best to prevent a rout. Insults in poor Latin being hurled by the victorious phalangists. Fabius, muttering a litany of hair-whitening curses. Antonius, by his side every step of the way. At the top of the breach, the blare of trumpets, signalling the advance.

The brothers stared at one another in horror.

'They're not trying to send us in again, are they?' asked Felix, doubting he had the courage to return to the cauldron of death below.

'The triarii are moving up,' said Antonius.

Disbelieving, Felix looked. His brother was right. Every triarius from the four legions on the field appeared to be marching towards the breach.

'Has Flamininus gone mad? The poor bastards will get slaughtered.'

'He wants the fortress taken at all costs, clearly.'

'There's no way through those fucking spears,' said Felix, remembering with horror how Pullo had died.

'We're not being sent back,' said Antonius.

A short time later, they reached the flat ground before Atrax's walls. Against the odds, they had survived. An odd sound reached his ears; it was his own, manic laugh. 'We're alive!' he said, repeating like a fool, 'We're alive!'

'Stand about like that, and you fucking won't be!' Livius was at their back, appearing from nowhere as Pullo had used to. 'Keep your shields up. Face the walls. Follow me, at the walk.'

Felix had never been gladder to obey an order.

CHAPTER XLIX

Irritated by the Epirotes' failure, Flamininus had watched the Illyrians' and Dardani' half-hearted attempt with rising anger. When the hastati had also come to grief, he'd felt the first niggle that the entire attack might fail – but had put it scornfully from his mind. The Macedonians were cornered, he had told himself, like rats in a trap. They were outnumbered dozens to one. His soldiers had proved themselves numerous times since the spring. He would emerge victorious, not the dog Philip. Contempt filled him that the Macedonian king wasn't inside Atrax. *He models himself on Alexander*, thought Flamininus, *yet he is not here to face me. It is I who lead in person, and I who shall triumph.*

A short time later, the battered remnants of the principes climbed down from the breach, and Flamininus began to wonder if he had underestimated the enemy. For this number of attacks to fail, the phalangists' position had to border on unassailable. Order the triarii forward, and many would die. Nonetheless, it took only a heartbeat to make the decision.

'Matters have come to the triarii,' he said, uttering the expression that had come into use after a particularly vicious battle with Hannibal some years before.

'Shall I send them in, sir?' asked one of his staff officers.

Flamininus' icy control fell away. 'Curse you, yes!'

The officer scrambled to obey.

It took time for the six hundred triarii of each legion to advance from their usual place in the third rank. Flamininus cared nothing for their neat, smooth-marching lines, and the way their polished helmets and shield bosses winked in the sun. He looked on with growing impatience as they made their way to the base of the breach. *Get in there and smash those Macedonian bastards*, he wanted to shout.

When the first triarii vanished from sight, the tension grew unbearable. Flamininus listened to the clamour and the shouts, trying to picture the scene. He imagined the seasoned legionaries breaking apart the phalanx the way a nut could be cracked with a hammer. Once the Macedonians panicked, the triarii would slaughter them like lambs.

A messenger arrived, bringing word that a foothold had been gained on one of the walkways, granting respite from the arrows and spears that had plagued the previous waves of attackers. Optiones left in the breach itself signalled for reinforcements, and Flamininus took heart. The tide was turning, he thought. Atrax would be his by the day's end.

Flamininus' hopes came to naught. Not long after, the noises arising from the courtyard changed in timbre. Screams outnumbered shouts. Men began singing in Greek. Cheering broke out next, making the outcome clear even before triarii appeared in the breach and began scrambling down towards the watching legions. Gone was their disciplined advance, their neat formation. In twos and threes, many helping injured comrades, they straggled down the mounds of broken masonry.

Perhaps half did not return at all.

Flamininus glanced at the sky in silent entreaty to the gods, but they were not listening. As if to reinforce the message that Philip had their favour this day, he saw ominous clouds hanging over the mountains to the west. A freshening breeze rose. Heavy rain was on its way. Autumn had arrived.

There was a sour taste in Flamininus' mouth. 'Cocksucking Macedonian cunts!' he said in a loud voice. He felt a perverse satisfaction at his staff officers' shocked expressions.

'Shall I send in more triarii, sir?' asked one.

'No, you fool. It's a deathtrap, in case you hadn't noticed. If those triarii couldn't break through, no one can.' Flamininus let out an exasperated sigh. 'Have the men fall back.'

'Fall back, sir?'

'Five assaults have ended in abysmal failure. The weather's changing. This is not the time of year to waste more soldiers' lives, or to start a siege.'

The staff officer quailed before Flamininus' withering look. 'I'll see to it right away, sir.'

Remembering the officer's face so he could make sure the fool was posted permanently to Rome – Flamininus could not bear subordinates who answered back – he aimed his horse towards the camp. It was bitter medicine to swallow that Philip remained undefeated. This was not how Flamininus had imagined finishing the year. His losses were by no means crippling, but defeat could not be denied.

Atrax was a bump in the road on a long journey, Flamininus decided, nothing more. The campaign had not been without success. His legions had forced their way through the Aous valley, and taken Phaloria and many other towns. Gomphi, just a short distance to the west, was in friendly hands, and much as he had been wary of leaving Atrax at his rear, the fortress would dissuade Philip from an attempt to retake his lost territories. Come the spring, Gomphi would offer the legions a direct route into Thessaly.

At the same time, Flamininus' brother Lucius would build on his successes in the east. Their simultaneous, two-pronged attack would see Philip contained within Macedonia *before* the hostilities had even recommenced. Matters could be taken up from where they were being left today, thought Flamininus, and the Senate would see that. There would be no repeat of Atrax, his official letter would say – in future, he would simply reduce enemy-held fortresses to rubble. Even if Galba was unhappy, there weren't enough grounds to remove him from office.

He would still be in command the following spring, Flamininus decided as the trumpets rang out behind him.

Victory would be his.

EPILOGUE

Demetrios and his comrades watched in delight as the beaten triarii clambered up to the breach. They cheered as the archers shot and shot, bringing down more victims. As the last legionaries vanished beyond the gaping hole in the defences, an odd silence fell. The enemy had been beaten, but compared to the size of their army, casualties had been few. After a short respite, another attack would come.

It didn't.

Well-diluted wine was issued, and the wounded tended to. Stephanos paced to and fro, and told the phalangists that they were *men*. That he was fucking proud of them. That although the fight was not over, he knew they could win.

Cheeks flushed from the wine – he had already drunk three cups – Demetrios applauded with the rest. When Zotikos told him that he was a proper phalangist now, Demetrios thought he would die with pride.

Trumpets rang beyond the walls. Excitement rippled through the ranks, tinged with a little fear. Men muttered that the catapults would pound the fortress again, to soften them up before another assault. Some said that the triarii were about to attack for a second time. Stephanos, who was still warming to his task, ignored the sound, and told his audience how their names would go down in history. He didn't notice the archers nearest the breach capering about and yelling. Finally, when men began to point, Stephanos looked, and fell silent.

An archer cupped a hand to his mouth. 'They're withdrawing! The bastard Romans are marching away!'

A stunned silence reigned, and then, as the phalangists realised what this meant, pandemonium broke out. Men cheered and shouted, and pounded the butts of their sarissae on the blood-soaked ground. Zotikos' usual reticence vanished; he broke away from the back of the file and danced about like an excited child. Kimon twisted to look at Demetrios; there were tears in his eyes.

'We did it! We beat the barbarians!' he shouted.

'Aye, we fucking did,' said Demetrios, grinning until it hurt.

AUTHOR'S NOTE

O ver the last ten years, I have had the pleasure of writing novels about pivotal moments in Roman history, from the second Punic war to the Spartacus rebellion and the battle of the Teutoburg Forest. This year I have turned to the invasion of Macedon and Greece in 200 BC. Little known nowadays, it was a development of huge importance, forever changing the Mediterranean world. It's not exaggerating to say that the conquest influenced the future history of Europe.

Only a quarter-century before, no less than five powers had existed around the body of water known to the Romans as *Mare Nostrum*, 'our sea'. These were Rome, Carthage, Macedon, Syria and Egypt. By 197 BC two powers, Carthage and Macedon, had fallen to the mighty legions. Syria and its Seleucid ruler were defeated in 190 BC, leaving the tottering Egyptian kingdom of the Ptolemies. With stunning speed, the Roman Republic moved from regional power to superpower. Many would argue that its path to empire was inevitable from this point onwards.

In order to help differentiate Romans from Macedonians/Greeks, I have used anglicised Roman words and anglicised Greek words when talking from the relevant characters' point of view. One of the exceptions in the Macedonian chapters is the use of the word Macedon. Another is Philip himself. By rights, I 'should' have used the word Makedon, and called the king Philippos, but the two are known to history by the anglicised Latin terms, and I felt to call them anything different would confuse. No doubt I made errors – if so, I apologise now! The broad brushstrokes of the story within these covers is true; so is much of the finer detail. Philip V of Macedon was a complex, mercurial character, at once capable of tactical masterstrokes and major miscalculations, of extreme cruelty and insane courage.

His early successes were due in part thanks to his stepfather

Antigonus Doson, who had left the kingdom in a strong position; his Common Alliance had stabilised the Greek city states and protected Macedon. Their relationship is unknown. Of Philip's opponents, Galba, Villius and Flamininus, one can say most about the last. There is no evidence that Galba was as devious as I have made out, nor any that he blackmailed Flamininus. The latter was that rare creature in Republican Rome: someone who managed to get away with acting like a king. He was also a man of contradictions: loving all things Hellenic, speaking Greek, yet overseeing the death of Macedonian and Greek independence. His elder brother Lucius was known as a degenerate; in 184 BC, he was expelled from the Senate.

Philip and Hannibal entered into a secret alliance in 215 BC; Xenophanes of Athens was the intermediary. Their arrangement was discovered and derailed in the chance fashion I painted. Philip engaged in a blitzkrieg-like campaign around the Hellespont in 202 BC, attacking many towns, including Kios and Abydos. Athens relied on the grain from the Greek settlements dotted around the Black Sea; whoever controlled the Hellespont put himself in a powerful position indeed. Although Euripidas and Neophron are fictitious characters, an Aetolian embassy did visit Rome at this time to request aid against Philip. They were rebuffed in the rudest manner, which must have made the Republic's turnaround less than two years later all the more galling.

The battle of Zama unfolded as I described; it was a sorry finale for the military genius Hannibal Barca. His army was ever a polyglot of races. The elephants he used were North African forest elephants, now extinct. Smaller than their African and Asian cousins, they were nonetheless a formidable weapon – if well trained. At Zama, Hannibal only had newly captured elephants, and in Scipio, he faced an opponent who knew how to combat them. It's possible but unlikely that Macedonian troops were present at the battle – my inclusion was a plot device. Aristotle recorded how vultures followed armies. I made up the escape of the prisoners after Zama, but the shocking fustuarium was a real punishment. So too was decimation; afterwards, the survivors were forced to camp outside the fort (i.e. in danger), to eat the barley normally reserved for mules, and to take off their military belts (I assume because it made them look like women). Scipio extracted three months' provisions for his army from the Carthaginians after Zama; he also paid every soldier 400 asses as a reward.

The expression *rem ad triarios redisse*, 'matters have come to the triarii', dates from the second Punic war; it means that the hastati and principes have lost, so send in the reserve, or we are up a certain creek without a paddle. Optiones were sometimes positioned at soldiers' backs; they used their staffs to push men forward. Centurions are recorded as having called their soldiers 'boys' as well as 'brothers'. The practice of advancing towards the enemy in silence is recorded during the Principate; it may have been used earlier. No evidence exists for the use of whistles by Roman officers, but their usefulness at close quarters cannot be denied.

In 201 BC, Philip launched another lightning-fast campaign in the Cyclades and Asia Minor, but bit off more than he could chew. The naval battles at Lade and Chios unfolded as I described. The siege of Chios town may have been in the summer, not the autumn. After it, Philip was trapped in Bargylia for almost six months. The exact manner of the king's escape is unknown, but he sent a slave into the enemy camp with false news and slipped out to sea under the cover of darkness.

The Roman emissary Lepidus sailed to Abydos, his mission to deliver to Philip the Senate's unpalatable and arrogant demands; Livy's description of their conversation is excellent. Flamininus' contact with the Rhodian and Pergamene ambassadors was invented, but it's likely that their visit influenced the Senate's dramatic about-face.

In my mind, the Centuriate's refusal to ratify the Senate's first motion for war with Macedon was entirely understandable. After seventeen years of brutal war with Hannibal, peace must have appealed to most men. Huge amounts of politicking and backstreet deals will have taken place in the months after; the violence is my invention, but political thuggery was a common theme in the Republic. Galba's speech to the Centuriate is recounted by Livy in vivid detail. Among the references in it were Hannibal's siege of Saguntum, a city in Spain allied to the Republic, an act which began the second Punic war, and the Mamertine mercenaries, who provided the spark for the outbreak of hostilities of the first Punic war (264–241 BC).

When the Romans advanced towards Macedon in autumn 200 BC, the praetor Lucius Apustius had elephants with him, as well as Numidians. It isn't clear if Antipatreia was taken using ladders, but Syracuse fell thanks to this method just a few years before. The brutal sacking of the town would have been a common reply to resistance. At thirteen, girls were women two millennia ago; distasteful as it is, rape of such females was widespread. So too was the cruel practice of leaving disabled, ill or female babies to die of exposure. It is worth mentioning Felix's dreams here. Post Traumatic Stress Disorder, PTSD, was almost unknown in ancient times – there is no body of evidence to suggest otherwise. The reasons for this must have been manifold but serve to show us how different from us ancient peoples were – we want to think that Romans were like us, but in so many ways, they weren't. Two thousand years ago, life was brutal. Death was ever-present – think infant and child mortality rates of 40–60 per cent by the age of ten, and a life expectancy of under thirty for women (thanks to childbirth), and about forty for men. Slavery and horrific public executions were normal throughout the Mediterranean; so too was widespread slaughter in war. In other words, the average person, whether Roman, Macedonian or Greek, was used to a great deal more violence and death than pretty much anyone is today.

Philip's crazy attack on Athens typified the man. The statues of youths outside Greek city walls venerated war dead, so the Athenians would have been enraged by his order to pull them down. No one knows what the mountain passes between Illyria, Epirus and Macedon were called; 'the dirty gates' is the translation from Turkish of one. 'The camp of Pyrrhus' is another location mentioned by Livy in this area. The clashes at Ottolobus and Pluinna unfolded as I described. Philip was lucky not to be killed at the former. I made up his men equipping themselves with Roman mail shirts taken from the dead, but Hannibal's soldiers did this after the battle of Lake Trasimene. The level of intrigue and the rivalry between Flamininus and Galba is my invention, but the two tribunes' opposition to his candidacy as consul is fact. Consuls were not elected by their fellows, but by the Centuriate. I felt a scene in the Senate would be more dramatic, however. Philip is known to have had spies in Rome; I like to think that Flamininus might have had the same throughout Greece but have no proof.

Aristophanes was a noted Greek playwright; *Frogs* is one of his most famous works. A bawdy comedy, its text survives. The assassination attempt at the theatre is my invention; so too is Herakleides' involvement.

The Tarentine was a real person; a lot of intrigue is ascribed to him, but it was my choice to put Herakleides in league with the Aetolians. His fate is unknown. During the winter of 199 BC, dissatisfied Roman veterans mutinied in Apollonia. When Flamininus arrived, he at once relieved Villius of his command. Soon after, he advanced up the Aous valley to meet Philip, where a forty-day standoff resulted.

Night attacks were rare, but did sometimes happen; Alexander the Great used them to great effect. The confrontation between Flamininus and Philip took place across the Aous. The standoff in the valley only ended when Charops, a local Epirote chieftain, guided a Roman force up and around the Macedonian position. Attacked from front and rear, Philip's army broke. The campaign progressed as I described, with Phacium, Phaloria and Gomphi all falling to the Romans and Thessaly being burned. Accounts of the battle at Atrax are scant, but in the confined space of the fortress's walls, Philip's phalangists were victorious over the legionaries.

The Macedonian phalanx was a formidable battle formation; by the time of Philip V, all Greek city states had adopted it. Cavalry had reverted to their earlier role, that of being subsidiary to the infantry. The structure of the phalanx is, like so much to do with the ancient world, open to debate. Thanks to the Greek historian Polybius, we are fairly sure that the basic 256-man unit (16 men wide, 16 men deep) was called the speira. Four speirai formed a battalion, which may have been called a chiliarchy, and four chiliarchies formed a strategia. Philip's phalanx was often referred to as having a strength of 10,000 men; Connolly and others have suggested therefore that his two strategiai each had five chiliarchies. Some of Philip's units were called white shields and brazen shields; copying Connolly, I decided to make these full strategiai in size. There is almost no historical evidence for phalangists engaging in training; the exception is Philip V, who insisted his soldiers train during this war. Trumpets were used to relay commands at distance, as with the Romans.

The oath taken by new recruits to the legions was known during the Principate; I think it logical to assume a similar one was used during the Republic. Legionary training lasted perhaps two to three months, and was brutally tough. The sword of the time, the gladius hispaniensis, was lethal, and it wasn't just a stabbing weapon. Livy describes how scared Philip's soldiers were of these blades, because of the ease with which they removed limbs. Romans used inches, feet and miles (the last was only a little smaller than the imperial mile). Greeks used feet – different to the Roman one! – and stadia.

Philip's helmet with ram's horns is attested. Peritas was a dog owned by Alexander the Great. Pankration was a brutal sport, much respected by all Greeks; Spartans were known for their gouging. Greek drinkers flicked wine at statues for fun; they diluted their wine less than the Romans. Weights shaped like bulls' heads were used in Greece. Lions were rare but still present in Philip's kingdom. The rooms I described in his royal palace were excavated in Pella, and probably date to the time of Philip II, Alexander's father. A stadium hasn't yet been found in the city, as far as I know. Nor has a theatre. It stands to reason, however, that such structures would have existed. Leprosy was common in ancient times. So were fires in Rome, where the upper storeys of larger buildings tended to be built of wood. Official fire brigades didn't come into existence until the first century AD. It's not known if 'million' was used by the Romans, so I used the term 'a thousand thousand' instead.

Despite what some people believe, people in ancient Rome cursed just as much as we do today – perhaps more so. Proof exists in the plentiful, lewd graffiti in Pompeii and bawdy Roman poetry. You might be surprised to know that the 'C' word was one of the commonest swear words. So too was 'cocksucker'. 'Fuck' is less well attested, but there is a Latin verb *futuere*, which means 'to fuck'. My more frequent use of the 'F' word compared to the 'C' word is nothing more than an attempt to spare blushes.

The Greeks were fond of swearing too. I liked the expressions 'dusty footed', 'sheepskin wearer' and 'tent sulker' too much not to use them. I also love 'mouse in the pitch pot' and 'knee high to a grasshopper'. Looking a gift horse in the mouth is a little controversial: it was first described around 400 AD, and we know that the Greeks didn't know how to age a horse by its teeth, but it's such a great expression I decided to use it anyway. The lines from the drinking song ('Pipe, pipe away . . .') are from ancient Greece. The orator Demosthenes' derogatory comments about Philip, Alexander the Great's father, come from his famous *Philippics*. Although the word 'barbarian' is often thought of as Roman, it derived from the Greek *barbaros*, which means foreigner, or someone who doesn't speak Greek. I love the theory that the word might have come from how non-Greek speakers sounded: 'bar-bar-bar'.

Titus Pullo was a centurion in Julius Caesar's army; he also featured in the excellent HBO series *Rome*: I found it amusing to name a character after him. Sarmentus and Messius Cicirrus were famous Roman clowns. Melankomas was a boxer famous for avoiding his opponents' punches. Tiberius Claudius Nero and Marcus Servilius Pulex Geminus were consuls at the time I described. So too were Villius and Sextus Aelius Paetus Catus. Minucius Rufus, Scipio Africanus, Gaius Cornelius Cethegus, Lucius Furius Purpureo and Cato were all politicians of the period. Perseus was Philip's son. Amynander of Athamania was a real man; the generals Philokles and Sopater served Philip.

There is a homage to the film *Gladiator* in the book – this one's easy to spot. I have again given a nod to Joe Abercrombie, the master of dark fantasy – 'laying someone in the mud' is my favourite of his phrases. The expression 'shoulder to shoulder' may have been used by Roman soldiers, but my intent in this book was to honour the modern-day warriors who play rugby for Ireland. I am a fanatical supporter of the boys in green, and the hashtag #ShoulderToShoulder is used on social media when showing support for the Irish team. The discus thrower is perhaps the most famous statue from ancient times; its sculptor Myron was famous even in antiquity.

The ancient texts are indispensable to an author of Roman and Greek historical fiction. Without Livy, Pausanias and to a lesser extent Polybius, Hesiod, Xenophon, Aristophanes and Diodorus, my task of writing this book would have been nigh-on impossible. Their words must be taken with a pinch of salt, but they are vital when describing events that took place more than two millennia ago. I own many texts, but I also make extensive use of the Lacus Curtius website, which has English translations of many surviving texts. My thanks, therefore, to Bill Thayer of the University of Chicago, who runs it. Find Lacus Curtius here: tinyurl.com/3utm5.

The modern texts on my desk when writing *Clash of Empires* include *A History of Greece* by J.B. Bury and R. Meiggs; *Roman Military Equipment* by M. C. Bishop and J. C. N. Coulston; *Greece and Rome at War* and *The Greek Armies* by Peter Connolly; Conway's *The Age of the Galley; Greek and Roman Mythology* by D.M. Field; *Ancient Greece* by Robert Garland; *The Complete Roman Army* by Adrian Goldsworthy; *Atlas of the Greek World* by Peter Levi; *Roman Conquests: Macedonia and Greece* by Philip Matyszak; *A Companion to Greek Religion* edited by Daniel Ogden; *Everyday Life in Ancient Greece* by Nigel Rodgers; *The Hellenistic Age* by Peter Thonemann; *Philip V of Macedon* by F.W. Walbank (without this superlative text, I would have been utterly lost); *Warfare in the Classical World* by John Warry; *Taken at the Flood* by Robin Waterfield (whom I am also grateful to for his help with planning a visit to Albania). Publications by Osprey and Karwansaray are often helpful, and I couldn't do without the *Oxford Classical Dictionary* (thanks to my father for that!). Thanks also to my friend Harry Sidebottom, a fellow author and Roman academic, for casting his eagle eye over the book. I'm relieved to say that he found just two errors, only one of which was embarrassing.

Many of you will know that I support the charities Combat Stress, which helps British veterans with PTSD, and Médecins sans Frontières (MSF), which sends medical staff into disaster and war zones worldwide. If you'd like to know more about one of the money-raising efforts I made with author friends Anthony Riches and Russell Whitfield, look up 'Romani walk' on YouTube. The three of us walked 130 miles/210 kilometres in Italy, wearing full Roman armour. The documentary is narrated by Sir Ian McKellen – Gandalf! Find it here: tinyurl.com/h4n8h6g – and please tell your friends about it.

More recently I have been helping Park in the Past, a community-interest company which plans to build a Roman marching fort near Chester, in north-west England. It's the most amazing project. Find it here: parkinthepast.org.uk. Thanks to all of you who continue to donate, support and help with the fundraising. Two readers who've been especially supportive in recent months appear in this book: Philippos is based on the inestimable Bruce Phillips, one of life's true gentlemen, and Livius is based on the wonderful Lesley Jolley. Thank you both. Kimon and Antileon are affectionate depictions of two of my oldest friends, Killian Ó Móráin and Arthur O'Connor. Here's to another three decades of comradeship! I am grateful to the ever-generous Robin Carter of Parmenion Books (check out his website!), and the many books he has donated to 'the cause'.

Thanks to my two new editors, Jon Wood and Craig Lye of Orion Publishing. Finishing this book sometimes seemed impossible, but you managed to extract it from me without toooo much pain. It's a more toned, pedigree beast because of your input – gratitude to you both. I'm thankful to my foreign publishers, in particular the team at Ediciones

B in Spain. Other people must be mentioned too: Charlie Viney, my wonderful agent and friend. Steve O'Gorman, my copy editor, a true professional. Claire Wheller, my fabulous sports physio, who keeps my RSIs at bay; Chris Vick, masseuse extraordinaire, who ensures that my back doesn't seize up. Thank you all.

And so to you, my fabulous readers. You keep me in a job, and I am always appreciative of that. I will say it again: anything not to go back to veterinary medicine! Please keep sending your emails and comments/messages on Facebook and Twitter. Look out for the signed books and Roman goodies I give away and auction (for charity) via these media. I should mention that after you've read my books, leaving a short review on websites such as Amazon, Goodreads, Waterstone's and iTunes is *really* important. Historical fiction is currently a shrinking market, sad to say. Times are way tougher than they were when I was first published in 2008, and an author lives and dies on their reviews. Just a few minutes of your time helps me more than you know – thank you in advance!

Last but not least, I want to thank my wife Sair and my amazing children Ferdia and Pippa for the oceans of love and joy that they bring into my world.

Ways to contact me:
Email: ben@benkane.net
Twitter: @BenKaneAuthor
Facebook: facebook.com/benkanebooks
Also, my website: benkane.net
YouTube (my short documentary-style videos): tinyurl.com/y7chqhgo

GLOSSARY

Abydos: a town on the Asiatic side of the Hellespont/Bosphorus. Abydus to the Romans.

Acarnania/Akarnania: an isolated area of north-west coastal Greece, allied to Macedon.

Achaea/Akhaia: a region on the northern coast of the Peleponnese.

Acrocorinth/Akrokorinth: the mighty Macedonian fortress sited at the neck of the Peloponnese; one of the 'Fetters of Greece' (see separate entry), it controlled access to the mainland.

aedile: a Roman magistrate tasked with running cities, water supplies and markets.

Aegean Sea: the body of water between Greece and Asia Minor, modern-day Turkey.

Aeolus: ruler god of the winds.

Aeschylus/Aiskhylos: a famous Athenian playwright of the sixth and fifth centuries BC.

Aetolia/Aitolia: a region in west-central Greece; an implacable enemy of Macedon.

agora: a Greek term for the place where people gathered. Typically in the centre of towns or cities, its Roman equivalent was the forum.

Ambracian Gulf: an enclosed bay between Epirus and Acarnania.

Antiochus III/Antiokhos III: the Seleucid ruler of Syria, a vast kingdom that had emerged after the death of Alexander the Great. An energetic and clever ruler, he reconquered large areas lost by his forebears. It will come as no surprise that he was on Rome's radar, as it were, at the time of the war with Philip.

Antipatreia: modern day Berat, Albania.

Aous, River: the modern-day Vjosa river.

Aphrodite: the goddess of sexuality and reproduction.

Apollo: son of Zeus, the god of healing, prophecy, poetry and music.

Apollonia: a city sited at the mouth of the River Aous; it allied itself with Rome in 229 BC and served as the main base for the military campaigns against Macedon.

Apsus, River: the modern-day Devoll river in Albania.

Ares: the Greek god of war, embodiment of the destructive but often useful aspects of war; his sons were called Fear and Terror.

Aristotle: one of the greatest Greek philosophers; he is known to have tutored the young Alexander the Great.

Artemis: the Greek goddess of women's and men's rites of passage, and of hunting.

Asia Minor: modern-day Turkey.

Asklepios/Aesculapius: the god of medicine. A major shrine to the god, the oldest in Greece, existed in Trikka, modern-day Trikala.

aspis/aspides: the small, round shield used by Philip's phalangists. Sheathed in bronze with a wooden core, the face was usually embossed. In shape it was a little concave, and about eight palms in diameter. The aspis was controlled with a band for the left arm, and a neck strap. Modern reconstructions weigh about 5 kg.

asses (sing. as): small copper coins, each worth a sixteenth of a *denarius.*

Athamania: a small region to the east of Epirus and the west of Thessaly.

Atrax: a vitally important Macedonian fortress situated in the Thessalian plain, east of Gomphi.

atrium: the front hall of a Roman villa, a courtyard with a pool to collect rainwater at its centre.

Attica/Attika: the territory belonging to the city of Athens.

Bacchus: the Roman god of wine. See also entry for Dionysos.

Bargylia: a town in western Asia Minor, north of Bodrum in modern-day Turkey.

Boeotia: a region of central Greece. Pronounced 'Bee-o-sha'. One of the most stylish and recognisable helmets from ancient times was the Boeotian, worn by cavalrymen.

Brundisium: modern-day Brindisi.

caltrops: the ancient precursor to the spiked chain used by police today to stop speeding vehicles. Four-pronged pieces of iron varying in height from 5 to 15 centimetres/2 to 6 inches, they were designed when thrown to land with one point uppermost. The Romans used them at the bottoms of ditches and on the battlefield.

Campus Martius: the Field of Mars was an open area just to the north of Rome where public meetings took place, and young men trained. During the Principate, it was built on.

Capua: one of the most important cities in Republican Rome. Now a small town north of Naples.

Carthage: founded by Phoenicians as a trading settlement in the eighth century BC, it developed into a mighty city state with territories covering the entire western Mediterranean. It fought three great wars against Rome, losing all three; at the end of the last (149–146 BC) it was razed to the ground. Note: its fields were *not* salted.

Carthaginians: natives of Carthage.

cenaculum/cenacula: the miserable, one-room apartments in which the majority of the urban Roman poor lived.

Centuriate (in Latin, comitia centuriata): a remnant of Rome's earliest political structure, it was largely defunct by the late third century BC. Its members were for the most part farmers, who would have had intimate experience of the horrors of the Hannibalic conflict, which explains their refusal to ratify the Senate's first motion for war with Macedon.

centurion (in Latin, centurio): the disciplined career officers who formed the backbone of the Roman army. See also the entry for legion.

century: the main sub-unit of a Roman legion, led by a centurion. Although its original strength had been one hundred men, it numbered eighty by the third century BC. Each century was divided into ten sections of eight soldiers, called contubernia. Two centuries formed a maniple, a larger tactical unit. See also the entries for contubernium, maniple and legion.

Cephallenia: modern-day Cephalonia.

Chalcis/Chalkis: a Macedonian fortress and the main city of Euboea. One of the three 'Fetters of Greece'.

Chalkidian: one of the commoner types of helmets in ancient Greece.

chiliarchy: one of the sub-units of the phalanx, comprising 1,024 phalangists. See also entries for phalangist, phalanx, speira and strategia.

chiton: the tunic worn by most Greek men. One large piece of wool or linen, it was folded in half and pinned at the shoulders and the open side.

Companion cavalry: although no longer the shock force of Alexander's day, these horsemen were some of the finest ancient cavalry. Their horses wore only saddle blankets. Wearing bronze or padded linen breastplates and Boeotian helmets, the Companions were armed with the xyston, a thrusting spear up to 5 metres/16.5 feet in length.

consul: one of two annually elected chief magistrates, appointed by the people and ratified by the Senate. Effective rulers of Rome for twelve months, they were in charge of civil and military matters and led the legions to war. Each could countermand the other and both were supposed to heed the Senate's wishes. No man was supposed to serve as consul more than once, but in times of need this was disregarded.

contubernium (pl. contubernia): an eight-man sub-unit of the century. The legionaries in each slept in the same tent, and shared duties.

Curia: the Senate house in Rome, found in the forum Romanum.

Cyclades/Kyklades Islands: an archipelago in the Aegean, close to the Turkish coast. About thirty are inhabitable. In the third century BC, they were variously ruled by Macedon, Egypt, Pergamum and Rhodes (see relevant entries).

Dardani: a wild Illyrian people whose lands bordered north-west Macedon (modern-day Kosovo).

Demetrias: a Macedonian fortress on the Pagasean Gulf; one of the three 'Fetters of Greece' (see also entry for this).

Demosthenes: the greatest Athenian orator, he lived from 384 to 322 BC.

denarius (pl. denarii): the staple coin of the Republic from its introduction around 211 BC. Before this, the Romans had used some of their own coins, notably the as, as well as Greek coinage from the cities of southern Italy.

dictator: an extraordinary supreme magistracy, used in times of military and later, civil crisis.

dignitas: a hard to define Latin word. Dignitas represented a man's reputation, his moral standing, and his values.

Dionysos: the Greek god of wine, intoxication, ritual madness and mania, he was Bacchus to the Romans.

Dipylon Gate: the double gateway in the north-west section of Athens' great wall.

Dodona: a shrine to Zeus in Epirus; also site of a third-century BC theatre which could seat 17,000 people.

drachmae (sing. drachma): the staple coins of ancient Greece. The word's origin is *drachm*, which means 'a handful', or 'a grasp'. Made of silver, they were minted by numerous city states. There were six obols in a drachma.

Drynos, River: the modern-day Drino river.

Egypt: after Alexander the Great's death, Egypt was ruled by the Ptolemies. By the late third century BC, it was in a weakened state but would totter on for another two hundred years.

Epirus: a region west of Athamania and Thessaly, and south-west of Macedon. Most of its tribes supported Rome in the war against Philip.

equestrian: a member of the lower class of Roman nobility.

Eros: the god of love.

Euboea: a long island to the north of Athens and Boeotia. Pronounced 'Yew-be-a'. The important fortress of Chalkis was on Euboea.

Euripides: a famous Athenian

playwright of the fifth century BC.

Euxine Sea: the modern-day Black Sea.

Ferentinum: modern-day Ferentino, a town in Lazio which lies 65 kilometres/40 miles southeast of Rome.

Fetters of Greece: the three fortresses of Akrokorinth, Chalkis and Demetrias (see relevant entries). Named by Philip V for their ability to keep Macedon safe from Greek hostility.

fibula: a brooch for fastening garments.

focale: the neckerchief worn by legionaries.

forum: the public space at the centre of Roman towns. Bordered by covered markets, civic buildings and shrines, it was where people met to do business, converse and witness court cases and public announcements.

fustuarium: a punishment meted out to legionaries for reasons including falling asleep on sentry duty, stealing from a comrade, desertion in the face of the enemy or taking off one's sword while digging a ditch. The guilty individual was beaten to death by the men of his contubernium, with either bare fists or sticks.

Gaugamela: the battle in 331 BC that saw Alexander triumph over the Persian emperor Darius for the second and final time. Today it lies in Iraqi Kurdistan.

Gomphi: a Macedonian fortress that protected Thessaly from attack to the west.

gugga: a Latin term of abuse for a Carthaginian, found in one of Plautus' comedies. It possibly means 'little rat'.

Gulf of Korinth/Corinth: the narrow body of water between the Peloponnese and mainland Greece.

Hades: the underworld for both Romans and Greeks. Elysium, paradise, was part of the underworld. So was Tartaros.

Hannibal Barca: most famous son of Carthage, he remains one of history's finest generals. Having initiated a fresh war with Rome in 218 BC, he marched an army from Spain to France and over the Alps to Italy. Although he inflicted massive defeats on the Romans, most notably at Lake Trasimene and Cannae, he never forced the Republic to surrender. Zama was his only major defeat; after it, he helped to rebuild Carthage.

hastatus (pl. hastati): twelve hundred young legionaries who stood in the first rank of each legion. They wore bronze breast and back plates, a single greave, triple-crested helmets, and carried shields. They were armed with one or two javelins and a sword.

Hellespont: the modern-day Dardanelles.

Hera: Greek goddess of royalty and marriage.

Hercules (in Greek, Herakles): the divine son of Jupiter/Zeus, famous for his strength and twelve labours.

Hermes: messenger of the gods; a deity worshipped by shepherds and travellers.

himation: larger and heavier than the chiton, this garment served Greek men and women as a wrap or cloak.

Hispania: the Iberian Peninsula.

hoplite: soldiers in ancient Greece. Citizens of city states, they were armed with spears and shields, and fought in a phalanx. Their spears were a good deal shorter than those used by Macedonian phalangists.

hoplitodromos: an immensely tough foot race for soldiers, who ran naked but wearing helmets and carrying shields.

Hydaspes: a river in modern-day India and Pakistan where Alexander the Great won one of his hardest victories, against the army of the Indian king Poros.

Ikaros/Icarus: a mythical figure who tried to escape from Crete using wings made of feathers and wax. Refusing to heed his father's warnings, the hubristic Ikaros flew close to the sun. The wax melted, and he fell to the sea and drowned.

Illyria: the lands that lay across the Adriatic Sea from Italy: including parts of modern-day Slovenia, Serbia, Croatia, Bosnia and Montenegro.

Issus: the site of Alexander's first victory over the Persian emperor Darius in 333 BC. Today it lies in south-east Turkey.

javelin: the famous Roman pilum (pl. pila). The third-century BC version was more primitive than that of the Principate. It consisted of a wooden shaft some 1.2 metres long, joined to a thin iron shank topped by a barbed head. The range of the javelin is thought to have been about 30 metres, with an effective range of half this distance.

Judaean: someone from Judaea, modern-day Israel.

Juno: the goddess of women, of civic matters and perhaps military prowess.

Jupiter: often referred to as 'Optimus Maximus' – 'Greatest and Best'. Most powerful of the Roman gods, he was responsible for weather, especially storms.

kausia: a Macedonian flat hat worn by men.

Khios/Chios: an important Ionian town on an island of the same name; situated off west-central Asia Minor, modern-day Turkey.

kopis: a curved, single-edged sword used by Greek soldiers.

Korinth/Corinth: the city sited on the narrow isthmus of land between the Peloponnese and mainland Greece.

krater: a large, two-handed vessel for serving wine.

Lade: a small island close to Miletus, off the coast of western Asia Minor.

Latin: not just a language, but a people.

legion: the standard large unit of the Roman army. In the mid-Republic, it was made up of four thousand two hundred legionaries: twelve hundred each of the velites, hastati and principes, and six hundred triarii. Three hundred cavalry were also attached to each legion.

lembi (sing. lembus): Illyrian galleys, often used by pirates. Small and manoeuvrable, they were powered by about fifty oars, and did not have a sail.

lictores (sing. lictor): attendants to Roman magistrates. Their number varied according the magistrate's rank: a consul had twelve, for example, and a praetor six. Each lictor carried a bundle of 1.5 metre rods and a single-bladed axe – symbols of the magistrate's authority.

Lithaios, River: the river that runs through Trikka, modern-day Trikala.

Locris: modern-day Locri in Calabria, Italy.

Macedon/Macedonia: formerly of little importance, the kingdom rose to pre-eminence under Philip II, father of Alexander the Great. By Philip V's time, its glory days had long gone, but it was still the dominant force in Greece.

Maenads: followers of Dionysos.

maniple: a sub-unit of the legion adopted around 300 BC. It's unclear exactly how many legionaries were in a maniple, but most academics agree a double century was probable. The maniple disappeared in the Marian reforms of the late second century BC.

Marathon: site of another of history's most famous battles, on the coast north of Athens. During the first Persian invasion of Greece in 490 BC, the Athenians and Plataeans inflicted a massive defeat on the Persians there.

Mars: Roman god of war. All spoils of war were consecrated to him, and few Roman commanders would go on campaign without having visited Mars' temple to ask for the god's protection and blessing.

Minerva: Roman goddess of war and also of wisdom.

molles: Latin word, meaning 'soft' or 'gentle', here used as a derogatory term for a homosexual.

Morpheus: the god of dreams for both Greeks and Romans.

Neptunus: Roman god of the sea.

Nubian: someone from Nubia, a region spanning modern-day southern Egypt and central Sudan.

Numidians: people from Numidia, an area that included parts of modern-day Algeria, Tunisia and

Libya. Their riders were some of the finest cavalry in the ancient world.

obol: a low denomination Greek coin made from copper or bronze. The name derives from a word meaning 'spit'. Six obols made one drachma.

Olympos, Mt.: the highest mountain in Greece. Situated between Thessaly and Macedonia, it was home to the gods.

optio (pl. optiones): the officer who ranked immediately below a centurion; the second-in-command of a century. (See also the entry for legion.)

Ottolobus: possibly near modern-day Lake Malik in Albania.

Paean: a song addressed to the gods, used by Greeks in personal, civic, political and military situations. I love the novelist Christian Cameron's use of it. (If you haven't read his books, please do!)

Pagasean Gulf: the modern-day Pagasetic Gulf in east-central Greece.

palaestra: a training school for boxing and wrestling. Often part of a gymnasium, an exercise and training facility for athletes.

palus: the wooden post against which recruits to the legions would practise their sword skills.

pectorale: a bronze chest and backplate about 30 cm/12" square worn by hastati.

Pella: capital of Macedon. By the third century BC it was a magnificent city with a central grid complex of streets.

Peleponnese: the finger-shaped peninsula held to the Greek mainland by a narrow isthmus.

peltast: originally a term for a type of Thracian light infantry, by the third century BC it referred to a class of soldier used by many Greek city states. Armed with a crescent-shaped wicker shield (the pelte) and a bundle of spears, they were fast-moving, dangerous troops.

Peneios, River: the modern-day River Pineios in Thessaly.

Pergamum: a kingdom in western Asia Minor formed after the collapse of the Lysimachian empire (which had been ruled by Lysimachus, one of Alexander the Great's generals). Governed by the Attalid family for a century and a half from the 280s BC, the kingdom allied itself with Rome against Macedon on numerous occasions. Attalus I was its king at the time of the events in this novel.

Perseus: eldest son of Philip V, later to be ruler of Macedon himself.

Persia: a mighty empire that twice invaded Greece. It was vanquished by Alexander the Great in the fourth century BC.

Phacium: a town in Thessaly. Modern location possibly near the Greek town of Zarko.

phalangist: a soldier who fought in the Macedonian phalanx.

His helmet was often simple but could have a crest. His armour was a bronze cuirass or padded linen corselet, and greaves. He carried an aspis shield and a massive sarissa spear (see relevant entries), and he probably carried a sword as well.

phalanx: long the staple fighting unit of the Greeks, this was akin to a battering ram, with thousands of men facing up to similar enemy formations while protected on the flanks by light infantry and/or cavalry. Adapted by Philip II and Alexander the Great to great effect, it formed the core of Philip V's army.

phalerae: sculpted disc-like decorations for bravery worn on a chest harness, over a Roman officer's armour. Phalerae were often made of bronze but could also be made of silver or gold. I have even seen one made of glass. Torques, arm rings and bracelets were also awarded to soldiers.

Phaloria: a town on the Macedonian frontier with Epirus. Its modern-day location would be west of Trikala.

pilos: a simple conical helmet worn by some Greek soldiers.

Piraeus: the port for Athens. Access came to the city via a double wall that ran all the way from the coast.

Plataea: a small city state north of Athens. Noted for being the only state to march with the Athenians to Marathon.

Pluinna: sadly, the location is unknown. The word may mean 'mountain', which doesn't help much in the terrain of Macedonia, Greece and Albania!

Pluto: Roman god of the underworld.

Poseidon: Greek god of the sea.

praetor: a Roman magistrate ranked below that of consul. He held only slightly less power (imperium) than a consul and performed similar civic and military duties. By the late third century BC, the war with Carthage had seen the number of praetors increase to four. Another two were added in 198.

Priapus: a minor Greek god of fertility and male genitalia, he was adopted with gusto by the Romans. Usually portrayed with a massive erect penis.

principes (sing. princeps): family men in their prime, these twelve hundred legionaries formed the second rank of a legion's battle line. They were armed and armoured similarly to the hastati, with the notable exception of a mail shirt instead of a pectorale (see relevant entry).

Propontis: the modern-day Sea of Marmara, which connects the Black Sea with the Aegean.

propraetor: a Roman magistrate given temporary extra powers (imperium). The positions tended to be used in war situations, when the two consuls and two praetors were occupied with other duties.

Prytaneum: the building in which the government of Rhodes sat.

Pydna: a town on the eastern Macedonian coast.

Pyrrhus of Epirus: one of history's most unlucky generals. He fought a major campaign in Italy against the Romans in the early third century BC, winning victories that were so costly they were almost not worth having: hence the term, 'Pyrrhic victory'.

quaestor: lowest of the Roman magistracies, the post was a stepping stone from the military to the political life. Quaestores' duties included administering public funds, as well as judicial and military duties.

Rhodes: the island first flourished during the wars of the Successors, when Alexander the Great's empire collapsed. A natural trading centre thanks to its five harbours, it managed to remain independent through the third century BC, albeit with close ties to Ptolemaic Egypt. Ever the enemy of pirates, Rhodes had territories among the Kyklades Islands and on Asia Minor.

Salamis: site of a massive Greek naval victory over the Persians and their allies in 480 BC.

sarissa: the long thrusting spear of the Macedonian phalangist. Between 4.5 and 5 m/15–16.5 ' in length, and used two-handed, it had a heavy butt spike that served as a counterweight. In battle, the first five ranks levelled their spears at the enemy, which must have been a terrifying sight.

Publius Cornelius Scipio: one of Rome's most famous generals. He cut his military teeth as a youth at the outset of the second Punic war. By its end, he was a shrewd and careful commander who had learned enough to beat the master Hannibal at his own game.

Seleucid empire: one of the kingdoms formed during the wars of the Successors, the bitter clashes between Alexander the Great's generals and followers. It was vast, reaching from the Mediterranean almost to India. By the late third century BC, it had just emerged from a difficult period thanks to the leadership of its new Seleucid ruler, Antiochus III.

senator: one of three hundred men elected from the senatorial class of nobles to stand in the Senate, the governing body of Republican Rome.

shield: the Roman scutum (pl. scuta) was an elongated oval, about 1.2 m tall and 0.75 m wide. It was made from two layers of wood, the pieces laid at right angles to each other; it was then covered with linen or canvas, and leather. Republican scuta had a central wooden spine that ran from the top to the bottom.

The scutum was heavy, weighing between 6 and 10 kg. A large metal boss decorated its centre, with the horizontal grip placed behind this. Decorative designs were often painted on the front, and a leather cover was used to protect the shield when not in use, e.g. while marching.

Signia: modern-day Segni, in Lazio, central Italy.

Sirens: enchantresses from Homer's *Odyssey* whose song lured sailors to their deaths.

Sogdia: a region lying in modern-day Uzbekistan and Tajikistan.

Sparta: also known to Greeks as Lacedaemon or Lakonia, which gave rise to the modern word 'laconic', the land of the Spartans spanned the central Peloponnese.

speira (pl. speirai): a 256-man-strong unit of the Macedonian phalanx. It measured sixteen men wide, sixteen deep. (See also Author's Note.)

stadion (pl. stadia): a Greek unit of measurement, roughly corresponding to 176 metres/577 feet.

strategia (pl. strategiai): a five-thousand-man strong unit of the Macedonian phalanx. (See also the Author's Note.)

subarmalis: a padded garment worn over a legionary's tunic and under his mail shirt. It served to dissipate the force of a blow from an enemy's weapon.

Syria: part of the Seleucid empire.

Tarentum: modern-day Tarento.

Tartaros: part of the underworld.

Tempe: an eight-kilometre/five-mile defile in the mountains between Thessaly and Macedon. It was the easiest route between the two regions but could be easily defended.

tesserarius: one of the junior officers in a century, whose duties included commanding the guard. The name originates from the tessera tablet on which was written the password for the day.

Thasos: a town and island of the same name, lying close to the coast between the Hellespont and Macedon.

Thermopylae: site of one of history's most famous battles. In 480 BC, King Leonidas of Sparta and his three hundred warriors, together with 6–7,000 Greeks, held off a vastly larger Persian army for two days. When the enemy appeared behind them, most of the Greeks left, but not Leonidas and his three hundred.

Thessaly: a region of north Greece. Essentially plains enclosed by mountains except for the Pagasean Gulf to the east, in the third century BC it was mostly controlled by Macedon; Aetolia held sway over smaller areas.

Thrace/Thrake: a region populated by fierce, warlike tribes – the Thracians. Today it would lie in parts of Greece, Bulgaria and Turkey.

triarii (sing. triarius): the oldest, most experienced soldiers in a legion. These six hundred men wore helmets, mail shirts and a single greave. They each carried a shield, and were armed with a sword and a long, thrusting spear.

tribune: one of six senior officers in each legion. During the mid-Republic, these men were of senatorial rank.

Trikka: modern-day Trikala, in Thessaly.

turmae (sing. turma): a ten-man cavalry unit. In the mid-Republic, each legion had a mounted force of 300 riders. This was divided into thirty turmae, each commanded by a decurion.

velites (sing. veles): light skirmishers recruited from the poorest social class. Twelve hundred were attached to each legion. Young men of perhaps 16 to 18 years, their equipment consisted of a small, round shield and a bundle of 4' (1.2 m) javelins. They also wore strips of wolfskin on their heads.

Via Appia: the road that linked Rome with Brundisium, at Italy's heel.

vitis: the vine stick carried by centurions. It was used as a mark of rank and also to inflict punishment.

Vulcan (in Latin, Vulcanus): a Roman god of destructive fire, who was often worshipped to prevent – fire!

wine: it is unclear when viticulture first came to Italy. It was practised by the Etruscans but could also have been introduced by Greek settlers. At the time of this book, Roman winegrowing had not yet reached its peak. Alban, Caecuban and Falernian were some of the most famous types.

xyston: the long thrusting spear of the Companion cavalryman. Up to 5 metres/16.5 feet in length, it had a metal butt spike and was held two-handed in combat, which is incredible when you consider there were no saddles being used.

Zama: site of Hannibal's defeat at the hands of Publius Cornelius Scipio in October 202 BC. Today the probable site lies south-west of Tunis, close to the border with Algeria.

Zeus Soter: Zeus was the most important Greek god, and ruler of the other deities. He was revered as the god of thunder and of the sky. Soter means 'the Saviour'; it was a title given to many gods.

Can't wait to find out what happens next?
Turn over for an exclusive extract
from *The Falling Sword*

The *Sunday Times* Bestselling Author

BEN KANE

THE FALLING SWORD

Can Greece resist the might of Rome?

Available from Orion Books in print, ebook and audio
from May 2019

ORION

CHAPTER I

Near Elatea in Phocis, autumn 198 BC

Despite the waning year, the narrow Phocian plain was bathed in warm sunlight. It was bordered to the north by mountains, on the other side of which lay Thermopylae, the 'gates of fire' where Leonidas and his Spartans had fought and died. South of these peaks the flat ground sprawled, bisected by a road that was as important now as it had been during the Persian invasions almost three centuries before. South of here lay Athens, open to attack. Harvest time was not long past; the fields were yet full of golden stubble. Neat rows of vines lined the road in places, their heavy clusters of blue-purple grapes an invitation to the thirsty traveller, or soldier.

Long trails of dust hung in the air, marking the passage of Titus Quinctius Flamininus' army. Six days had gone by since its defeat at the Macedonian fortress of Atrax, eighty miles to the north-west. Its dead buried, the injured in wagons or left behind, it had come south-east to protect the Roman fleet, at harbour nearby. Other than the keen-eyed vultures following the legions from above, few creatures were abroad. The approach of such a host meant many things, none good. Local farmers had fled with their families and animals, a good number taking refuge inside Elatea, the town outside which the first of Flamininus' troops were deploying.

The Roman vanguard had spread out, forming a protective screen for the rest of the army to deploy behind. Among the *principes* stood a friendly faced man by the name of Felix. Black-haired, sallow-skinned, he stood a head taller than most. He stared at the walls of Elatea with sullen resentment; so did his brother and his comrades. Elatea, with its defenders atop its walls, was a sharp reminder that the war wasn't over. More of them would die here, thought Felix grimly. Not many, perhaps, but some.

Wise to the proximity of their acting commander Livius, no one complained. Instead the principes leaned on their shields, drank sly mouthfuls of wine and waited, for orders, for time to pass.

Nothing would happen before the next day, Felix judged. After the cavalry and scouts, who travelled in front of the army, his unit had been among the first to arrive, which meant that at least three more hours would pass before the last of the miles-long column caught up. The wagons, laden down with supplies and the dismantled catapults, travelled slowly, and the score of war elephants did too. Stragglers would still be trailing in after the sun went down, and until they were told otherwise, Felix and his comrades had to watch out for a sally by Elatea's defenders.

An attack seemed doubtful: this was no mighty fortress built to protect Macedonia's borders, but a small town with a fortified rampart. The majority of its garrison would be bakers and carpenters, smiths, leather workers and wine sellers, not soldiers. They would certainly not be the phalangists of Atrax, on whose *sarissa* spears the legionaries had broken like waves on a harbour wall. Their centurion Pullo had been the most grievous loss, but plenty of ordinary soldiers in the century had fallen too, among them Felix's always-laughing friend Mattheus. Others had died during battles earlier that summer. Felix's original *contubernium* tent group was down to three men: him, his brother Antonius and Fabius, the crusty old veteran who snapped whenever anyone asked if he was related to Fabius 'the Delayer'.

'Won't be long now,' said a voice.

Felix started. Livius was an *optio*, but he had the unnerving centurion's knack of appearing when one least expected it. He had been in command since Pullo's death. Felix threw him a curious look. 'Until what, sir?'

Livius grinned, revealing the gap between his front teeth. 'Until you can start digging. The second half of the legion is almost here.'

Constructing the defensive ditch that would surround their camp, and after that, the rampart, was better than fighting, but Felix was unable to muster any enthusiasm. 'Aye, sir,' he mumbled.

'It's been a long march. I'll see that there's a ration of wine issued tonight.' Livius walked off, leaving Felix open-mouthed. The journey from the fortress where Pullo had fallen had been simple, and through easy terrain. The only difficulty had been the grief weighing them down, and Livius had just acknowledged it, albeit indirectly.

434

'He's a good officer,' said Felix under his breath.

'More's the pity that he won't become our centurion,' said Antonius. Shorter, more serious than Felix, he was four years the elder.

Rumour had it that those in command had been impressed with Livius' holding together of the shattered century after Pullo's death. Promotion to the centurionate wasn't unheard of for similar feats of bravery, but it was something that none of the principes wanted for Livius, for it would mean losing him as well.

'Gods will it that he'll stay with us,' said Fabius, giving his phallus amulet a rub. It was the norm for surviving junior officers to remain in place.

'Who's the new centurion going to be?' said Felix.

A chorus of I don't knows filled his ears, and he grimaced. There was no reason for his comrades to have any more idea than he. Don't let it be a cunt like Matho, he prayed. Both brothers had served in the legions during the war with Hannibal; five years before, they had been dishonourably discharged by the malevolent Matho after the battle of Zama. Civilian life had not worked out for the pair, and when war was declared with Macedonia, they had risked their lives by joining the army again. Capricious to the last, the goddess Fortuna had again crossed their paths with Matho. The only witness to their final confrontation with him, which had resulted in Matho's death, had been a Macedonian – a youth who was fortunately dead.

'We need new men too,' said Fabius. 'Who ever heard of a contubernium of three?'

'I don't see that happening any time soon,' observed Antonius.

'More likely that we get shoved in with another tent group that's in the same position.' Felix raised his voice so it could be heard. 'Let's hope it's not the shower of bastards in the next rank.' He grinned at the shower of insults and threats that came by way of response.

The next few hours were spent in similar fashion. Wise to their need for diversion from the grim reality of life, Livius let them be. Other than the occasional wink of sunlight off a helmet, there was no activity atop Elatea's walls. This was also heartening, as was Antonius' observation that the defenders were shitting themselves at what would happen in the coming days.

*

Darkness blanketed the Phocian plain. Inside Elatea, dogs barked at one another, in the annoying way dogs do at night. Peace reigned over the great camps built by Flamininus' legions. Sentries paced the walkways, checked on every so often by junior officers. A short way beyond the ditch facing the town stood the catapults that would soon wreak havoc on Elatea's defences. The hour was late, and most men were abed. Among the neat lines of principes' tents a handful of fires still glowed, including that of Felix, Antonius and Fabius. Orders had come in at sunset. An attack on Elatea was planned for the next day; the principes would be taking part. This unwelcome news had seen the wine procured by Livius left unfinished. No one was stupid enough to get rat-arsed drunk with a fight in the offing. By unspoken consent, the assault went unmentioned.

'What will you do after the war?' Fabius inched his toes closer to the glowing embers, and then eyed Felix and Antonius, who were lounging on their blankets on the other side of the fire. 'You left your farm once before – could you go back to it?'

'I'll give it another try,' said Antonius, as he had each time the topic had been discussed during the previous two summers' campaigns. 'By the time this war is done, I should have enough coin to buy mules and a slave. That will make life a good deal easier.' He glanced at Felix, trying to gauge his interest, but Felix pretended not to see.

Fabius, who knew only that their farming life had been brutally hard, grunted. His gaze moved to Felix. 'And you?'

'What will you do, old man?' countered Felix.

'Me? Same as I've always said. I'm going to buy a tavern and slowly drink myself to death.'

Felix snorted. 'How long will that take?'

'Many years, I hope.' A rare smile appeared on Fabius' face. 'Why don't you two come in with me? You're young and strong – taverns need men like that around. With you around to keep me straight, I'll last into my sixties.'

'It could only be better than our last experience in the trade,' admitted Antonius. 'My ribs hurt just remembering it.'

Felix rubbed his jaw, which had ached for days after a fight with a brute who'd nearly had the better of the two of them. 'Where would it be?'

Fabius gave him a look. 'I'm from Rome. Where else would a man want to open a tavern?'

'There are plenty of shitty areas in Rome,' challenged Felix.

'D'you think I came down with the last shower?' retorted Fabius. 'I know that. We would decide on the location together.'

Felix glanced at Antonius, and then at Fabius. 'Equal partners?'

'As long as you can come up with a third of the coin each, aye.' Fabius spat on his hand and shoved it at Felix.

Felix held back. 'What d'you think, brother? Running a tavern has got to be better than working a plough day in, day out. Better than breaking your back at harvest time too.'

Antonius' eyes met his, and moved to Fabius, who nodded encouragingly, before returning to Felix. 'Aye, why not?' he muttered. 'If it doesn't work out, the farm will still be there.'

The three shook hands, grinning. Fabius produced a skin of wine, an event so rare that Felix declared it to be another reason for celebration. Under normal circumstances, this acid comment would have soured Fabius enough to make him refuse to share, but tonight he merely grumbled about youngsters having no respect for their elders and betters. The skin travelled around the fire, and the three partners took small sips as they discussed their new enterprise.

Fabius was the first to nod off. One moment he was enthusing about the wines he could buy from an old contact with a farm south of Rome, the next his chin was on his chest and he was gently snoring. There was no response from Antonius, and Felix saw with amusement that he too was almost asleep. Felix prepared to stir himself. It wasn't that cold, but the fire had burned down to embers. Despite the wine-warmth coating him, the tent was only a few paces away, and was worth getting up for. Tipping up the skin, he swallowed a few last drops. It had been a decent vintage, he decided.

He nudged Antonius and Fabius into wakefulness and went to empty his bladder in the latrine trench, which was close to the wall nearest Elatea. Job done, Felix smoothed down his tunic and turned to retrace his steps. He aimed an idle glance at the walkway, thinking he hadn't heard a sentry's tread while he'd been pissing. There was no one in sight, which was curious. He moved back a little, to see more of the earthen rampart, which stood tall as two men. Not a soul.

He felt a prick of alarm. Sliding his feet now so they made no sound, he paced twenty and then fifty paces along the base of the wall. There were no sentries to be seen, but a telltale prone shape made his mouth go dry. Felix studied the nearest tents, but could see and hear nothing to suggest that attackers had entered the camp. He warred with himself for a moment. Scream a false alarm, and he would be punished. Better to check on the man, he decided, stealing towards the nearest ladder.

He crept up it, heart pounding, eyes darting to left and right along the walkway. Halfway up, he spied a second figure slumped in a sitting position. It had to be another sentry. Ill deeds *are* afoot, thought Felix, his pulse quickening. The Elateans weren't without spine after all. Crouching below the top of the rampart, he sped to the nearest sentry. The man lay face down and still as stone. A dark pool around his neck was grim warning of what had befallen him. Felix dipped his fingers into the liquid to be sure, and wished he hadn't. A grappling hook lay nearby, and from it a rope snaked over the rampart – this was how the enemy or enemies who'd slain the sentry had climbed up. He couldn't see a soul along the entire walkway, which meant this wall was undefended, but bizarrely there was still no sign of attackers within the camp.

He risked a look over the fortifications, and his eyes widened. Around the two large catapults that had pounded a hole in the walls of Atrax, dozens of figures loomed. Torches flickered in their hands; the distinctive tang of pitch carried through the air.

Felix leaped to his feet and bellowed the alarm with all his might.

Heads turned among the attackers, and their efforts to light the catapults grew more urgent.

Felix could hear sentries on the other walls taking up his call; there were men stirring in the nearest tents. It was slow, however, too slow. Flames were licking up the side of one catapult, and the attackers had moved on to the second weapon. He wondered about rousing Antonius and Fabius, but that would also take too long. Cursing himself for a fool, Felix stripped the dead sentry of his baldric and sword. He tossed the man's javelin and shield into the defensive ditch, checked the grappling iron was secure and clambered over the rampart. Down he went, hand over hand, balancing his feet against the wall. He paused at the bottom to stare at the attackers. None appeared to have noticed his descent. Not that they'd worry about one man, Felix decided grimly. He peered into the ditch, thinking, one slip and I'll end up on a caltrop, if not two. There was nothing for it, though. Sitting on his arse with his hands on the edge, he eased himself down.

He gingerly found safe footing, and then crouched to spot the shield and javelin. Fortuna smiled on him; they had landed close by. Probing for caltrops with his fingertips, he retrieved both and heaved them over the lip of the ditch. Praying that no one was waiting to brain him, Felix scrambled out of the trench.

No one had noticed. Although there was good light now from the first burning catapult, the attackers were absorbed with trying to set the second piece ablaze. For some reason, it had not ignited with the ease of its companion, but given their frantic efforts, it wouldn't be long going the same way. Felix wavered. He had raised the alarm; he could not put out the fire alone, and the attackers would soon be driven off. Why throw his life away?

One of the attackers turned and saw him.

Felix had time to think what an old bitch Fortuna was, and then he was beckoning to imaginary comrades and shouting, 'Come on, brothers! With me!' He threw the javelin, spitting one of the enemy between the shoulder blades. Then, roaring as if he were a century of legionaries, not one, he drew the sword and ran towards the burning catapults.

The man who'd seen him was nervous. His badly aimed spear hummed past, nowhere near Felix.

Felix was on him in another heartbeat. The shield boss slammed the man backwards, onto his arse. Felix left him behind, closing on a second man who, panicked by his wild face, turned to flee. Felix stabbed him in the back, and drove on. Two attackers joined forces, one going left of Felix, the other right. I'm dead, he thought. They'll have seen I'm alone. He made a snap judgement; the one to his left was no more than a youth. Dart forward. Punch with the shield. Stab with his sword, and the youth went down, mewling like a babe ripped from the tit.

Felix spun, wary of the second attacker. The man was hanging back, however. Paunchy, holding his shield and spear like a new recruit, he was no soldier. Felix felt a glimmer of hope. He charged, not seeing the discarded torch underfoot. Skidding, balance lost, he stumbled forward and fell flat on his face. A cry of triumph rose from his opponent, who stepped in, spear raised high.

'ROMA!' The cry was some distance off, but it was being made by scores of voices. 'ROMA!'

Felix flinched, still expecting a spear in the back.

The blow didn't fall. Feet pounded. Men cried to one another in Greek.

Felix rolled over, unable to believe his luck. A trained soldier would have killed him before running away, but the paunchy man had given in to fear, and saved his own skin.

An odd peace fell. Wood crackled. Heat radiated from the catapults. Felix got to his feet. Both artillery pieces were ablaze now; attempt to put out the fire and he would get badly burnt. He stood back, deciding that Fortuna had been tempted enough for one night.

The siege of Elatea was going to be more difficult than everyone had assumed.

Help us make the next generation of readers

We – both author and publisher – hope you enjoyed this book.
We believe that you can become a reader at any time in your life,
but we'd love your help to give the next generation a head start.

Did you know that 9% of children don't have a book of their
own in their home, rising to 13% in disadvantaged families*?
We'd like to try to change that by asking you to consider the role
you could play in helping to build readers of the future.

We'd love you to think of sharing, borrowing, reading, buying or talking
about a book with a child in your life and spreading the love of reading.
We want to make sure the next generation continue to have access
to books, wherever they come from.

And if you would like to consider donating to charities that help
fund literacy projects, find out more at www.literacytrust.org.uk
and www.booktrust.org.uk.

Thank you.

hachette
CHILDREN'S GROUP

*As reported by the National Literacy Trust